'Please don't lea hoarse. 'Not now ... a co month ... Owen will still be there, it w... make any difference. And you're far too young to rush into marriage ...' There was a note of helpless panic. Tears were welling up in Megan's eyes. 'I need you here, I must have someone — someone that I love.' She didn't even try to disguise a sob.

'Of course I'll stay on for a bit, if you want me to,' Megan said, unyielding; each wanting desperately the unstinting love and approval only the other could, and would not, give.

When Vera didn't reply, very slowly — and thinking hard of Owen — Megan began to move towards the beacon of the lamp, shining at the end of the corridor. Her mother was crying quietly and openly behind her now.

It was the longest walk of her life.

by the same author

DANCING LEDGE
CHOICES
SUMMER SECRETS
BLUE DUSK

Mother Love

SUSAN GOODMAN

For Tim, this year

A *Warner* Book

First published in Great Britain in 1992 by Michael Joseph
This edition published by Warner Books in 1993

Copyright © Susan Goodman 1992

The moral right of the author has been asserted.

*All characters in this publication are fictitious and
any resemblance to real persons, living or dead,
is purely coincidental.*

All rights reserved.
No part of this publication may be reproduced,
stored in a retrieval system or transmitted, in any
form or by any means, without the prior
permission in writing of the publisher, nor be
otherwise circulated in any form of binding or
cover other than that in which it is published and
without a similar condition including this
condition being imposed on the subsequent purchaser.

A CIP catalogue record for this book is
available from the British Library.

ISBN 0 7515 0129 8

Printed in England by Clays Ltd, St Ives plc

Warner Books
A Division of
Little, Brown and Company (UK) Limited
165 Great Dover Street
London SE1 4YA

Prologue

1939–40

Love . . . is the greatest thing,
The oldest yet the latest thing,
I only hope that fate may bring
Love's story to you.

Chapter 1

'Vera Bowen — *you* know, the actress,' was what people said about her that spring. She was now a recognizable theatrical name, almost a star. She was at her best then: lithe, thin as a rail, nearly six feet tall, with porcelain skin and thick, manageable brown hair. Her eyes were very pale blue, slightly protuberant — and inclined to stare. Her nose was straight, a whisker too long. She had never been pretty. Her great asset was her remarkable figure and the pared-down, sophisticated style she had evolved — with single-minded narcissism — to clothe it. She depended totally on her appearance, and the way she moved, to make an impression. She was also, disconcertingly, inclined to say exactly what she meant — largely because she didn't know how else to express herself. This was frequently interpreted as wit. Vera herself had started to be aware of this, and was learning to turn what was genuine gaucheness to her own advantage.

In the early months of the year there was a good deal of optimism throughout the country that war could still be avoided. The Munich agreement, 'Peace in our time', had been signed — and everyday life continued, people hoping against hope; 'No war this year — or the next' became the slogan of one of the tabloids. At top London nightspots, 1939 had been ushered in with hectic lavishness — bagpipes at the Café de Paris; banks of daffodils and mimosas at Quaglino's. Spring came early that year, too, at the beginning of March, with brilliant, sunny days under deep blue skies — raising spirits even further.

It was around this time, sensing her particular talents, that the playwright/impresario Brian Worth started taking Vera Bowen out and about quite a bit. She had no one special in her life at that moment – and Brian Worth never did. When a replacement was suddenly needed for the spectacular second lead in a new comedy that had just opened to rave notices – and looked set for a long run – he made a few phone calls . . . And the part went to Vera Bowen who had a small but noteworthy triumph. Which was how, close on thirty, and having spent more than half her life on the boards in one way or another, she came to the public's notice.

One golden Sunday morning in April Brian took her to a lunch party at the Savoy, given by an American heiress he had known for years. 'You can't be overdressed for this one, duckie,' he told Vera. So she wore a superb black gaberdine suit with wide, sharp shoulders and a feathery hat pulled down to one pencilled eyebrow. A silver fox stole was slung about her neck.

There were cocktails first in the smart American bar. Robert Brandon arrived late, a good ten minutes after they were seated in the restaurant overlooking the river. He caused a stir – you couldn't miss him: perfectly groomed and tailored, his cigarette held nonchalantly as his chair was pulled out. Waiters always made a fuss of Robert Brandon. He was seated on the right of their hostess, Babs somebody, bending confidentially towards her, totally at ease, talking amusingly.

Vera, bored, was being monopolized at the other end of the table. But she had noticed him – with a jolt – the moment he appeared. She took it all in: the flashing smile, the assurance, the darkness; the narrow moustache that suited him to perfection. About forty, she decided, perhaps a year or two older. Towards the end of the meal they caught each other's eye across the luncheon débris – white nappery, coffee cups, half-empty wine glasses, cigarette smoke. His eyebrows, heavily marked in a slanted V, were remarkable; and Vera always had a mesmeric effect. They both smiled briefly and turned away.

Somebody sitting near Vera said jokingly that Robert Brandon – did she know? – was one of the most eligible men in London. He went for older women, mostly married, and the family were getting jittery, he'd heard, because he was an only son. Listening in, Brian Worth murmured, 'Arrogant so-and-so, I'll bet. I know the type.' Although they were finally introduced when the party was breaking up, they hardly spoke. So Vera was quite taken aback when he telephoned her flat the next morning and asked her out to supper that night.

'Yes,' she said immediately. 'Just give me half an hour after the curtain to change.' She avoided a lot of social contact — so she wondered why, all of a sudden, she should feel like the cat who had swallowed the canary.

He picked her up at the theatre, striding through the stage door, wearing white tie and tails as though he lived in them. Just one look undid Vera. Born in a slum, she was never convinced she was out of it for good.

'I very much enjoyed the play, by the way,' he told her, turning quickly to look at her as he eased the car through the crowded, light-splashed streets around Piccadilly. He was taking her to the Four Hundred, which was becoming the most fashionable nightclub in London. 'It's an amusing caper. And the part is absolutely perfect for you.'

'Yes, I know.'

'You're very confident.' She could sense he was smiling; there was an electric tension between them even there.

'No.' Her chin was sunk in the mole-grey velvet of her evening cloak. 'But it is. *You* thought so . . .'

Vera knew exactly what she wanted to eat; she never dithered. 'Smoked salmon and scrambled eggs.' He ordered the same. They drank champagne, Pol Roger — and they danced. '*Blue Moon . . . now I'm no longer alone . . .*' the band's singer crooned silkily through the microphone. And from that first intimate embrace on the dim and crowded floor they were physically hooked. And they knew it. In her silvery high heels, Vera was as tall as he. Thigh matched thigh as they moved to the syrupy, evocative music. She was wearing a slinky, strapless dress and her bare arm slid across his shoulders, just touching his neck. Their eyes were level.

Back at their table where small, shaded lamps gave pools of light, Robert Brandon kept up the smooth stream of conversation that he was so good at. Vera learnt that after a long spell in the Guards he was beginning to manage his uncle's estate — Cloverley Court in Wiltshire — which he would inherit; a title, too, apparently. His father and two brothers, Robert's uncles, had been killed on the Somme within months of each other. He had come late to politics, but he was taking them very seriously indeed these anxious days. He expected to be adopted as the local Conservative candidate at the next general election. His mother, who still lived there, had brought him up at Cloverley. He adored the place but London — he gave that quick, dashing grin, — had such attractions ... He had a house in Chester Square and he was lucky he had marvellous servants who spoilt him. She must come and dine. And she? Lighting cigarettes for them both, eyes narrowed, he was watching her closely.

'My Dad's dead. He was a trapeze artist. Best in the business on a high wire.'

'I see ...' He was intrigued. This sort of thing was new to him, Vera could tell.

'And your mother?'

'Works in a pub.'

'So how did you — make your way on the stage?'

'The hard way.'

He threw back his head and gave a shout of laughter. 'Meaning?' He leant towards her — and she saw that his eyes were a dense grey-green.

'Oh, provincial tours, dirty digs and landladies. Drafty dressing-rooms, auditions. A bit of singing and a bit of dancing ... walk on parts to begin with.' Vera was no good at words. And the less she thought about all that the better. It beat her how anyone believed there was glamour about the stage, the bottom end anyhow. It was only toffs like him that did.

'I thought as much.' He ground out his cigarette. 'I adore this song — let's dance ...'

He took her wrist and went on holding it as she made her way ahead of him through the tables.

'Love . . . is the sweetest thing.
What else on earth could ever bring
Such happiness to everything . . .'

They made a sensational couple, attracting glances even there in the glowing semi-darkness; several people recognized Vera. They danced very close, not speaking, and not moving much. When they were walking off the floor, Robert raised an arm and nodded towards a man a few tables away.

'He's just gone back to his regiment, the fellow over there. It's absurd all this talk of war — a rush to madness, insanity . . .' He sounded angry.

'Why?'

'Why? Didn't we learn anything from the Great War — and the slaughter? We should treat with the Germans, not fight them. They're too like us. My God, the Royal Family is more German than British.'

'We might have to fight.'

'Not if some people, people of importance, have anything to do with it.'

He sounded grim, as though his mind had veered elsewhere. Vera shrugged. Politics bored her and this wasn't the time or place. Fancy him getting so steamed up . . . She held out her glass and when he had refilled it, he bent his mouth to her fingers. She shivered.

He drove her back to the mansion block in the heart of Mayfair where she had a small flat and saw her up in the lift. Thanking him formally, closing the door, Vera looked down and saw the toe of his polished evening shoe inching forward. She took hold of the ends of his white silk scarf and pulled . . . The door shut behind him.

She led him down the narrow corridor to the bedroom — where there was a soft light on by the bed. She threw her bag and cloak on to a chair and stood with her back to him, looking over her shoulder, her eyes never once leaving his face. She reached behind — and her dress slithered to a heap on the floor.

She stood there in lacy knickers, suspenders, silk stockings, silver shoes; the long white scarf — his — round her neck, draped over her bare breasts. Slowly, she turned until she was directly facing him, her long, supple body flawless and silken in the pale light. He didn't say anything, didn't move — but his eyes were on her everywhere. She touched the scarf. *Then* he moved . . .

'No — don't . . .' he said — urgent.

His coat was off, and his tie. He came towards her, tearing at his shirt, pulling down his braces. He ripped at the scarf and half threw her on to the bed. He came into her quickly — very hard and without much tenderness. It was exactly what they both wanted. He dressed briskly. At the bedroom door, he turned and came back to her. He was smiling again, his normal self, and his hair was ruffled. He kissed her for the first time.

'This is extraordinary,' he whispered.'Quite extraordinary. I'll pick you up at the theatre — tonight.'

He let himself out and she heard him running lightly down the stairs. Although the flat was on the fourth floor, in all the time she knew him, when he was alone he never once took the lift.

Vera switched off the light and lay there for quite some time. Robert Brandon was her second lover — if you could call Jim Trickett a lover. He had been, and a competent one; he'd taught her everything she knew. But he was her protector, really, and they'd been happy enough in their way those seven years, Jim going back and forth between the flat and his invalid wife in the big, ugly house up north while she was in and out of the theatre. He had given her the only bit of security she had ever known: this flat and a nest egg to go with it. She still remembered the stunned disbelief she had felt when that letter from a firm of solicitors in Manchester had arrived on the doorstep, telling her that he had died of a sudden heart attack at his factory — and that these were their instructions . . . There were one or two papers to be signed — and they made it clear that they did not expect to hear from her further. As if she would do any such thing . . . Poor old Jim, he'd been down in London with her all that week, looking a bit tired, but cheerful enough. That was more than a year ago.

Now, she was almost a star.
Now, she had met Robert Brandon.

If Robert Brandon had any serious relationship when they met, Vera never knew about it. He picked her up the next night after the play, and the next, and the next. Sometimes they went to nightclubs, sometimes to his house where his servant, Peters, looked after them with well-trained discretion. Everything was left ready in the first-floor drawing-room — sandwiches, drinks, a flask of coffee. On cool nights, the fire was lit. They always ended in bed, usually hers. She told Robert, embarrassed, that she hadn't the nerve to meet Peters' eye in the morning.

'Who would ever suspect you of such prudery?' he murmured, amused, his mouth moving down her shoulder.

Robert Brandon had hundreds of acquaintances but few close friends. Some of these were introduced to Vera — in clubs or restaurants or at his house; they were intrigued to meet this rising stage actress who looked as if she was becoming a serious star. If she didn't count Brian Worth, the daily housekeeper Flo, her agent and a handful of theatrical contacts, Vera Bowen had no friends at all. In her years with the late Jim Trickett, she had kept herself strictly to herself, which suited them both. In any case, people didn't interest her much, all her energies had gone into her appearance and her work and the struggle to keep going and get the next part. In the theatre, she was totally disciplined — on time, word perfect, every hair in place: characteristics which had often triumphed over prettier, more talented girls.

Except on matinée days, they lunched at the Ritz or the Berkeley or Ciro's or Oddenino's. Occasionally, Robert invited one or two friends to Chester Square. In private he was often preoccupied and silent, moody, lost in thought as though wrestling with deep inner concerns. But as Vera didn't see much point in talking unless there was something specific to say, this never worried her. And neither did Robert's sudden cancellations when a whispered word from Peters called him to some mysterious meeting or a long secretive telephone conversation.

Every Friday morning he disappeared to the country, to

Cloverley Court. This, for Vera, with its implications of a life about which she knew nothing, and from which she was totally excluded, was much more threatening. Towards the end of May — and in June, and July — he took to reappearing on Sunday afternoons, taking the steps to her flat two at a time, standing at the door with that debonair smile, tanned and refreshed; Vera would be weak with the relief of seeing him. They would spend every minute together until she left for the theatre on Monday evening. For both of them, their sex was addictive.

There was a photograph of her in the *Tatler* that May, looking sulky and soignée, taken by Beaton. Vera dressed to the hilt, with flair and style — and her height and her figure displayed clothes stunningly. She had kept on Flo, who was a confidante of a sort and a marvellous lady's maid, satisfying even Vera's quest for perfection. And the play continued to be a hit, everyone talking about it, wanting to get tickets.

Despite the growing sense, after the early flurries of hope, that war was inevitable, the London Season was as brilliant as ever that year. On the surface at least, no one was greatly fussed by the ominous international scene. Hitler or no, débutantes in white dresses and feathers in their hair curtsied in a series of glittering courts at the Palace. And night after night hostesses produced dazzling dinners and balls and entertainments. Robert Brandon took Vera to a late reception at one of the great houses in Park Lane, holding her arm possessively as they swept in through the portico, past a group of photographers and excited gapers. In a sea of pastel ballgowns, Vera stood out superbly in dead simple gold lamé. It was like a stage to her — and she created an impression all right. Everyone turned to look at her and Robert liked that, she knew.

One night, she presided at a small supper party he gave at Chester Square. He watched her from the other end of the table — her skin creamy against the black dress, her hair set in deep, glossy waves. She didn't say much. Her background was still a mystery; she made no secret of it, but she wouldn't talk about it openly to anyone, apart from Robert. Someone asked her a question and she looked over at him. He caught her eye and saw the sudden, panicky insecurity before he leant across and smoothed over the conversation. No one else at that table would have suspected her vulnerability. He was very gentle with her later, and for the first time she stayed. When Peters brought tea in the morning, impassive, two cups on the tray, she lay very still with her eyes closed.

The following week, they went to a box at Ascot, Vera dressed in wide red and white silk stripes and a huge white picture hat swathed in tulle.

'We're two of a kind,' he told her, driving her back to London.

'How?'

'Loners essentially. Cold, ambitious . . .'

She removed her white glove and put her hand on his thigh. 'Go on.'

'Self-centred . . .'

Her long fingers, tipped in crimson, moved upwards.

'Bitch . . .'

He shot her a dark look – but he was amused, she could see, his mouth curving. They were both suddenly, violently, excited – as was the way with them. Robert swerved off the main road, driving furiously across-country until he came to a deserted lane. He stopped the car, scooped a rug from the back seat and dragged her out. Grabbing her hand, he pulled her into a field, Vera tottering on her flimsy high heels, holding on to her hat, protesting, Robert in his elegant morning suit. It was a grey day, starting to drizzle. He flung her down on the rug by a hedge, his hand pushing up her skirt, his mouth on hers. She wanted this quite as much as he did; they knew everything about each other physically by then. The sounds of ripping silk and Vera's cries fell on the new wheat and the gently dripping greenery. When they finally reached the outskirts of London, more or less composed, Vera saw that she had left her hat in the field.

That night, she played her part with a particular edge and brilliance. It was towards the end of the second act that she looked down and saw Robert in the stalls. She hadn't expected him to be there and the sight of him almost took her breath away. Beneath the words which came automatically now a painful realization formed for the first time: *how am I going to live without him?*

In the early hours of the following morning, dancing very close in the intimate darkness of some nightclub, Robert murmured, 'Now who is going to find that beautiful, rain-sodden, white hat – and what are they going to think when they do?'

When she whispered something short and vulgar – gutter language – into his ear, he threw back his head and laughed and laughed. And for a glorious moment she held him, she knew, in the palm of her hand.

Chapter 2

They were having tea at Gunter's on a warm afternoon late in July when Vera became aware of someone standing over their table. She looked up and saw a striking older woman, dressed entirely in dove grey, her hair swept up under the wide brim of her hat. Her chin was raised and she carried herself superbly. She was looking at Robert who was already on his feet.

'Mama . . . Miss Bowen . . . Vera, my mother . . .'

Clementine Brandon pointedly ignored Vera's outstretched hand and spoke directly to Robert. It was something about a houseparty, orders to be given and arrangements to be made. She spoke coldly and clearly in the unmistakable accents of the British upper classes. Vera, usually indifferent where other people were concerned, blinked and stared. She took Clementine Brandon, instantaneously, for the enemy she was.

'Of course I'll see to it,' Robert replied impatiently, equally cold. 'I'll do it, I say.'

'Very well, Robert.'

She swept out as though Vera simply weren't there. Vera, her temper rising by the second, thought that she might have been watching them across the room for some time. When they were together, she and Robert, they never took much notice of what was happening around them. And it was likely that his mother had heard the gossip; they had been out and about in London enough that summer – heads turning, people whispering. Vera glanced at Robert – but his expression told her nothing. He was dealing with the bill – urbane, unruffled, dark and handsome as any Hollywood film star. He glanced at his watch.

'Shall we go?'

She didn't trust her voice.

He took her arm as they walked silently into Park Lane in search of a taxi.

Finally, fuming, Vera burst out, 'You call that manners? You call that being a lady?' Elocution thrown to the winds, the last word came out pure cockney – *'loidy.'*

'Vera – I'm sorry – look ...' He was still holding her arm as they stood and faced each other. The dusky pink crêpe dress and matching hat accentuated her very pale blue eyes. He couldn't quite suppress the trace of a smile – which she saw. 'I mean, you know the situation ... the family ... I told you, when we met ... you must understand ...' He shrugged. His natural arrogance, his maddening good looks, enraged her further. She tore her arm away. Her matt, powdered skin was flushed.

'Not bleedin' loikly I don't.' Cockney again. She was furious, breathing hard; she was letting herself down – she knew it, and she didn't care. She was sounding exactly like her own mother, Nellie Bowen, who served behind the bar in the Mason's Arms in one of the dreariest parts of the East End of London.

'Vera – it was inexcusable, I know. It was appallingly rude. But you must realize that my mother is a professional widow. I was brought up in a house of mourning. Good God, since I was a boy I've never seen her in any garment that wasn't grey or black or purple. In a terrible way, she's made me – and Cloverley – her life. And I can't say I've been entirely satisfactory.' He smiled right at her with a good deal of charm, but she glared back, not giving an inch. 'I've got a lot of commitments,' he went on seriously. 'I haven't told you much, but my uncle isn't well, so I often have to deputize.' They were standing in the middle of the pavement, oblivious, people walking briskly round them. 'I've got to take over the estates, in Scotland, too. There's nobody else; it's expected of me. And I've got other decisions to make, political ones, which I'm finding difficult. In fact, I've got a hell of a rough meeting tonight which will run until God knows when. Then I've got to spend some time in the country, sorting things out.'

'I must go,' she said abruptly.

He raised his hand for a taxi that was lumbering towards them. She had to get back to the flat to Flo, to rest, before she went to the theatre. He knew that. He opened the door and she got in, sitting forward on the seat as he spoke to the driver and handed over money.

'Will I see you on Sunday?' she challenged.

'I don't know,' he said gravely.

She nodded and sat back, looking straight ahead. The expression of hopelessness on her face, the first time he had seen it, touched him more than she could have imagined. For two pins, at that moment, he would have dived into the cab and pulled her to him and kissed the unhappiness away and said – what?

He slammed the door shut and made a kind of salute as the taxi moved off into the traffic streaming down Park Lane.

It's expected of me . . . it's expected of me . . . The phrase went round and round in Vera's head as they ground through the streets of Mayfair. Yet, she thought, with a stab of fierce satisfaction, Robert *hadn't* done everything that was expected of him – not by a long shot he hadn't. For one thing, he hadn't married suitably as that old cow of a mother must have hoped. He was past forty and he hadn't produced an heir for that precious bloody house of theirs. And he had some very queer ideas politically, if you asked her – take this cloak-and-dagger nonsense he was involved in about not standing up to the Germans, as if she hadn't twigged what all the secret meetings with those other nobs were about this summer. They were like a lot of school kids; and it was downright treason, if you asked her. And now – horrors – he was involved with an actress. Serve her damn well right, the rude bitch.

During August, Robert was seldom in London. He explained to Vera, rather hurriedly, that he was up to his eyes in work at Cloverley, in the estate office, and beating the drum with his agent in the constituency. The inevitability of war had generally been accepted by then, and people were snatching their last peacetime holidays, hoping for the best but making serious plans for the worst. At the end of the month, when they were having a late drink at the Chester Square house, he told her, with no further explanation, that he had rejoined his regiment.

'But I thought . . .'

He swallowed some whisky, sprawled back on the sofa, totally at ease, as he always was with her. Just one lamp glowed in the drawing-room where they were sitting. It was very quiet and the windows were open on to the warm night air. Out in the blackness, in the square beyond, the dry leaves rustled faintly.

'I changed my mind,' he said flatly. 'I thought it through from all angles and I wasn't prepared to go on with it – the plan for peace, such as it was. So I resigned from the committee. Can't miss out on all the fun, can I? You're such a long way away, Vera. Why don't you come over here?'

Soon after war was declared – on Sunday, 6 September – Robert disappeared on training exercises. He managed the occasional phone call and one weekend, at the end of October, he turned up unexpectedly having told no one. He looked leaner and fitter and more sombre. They spent Saturday night alone in Chester Square; the servants, even the faithful Peters, were away. The next day they lunched outside London at a famous inn on the river. Deliberately, they did not talk about the war and what might happen and the dangers ahead. They enjoyed the good meal and remembered some of the amusing things they had done last summer – which already seemed a world away. And the play, Vera said, was still going strong. She was keeping her fingers crossed, but it looked as though they would carry on right through the winter. They were all getting a bit fed up with it, of course, but it was steady work and good money.

After lunch, Robert announced that he was taking her for a drive.

'Where to?'

'Wait and see.'

He drove fast across-country, finally stopping in a copse amid gentle green downlands.

'Where are we?' Vera leant back, turning her head to look at him. Wine at lunch always made her drowsy.

'Get out and I'll show you.' He smiled mysteriously. 'I want to surprise you . . .' He took her hand and led her through the trees. There was a pale sun in the luminous sky and the leaves were the colours of beaten gold and copper. 'Are your shoes up to this? Good girl.' Vera was wearing wide, fashionably draped trousers, a tailored, rather mannish jacket, and brown brogues.

'Robert – where . . .?'

'You'll see in a minute. We're coming this way' – ducking under a low branch – 'because it was my secret entrance when I was a boy.' They emerged on to a low ridge. Beneath them, in a valley hung with faint bluish mist, was a wide expanse of parkland dotted with fine oaks. A curving drive, just below, led to an Elizabethan country house – mellowed pink stone, timbered, curling turrets – so settled it seemed a part of the surrounding landscape.

Vera gasped.

'Cloverley,' he said. He put his arm round her shoulders and she leant against him. They stayed like that for a couple of minutes – then she turned to him. Her face, which was never pretty, could be infinitely alluring, as it was then – her eyes enormous, her face pale and her mouth made up a pillar-box red. Except on stage, she could never dissimulate.

'Robert,' she said clearly. 'I want us to have a child.'

A flock of birds flew overhead and there was a tantalizing smell of woodsmoke.

He dropped his head and picked up her hand and kissed it for a long time.

They slithered down a path to the drive arriving at a spot quite close to the house. Robert pulled her up the broad steps and strode ahead into the dim, galleried hall. He shouted several times, flinging open doors. Vera stood looking about her, nervous as a cat beneath the studied poise – although no one would have guessed it.

'My mother and Angus are in Scotland.' He grinned at her over his shoulder. 'In case you wondered. Oh, there you are Mrs Barrow . . .'

There was dither and consternation as the place roused into life. A manservant appeared, red in the face, pulling down his shirtsleeves. They had not been told, they hadn't expected, they hadn't heard the car... Madam this, Sir Angus that ... Robert settled them down.

'Tea in the library is all we want, Foster. We've got to be off back to London.'

He then took Vera off on a whirlwind inspection of the house, pointing out various features with careless familiarity. The principal rooms with panelled walls and moulded ceilings and huge, cavernous fireplaces were hauntingly beautiful in the fading autumn daylight which cast soft shadows. Daunted by the scale of it – room after room, wide corridors, unexpected crannies and casements – Vera was astonished that such a grand place could also seem homely. It was full of books and flowers and family photographs and squashy, lived-in sofas and deep armchairs. Robert mentioned casually that there was talk of evacuating a small private boys' school there from near London.

'There are two enormous Victorian wings behind, vile additions, which are hardly used so it could easily be accommodated.'

On their way back down the wide staircase, Vera hesitated in front of a full-length portrait of a young woman. Exaggeratedly tall and willowy, she looked out at them with delightful candour – wasp-waisted in her white satin dress, hair piled high, a pearl choker round her long neck.

'Who's that?' The eyes and the distinctive dark brows, winging upwards, were the image of Robert's. 'You look ever so like her.'

'Yes? Other people have said so, too. She's Cordelia, my American grandmother, the mother of four Brandon sons. Her father came from nothing and made a pile in railways. She married another Robert Brandon some time in the 1880s, which explains why Cloverley has a sound roof. Toldini painted her soon after their marriage. My father resembled her too, by the way. She was much liked, very warm and natural – people round here still speak of her.'

Tea was laid on a low table in front of the fire. The butler, uniform now in place, hovered. Mrs Barrow appeared, flustered and asking unnecessary questions. In addition to Robert turning up out of the blue late on a Sunday afternoon, Vera's actressy figure in her flaring trousers — not at all the sort of outfit they were used to seeing on ladies — flummoxed them utterly. Robert waved them away and pushed a plate of scones towards Vera. It was getting dark and the fire and the lamps burnished the books which lined the walls and the shabby old leather furnishings. They lingered, not saying much, drinking tea. Robert looked hard at Vera, then into the leaping flames. He put his cup and saucer down on the floor with a clatter.

'We ought to be making a move,' he said moodily, not stirring.

Vera held her hands out to the fire and the bracelets which she always wore jangled.

'We'll have to go back to the car your way, through the woods, won't we?' she asked.

Ignoring, or not hearing, the question, 'I love you, I suppose,' he said coldly, looking at her without kindness. He had never used the word 'love' before — to anyone.

Vera drew in her breath. She felt panicked — by the house, the servants, the understated grandeur; the glimpse of what it was like to belong to a family where a heritage like Cloverley was handed down and down — and *she* with her grim East End childhood. But it was the harshness in Robert's voice that destroyed her. She had no notion of how to respond. There was no script here. Helplessly, she reached for her bag and stood; and, turning blindly, Vera, who rarely made an awkward move, caught his cup with the toe of her shoe and the delicate china shattered.

'Oh God — damn ... I'm sorry.' She dropped to her knees, biting her lip, suddenly fighting tears — and she hardly ever cried. Breaking the china, just as she was losing her composure, had shocked her badly. Her hands were shaking.

'Leave it, it doesn't matter, it's not of the slightest importance.' He got up, looking at his watch impatiently as Vera went on picking the shards from the carpet. 'Oh, do leave it, Vera.' He sounded exasperated. 'It's my fault anyhow for leaving the bloody thing on the floor. They'll see to it.'

17

'They' – those servants who saw right through her.

And when she still didn't look up or answer, 'We really must get going, you know. I'm due back by nine.' They made their way back to the car using Robert's torch. It was a pitch-black night. Twigs cracked under their feet and the darkened woods which had been so full of light and colour earlier were ghostly and alien. There was an electric emotional tension between them. Opening the car door for her, he pulled her against him.

'Would you marry me?' he asked curtly.

Vera's 'Robert – yes' died in a whisper against his chest. He kissed her once, roughly.

It was a hellish drive through blankets of fog, what lighting there was too dim to make much difference. When he dropped her at her flat, both of them tense and tired, he only said, 'I'll phone when I can. It may be difficult.'

He then vanished again, phoning occasionally and sending a few notes, which said nothing of importance and didn't even give an address. She believed he was in the West Country, somewhere near Salisbury Plain. Missing him desperately, terrified of being out when he phoned, Vera let her life dwindle to the flat and the theatre. Only Brian Worth had any inkling of the passion of her private life. This was the time of the phoney war – unnaturally quiet, everyone on edge, waiting. Knowing every nuance of the part, Vera kept up her usual polished performances. They had never had more responsive audiences and they were playing to full houses night after night.

In the end, Robert phoned, not long before Christmas. He had ten days' leave starting the following week and he would be spending most of it at Cloverley. To Vera, hanging on every word, he sounded almost impersonal. There was no suggestion that she should join him there. He had to be in London on the Friday; he would come round to the flat mid afternoon.

But it was after five when he eventually turned up, although he knew that she never left for the theatre later than six. After hours of nervy pacing and smoking, she heard him taking the stairs two at a time, whistling. Suddenly come vibrantly to life, she opened the door before he rang. His uniform, expertly tailored, looked extremely smart — and Vera thought he seemed boyish and rather pleased with himself. He made some airy apologies — he'd had to give lunch to a young relative of his mother's and it had gone on longer than he had anticipated — before aiming his cap towards a chair and crushing her against him.

Some time during the next hour, Robert produced a small red leather box from a Bond Street jeweller. Inside was a brooch in the shape of a star, made from small diamonds.

'Oh, Robert...'

It was the one expensive present he had given her.

'Pretty, isn't it? It's early Victorian. I looked, and it was the only one that seemed right for you.'

But for all their passion, dancing through the early hours, intoxicated on Pol Roger and each other, something had changed in Robert since that autumn night in the woods above Cloverley. Vera — dimly — sensed this. He stayed at the flat that night. And the next. They were both reckless.

'I can't get enough of you,' he muttered, waking her at some unearthly hour that last morning. Neither slept a wink before daylight.

Vera watched him grimace in the mirror as he did up his tie. She stood just behind him, hands thrust deep into the pockets of her long silk dressing-gown. She dreaded this parting.

'When will I see you again?' She sounded as she felt — hopeless.

'I don't know. There are rumours in the mess... this absurd bloody war is going to be hotting up soon.'

The war — that he didn't believe in, yet was about to fight. She thought of that house and the family; from his father and three brothers there was no heir, just Robert.

'I hate it when you go.' She was desperate now. If only she could find the words to bind him for ever. Or, perhaps, a son... He buckled on his belt smartly; precious seconds were ticking by. Turning, he put his hands on her shoulders.

'Look, it's a dreadful time. The uncertainty is the worst, waiting for the rough stuff to begin.'

He kissed the tip of her nose as she closed her eyes very tight. Her hands were clenched in her pockets. When she didn't answer he said, 'You'll look after yourself and stay safe — you won't run away, will you?'

He looked as handsome and young as he did the first day she saw him across the lunch table at the Savoy.

'We're happy together, Robert,' she whispered, playing her last card. 'We *are*. We — we — match. I want . . .' But her voice wouldn't come.

'I know.' He held her briefly. 'But we can't.'

And he was gone.

Leaning out of the window, she could see his car parked in the street below. She watched as he threw his bag into the back, slid into the driver's seat and zoomed off, to Cloverley.

He did not appear again during his leave, but he phoned the night before he went back to his regiment. Things were starting to move at last, he said, and this was a relief. He had received his orders — but he couldn't, she understood, say any more. He would be in London soon and let her know. If he was missing her as she was him, he didn't say so.

With agonizing slowness, it seemed to Vera, grey January gave way to a freezing February. Day followed day followed day . . .

The doctor shuffled some papers on his desk, coughed once, and told Vera what she already knew — that she was pregnant. By his reckoning, the child would be born early in September.

'If there's anything Miss — er . . .'

'Bowen.'

'Miss Bowen. Of course. If there is anything at all I can do . . .' He looked keenly at his patient over the top of his glasses. An actress in a popular play. He couldn't remember offhand what it was called, but his nurse had seen it and thought it excellent. Chester Moore was a worldly man, close to sixty, with a large and lucrative Mayfair practice. In his time, he had seen most human situations at close range. This one was unexceptional, probably rather a sad case; but he assumed that she would be well looked after, financially at least. 'Frankly, how you proceed is entirely your own decision, of course, Miss Bowen. But if you would like to discuss arrangements for your care and the birth of the child . . .'

'Thank you Doctor.'

She had come to see him once before with Jim, when he'd had one of his bad turns, and taken to him. She stood, shook his hand, and left.

She went straight to the theatre from Dr Moore's consulting rooms and gave one of her most scintillating performances. She wouldn't think of the future, not yet. She would keep her head and her iron self-discipline, and bide her time.

Two days later, Robert phoned. It was a terrible line; they could barely hear above the crackling. He was crisp and cool and business-like. Could she meet him at Chester Square on Sunday night? It would have to be late, about ten, as he was tied up earlier; he would explain when he saw her.

She made her way by taxi through the bitter and blacked-out London night. Robert answered the front door, pulled her quickly inside and embraced her as he removed her cape. They went straight upstairs to the drawing-room. As so often during the past year, Peters had left everything ready. The fire was lit and the exquisite furniture gleamed in the lamplight; the heavy curtains were tightly drawn. Robert was solicitous and charming, and just a little distant. Vera had the feeling that his mind was elsewhere. There was a pile of papers that looked like accounts beside a chair to one side of the fireplace.

The telephone rang in the downstairs hall.

'Drat! I shan't be a moment, I swear. Sit and be comfortable.' He dashed back down the stairs. Vera strained to listen through the open door. He seemed to be talking about administrative problems — Cloverley no doubt — and she was certain that he was speaking to his mother. When he came back, she was standing in front of the fire. The ruby-red tube of a dress accentuated her height and her willowy slenderness.

'You're looking as wonderful as ever, thank God,' Robert told her. 'Good for the troops' morale – mine at least.' Bending over the drinks, suave, smiling across at her, 'What will you have, my sweet?'

Vera moved her neck a fraction so that she was looking straight at him, the deep red collar dramatically framing her face. That was when she told him. She watched impassively as his confident smile faded.

After the first appalled comprehension, Robert took a deep breath and made some rapid and conclusive mental decisions. He fixed them drinks without saying anything and came over and pulled her down on the sofa beside him. He handed her a drink and took a large gulp of his.

'You're quite sure of this?'

'Quite sure. I've seen a doctor.'

'My poor darling, what most terribly bad luck.' His hand massaged her shoulder. 'Christ, I'm so sorry. But you're not to worry – about anything. Drink up – it will do you good. And God knows I need it . . .'

The fire leapt and sparked and sent waving shadows around the elegant room. Vera's mind was blank.

He then told her, with what seemed to her quite breathtaking callousness, that arrangements would be made, he knew just the man, 'a proper doctor, not a quack'; he'd see to everything in the morning. Peters would take her; he would get the address, the bill would be settled immediately. He sounded perfectly assured and in control, quite as though he was dealing with some troublesome estate problem.

Vera started breathing in shallow gasps. She had a confused mental image of that night in the woods at Cloverley. Clearly, there was to be no more talk of love or marriage.

'But what if I don't want that – an abortion?'

'Vera, darling, be sensible. Everybody's life is in limbo at the moment. And I was going to tell you, it's why I'm in London –'

'What?'

'We're off to France to join the BEF – hush-hush, incommunicado, all that stuff.'

22

'Oh, Robert – no!' Fear shot through her.

'Yes, any day now. We move down to the coast tomorrow, and after that it's just a matter of time before we go over.' He got up and poured himself another whisky, neat this time. 'It's anyone's guess what we'll find over there. But I suppose if one's in a war one might as well see some action.'

He came back to the sofa, put his arms round her, and started kissing her neck. The drink and his decisiveness had steadied him after a few nasty moments – and just the sight of her could arouse him anywhere.

'It's not what I want,' she repeated stubbornly, drawing away. She took a sip of her drink, almost gagged, and put it down.

'Darling, I do understand. It's difficult for you, it must be, for any woman. But be reasonable; we're all living with terrible uncertainty these days. One simply can't make plans for the future. And look at your career – it's dazzling, going so well, everything you've fought so hard for.' He kissed her cheek and her hair as she sat still as a statue. He told her how wonderful she was, how extraordinarily talented and stylish, and what fun they'd had together – and would again. 'You're as cold as ice,' he said, warming her long, beautiful fingers in his hands.

Not long after, she asked him to take her home.

'I'll organize everything in the morning,' he told her as they left the house and stepped into the darkened square. He took her arm. 'You'll go through with it, won't you?' He sounded guarded.

'I suppose so.'

Chapter 3

The next week, still wearing her coat and hat, Vera stared out of a bedroom window on to the frozen suburban garden below. The room was starkly arranged as a makeshift surgery, with a simple bed, a strong overhead light, a table with some instruments and piles of white towels. She stayed like that for a good ten minutes; then she turned and left, shutting the door behind her. She was pulling on her gloves as she came down the stairs, hideously patterned in orange and yellow carpet.

The doctor opened his study door.

'I've changed my mind,' she said, very composed and elegant, her chin deep in her fur collar and her face half hidden by the dark felt hat.

'What's that?' He looked decidedly put out. 'Now – now – just wait a minute. This is an emotional decision for any woman, it's bound to be. Come in here and we'll talk.' He had a nervous tic in his cheek and he sounded anxious. 'The responsibility . . . and you seemed so certain . . . and I won't be able to see you again, you understand, Mrs James.'

'I understand.' Vera thought he might have recognized her, although Robert, making the arrangements that last frantic morning, had naturally used fictitious names. 'The account will be settled in full as agreed.' After looking quickly up and down the road, he let her out of the front door. Peters, glued to the pages of a sporting tabloid, was parked a couple of houses down. During the drive back into London, from time to time he shot glances at Vera as she gazed out of the window.

Handing her out of the car near the flat, he said casually, 'I'll be shutting Chester Square now, "for the duration", Mr Brandon said. I'll be joining up myself any minute, so it's for the best, isn't it?' He watched her with undisguised insolence. 'No use leaving it empty with all them furnishings and pictures. Mr Brandon didn't mention it, then?'

'No . . . no, he didn't.'

She had never liked, or trusted, Peters. Stricken, she fought down a wave of panic.

'Then where – how . . .?'

Her throat was so dry she was croaking.

'Mr Brandon can be reached via Cloverley Court. Any important correspondence will be forwarded to him in France. He told me that particularly.' He coughed politely. 'Will that be all then, *Madam*?'

She wrote, waited, and wrote again – to Captain Robert Brandon, to Cloverley Court in Wiltshire. They were short, stilted letters saying only would he get in touch with her at once, that she needed to see him urgently. There was no answer, from Cloverley Court or from France.

The freezing winter was followed by a warm and miraculously beautiful spring. The cherry tree in the courtyard, just visible from the living-room of Vera's flat, burst into a halo of pink blossoms. Vera left the play, pleading exhaustion. She could get by for the moment on the small annuity Jim Trickett had left her, and she had put herself in the capable hands of Dr Moore. Now obviously pregnant, she rarely left the flat. Flo came every day and saw to the cleaning and such food as she needed. Brian Worth often popped in. Because he was her only friend – and because she had to have some human contact – she had told him everything in as few words as possible.

'You're mad, dear girl; never say I didn't tell you. Throwing your life away . . .' He sighed ostentatiously.

'I couldn't do it,' she said stubbornly.

'Pity.' He'd known it was a mistake, this Robert Brandon business, from the beginning. These misalliances rarely worked, and she had taken the affair far, far too seriously. All the same, he was loyal – and crafty. He brought her goodies from Fortnum & Mason and bits of theatre gossip. Most importantly, he was writing a play with her in mind for the lead; the hard and flighty Gina Hollis would be her creation. Vera's particular talents were uniquely suited to his style as a playwright: he had recognized this for some time. When he came for a drink in the evenings, they would read the play aloud, playing all the parts, changing and revising as they went. Vera even hit on the title – *Partners in Paradise*. This was her one bright spot amidst the unhappiness and boredom and uncertainty.

With the end of May came Dunkirk. Like the rest of the country, Vera stayed glued to the wireless during those hot, sunny days when the whole country was in mortal danger. Was Robert safe? Had he been rescued by one of the 'little ships'? Was he alive?

She waited – and still she heard nothing.

One morning, about a month later, on an impulse she telephoned the house in Chester Square. Expecting the rings to echo in the empty house, she was astonished when the phone was picked up immediately. It was Peters.

'Oh, good morning, Madam.' He had just dropped in, he said, to make sure everything was in order. He was off back to camp in the afternoon. 'The Major? Oh, he's on the mend now.'

'He . . . he . . .'

'Very badly wounded indeed he was, nearly a goner. Just before Dunkirk it was. Held the buggers off, they did – begging your pardon, Miss – so's more of our chaps could reach the coast. For sure he'll be decorated. They got him in the right shoulder – he lost an arm, near as dammit. It was touch and go for a bit, but they're pulling him round, nursing him at Cloverley now.'

'I see – well, thank you, Peters.'

Clementine Brandon came out of the library just as the telephone rang. She had a sheaf of papers in one hand, her glasses in another and a sweater was flung round the shoulders of her ivory linen dress. A born organizer, she had been making the final arrangements for the school that was to be evacuated to Cloverley.

'I shall take it, Foster,' she announced as the butler creaked out of somewhere. The great panelled hall was dark and shadowy even on that hot summer morning. The single downstairs telephone in the entire house was in a curtained alcove off the hall. Unlike his nephew, Angus Brandon did not hold much with modern communications.

'This is Cloverley 74.'

There were some silent seconds. This was not the call, concerning beds for the dormitories, that Clementine Brandon had been expecting. Neither did it take her entirely by surprise. Both the letters that Vera Bowen had written to Robert had been intercepted and read by her – and immediately consigned to the fire. She was fully prepared to end the distasteful business once and for all.

'My son is recuperating, out of danger now . . . No, there is no question of his being disturbed . . . I shall, certainly . . . good day, Miss Bowen.'

Making her way serenely back to the library, she heard a car pull up noisily outside, and minutes later, the butler showed a large, untidily dressed young woman into the library.

'Ceci, dear.' Clementine Brandon rose and held out her hands. 'How angelic of you to come over so quickly. I was afraid I might have left it too late to catch you – I thought you were off to the WRNS?'

'I am soon, I hope. Daddy's having a fit, of course, but then he would, wouldn't he?'

Cecilia Neville was the daughter of a distant relative of Clementine Brandon's, who lived near by. At twenty-one, Cecilia was outgoing and confident: a country girl, thoroughly at home with dogs and horses, and blissfully unconcerned with her appearance. She had a high colour, a marvellous complexion and very dark glossy hair which tumbled to her shoulders. Over the past Christmas period, the two families had seen a good deal of each other. Robert, who had been edgy and bad-tempered, had taken some notice of Cecilia Neville for the first time – and despite the age gap, he seemed to find her company refreshing. She made him laugh and coaxed him out of his black humour. Clementine Brandon, hardly daring to hope, knew for a fact that they had lunched together in London.

'He's a funny old thing, your father. But it's adorable of you to answer my SOS about Robert. He was very bad, you know, I really was in despair.' She looked strained and there were dark shadows under her eyes. 'The doctors think his arm will never be right, but at least it was saved. He's improving a little every day, I think. He's outside now, getting an airing for the first time since he came back from hospital, and I thought a bit of youthful companionship would do him the world of good. You can stay to lunch, can't you?' Linking her arm through Cecilia's, she went on, 'Let's go out and find him. Don't be shocked by the way he looks. I didn't tell him you might be coming, so it will be a pleasant surprise.'

Robert Brandon lay in a hammock at the far end of the lower lawn, idly swinging between shade and sunlight. His shoulder, wedged against a cushion, was slightly easier today. He flapped at a cruising wasp. The recent weeks were a painful blur punctuated by too vivid memories of war: skirmishes with the enemy which culminated in a desperate attempt to hold part of a French town, just back from the coast, already decimated by the Germans. His men were pushed to the limit, dropping like flies; German bombers overhead strafing. Every hour counted, as behind them the ragged lines of exhausted troops trudged towards the beaches. After he took that bullet, his memories became incoherent – pain, voices, a stretcher, more pain, a lorry jolting over rough ground. He couldn't make much sense of anything after that; the fever and the sweating and the chills had set in. There was a hospital; nightmares; devastating weakness; pain again.

Somehow, cutting a swathe through regulations and red tape, Clementine Brandon had arrived and insisted that he was brought back by ambulance to Cloverley. Gradually, the fever had come down and he began to eat a bit. He was still weak as a kitten, gaunt, white-faced. He moved his shoulder – and grimaced.

And another reason that he knew he was on the mend was that his thoughts turned increasingly to Vera Bowen, with a yearning and a tenderness that astonished him . . .

He pushed against the ground with his foot and the hammock swung gently to and fro.

He had lost his head – and perhaps more – over her last summer; there was no doubt about that. She was enigmatic, elegant, with a body made in heaven: just the thought of those shoulders melting seamlessly into long white arms and his senses stirred agreeably. She was easy to be with, too, she could be amusing – and she didn't mind silences when most women sulked. He was not without a conscience where she was concerned, either. He had done the honourable thing – what else *was* there to do in the circumstances? – but although he hadn't believed so at the time he wasn't finding it easy to remove her from his life, the way he always had before when a relationship ended. Not that there had been so much as a postcard from her in the mountain of mail he had found waiting for him: not one word since that morning he'd left London with the regiment.

If he saw her again, it would be playing with fire – he knew that. It had been touch and go in the autumn, he could easily have done something absurd like marry her. He had wanted to, one magic and moody afternoon down here – suddenly, desperately. (Marry he must, after all.) But the fact was that he, who had no time for women except in what he considered to be their place, admired Vera Bowen. Everything she had achieved had been through her own efforts. And there was more. The vulnerability beneath the enamelled exterior turned his guts to water. What did they call it – love?

There was no question of writing, not with this arm. But to hear her voice, tonight, perhaps, from that absurd telephone in the alcove . . .

He fell asleep still thinking about her, and smiling. When he opened his eyes, he saw, or believed he saw, two figures walking across the lawns towards him. Behind them, through the heat haze, rose the dark romantic outline of Cloverley. The figures came closer: his mother and young Cecilia Neville. In his weak and disorientated state, they melted into one in his vision. And there were similarities in the two women which he hadn't realized before: both were tall and dark eyed, both carried themselves well. They floated on towards him . . .

'Robert,' Clementine Brandon called, her voice cutting through the soft summer air. 'You're not asleep, are you? I've brought you a visitor. Can you guess? Ceci has come over specially to cheer you up.'

That afternoon, after hours of anguished indecision — walking distractedly round the small sitting-room, lighting cigarettes and stubbing them out — Vera Bowen made up her mind. For the first time in several years she got in touch with her mother because she needed her. She asked her to come round to the flat tomorrow. And Nellie Bowen, wondering nervously what on earth all this was about, agreed.

Chapter 4

And all that, Vera thought disgustedly, turning her face to the wall, all that for a *girl* ... In all the boring, lonely months of waiting, she had never seriously thought that the child would not be a boy.

The starched sheets felt scratchy against her bare arms and there was a faint smell of disinfectant. The discreet clinic, where she had just given birth, was in a quiet, leafy street of solid family houses just north of Regent's Park. It was a warm September evening in the fateful month of September 1940. Every so often, as she lay there like a dead thing, people came in and poked and prodded and murmured reassuringly and left.

Some miles away there was a German air raid in progress. Less than a week ago, a V formation of enemy planes had appeared like a flight of silver birds out of the cloudless late afternoon sky. By evening, London glowed an angry red; the Blitz, so long expected, had hardly let up since.

The door opened again and Vera heard voices in the corridor. 'God Almighty, the East End's not half getting it again tonight, the sky's lit up like ...' The door was firmly shut and heels clicked bossily over the bare floor.

'Now, Mother,' gushed a nurse somewhere close to Vera's face, 'we're a dear little girl, aren't we? And a nice size, just over seven pounds, all cuddled up in our sweet pink shawl. A rosebud mouth and such pretty eyebrows we've got.'

'Go,' Vera commanded weakly, opening her eyes a fraction. 'Please leave –'

'There, there, such a pretty little thing,' cajoled the nurse. In her time, she'd seen plenty of these spoiled society madams, acting like no one had ever been through a confinement before. And she'd made enough fuss about it, Lord knew.

'– *Me alone*,' hissed Vera.

The nurse was taken aback at this; but she wasn't used to putting up with any nonsense. She was holding the baby for her mother's first close inspection. Had she the energy, Vera would have screamed at the woman to take herself, and this newborn daughter, as far away as possible. As it was, making an effort and turning her head, she saw the tiny face quiet in the soft blanket: dark hair, distinctive slanting eyebrows, neat features.

Robert – all over again . . .

Nothing had prepared her for this shock of recognition – and she could hardly stop herself from crying out in anguish . . . *Robert, Robert* . . . A wave of black despair washed over her. Tentatively, she reached out and touched the baby's cheek – her daughter, and Robert Brandon's: so small; so perfect; so helpless; so familiar. Still weak and woozy from the anaesthetic, her emotions raw, she longed with every fibre in her body to snatch her from the nurse's arms and hold her and hold her and never let her go. Another part of her mind – the rational part that had taken stock and realistically planned some sort of a future for both of them – warned: *caution*. Vera could feel her whole body, even her fingers, trembling. As she went on stroking her daughter's cheek – wordless, expressionless – the baby moved her head and snuffled into the blanket.

The nurse, unused to such a feeble display of motherhood, stood back, removing the infant from Vera's touch, muttered something about some people being 'ever so funny', and marched smartly away from this unnatural mother.

Vera lay back, eyes closed, wetness spilling down her cheeks.

'It's the docks again, but they drop them anywhere to lighten the load. Coo – that was a close one!' There was a whistle and a thud and the building shook slightly. 'But it's the docks they're after . . .'

The door shut firmly.

The East End . . . the docks . . . alarm briefly pierced Vera's unhappy self-absorption. Those brief minutes with her daughter – shocking and painful and loving – had changed her instincts for ever. It was *her* life that mattered now. And with Nellie? In the thick of all this? Her eyes opened – wide and fearful. It was a terrifying thought: bombs hurled down on that flat, grimy area of London with its maze of narrow, overcrowded streets and alleyways and market stalls, where you could literally smell the poverty. Vera knew it all too well. With steely discipline – and a bit of talent – she had managed to claw her way out of it. But her mother was still there – and her grandmother, Gran Gubbins, a toothless old harridan, loathed by everyone, who kept the corner shop two streets away. And despite the present danger, she knew instinctively that she could entrust this precious infant daughter to her mother. This was her one crumb of solace. Not that she had any choice in the matter, she thought bitterly – crying silently, weakly.

Vera had telephoned Nellie Bowen a couple of nights ago at work at the pub, telling her that she was going into the nursing home. Nellie had sounded spunky and cheery as ever above the background din. 'Keepin' well, are you, luv? You'll be glad when it's all over. Now you jus' get your Flo to let me know.'

There was another whine and crunch, closer this time. Vera was thinking confusedly: poor baby, not her fault after all ... what a world, what at time to be born into.

The door opened again. 'I've just popped in to see how you're getting along.' This was the older nurse, the one Vera had taken to, with iron-grey hair tucked up under her cap and strong capable hands. It was her calm and authority that had got Vera somehow through the ordeal of labour until she was at last wheeled screaming into the delivery room, gasping for oblivion.

'Not too bad. A bit sleepy.'

'It's the gas that does that. You'll be right as rain in a day or so.' She had looked at Vera sharply when she was admitted the previous evening. Vera fancied she knew who she was despite the dark glasses, no make-up to speak of and the drab navy maternity dress. She was having weak pains that had, maddeningly, stopped. But Dr Moore insisted that she stayed in the nursing home to be on the safe side, because of the situation – as everyone was saying about everything these days. The baby was due at any moment and she didn't want to get caught out in a raid.

'Look, I'd lie on my stomach if I was you. Sleep on it, too, if you can.' The nurse turned her deftly, tucking in the sheets. 'You'll get your figure back quicker that way.'

'Thanks.'

Suddenly, Vera was close to tears again – utterly alone, bleeding for Robert, physically and emotionally exhausted. She meant her thanks for more than a bit of professional wisdom; for staying sympathetically close all the hours when she was in pain and frightened. Undone by kindness, she had a sudden wild urge to break down and tell her everything. But she could rarely show her feelings naturally – not even to Robert. They emerged only in brittle lines, written by others, under bright stage-lighting. Blinking, she muttered 'Thanks' again.

'It's what I'm here for. Now you get some rest. I'm going to make a dash for it while it seems a bit quieter. They say you could see to read in Piccadilly at ten o'clock last night. I'll look in again tomorrow.' She gave Vera a reassuring pat on the shoulder, and she was gone.

Soon, lying on her stomach in the blacked-out room, Vera heard the 'All Clear' wail.

Across London, raked by bombs and lit by fires, Nellie Bowen heard that 'All Clear' as she huddled with the rest of them in the beery cellar of the Mason's Arms. The pub was in Parchway, a couple of miles to the north of the East End and the docks. Too close for comfort to all *that* if you asked Nellie . . . The rival pub on the opposite corner had been badly damaged a couple of nights before, evacuated and boarded up 'in the interest of public safety', as the notice said.

It had been bad again that night – and it wasn't over yet, not by a long shot. Nellie could swear that there had been a direct hit in the next street, or the one behind. Glances were exchanged in the semi-darkness. They had lived in those streets all their lives. They were thinking, Who's bought it this time, then?

Minutes after the wailing crescendo of the 'All Clear', Nellie was standing with her hands on her hips in her accustomed place behind the bar. They were all momentarily lightheaded with relief.

'Got rid o' them bastards for a bit. What's it to be then, luv?'

Petite and quick-moving, Nellie Bowen was still a pretty woman with her neat little features, a turned-up nose and lovely creamy skin. Her thick brown hair was greying a bit these days and she was spreading round the bottom; but when she smiled, her eyes lit up and crinkled – and most people were inclined to smile back. Everyone loved Nellie, the pert, warmhearted cockney with a wink and a grin and bit of chit-chat all round. Nothing got Nellie down for long. She was naturally talented, too, musical to her fingertips. She sang like a bird, sweetly and from the heart; give her any popular tune and her toes started tapping and she was off and away. Nellie Bowen's Saturday night sing-alongs in the Mason's Arms had been attracting custom in that part of London for as long as she'd worked there, over thirty years now.

They were already standing three-deep at the bar as Nellie reached for a couple of mugs and started pulling pints. Since the 'All Clear' had sounded, both the doors had been pushed open and men and women, some with children in their arms, trooped in, crowding the grimy old Victorian pub.

'Three 'alves, darlin'? Comin' right up.'

Nellie had never known anything like it, these past days with the bloody Blitz, except round Christmas. The chatter and the cigarette smoke and the too-loud laughter were already deafening. Fear did that to people, Nellie noticed.

Her mind darted to her only child, Vera. She was in the posh nursing home now. That uppity so-called housekeeper, Flo, had phoned and left a message at the Arms this afternoon; but there had been no further news. For all Nellie knew, she could be having the baby at this very moment. It puzzled Nellie – and hurt her inside a lot more than she let on – that she, with her friendly ways, should have become so estranged from this dazzling actress daughter of hers. She was proud of her, of course, but she was like a stranger; had been for years. Nellie had to pinch herself sometimes to make herself realize that this creature, got up to the nines, who talked as if she had a plum in her mouth, really was her Vera. To be fair, she was generous enough from time to time — although Nellie found she didn't much want her generosity. She had everything she needed, ta very much — and that wasn't a lot.

And to think that it was she, Nellie, who had been the stage-struck one in her youth; she who had coached and chivvied and encouraged the sullen teenager, Vera, suddenly grown much too tall, all legs and neck and arms. It was *she* who had thought that possibly, just possibly, she might have inherited a bit of her late dad's talent. And there was no one to touch Alf as a trapeze artist, on the high wires, when he was in his heyday — before the Great War, that was.

So one Sunday afternoon, in the shabby front room of the narrow terraced cottage in Trout Lane, Nellie had forced Vera to get her head out of one of those trashy books from the library she'd taken to reading, wound up the gramophone, and put her through her paces: a popular song barely discernible through the scratches, a few steps, a bit of singing and a bit of dancing. Everything that came to Nellie as naturally as breathing. It wasn't like that for Vera — but she wasn't bad. She had her father's timing, all right, and with her white skin and tapering fingers she looked, well, unusual. There wasn't an ounce of puppy fat on her, not like most girls her age. Even Gran Gubbins, who had disliked the taciturn Alf Bowen on sight and felt the same about his daughter — she always said the pair of them had eyes like pale blue boiled gooseberries — grudgingly admitted that. It was only with her thick, pretty brown hair that Vera took after Nellie.

'Two gins? Let's make 'em doubles then ... Right, dear? And 'ere's to our boys givin' 'em what they asks for over there.'

Nellie winked, swiping a spill, pouring tonic. Make 'em smile, that was Nellie's motto. She worked quickly and automatically. She sometimes thought she could do the bar at the Arms in her sleep. And these days you never knew when the blinking siren was going to start up again. She slid the glasses across the bar, handed over the change and went on to the next customer. 'What's it to be then, darlin'?'

Miss High and Mighty, that was her Vera. Not good enough for 'er, I'm not, that's the fact of it, Nellie would sniff to herself, sticking her nose in the air. All the same, she thought bitterly, the moment she was in trouble, in the family way, who did she send for, if you please? *Her* – that's who. No mention of the father, nothing like that: just the bare facts that her ladyship had decided to go through with it, and after the birth, she wanted Nellie to look after it. For the time being, at least. She'd see to the finances for both of them. There was a new play, it was almost certain, and she'd be starting rehearsals shortly.

Despite her own dismal experience with Alf, Nellie had remained a romantic at heart. This was her daughter, after all. The questions tumbled into her mind: Do you love him? Is he handsome? Is he rich? Will you be getting married?

'When are you expectin', then?' was all she could manage, looking round to see that nosy Flo wasn't in the room.

'September. The second week, the doctor said.'

Vera. Cool as a cucumber with her la-di-da accent – she never learned to speak like that roundabout Parchway – smoking one cigarette after the next in that flat of hers in Mayfair. Nellie had never plucked up the courage to ask how she came by that. And Nellie had sat there on the hard couch with her hat clamped on, twisting her hands in her lap, struck dumb as she always was in the presence of this daughter who had a funny way of moving, as though she was swimming under water. And all the time that Flo flounced in and out of the room looking at her as though she was something the cat had brought in.

'More tea, madam?' *Madam* ... And you couldn't call this tepid dishwater with a scented smell tea. Give her a decent brown cuppa any day – something stronger, more to the point.

'Well now, Vera,' Nellie had said at last, nervous and sweating under the tight crown of her felt hat. 'I don't know 'ow I'll manage, I'm sure. A baby takes some lookin' after. I've got my hours at the Arms. And I'm not as young as I were, mind.'

'Get the back bedroom fixed up. I'll arrange to have everything you need sent,' Vera cut in, leaning forward to get at the cigarette box. She'd hardly touched her tea – not that Nellie could blame her for that. 'And I'll send an allowance, weekly.' She paused to click open the heavy lighter. 'So you won't have to go out to work unless you want to — and surely you can arrange to get some help? You ought to get on the phone, too.'

Despite herself, something stirred then deep in Nellie's guts. Would it be a boy or a girl? Doris Brown across the street was saddled with twin grandbabies, lovely little kiddies, her Lizzie off living it up in the WRNS. All the neighbours pitched in to help. Nobody thought to ask about the father. And now here was her Vera; who would have believed it?

But all that was back in the spring, before this devilish bombing and such-like started; the war hadn't seemed real then. She'd seen Vera only once since, when she came to check that all the baby things had arrived. When she phoned the Arms a couple of nights ago, she sounded as cold as ever. She was expecting to go into the nursing home any moment now, she said. And instead of all the things Nellie desperately wanted to say — shall I come with you, luv? Don't be frightened, we women all get through it somehow — she found herself chattering on about Jerry being good for business in the pubs.

She always had been one for babies, herself; although with Alf gassed in the trenches when Vera was a child, his nerves done in, she'd been glad enough she'd only had the one to watch out for and feed. After he was invalided home, poor old Alfie was no good to man nor beast. With that shake, they couldn't take him back in the troupe, and the high wire was all he'd ever known. His chest was affected, too: cough, cough, cough; thinner and thinner. So he got odd jobs on and around the river when he could — every last penny gone on drink. It was Nellie's takings at the Mason's Arms that kept them, and they'd hung on to the little house in Trout Lane, although many a day they'd known real hunger. Things were bad then, back in the early twenties, if you were really poor.

Vera was ten when Alf fell, or jumped, into the Thames one foggy November night and was pulled out and identified two days later. Not much use as a husband, Alf hadn't been, although, give him his due, he'd put all his savings into buying the cottage when they got married. It seemed a miracle at the time, a place of their own with an indoor lavatory. And the good-humoured Nellie bore his memory no ill will.

Now she was left with my lady Vera. And this mysterious baby...

Just before closing, Nellie jumped when the phone by the bar rang, spilling the beer she was pouring. But it wasn't for her – and soon the siren went again.

Chapter 5

Brian Worth came to visit Vera at the nursing home three days after her daughter's birth. He swept into her room, carrying an armful of cloying lilies, newspapers and the latest batch of smart magazines. He also had a Harrods shopping bag containing gin, a large bottle of tonic water, a lemon, and a small knife. As a director, Worth was famous for his attention to detail. Once the nurse had been dispatched with the flowers, he seized the glasses on the bedside table and began to pour.

'A bit early, isn't it?' inquired Vera, raising her fine eyebrows. She lay back on a heap of pillows, in a cloud of cigarette smoke, wearing a jade crêpe de Chine bedjacket. She had managed some make-up and her hair was sleekly brushed.

'Nonsense, darling, it's tea-time at least, and this stuff is getting very precious. Pity there's no ice.' He handed her a glass. 'Here's to the new arrival,' he said, sitting gingerly in the chair by the side of the bed, his trousers perfectly creased beneath his silver-buttoned navy blazer. He had just the right amount of cuff showing – and a silk handkerchief spilling from his pocket. He was nearly fifty, but relentless dieting and a perpetually active intelligence kept him looking younger. 'Where is she, anyway?' He looked round warily. 'I'd adore to see her, don't you know.'

'All right,' Vera agreed indifferently. 'We'll ask Nurse when she brings the flowers back. I never thought it would be a girl. *Never.*'

Brian Worth noted her vehemence, and didn't like it. He was staking his new play on Vera and he didn't want any more nonsense. He'd stood by her during all this upheaval, but now she had to behave. 'It wouldn't have made the slightest difference if it wasn't,' he said severely. 'Not the slightest.' He'd warned Vera concerning Robert Brandon; he knew something about the way the world worked. As she didn't answer, he said, 'Anyhow, what have you called her?'

'Megan.'

'Darling girl, what on earth for?'

'I like it.'

'I see. And who does little Megan look like?'

'*Him* . . . God, it was awful. Having her . . .'

Brian raised a languid wrist. 'No details, please, I couldn't bear a *single* one. Anyhow, you *look* healthy enough,' he added spitefully. He had taken in the hair and the well-applied make-up. 'Nice and calm and rested. Not like the general population, trooping in and out of cellars, losing our beauty sleep.'

'I'll be doing the same soon enough.'

'And you've got to put all this behind you,' he said crossly. 'You're not the first, you won't be the last, you've made sensible arrangements with your Ma . . .'

'Flo phoned the Arms?'

'Of course. I promised, didn't I? But as I say, you've got to get on with things, sweetie, get the famous figure back, look after yourself. Best foot forward, if you please. Because I've brought some very good news.'

'You've found a theatre?' Vera sat bolt upright.

'Precisely. *Strangers in Paradise* opens in January, just as we'd planned, at the Fortune. We'll finish the casting in a week or so. I'm keeping my fingers crossed.' He passed a hand over his carefully waved hair and looked smug. He was utterly confident of his talent; he always had been. Vera was no great actress — but she had her points. She delivered his witty, and often bitchy, lines with deadpan aplomb. She took direction, she didn't have any tiresome ideas of her own. And nobody moved a snake-hipped, almost six-foot body across a stage like Vera Bowen; nor would anyone look more seductive in the type of bias-cut satin evening dress he had in mind for the final scene.

'And rehearsals?' The gin was having an effect, relaxing her, pushing away the heartache that was like a physical pain in her side.

'As soon as you can make it, darling – and on you get with stardom and creating the rôle of Gina Hollis.'

'I'll be out of here next week.' She crushed out her cigarette. 'Ask Flo to pass that on to Nellie, would you?'

When the sleeping Megan was duly brought in, Brian saw at once that the small face framed in dark hair bore more than a passing likeness to Robert Brandon. He then left as soon as he decently could. With the Blitz about to rain down on them again at any moment, social excuses were no longer necessary. Vera stowed away the gin, pulled the pile of newspapers and magazines on to the bed, and lay back, gazing up at the ceiling.

So *Strangers in Paradise* was going to work, after all. The plot was ridiculous, but the dialogue was crisp and amusing. She would wear – marvellously – some wonderful clothes. It was a recipe for elegant escapism which a nation at war seemed to thirst for. With Brian Worth's name, it was unlikely that it wouldn't be a hit – and she a star. It was the one thing that had kept her going during the interminable hot summer, waiting and waiting, agonizing, hoping, too, until that telephone call one summer morning to Cloverley Court had left her stunned, still holding the receiver, long after the person on the other end had hung up.

Robert, she had realized at once, would never be told. His mother had been out to defeat her from that first icy look at Gunter's. But it was Robert who had taken the final decision, she thought bleakly; in the end, it was she who hadn't mattered enough to him.

She moved restlessly on the uncomfortable bed and started to work through *Strangers in Paradise* in her mind. She owed everything to this acting lark. Without it, who knew if she would ever have been able to dig herself out of Trout Lane and the East End? She groped for a cigarette. It was Nellie who had encouraged her, she had to give her that. She'd coached her a bit, got her going; and it was she who had seen the notice – the Great

Kiddies Talent Competition – on that day trip to Westend-on-Sea, Whitsun 1924.

When she closed her eyes, it was as clear as if it had been yesterday. The muddy tide swept out and the sparkling lights came on in a shower of winking diamonds. A kid like her was swept up in the cheerful vulgarity of it all – the brilliantly lit pier, the amusement arcades, the stalls selling cockles and mussels and bright sticks of rock. Nellie saw the poster and it somehow struck a chord. A talent contest; now why shouldn't she have a go – her Vera? She looked a treat in a navy serge dress with a sailor collar, her only decent garment, her long hair tied back with a ribbon. But Vera pulled a face and pouted. In the end, she agreed to go in for it only because Gran Gubbins, who she hated, cackled so hard at the very idea.

When her turn came, she stood stock still in the spotlight on the rickety stage with her shoulders back and her arms by her side. She was half a head taller than any of the other contestants. She looked right out into the distance while the accompanist banged away at the tinny upright piano. She waited; her timing was instinctive. People standing round the edge quietened and craned to get a better view. She sang straight and clear, just as Nellie had taught her. It wasn't Nellie's pure birdsong call, but it was all right. There was some respectful clapping when she finished. And she won.

They were standing, dazed, Vera clutching an enormous box of chocolates – her prize – when a tall man appeared from behind and tapped Nellie on the shoulder. She whirled round. Removing his hat, he congratulated Vera and, speaking to her directly, handed her a white printed card. It read: 'Ben Maynard – theatrical agent.' He was on the lookout, he said, for talented youngsters to appear in an all-children production of *The Mermaid*. Having seen her performance – he smiled nicely – he was certain 'the young lady' would be suitable and he could 'confidently offer her a fee of one and a half guineas'.

'Of wha'?' Nellie shrieked, looking faint.

'Shut up, Ma,' snapped Vera.

'But I can' afford that,' cried the bewildered Nellie.

'Er – per week.'

'Don't be daft, Ma,' hissed Vera. ''E pays us, see.'

'Now, Vera, you jus' wait . . .'

'Yes,' said Vera to this stranger.

Ben Maynard – she'd been lucky there all right, lucky to have been spotted by him on a holiday evening in the tacky seaside playground. And she was only a kid; she knew nothing except that somehow, some time, she was going to get out of the grime and poverty of the East End. It turned out that he was an agent in a substantial way of business, and he was fair. He kept his word and got her the job in *The Mermaid* extravaganza, as one of a chorus of forty children shivering in gossamer cheesecloth. It was then that Vera decided, once and for all, that any life she could cling to in the theatre was preferable to Nellie and Gran Gubbins and 5 Trout Lane.

For his part, Ben Maynard recognized grit when he saw it. From then on, he had kept Vera mostly in work – a bit of dancing, a bit of singing, a bit of acting, to begin with. He saw to it that she had singing and elocution lessons. No one ever had to teach her much about how to stand or move on a stage and she never turned up to auditions without knowing what was expected of her. She learned how to make the best of herself from an early age. Some of the secondhand clothes, all she could afford, which she picked up from East End market stalls were eccentric – but she always created an impression. She went on growing and she made her unusual height work for her: she was noticed.

Looking back now, the years were blurred. Scrimping and saving to buy a dress or a pair of shoes, she was often hungry. She kept herself aloof from the backstage gossiping and the camaraderie. Between engagements, she returned, sullen and wretched, to Trout Lane, where she locked herself in the small, dingy back bedroom and had as little as possible to do with anyone, including Nellie.

A late afternoon hush had settled over the nursing home. Visitors had left, and apart from the odd car passing outside, the place was as quiet as the country. Vera was still exhausted from the long labour and the drink had made her sleepy. She started to doze ...

Her second bit of luck, no doubt about it, was when Jim Trickett marched into her life. It was in Manchester, outside the stage door, where she had a small part in some frothy comedy. He was there, waiting, when she came out; quietly confident, clutching a large bouquet of red roses, he was a short, stout middle-aged man with a ruddy face, who looked people disconcertingly straight in the eye. Starving hungry and almost penniless, Vera accepted his offer of dinner, something she rarely did with anyone. His name was Jim Trickett, he told her in his flat north-country accent as she wolfed down her first good hot meal for weeks. Watching her carefully, he came to the point at once. He'd sat through the play three times — 'There's nowt to it, is there?' — and picked her out from the start. His wife was an invalid; they had no children. And his textile business was comfortable, very comfortable indeed; in fact, the company was expanding south to London. He'd have to spend a couple of nights a week there from now on. He'd bought a lease on a small flat in a big block in Mayfair: nothing fancy, but pleasant enough. He didn't want to be there alone. If she moved in, she could have the run of it: he'd make few demands; she'd not find him ungenerous. But he wanted to know she'd be there when he was down; he was firm about that. So in future, she should only take on jobs in London. That was all. And they'd see how they went from there. She wasn't to say anything hasty; she was to think it over. But a bargain was a bargain — and Jim Trickett had never broken one in his life.

All in all, it seemed a good deal to Vera Bowen at twenty-two, and the following night she told Jim Trickett so. They shook hands, and the deal was on. Two weeks later, Vera was settled in the flat, nervously asking the housekeeper, Flo, what she thought Mr Trickett would want for his dinner that night.

Astonishingly, the arrangement worked remarkably well. She was a virgin when she went to Jim Trickett — and he taught her everything, patiently, gently and sometimes exotically. Soon, trusting him, she started to enjoy his lovemaking. And he was proud of the way she looked. She found a good dressmaker and someone to make her hats, and it was Jim Trickett's pleasure to buy her the bits and pieces of jewellery and accessories that she craved. Ben Maynard, tickled to death at Vera's falling on her feet so satisfactorily, started coming up with better parts in London theatres. Everything went along smoothly enough until the day the letter from the Manchester solicitors arrived in the post. Soon after that, she started seeing Brian Worth. Then came the plum part in the West End hit — and one Sunday morning, there was the luncheon party at the Savoy.

A nurse woke her, bustling in with a cup of tea. 'I looked in a couple of times and you were off in the land of nod, all right.'

Vera winced at the gratingly cheerful voice. 'Tired,' she muttered, suffering her pillows to be plumped and the sheet smoothed.

'That's right, you have a good rest while you can. There's nothing very jolly on the news today, I can tell you.'

When she left, Vera sighed and sat up and picked up *The Times*, skimming through it: Mr Churchill's speech, pictures of bomb damage, the King and Queen meeting an ambulance crew . . . She came to the social page and as her eyes raked downwards, one name leapt out at her: *Major Robert Brandon*. Reading on, she learnt that: 'Owing to the international situation, Major Robert Brandon and Lady Cecilia Neville were married quietly yesterday at St Mary's Church, Cloverley, Wiltshire. A family luncheon was held afterwards at Cloverley Court.'

For a few moments Vera held on to the paper as though she had been turned to stone. Shock followed — and her mind cleared with the short, sharp pain of it. She struggled up from the pillows and threw off the covers. She felt stifled; she could not stay in that room a second longer than she must. Every bit of steel instilled over the years buoyed her. And her self-discipline — and her pride. Her one thought was that she must get up and out of there, get on with her life, and her daughter's. *Now* . . .

When the nurse came to answer her ring she found her already dressed in the maternity outfit she had arrived in, carefully repairing her make-up. Her belongings were packed. Appalled, the nurse started remonstrating. 'Matron ... Dr Moore ... he was up all last night, we don't know when to expect him next ... the baby ... can't possibly be allowed to discharge yourself.'

Vera snapped shut her handbag and cut her short.

She wanted the use of a telephone, instructions for the baby's feed and as many full bottles as they could spare.

Seeing that there was nothing to be done — and as everything, she despaired, was topsy-turvy these days — the nurse went off meekly to do as she said.

An hour later, a black taxi shuddered up to 5 Trout Lane. Nellie, who had been expecting them from Flo's urgent message, ran to the door. She was flustered and anxious, and deliriously excited. She didn't even notice Doris Brown, with a toddler on either arm, watching from across the way. She hardly looked at Vera as she stepped gingerly out of the taxi; all her being was concentrated on the pink shawl which her daughter was holding stiffly, away from her body. She put out her arms and took the baby, cradling her instinctively. Inside the folds of the blanket, she looked down on a tiny, sleeping face.

'There now, your Nan's got you.' Nellie's face shone and her dimples showed. She led the way back into the dark little house, through the narrow doorway. By then, a few of her neighbours had clustered on the pavement, heads together, wiping their hands on their pinafores.

Vera supervised as the driver brought in two canvas bags. 'Leave them there, and wait. I won't be more than a minute or two.'

The door banged shut.

Standing in the poky hall with its grimy rose-patterned wallpaper, Nellie tore her eyes from her three-day-old granddaughter and peered up at Vera. Her figure was hidden by the shapeless navy dress, but even in the dimness she could see that she was terribly pale and there were circles under her eyes. She must have had a hard time, and she shouldn't be standing about, it was too soon; she must rest up. But she never could say these natural, womanly things to Vera.

'Come on in, then.' Nervously, she nodded at the front room but Vera didn't move. 'All right, are you, dear? I didn't 'alf get a fright when I 'eard from your Flo jus' now. It's ever so soon for the two of you.'

'I'm all right. I wanted to get out of there. And the baby, Megan, is healthy; good, too, so the nurses said. She sleeps well and feeds well. I've got the bottles and the instructions here, in this bag. Enough to keep you going until tomorrow.'

Nellie thought, she doesn't sound as though this mite had anything to do with her at all. And not a mention of the father, either. Off in the forces, most likely. There was no talking, proper talking, with Vera. She could feel the warmth of the baby through the blanket. Gently, she freed her face. Lots of dark hair – and pretty into the bargain. And her own. She loved her already, bless her little heart.

'You've got everything you need?'

'Plenty – and more. The back bedroom's chock-a-block.' She looked down again as the baby stretched and yawned. 'I'll give 'er 'er feed – there's plenty round 'ere will give me 'an 'and if I need it.'

'These damned air raids . . .' Vera sounded terribly strained.

Nellie could swear she was swaying about. She ought to get off her feet, and quick. But she said, 'Don't you worry, we're out of the worst of it 'ere.' Not true, of course, and Nellie had a plan concerning *that*; but she had no intention of telling Vera.

'Well, in that case . . .'

Nellie sensed Vera's unhappy tension, but she felt powerless to help, as always. 'You get on back 'ome. Them sirens'll be goin' soon, like as not.'

'Give me a ring in a day or so. I'd like to know – how you're getting on.' Vera stood awkwardly with her hand on the doorknob. She did not touch her mother or her daughter. 'So if you're all right with her, I'll be off to the flat. I'm not feeling all that grand.' She seemed to want to say something more but couldn't find the words.

'Your Flo'll see to you, I expect,' Nellie said absently. Her attention was on her granddaughter now. 'T'ra then, luv.' She'd put the baby down for a bit, she was sleeping lovely, while she sorted out them bottles and such.

Moments later, Vera reopened the door holding a bottle of gin, which she thrust towards Nellie.

'Here. Take this, I've got plenty.' Her voice sounded thick and strangulated. Just as Nellie grabbed the gin, Vera lunged towards her and scooped the sleeping baby from her arm.

'Careful now!' Nellie gaped as she watched her daughter clutching the baby to her, half bent as though in agony, her shoulders heaving. 'There now, luv, don' take on so.' Nellie was awkward: she hadn't seen Vera in tears, not since she was a little girl. With her back to what light there was and her head down, Nellie couldn't see Vera's face. Then, with a gasp of pure pain, Vera gave the baby back to her and stumbled out through the door.

Nellie listened as the taxi ground off.

'Poor soul,' she said aloud. At best it was a difficult time for a woman, right after giving birth; everyone knew that. And the bloke, whoever he was, must have let her down badly: no doubt about that at all. Nellie gave a little skip as she smiled down at the baby, still sleeping like an angel, a tiny fist curled up by her chin. Then, pushing Vera and her unhappiness right out of her mind, she carried the baby carefully up to the small, newly painted bedroom overlooking the back yard, which had been Vera's years ago. It was looking a treat now, all pale yellow and white with new curtains, made by Nellie, fluttering at the window. Vera had decided on it when she came by in the summer; she had given Nellie an envelope stuffed with cash to get the decorating done. Megan settled into the cot without waking — and Nellie, singing away softly and happily, ran back down the stairs.

That night there was a raid that lasted well into the early hours. Immediately after the siren went, Nellie calmly put her plan into action. And Megan spent her first night at home — and many thereafter — tucked cosily into her brand new carrycot, in the beery safety of the cellar of the Mason's Arms.

Part 1

Megan

Chapter 6

'Please would you tell me who my father is?'

When Megan uttered the sentence she had been rehearsing in her head since lying in bed very late the night before, her mother seemed not to have heard. She was studying the menu of the genteel restaurant, just off one of London's main thoroughfares, where she had taken Megan for lunch before a shopping expedition. Only a sudden movement of her elegant, vermilion-tipped hand gave her away, indicating that the ever-present raw nerve had at last been touched again.

On the verge of adolescence, Megan was slim and graceful, still childlike in her plain blue cotton dress. Her thick dark hair sprang back off her forehead. Her eyes were deep, dense grey beneath arrestingly slanted brows; her faintly olive skin was dusted with freckles. She was – almost – beautiful. And she was concentrating totally on her mother – who gave no sign that she was even listening.

'Creamed chicken and mashed potato,' Vera read aloud, with distaste. 'Perhaps an omelette?' With her glasses perched on the tip of her nose, her eyes travelled downwards as her fingers drummed on the tablecloth. This wasn't the kind of establishment she would have dreamt of patronizing if she hadn't had Megan sullenly in tow. The understated elegance of her designer clothes, her hair swept up in an immaculate chignon, contrasted oddly with the harried, untidy women shoppers at adjoining tables.

'I do want to know,' Megan began again, desperate, her voice unsteady. 'I *must* . . .' She leant across the table, her body tensed.

'An omelette, definitely. Ham perhaps – otherwise plain.'

Vera discarded the menu and removed her glasses, revealing the pale, protuberant eyes with greyish powdered lids.

'...'oo my father is,' Megan hissed.

'*Who* not '*oo*, Megan,' Vera said coolly. 'Aitches are to be pronounced, not dropped. I did hear you the first time. And the answer is no.'

Megan blinked and swallowed and her lips parted. 'But –'

Every summer, Vera Mortimer – née Bowen – and her husband, accompanied by mountains of luggage, spent a month in the south of France. On the way there and back from New York, where they lived, they stayed in London, partly for some serious shopping for Vera, partly to visit Nellie and Megan in Trout Lane.

For Megan's part, she had dreaded these sudden, regal appearances for as long as she could remember; they disrupted the cosy, shabby little house where she and Nellie Bowen lived so contentedly, causing her friends to gather, tittering, on the pavement – a couple of mothers in aprons, hair in curlers, shuffling behind, every bit as curious as the kids. 'Meg's Mum's 'ere again, see.' The word flew up and down Trout Lane, the shiny chauffeur-driven car sticking out like a sore thumb in the grimy street that was only slowly recovering from war damage.

This was the latest visit, going awkwardly for them both.

'I know what I'm saying, Megan. And I know what's best in this instance, for all concerned.' Vera spoke, at least, with complete assurance. 'This is something you have to accept from me.' For the first time in her life – and Megan was dimly aware of this – her mother was speaking to her seriously, almost as an equal. She drew in her breath. 'The circumstances of your birth belong to part of my life that was over long ago. Finished.' No flicker of expression crossed her face, but her long fingers moved restlessly on the table. 'You have been well looked after, Megan. Nellie – Nan – is devoted to you. It was best to leave you with her, even after I married Eddy.' It would have broken her mother's heart to have taken four-year-old Megan away – and she'd brought her up well, she gave her that. The child had manners, of a sort, and the cockney accent couldn't be helped for the moment. All the same, if she'd had to do it over again ... frankly, she was getting heartily tired of Megan and her 'Nan this' and 'Nan that' ... She was *her* daughter, after all, and she resented these absurd twinges of impatient jealousy of Nellie Bowen — her own mother — that were building up in her. 'And Eddy has always been very concerned for you, very father-like.'

'It's not the same.' Megan's chin came up and her eyes — which were sometimes green and sometimes grey, fringed in very dark lashes — blazed. Although it was true that she was fond of Eddy Mortimer. When she was younger, it was he who had taken her off on outings while her mother was shopping or getting her hair done. He was patient and humorous; unlike how she felt with her mother, whom she never seemed able to please, Megan felt at ease with Eddy. And she thought that he, too, enjoyed their visits to the zoo and afternoons wandering through Hyde Park cheerfully licking ice creams. Also, he was chattier and funnier when her mother wasn't present; she had particularly noticed this. 'I do like Eddy — I do — but it isn't the same,' she repeated, stubborn. 'It *isn't* ...'

Vera considered her daughter; her pretty face above the neat dress and white sweater; her air of innocent puzzlement; those disturbingly familiar eyes, which still had the power to make her wince ... She felt it then, at that very moment; how different their lives, hers and Megan's, would have been if ... if ... She pulled herself up sharply. She felt quite dizzy.

'No,' she said quietly, meeting those eyes honestly. 'No, it's not. But I've given you my answer and let that be an end to it. But what brought this on, all of a sudden?'

It wasn't 'sudden', but Megan was helpless to explain it to this mother who was almost a stranger: admired, unapproachable, occasionally feared. She had wondered all her life, for as long as she could remember. *Of course she had*. She day-dreamed about him often, inventing impossibly romantic and far-fetched stories based on films she had seen; and sometimes she dreamed of a faceless presence who was always a man and always dark, who she believed when she woke up — heart pounding, frightened — might be *him*. Nan didn't know anything at all — Megan was quite sure of that. And she didn't like talking about it either.

Megan deliberately stopped telling her now when she had had one of her disturbing dreams.

'Boardin' school, I suppose,' Megan muttered. She couldn't explain this, either. But in her wretched state, not knowing where to turn — even Nan seemed to take this awful school idea in her stride — the unknown 'he' seemed to represent her only possible ally. Megan concentrated hard on the thick, white plate in front of her. She desperately wanted Nan. For reasons she did not in the least understand, she knew she was about to burst into tears. For one terrible moment she thought she was going to rush out of the restaurant, away from her mother and the frightening mystery of her birth for ever. She forced herself to stay put.

'Boarding, with a g,' Vera was correcting automatically. 'Now listen, Megan, I know this came as kind of a shock to you . . .'

She remembered, uneasily, how when she had broken it to Megan in the grimy front room at Trout Lane a few days ago, the girl had become almost hysterical, screaming that she wasn't going to leave 'my Nan', that this was her ''ome'. But Vera, backed up by Eddy, had made up her mind. The sight of Nellie Bowen when she opened the door that day, carpet clippers flapping, apron stained, grinning saucily, was the final straw. 'Well, I be blowed, if it isn't 'er Ladyship 'erself . . .' She dropped a curtsy none too steadily as Vera swept past into the familiar smells of stale cooking and the depressing sight of flaking paint. No, Megan should have all the chances that Vera never had — education, polish, the right contacts. And she must be taken away from Nellie Bowen and Trout Lane as soon as possible. It was obvious that she was beginning to look after Nellie, not the other way round, running all the errands and doing the shopping. Vera wondered if her mother went out much these days except for an occasional trip to the Arms. A good, middlebrow boarding school for Megan was the logical next step, she was convinced; enquiries had already gone out from their hotel suite.

'*Must* I still go?' — those eyes, huge with misery, tugged at Vera's heart. All the fight had gone out of her; she was a child again.

'It's for the best, Megan,' Vera said gently. 'I've heard very good things about the school we've chosen. Eddy is trying to arrange for the headmistress to come to see us at the hotel later today — you know that. It will be hard for you at first, but you'll soon settle down and make friends.'

Megan, abject, said nothing. Suddenly, Vera badly wanted to take her hand, lying limp on the table between them. She wanted to — but she didn't. She had never found physical contact with Megan easy; even as a baby she had always clung to Nellie. Then a waitress appeared, and the moment passed.

'Now,' Vera said briskly. 'Let's order some lunch and get on with our plans. We haven't all that much time.'

Megan picked up the menu; she was, after all, quite hungry. 'All right,' she said in a squeaky little voice, which was almost lost in the cacophony of sirens that suddenly erupted in the street outside. Fire engines, police cars, screamed their way urgently through the traffic. Automatically turning to watch, Megan didn't notice her mother tense and catch her breath.

April 1944: the warning wail — the air-raid siren — again. And the new, nerve-tingling horror of buzz bombs had to be faced now: the eery whine, the cut-off, the agonizing wait for the explosion. Weary to the bone, the whole cast, down to the last elderly stagehand, dreaded the very sound: anxiety, for relatives as well as themselves; danger, possibly death; the performance fractured — or scuppered altogether.

Vera was slimmer and trimmer than ever, looking marvellous — quite as good off-stage as on. And anyone who saw her in the bias-cut, halter-neck white evening dress in the last act of *Partners in Paradise*, swanning gracefully down a staircase to deliver her final lines, agreed that she presented an unforgettable theatrical image. She had the discipline and the dedication of a real trouper. Even the rest of the cast, who by and large thought her hard and unfriendly, gave her that. Through all except the worst of the bombing raids, Brian Worth's show went on: sophisticated, witty, inconsequential and superbly dressed, it provided the perfect antidote to a war-weary population.

Necessity had turned Flo into a superb seamstress. With dash and daring, she had recently made the heads of Vera's magnificent set of fox furs into a modish hat. Vera was wearing this, tipped forward over one eye, with a pretty powder-blue suit, when she lunched one spring day with an uncommonly tall and skinny American Air Force officer. She had been seeing him on and off over the past couple of months, and she thought she rather liked him. He had a certain quiet charm about him, and although he couldn't be far off forty he was still a bachelor, unlike most of the brass hats that came knocking on her dressing-room door. He was stationed in Norfolk, but he managed to get down to London fairly frequently. Perhaps it was his unusual height that made him self-conscious; he never had a great deal to say. He was clearly dazzled by Vera's star status, and he treated her with old-fashioned restraint. Vera, whose emotional life after Robert Brandon had been a cold emptiness, found his exquisite manners soothing. And from hints he dropped – his travels with his parents before the war and the kinds of places they stayed in – Vera rightly deduced his background to be both wealthy and educated.

Towards the end of the meal, and with a good deal of hesitation, he told her that through friends of his mother's he had been lent a furnished house on the river at Henley. He hadn't been able to use it, and thought it unlikely that he ever would. He gave a wry grin when he told her that he had brought the key with him, and written down the telephone number of the resident housekeeper: with the new menace of rockets – his nice, plain face creased in a worried frown – would she not consider using it herself, at least for weekends, to get out of the worst danger and get some rest?

Vera put down her coffee cup. There was a distinct click at the back of her mind. Although he had no inkling of this, she had been searching for months for a way to get Megan and Nellie out of London. The thought of them clinging on in Trout Lane, buzz bombs exploding at any hour of the day or night, was becoming a desperate worry to her. Possibly – just possibly – this was the solution. When they said goodbye, Vera reached up to kiss him on the cheek with a lot more warmth than she had ever done before.

'Eddy Mortimer,' she said. 'What a very kind and thoughtful man you are.'

*

'Oh, its you Vera! That's a surprise. Come on in, then,' Nellie said, her face falling, wiping her hands on her overall. Her hair was twisted up in curlers, topped by a brightly coloured turban. It was eleven o'clock the next morning, grey and cloudy, with a chill wind blowing. 'Meg's down for 'er sleep, but I got the kettle on for a cuppa.' She led the way into the front room. It was cold and dark and dusty; she and Megan more or less lived in the warm fug of the kitchen at the back. 'I shan't be 'alf a mo'.'

Vera perched on the edge of one of the cheap, worn armchairs and glanced around. The room hadn't changed since she was a child: the same linoleum was on the floor where she had learnt her first dance routine, partly covered by a piece of drab carpet. The walls were bare except for a wedding photograph of her parents, her father grinning foolishly above a stiff collar, his pretty bride Nellie, a good foot and a half shorter, clinging to his arm. The net curtains were stiff with dirt.

Nellie came back, carrying two cups of strong, sweet tea.

'There now.' She handed one to Vera and sat opposite. Her face shone with happiness; Vera had heard her singing away while she waited by the front door. She was looking more like a young mother than a grandmother. Her mother's natural cheerfulness had always astonished Vera, who could never see what she had to be cheerful about. But she was certain that no one could look after her Megan with more care – and love.

Because it was a fact that the hasty arrival of three-day-old Megan at 5 Trout Lane, bang in the middle of the Blitz, had transformed Nellie Bowen's life. She hadn't pulled a single pint since. She still had no idea who Megan's father was, and she scarcely gave it a thought. It was wartime after all, and illegitimacy had always been an accepted fact of life around Trout Lane. To Nellie, every tiny progression of Megan's – learning to sit, first steps and beginning words – seemed a small miracle. She had never felt this way about Vera when she was little, she sometimes thought guiltily; standoffish, she'd been, even as a youngster. But it was a pleasure to Nellie to push Megan up and down the road, stopping to gossip with neighbours, popping in to Gran Gubbins's shop. Even old Gran loved little Meg – and she never could be doing with Vera.

'I thought I'd come over today,' Vera explained, putting down her tea and riffling through her bag for her cigarette case. 'I haven't seen Megan in a while.'

'She's runnin' now, into everythin' — can't turn me back, not for nothin',' Nellie said, smiling fondly. 'Wears me out, she do. I'll get 'er up for you jus' now.'

'Oh, let her have her sleep, Ma,' Vera said quickly, offering her mother a cigarette, which she snatched. 'I really wanted to have a word with you about something else now that we've got time.'

'What's that then?' Nellie enquired cautiously. She was always on edge around Vera. It wasn't the money; she sent that regularly and generously and she had more than enough to manage. It was just that when she turned up in Trout Lane, none of them was ever at ease. Vera was awkward with Megan, to whom she was a stranger, and anyone could see that Vera didn't have a good touch with babies, try as she might. Megan sensed tension and was unusually tetchy. And for Nellie, there lurked the terrible fear that Vera might one day exercise her rights and take her Meg away from her.

'Listen, Ma, I've been given the run of a house, near Henley,' Vera said, looking round for an ashtray and settling for the saucer. 'Right on the Thames. It's furnished and heated, someone comes in to look after the place . . .'

'You use it, then, Vera. Go on. Need a rest, you do, with wearin' yourself out every night. You look ever so tired, dear.' Nellie sensed danger.

'I wasn't thinking of that. I thought . . . you and Megan . . . it would get you out of — all this, for a bit.' She waved a hand indicating the house and the bomb-scarred streets. 'There's a bit of a lull in the bombing now but it won't last.' Coming in the taxi, Vera had noticed the pathetic gaps in the rows of houses near by. 'There are rumours it could get a lot worse before we're finished. And the big push into Europe is going to come soon — they'll fling anything they've got on London. You'd be safe from all that out in the country.'

Nellie was on her feet, hands on hips. 'What — 'Meg an' me?'

'That's right.' Vera eyed her coldly. She hadn't expected her to give in easily, but Megan's safety was her priority. She was dangling a key to the house, given to her by Eddy Mortimer, which she had just dug out of her bag.

'Now let me tell you, miss, if you think . . .' Nellie began, when they heard definite sounds from upstairs — 'Nana, Nana, Nana, Nana', accompanied by rocking and creaking, getting louder. Megan was standing up in her cot, calling for Nellie. Nellie stopped in mid sentence and flew up the staircase. Vera made no effort to follow her. She turned when they came down. Nellie was carrying Megan, who clung to her, her face hidden against her neck. She had on a pink woollen smocked dress, which Vera had wheedled out of one of her illicit sources, and a white cardigan knitted by Gran Gubbins; Nellie had tied a pink ribbon in her hair.

'Go on then, luv,' Nellie coaxed. 'Look, there's your Mum come to see you. Now be a good girl, Meg.'

Shyly, Megan turned and looked over her shoulder.

The sight of Megan always caused in Vera that familiar ache, dulled now from the hopeless longing she had felt on the night of her birth, but still tender. The shiny-dark hair, grave grey eyes below winged eyebrows; and, when she chose, a radiant smile.

'Hello, Megan.' Smiling, melted, Vera held out her arms as Megan turned back and clung to Nellie even more tightly. 'Come to me for a bit, darling.'

'She's shy, an' she don't see you that much, do she?' Nellie bristled, thinking, as she always did, that Vera had no business having babies, she didn't seem motherlike somehow. 'Give 'er a minute or two to get used to you, Vera.' She returned to her tea, holding Megan on her knee.

'I wish you'd think about that house, Ma,' Vera said, frowning. 'Apart from the danger of staying on in London, think how nice it would be for Megan to have a garden to play in.'

'What — leave Trout Lane an' go settin' up 'ome in some country 'ouse? Not bleedin' loikely, I won't,' Nellie said indignantly. 'We're right as rain 'ere, aren't we, Meg?' Vera didn't know about the nights in the cellar of the Mason's Arms, and Nellie had no intention of telling her. She must think they stayed under the stairs when things got bad. As if she was that daft.

Megan slipped off Nellie's knee and stared doubtfully at her mother. She stuck her thumb in her mouth, still holding on to Nellie. Vera sank to the floor and took something out of her bag — sweets wrapped in cellophane and tied with a bright ribbon.

'I've brought you a present, Megan. Come and get it. Here . . .' She held out the sweets. Reluctantly, Megan began toddling towards her. 'Look, Ma, what I'm telling you is that it's not safe to stay in London, not with a child.'

'We're stayin' 'ere.' Nellie's mouth shut mulishly.

'In that case, I'll have to think about Megan, won't I? And I might have to make other arrangements.'

At that moment, inches away from her mother, reaching out for the bag of sweets, Megan caught sight of Vera's fur hat. Repelled and terrified, she dropped the sweets and staggered back to Nellie, wailing. As Nellie swept her up and began comforting her, Vera muttered, 'The time . . . and a matinée at two today . . .' and fled, throwing down two unopened packets of cigarettes as she went. Megan was still shrieking at the top of her voice as she made her way down Trout Lane and came upon the welcome sight of a stray taxi.

All the way to the theatre, Vera sat with her head thrown back and her eyes closed, the terrifying responsibility of loving another human being — Megan — weighing her down. And no one to share it with . . . Although her visits to Trout Lane were never very satisfactory, seeing Megan, and leaving her, always tore Vera up inside. Damn that stubborn old Nellie. Over and over again she thought, I must get Megan away from London . . .

And where was Robert Brandon? The old familiar ache, the despair which she had fought her way through, came back to hit her in great waves, battering at her defences. Was he still on active service, despite his serious wound? Was he in some high-up desk job, perhaps at the War Office? Or was he at Cloverley, with — ?

The taxi drew up outside the stage door and stopped, shuddering, as Vera groped her way out.

Chapter 7

Megan, recovering from the outburst which had taken all her reserves of inner strength, ate her way through a stodgy lunch. It was a silent meal. As Megan noticed, her mother hardly touched her food, only drank cup after cup of black coffee. She looked edgy and distracted and as soon as Megan had finished, she whisked her straight off to the shops. Owing to Vera's perfectionism, even the simple task of buying Megan some cotton clothes took a long time. The colour was wrong, or the skirt fell awkwardly; shoddy buttons and drooping hems were immediately pounced on. Vera's demands caused black looks from shop assistants, which embarrassed Megan dreadfully. Only her thick, dark hair, which responded at once to a comb and scissors in expert hands, really pleased her mother.

They arrived back at the hotel, Megan trailing behind carrying the parcels as Vera marched through the marble hall, into the lift and up to their usual suite. In the plush sitting-room, Eddy Mortimer was lounging back in an armchair hidden behind the *Herald Tribune*, a glass of Scotch at his elbow. He immediately dropped the paper and rose to greet them. Because of his stoop, he appeared a lot less tall than his full height; but even so, he towered. His short, greying hair emphasized his ears, which Nellie Bowen said stuck out like jug handles. He grinned at them sheepishly.

'Well, now, you're back in good time. I wasn't expecting you yet a while.' He cleared his throat. 'Did you have a successful day, ladies?' He took in the packages draped about Megan, and winked at her conspiratorially. Megan gave him a wan smile.

'Not bad. We did what we had to, didn't we, Megan?' Vera picked up a pile of letters and messages and started going through them. 'The service in this country is God awful – like the weather.' It had been a particularly sunless week, and now it was starting to drizzle. 'I'll send down for tea,' Vera said, eyeing the glass of whisky disapprovingly. 'Megan and I could do with a cup.' After she had told Megan to take the parcels into the bedroom and unwrap them, she went to the mirror, automatically checking her appearance, toying with a chunky gold earring. Eddy watched her every move, his eyes like an adoring spaniel's. 'Oh, I almost forgot.' She wheeled round to face him. 'Did that woman from the school call – Miss Hopham? She thought she might be able to come round and meet us today.'

'Yes, dear. She did, dear. She's definitely coming.' Eddy peered about. 'I took all the information down – it's over on the desk.' He loped across the room. 'She'll be here at five thirty. I said I was sure you and Megan would be back by then.'

'Good. Then we can make a final decision on the school. And Eddy –'

'Yes, dear?'

Vera frowned. 'I had an idea, at lunch. I thought it would be sensible if we took Megan to France with us this year. Ted and the nurse are flying over for two weeks, so why not Megan? It would – I don't know – take her mind off things – leaving Nellie, going away to boarding school – and it's high time she saw something of the world other than Trout Lane . . .' Her voice tailed off vaguely.

'I think that's a very good idea, sweetheart. I don't know why I didn't think of it myself. I'll call the hotel in France right away.'

'And you made the reservation for supper tonight, after the theatre? You know Brian Worth is joining us.'

'Oh yes, dear.'

'That's good.' She began walking towards the bedroom where tissue paper and wrapping was crackling noisily. 'And order tea, would you, Eddy?'

'Sure thing, at once, dear.'

*

After telling Megan that this year she would be coming with them to France on holiday, Vera sent her off back to Trout Lane accompanied by Eddy. She could feel a migraine coming on, she said; and she was prone to them these days. It had been cloudy and heavy all day. They were going to the theatre tonight, so she wanted to rest and be quiet. When they had left, Vera lit a cigarette and stood by the heavy curtains, leaning her head to one side of the window, staring down at the street.

A mist of fine rain was coming down steadily now, emphasizing the greyness of the buildings. Even the passers by, hurrying home from shops and offices, looked drab. The scarlet streak of a bus was the only bit of brightness to be seen. Used now to the colour and the pace of New York, where she took for granted all the new-world luxury which wealth could buy, when she came back to London, Vera was always struck by the lethargy and the ordinariness. It was as though the war — which they had all endured, God knew — had ripped the guts out of the place; some vital spark needed to jolt it back to life was missing. Even the brilliant coronation ceremonies and the new Queen, by whom the whole country was apparently besotted — though she seemed rather a dull young woman to Vera — had failed to provide the needed lift-off.

Vera turned restlessly away, stubbing out her cigarette and pushing her fingers through her hair. She had been truthful enough about the migraine: her head was throbbing fiercely. Megan's pent-up outburst had shaken her badly. It wasn't that at the back of her mind she hadn't been expecting such a scene for years: she had — of course she had. It was just that . . .

Holding one of her hands in front of her, she saw that it was shaking; her breathing was fast and uneven. Tantalizing memories came tumbling into her mind, blotting out the here and now . . .

She glanced at her watch. She had no doubt at all that Eddy would stay on to have a drink with Nellie; neither of them could ever say no to that. But at least it would leave her a decent amount of time alone before they had to dress. Going to the bathroom, she poured a glass of water and shook out two pills. When she had changed into a dressing gown, she pulled the curtains and lay on the bed, forcing herself to think of nothing and no one, waiting for the darkness of blessed oblivion.

On that same April morning in 1944, at precisely the same time that Vera Bowen was met by Nellie on the doorstep of 5 Trout Lane, Robert Brandon walked out of the library at Cloverley Court. Halfway across the hall, he all but crashed into a boy who was speeding across, making for the front door. It was only the boy's lightning sidestep that prevented a collision.

'For Christ's sake ...' Robert Brandon, not known for his even temperament, reacted furiously. 'You're going very fast, young man.' He glared at him. 'As you are now attending the school, in the other wing, there is no reason for you to be using this part of the house at all.'

'Sorry, sir.'

He was about fourteen, neat in his school uniform – grey trousers, tie and blazer. He was slightly breathless and his black eyes were alight, but he kept his poise. There was no trace of gawky adolescence. He spoke perfect English with a decided French accent. 'We have no lessons until ten o'clock this morning and Lady Ceci asked me to run down to the stables to deliver a message.'

'Well, then, watch where you're going,' Robert Brandon told him irritably. Cecilia Brandon's adored King Charles's spaniel was yapping at his ankles.

'I will, sir. Sorry, sir.' Slowed to a sedate walk, he headed for the massive front door.

But Robert Brandon called after him angrily. 'Not that way. You've no business using the main entrance. Use one of the side doors, or go through the kitchens. And remember that in future.'

The boy turned, startled, and inclined his head slightly. 'Of course, sir.' He began walking in the direction from which he had come rushing out only seconds before.

Robert Brandon, still glowering, started up the stairs. High above, on the nursery floor, he could hear his three-year-old son James's yells developing into a full-blown tantrum.

'I don't know why on earth that boy still has to hang around the house, Ceci. He damn nearly knocked me over just now. Why can't he live in the back wing with the school, like the rest of them?'

Cecilia Brandon, who was sitting at her desk in their large, ornately decorated bedroom, looked up, surprised. She was dressed to go riding in jodhpurs, shirt and a tweed hacking jacket. She had the fresh, vivid colouring of someone who spends a good deal of time out of doors.

'Alain, do you mean? Alain Gesson?'

'Yes.' He strode over to the wide fireplace where a small fire was smoking unpleasantly and giving out little heat. 'Why on earth does he have to walk around here as though he had a right to it?' He kicked at the log violently with his shoe.

Cecilia Brandon said quietly, 'You know the story, Robert. Or part of it. I wrote to you about it — and you've seen him here whenever you've come on leave.' Robert said nothing, so she went on patiently in her pleasant voice — which was inclined to be loud, but always easy on the ear. 'He's a Jewish child, you know that, his parents fled from Paris hoping to escape over the Pyrenées into Spain. They were hidden in the cellar of the house of a doctor in Perpignan who was a member of the Maquis. The Germans had closed most of the routes by the time the Gessons got there. All I know about Alain's background is that his father is an architect, he never speaks of him. Anyhow, they had the chance to get the boy out to Spain in the care of nuns who had managed to get forged papers, and they took it. When he arrived in England, he was looked after by one of the refugee agencies . . .'

'There must be plenty of people — Jewish families for that matter — who could have taken the boy in. I fail to see why he had to settle here.'

'Peggy Loveday brought him — she's done the most marvellous war work, as well as acting as your agent now Dick is at the War Office. Anyhow, the agency contacted her to try to place him.'

'Why was it so difficult?' Robert turned and looked at her, challenging.

'There was a reason ...' Ceci hesitated. Head over heels in love with her husband as she was, she was in no way intimidated by him.

'What reason?'

'He wouldn't speak — not a word, in French or English, although he obviously took everything in. And even well meaning people didn't feel they could cope with that.'

'Hmm — well, he's not short of a word or two now, or not that I've noticed.'

Flushing, Ceci said angrily, 'No — no, he's not. He's clever and he's well mannered and everyone here likes him. He's got tremendous charm. He's learned the language amazingly well and he goes out of his way to be helpful. He's streets ahead of the other boys in the school. And that's a credit to him, and to us.'

'What on earth do you mean?'

'I mean — Oh Robert ...' Her voice softened; she was almost pleading with him. 'When Peg brought him he looked like a dead thing. He was as white as a sheet, black eyes staring. He had been torn from his parents — he hasn't heard a word of them since; he had nobody and nothing in the whole world. And yet he had some indefinable dignity. He stood there very straight, pathetically young, with a battered satchel he had brought out with him slung across his sweater, and I thought of James with Nannie in the nursery and all the security he's got, and my heart went out to him.'

'Evidently.'

'Poor Peggy was at her wits' end to know what to do with him.'

'I've got a lot of admiration for Peggy Loveday, and Dick — he is my agent, after all, or will be again, one hopes. But I think you fell for emotional blackmail here, Ceci.'

'I did not.' Ceci was furious, her head thrown back. 'I made my own decision, Robert, to keep Alain here, to make this his home. And I'd do the same again. God knows we've got enough room. I asked him to stay at Cloverley and he said, 'Yes, if you please, madame,' in English. They were the first words he had uttered since he left his parents months before.'

Swallowing hard, she got up from the desk very quickly and joined Robert beside the unsatisfactory fire. For most of this leave, Robert had been moody and difficult and restless. Ceci suspected that his shoulder was acting up again, only he didn't like admitting it. He looked tense and pale and his face was drawn.

'This is the most bloody awful excuse for a fire,' he said irritably, coughing. 'Can't they do better than that? There must be plenty of wood around.'

'I'll deal with it, leave it to me,' Ceci soothed, coping generously with her husband's uncertain temper. She slipped her arm through his, firmly changing the subject. 'Look, can't we go out for a ride? It would do us both the world of good. Do say yes, Robert. I've sent a message down to the stables already. We haven't got a lot of time left together.'

'I realize that,' he said sombrely. 'I'll have to be off early on Thursday. The big push into Europe is coming soon and we're all very stretched.' He had ten days' leave, of which a week had already passed. 'But I can't spare this morning, Ceci. I'm expecting a phone call from the solicitors in London. Perhaps tomorrow — we'll keep tomorrow free.' He grasped her shoulder and pulled her closer; but his mood had not lifted. 'Back to work now. If I don't get to grips with some of the estate problems today, I never will. With Angus ill and in Scotland, things are falling to rack and ruin. If it weren't for you and my mother, I don't know how we'd keep the place going at all.'

Robert returned to the library, and Ceci went back to her desk. But she found it hard to concentrate on the household bills and correspondence. The girlish crush she had had on Robert Brandon still lingered; even now, it sometimes seemed unreal to her that they were married at all. She thought back to their sudden courtship in that hot summer of 1940 when he was recovering slowly — it was still touch and go then whether his arm would heal satisfactorily, and she was with him day after day after day; his abrupt proposal which she so rapturously accepted; Clementine Brandon making the wedding arrangements almost before anyone else realized what was happening ... And yet, coming from such a similar background to Robert's, and very distantly related, she had fitted with ease into the life at Cloverley and in the village, even under the difficult wartime conditions. Buxom and cheerful, completely natural and a quintessential countrywoman, she was popular with everyone.

And even Clementine Brandon was supremely happy with the match, coming at a time when she despaired of any such thing happening. Her only slight misgivings concerned Ceci's breezy self-confidence which led her to rather extravagant gestures. Take the French boy, Alain Gesson, for example. It was perfectly understandable that she should have wished to help out Peggy Loveday; there was no reason why the boy should not have been housed temporarily. But dear Ceci, without a word to anyone – let alone to her – took it upon herself to settle him in one of the nursery bedrooms, find him clothes, arrange for English lessons. Nannie, who had come to Cloverley as nurserymaid when Robert was an infant, stayed on, and now looked after young James, was Clementine Brandon's firm ally. And Nannie had been anything but pleased.

'A foreign child? In my nursery?' she had said, folding her arms and looking Alain up and down. He wasn't at all the sort of boy she was used to dealing with, she could tell that for a start. 'I don't like it, Lady Ceci, I don't like it at all. I don't know what Mr Robert will say – or Madam, come to that. As if we didn't have enough boys round here, with the school evacuated.'

But Ceci told her, quite sharply, that there was a war on and they all had to do their bit and have a generous outlook. There was no arguing with her. The next thing Nannie knew, Lady Ceci was taking him about with her, teaching him to ride, working with him at his English. And although he went straight into the school, every weekend he still took his meals in the dining-room, like one of the family. It wasn't right, in Nannie's opinion, it wasn't right at all.

Talking over a cup of tea late at night, as they often did, Clementine Brandon and Nannie had words about it, heads nodding in agreement. They were also of the same view that Ceci

Brandon was, as Nannie put it, 'too physical a young woman to take easily to childcare'. She was far happier mucking out a stable or chasing round on Robert's political affairs than looking after James, whom she sensibly left in Nannie's capable charge. Robert always said that Nannie was the only friend his mother had ever had – and Ceci believed him. He knew that, during the dreadful years of the First World War, when the three telegrams had arrived one after the other in a space of months – three brothers killed on the Somme, a fourth, Angus, badly gassed – after breaking the news to old Lady Brandon, it was to Nannie she had come quietly in the night; it was with Nannie alone that she had wept, letting down the elegant and formidable façade that she had maintained through thick and thin ever since. And it was Nannie who, during one of their late-night sessions, had urged her to speak her mind strongly to Mr Robert concerning Alain Gesson – which was what Clementine Brandon was now resolved to do.

Half an hour later, Robert came bounding back into the bedroom, all lightness and charm, handsome in his countrified tweeds, saying that he was sorry he had acted like a bear with a sore head – 'Forgive me, Ceci' – but his mother had just waylaid him in the library, they had had a good chat, and he was going to say something to her which he knew she would take reasonably.

He came and stood behind her and put his hands on her shoulders.

'What's that, Robert?' It was an effort for her not to turn to him instinctively – but she didn't.

'It's about young Alain Gesson ...'

'What about him?'

'Ceci, darling, don't be cross, but I do want him out of this house, out of Cloverley, except when he's attending the school. And as soon as possible. I'm quite firm on this. And my mother would like it also.'

'She would do.'

'Yes, well – perhaps. But in this instance, I entirely agree with her.' He held her shoulders tighter. 'Surely it can be arranged, can't it?'

Ceci said quietly and steadily, 'It's because he's a Jew, isn't it?'
'Possibly.'

After some moments of silence, Robert went over to the window and looked out on to the early spring landscape. Although the trees were coming into leaf, there was still a wintry feel about. Ceci sat perfectly still, staring straight ahead.

Turning to look at her – smiling, good-humoured now – Robert told her casually that he had made some phone calls and he was slipping up to London for a few hours to deal with business matters. It was all boring stuff – the family solicitors, his tailor, nothing that would remotely interest her – and he'd be home long before dinner. 'And we'll definitely have our long ride tomorrow. That's a promise. I know there's a Conservative meeting this afternoon, but my mother said that you and she would kindly represent me. What would I – or Cloverley – do without the pair of you?'

Ceci was still at her desk, thinking hard, when she heard the taxi taking Robert to the station. Later, she drove Clementine to the meeting which was being held at a neighbour's house. To save petrol, Ceci was using the farm's Land Rover, wrenching round the wheel, clutching and double declutching with a good deal of brio. This was the kind of driving she revelled in.

'I bumped into Peggy Loveday this morning, when I was visiting someone in the village,' Ceci yelled above the raucous motor. 'She and Dick spent a few days together in London last week. She said it was very gay, lots going on, and plenty of good food. They managed to get tickets to *Partners in Paradise*. She said Vera Bowen is absolutely smashing in it. All the men in London are in love with her, especially the Yanks.'

Hanging on for dear life, hair, hat and gloves perfectly in place, Clementine Brandon murmured faintly, 'Really ... fancy that now ...'

Vera saw him at the end of the first act when, as the glamorous Gina Hollis, she was required to walk to the centre front of the stage, cigarette holder in hand, turn and glance down over her shoulder towards the audience. The opulent set gleamed behind her – brocade curtains, deep pile carpet and showy antiques – while her co-star went through the frenzied motions of a cuckolded husband.

A hallmark of Vera Bowen's career as an actress was her professionalism. No matter what was happening in her private life, she never failed to give her usual competent performance – and occasionally, she was superb. So it was on that chilly April day in 1944, even though, coming straight from Trout Lane, she was worried sick for Megan's safety.

Robert Brandon was sitting in the second row of the stalls. He had lost weight, but his dark, impressive good looks were unmistakable; his staring eyes beneath his heavy, slanted brows made him appear severe, in contrast to the rest of the audience who were smiling and titillated. It was she he was concentrating on, not the play. Frozen, she allowed the smallest pause. The so-familiar lines stuck in her throat; but she turned back, flinging out her arm with elegant nonchalance, and delivered into the tiny silence the five crushing lines that ended the act and brought the curtain swishing down to loud applause.

During the interval, fussed over by Flo, she changed her costume and adjusted her make-up. A dusting of powder, more rouge: he should not see her pale. Over four bloody years, she thought bitterly, flicking on mascara; four whole bloody years. And not a word. After all that...

Glacially composed, she got through the second and final act with even more polished perfection than usual. The applause was rapturous. Taking her curtain calls, Vera looked everywhere but down – and when she did, bowing gracefully for the last time, she saw that the seat where Robert had been sitting was empty.

She had barely sat down at her dressing-table when she saw him in the mirror, at the door, behind Flo who was attempting to block his way. But it was no good, he had taken control as he was accustomed to doing: flashing a smile of recognition at Flo, he patted her on the shoulder saying how good it was to see her again and the play really was as marvellous as everyone said and he would so appreciate a few minutes alone with Miss Bowen if she would be so kind as to . . .

Watching this, still through the huge mirror ringed with lights, Vera wondered later whether something — notes? — had been unobtrusively slipped into Flo's pocket. Robert was good at that sort of touch; and Flo always had had a weakness for him, despite everything.

Seeing the door shut and Robert leaning against it, Vera had a sense of total unreality. She turned slowly and faced him, chin raised, still in full theatrical make-up and the slinky white satin dress of the play's finale.

How she had longed for anything of him, anything at all, tossing and turning through long, anguished nights; when Megan was born; hearing snatches of some remembered tune —

> Love is . . . the strangest thing,
> No song of birds upon the wing
> Shall in our hearts more sweetly sing
> Than love's own story . . .

Time after time she had thought, wrongly, that she had glimpsed him in a crowd, her heart thumping wildly. Now she felt only emptiness and exhaustion. Matinées always wore her out. And tonight again . . .

'I had to see you.' The smiling charm exerted for Flo's benefit was wiped clear from his face. There were hollows in his cheeks. He seemed so much older; all the debonair, man-about-town verve was quite gone. Those piercing, dense grey eyes were the only live thing about him.

'Did you, now?' Not a disciplined actress for nothing, Vera countered the shock of seeing him again — his nearness, his fatal familiarity — by careful, measured breathing. She felt along the dressing-table, past the vase of massed spring flowers sent by Eddy Mortimer, the gentle American giant. 'Cigarette?' She took one, and offered the box.

He shook his head. 'I couldn't stay away, not any longer, not when I saw you today, on stage.' His lips were barely moving.

'Oh, but you did, Robert,' she said in a hard voice, staring coldly. 'You did stay away. Four years and — let me see —'

He crossed the room to where she was sitting, took the lighter from her and flicked it. She bent to the flame. Not one of their four hands, almost touching, was quite steady.

'Two months . . . that's right.' Her head thrown back, she drew on the cigarette. She said, very slowly, 'February 1940. A Sunday night in Chester Square.' In her misery, facing the rejection she had half expected, she had thought then on that cold black night that she would never be warm again.

'I wanted to finish it. I had my reasons,' he said brutally.

'Oh, yes — class, background,' she said ironically, moving her head slightly. 'But we knew that, didn't we, from the beginning?'

He shrugged. 'If you will . . .'

'Then why are you here now?' she challenged. She looked almost beautiful; her face was thinner, exposing good, high cheekbones.

He didn't answer; his passionate look was enough, striking remembered feeling deep inside her. Oh God, she thought, Oh God . . . Shaken to her core, she turned back to the dressing-table and began to take off her glittering paste earrings. He stood behind her. All her movements were slow and graceful, her seamless arms and shoulders a pale ivory, her brown hair, carefully lightened, perfectly shaped and set. In their dizzying months together he had watched her do this time after time, impatient to be off with her to some party or nightclub — or to bed. It was what he wanted now, more desperately than he had ever done before. War had peeled the frothy social layers from them all.

'I've regretted, many times, the way that it ended — and that it ended at all.'

Unclasping a bracelet, she looked up. Their eyes met — and locked — in the mirror.

'You asked me to marry you once,' she said flippantly, smiling as though she were still on stage. Her success and all the trappings of stardom had given her confidence, at least. And she was easier now that the first ghastly shock of seeing him had worn off. Coolly, she removed a second bracelet without looking away.

'I'm not proud of my behaviour.'

'I had the child after all,' she said matter-of-factly, still looking right at him. 'I wrote. Twice. To Cloverley — it was the only address I had — saying that I had to get in touch with you, urgently. You didn't get the letters?'

He hadn't, of course. She had always wondered and she could tell in a flash from his sharp intake of breath, his curse — even before he pulled her so roughly from the chair, held her wrists painfully tight, thrust his face within inches of hers. Certain knowledge struck her like a bolt of lightning: Clementine Brandon ... It all fell into place. Perhaps, deep down, she had known it all along.

'What?'

'I said, I had the child. A girl. Born, as it happened, the day before you married.'

She had gained assurance and a cutting edge — pain, as well as recognition, had done that much for her.

'Jesus Christ! A child? Letters? *Our* child? And what letters?'

She might never have said the word 'marriage'. 'And I telephoned, after you were wounded. Peters told me. I was informed that you mustn't be disturbed. Don't, Robert, you're hurting me.'

His grip tightened. 'My sainted mother, no doubt,' he spat through gritted teeth.

And although Vera had thought herself armoured against it, at that second the loneliness and the humiliation and the hurt overwhelmed her in a great wave of longing. Oh God, why did he have to come back now, just when everything was going so well — the play, her social life, the possibility of Broadway ahead. And Eddy, who was rich and kind and adoring, whom she really was beginning to like ...

'Yes, I spoke to her. I got the cold shoulder, naturally. But *you* never ... *you* made no attempt ...' She was bitter and accusatory with all the pent-up bile. This was agony, after all; as if it could be anything else.

'All men are weak. Didn't you know that, Vera? Didn't you? Oh Christ ...' It was almost a groan. He let her go so abruptly that she staggered back against the dressing-table. 'But I thought we had decided, before I left — I arranged for the doctor...' He pushed his hand through his hair; he looked utterly distraught.

'*You* had decided' — her anger flared. 'I made my own decision.' She started to shake like a leaf, uncontrollably. Flo hadn't even had time, as she usually did, to put a wrapper over the bare satin dress.

'Come...' Robert's voice dropped and he held out his hands: she thought that there were tears in his eyes. He was watching her differently, all the anger and tension smothered by the tactile heat between them.

He took her in his arms, his eyes closed, hands moving caressingly down her neck and shoulders, as she fell against him. He always had had unerring authority where she was concerned. He had always taken the lead, in everything.

'I loved you. I couldn't...' — barely audible against his chest.

'I'm sorry,' he muttered, almost humbly. 'I didn't realize — until it was too late — how much I cared. I couldn't... I wouldn't... And I was ill for months. But the child... If only I had known, I would have done something. I would have come to you when I could. You must believe that.' She did. But it would have made no difference; she knew that, too. 'I thought that I could walk away from you. Over, finished, done with. I always had before, from other women.' His mouth burnt against her cold skin. 'I sensed you were different for me. But I fought it, I wouldn't give in, I pushed it away.' He began speaking rapidly, urgently. 'Look, Vera, you must let me help you, in any way, and with the child, you *must*.'

She needed help so badly then: given Robert's authority, Megan would be safe. Vera could feel herself faltering...

He held her away from him, his hands on her shoulders. There was some grey in his hair and his face was chalky white. His expression was a mixture of hunger and longing and regret. He was deadly serious. She shook her head; she had never felt so drained, so tired.

'Vera, please...'

'Never.'

'Then tell me where...'

'No.' She wrenched herself from him, wilting, sitting down at the brightly lit dressing-table, loaded with flowers and cards and cosmetics. Outside the door she could hear the cheerful shouts of the stage hands whistling, something heavy being dragged. 'It's better to keep it this way – for both of us. For the child, too. And you are, after all, married.' Her voice had the caustic edge again, dredged up from somewhere. Had he left that suitable wife at Cloverley, made some excuse to come up to London? And did *he* have a child now too – a son? He didn't say, and she wouldn't ask. She longed for Flo and normality and a strong cup of tea. She could not let this go on much longer.

He said steadily, 'That doesn't mean we can't see each other – or that I can't make – some amends. No one need know. I can't leave you like this, Vera, I can't. You must see that. It is, in any case, the very last thing I want to do.'

He started pacing up and down behind her, darting glances, looking desperate. She knew that he was desperate – now. As for herself, she was fairly sure in her clearsighted way that there would be nothing else like this in her life again – or for him probably. God knows, she wanted him, and only him, on any terms at all. Yet some sort of steely pride won out: a sense of survival, perhaps, that she hadn't known was so strong in her.

She heard herself saying calmly and with dignity. 'It's too late for us, Robert – much, much too late. And nothing you say can change my mind. So please go, now...'

He stopped pacing and looked at her for a long moment. 'Very well. If that's what you want.'

She watched in the mirror as he blundered out of the door. She didn't remember anything else until she came to, lying on the sofa with Flo fussing and tucking round rugs and producing a hot water bottle and scalding tea.

'He went,' she said brokenly, propped on her elbow.

Flo pursed her lips. 'You'll 'ave to do your face again,' she said. 'It's not 'alf a mess.'

Chapter 8

Over in Trout Lane, Nellie greeted Eddy and Megan good-humouredly enough and remembered her manners sufficiently to turn the television off. Megan, after telling Nellie excitedly about the holiday in France, immediately skipped off into the street to find her friends.

'Come on in, then. I fancy a cuppa myself,' Nellie said to Eddy, eyeing the expensive-looking carrier bag he was holding. Despite the wispy grey hair and the drab wash-cotton dress which was none too clean, there was still something girlishly beguiling about Nellie Bowen; her lovely smile reached right up to her blue eyes. Eddy Mortimer grinned down at her affectionately. As she stuck the milk bottle and the big brown teapot on the table, chattering away like a magpie, Eddy shrunk his great length into one of her kitchen chairs.

'Jus' like Vera, that is,' she said, pouring the hot, dark liquid. 'Always on about somethin', never satisfied. Now she wants to 'ave a go at my Meg, takin' er off to France, sendin' 'er to some posh school . . .' She looked Eddy squarely in the face. 'I never did see eye to eye with Vera, mind, never.'

Eddy Mortimer cleared his throat. He had a horror of conflict of any kind, so he said hastily, 'I thought you might be able to use these, Nellie.' He reached into the carrier bag and pulled out a bottle of whisky, expensive chocolates and two cartons of cigarettes.

Nellie brightened visibly. 'Well, now . . .' She sat back, admiring. 'There's a treat. Tell you what, 'ow about a drop o' that in our tea? Set us up proper it will.'

They were still at it when Megan came back. Eddy looked at his watch, horrified that it was so late. 'I must dash, Vera might want . . .'

'Aw, let 'er wait – do 'er good. 'Ave a look at our plants out the back. Come up lovely this year, 'aven't they, Meg? An' not much sun, neither.'

After he had admired the profusion of petunias and begonias and geraniums, brilliantly colourful in the drab little area, Eddy scampered back off to the West End like a large and terrified rabbit.

'She don' deserve 'im, your Mum,' Nellie mumbled, taking out the bread and setting the frying pan over the flame. 'She's no company, Vera. And 'e's lonesome. There'll be trouble, you mark my words.'

'It's just that Eddy's shy, Nan. He's afraid of people.' Megan spun round. 'I'll be in France next week, Nan,' she said, pirouetting. As for going abroad, she was half excited, half terrified by the idea. Only one of her friends had been to France – on a day trip to Boulogne – and she'd been seasick crossing the Channel both ways; the food there was something terrible, not fit for humans, her Dad said. But France, like Miss Hopham's dreaded school, wasn't something she could talk to Nan about. Stopping dead in her tracks, Megan thought: and I've been able to tell her everything until now, everything . . .

'Wha's that, luv?'

The television was on full blast now – and Nellie's hearing wasn't what it had been.

'Oh, nothing much, Nan. Can we eat soon?'

Later, when she was doing the dishes, Megan said, 'I asked 'er today 'oo my Dad is, I did, Nan.'

There was a temporary lull in Nellie's television schedule and the kitchen was unusally quiet.

'Go on, Meg, you never did!' She was thunderstruck. 'She never said. Not nothin', ever. An' it's bin all these years . . .' Her mouth was open.

'I asked 'er, I did.' Megan's chin came up, and she looked

defiant, standing there with a greasy, soapy plate in either hand, her greenish eyes compelling beneath the remarkable eyebrows. But she wouldn't . . .'

Nellie shook her head. 'You won't get nothin' out of 'er, Meg, luv.' She felt about nervously in her apron pocket for a cigarette.

'I will one day – you wait.' She turned and plunged her hands back into the sudsy water.

'Maybe, luv, maybe . . .'

Relieved, Nellie turned back to the television and a shimmying foxtrot which set her foot tapping. She had long ago given up that mystery. It had been wartime after all, everything turned upside down. And she'd kept her word, Vera had; looked after them both. Meg was Meg – that was all that mattered to her. And it was Nellie Bowen's private opinion that whoever her father was, he'd given Vera Bowen – now Mortimer – her comeuppance. Which had given Nellie, in turn, no small satisfaction.

The play which Vera and Eddy Mortimer saw that night with Brian Worth ended just before eleven.

When they made their way outside on to the crowded pavement, Eddy, who was guiding Vera by the arm, said over the confusion, 'You stay here with Brian, dear. I'll go find the driver. He said he'd be waiting round the corner about now.' And he slid off through the crowd, a good head and shoulders above it.

'Such a comfort, Eddy is,' Brian Worth murmured, standing very close to Vera as people milled around them.

Vera thought, he hardly changes with the years – as well turned out as ever, sleek with success, although his reputation was a bit passé these days. He had a new play headed for Broadway in the fall, but the out-of-town reviews had been disappointing.

'New York money and Old Guard status – you *did* do well for yourself, darling, but you always were such a clever girl.'

'Eddy and I are devoted,' Vera said icily, drawing the cashmere wrap around her. 'God, it's cold, even in July – what a climate.'

All of which Brian Worth disregarded. 'And while I've got

you to myself for a tiny moment, I must tell you — gossip, gossip — that your old friend R.B. is being tipped for big things politically. An MP you know — and wildly ambitious. He's hardly ever off the front pages — speeches all over the place and photographs, striding about, shaking hands.'

Damn him, the wily old queen. He'd got her trapped, standing there with no chance to escape. She supposed she would have to listen, although nothing in the world would induce her to use Robert's name. So she stared across the noisy street which was jammed with cars and taxis and people weaving in between. Her profile was striking — she was Nefertiti-like that evening with her elongated neck, longish nose, her hair pulled back and up and heavy gold and diamond necklace and earrings. He was a devil, Brian; he always had been under the charm. He'd been kind to her years ago because he needed her: there was no other reason. She had bared her soul to him once, and regretted it ever since.

'Yes?' she said indifferently.

'Oh yes, indeed. He made a name for himself in Parliament very quickly. He's got rather a following among the right wing and it's whispered that he's got the mood of the country right. People are tired of too much "equality", if you get my meaning, all this immigration that's going on. "Britain for the Brits" is Brandon's theme song.'

All very smooth, typically Brian. She knew about Robert's political leanings and odd ideas. He was watching her closely; he was enjoying this hugely.

She turned and smiled brightly. 'Oh,' she said — brittle, not inviting confidences, 'that's good.'

'We were at the same charity performance recently,' he went on casually. He slid a silver cigarette case from his pocket and offered it to Vera. She shook her head. 'His wife was with him rather a large, jolly woman, I thought, probably terribly horsy. A nice gutsy laugh. She's popular, one hears. She gives large private lunches in London which are becoming rather famous, a sort of salon where various odds and sods can mix. And how's little Megan, by the way?' he asked innocently, his eyes gleaming.

'She's fine, growing up fast. Sixteen in September. As a matter of fact, she's coming to France with us next week,' Vera said blandly, masking her fury.

'Heavens, how time does fly . . .'

Absurd that any of this should still rankle – but it did. All of it. Somewhere across this town, beneath the rainy, scudding grey clouds, *he* was . . . Or in the country, in that house; or perhaps in a villa in one of the choicer parts of Europe with his large, horsy, laughing wife. She was beside herself with anger at Brian, for telling her this, for revelling in it – which he was. Where the hell was Eddy, anyhow?

'We've booked for supper at the Caprice,' she said coldly. 'You'll be joining us, will you?' She was not inviting, although she had asked him earlier in the day.

'But, of course, darling girl, with pleasure.' His cigarette was held nonchalantly high. Around them, the crowd was starting to thin. 'Ah,' he cried. 'There's Eddy at last, waving us over.' He took her arm. 'Off we go. So much more satisfactory for you, *this* life, Vera darling, your heavenly New York apartment and all the entertaining and the travelling, than the Brandon thing. It would never have worked, not for a minute. I know Robert Brandon's type, darling, I always have.'

But Vera wasn't falling into that trap. 'I enjoyed the play,' she said loudly. 'I thought it was rather good – interesting, at least. Eddy did, too – we always enjoy the same things. What a pity you've never written anything with a bit of weight to it, Brian. No one seems to want the pretty, witty plays now, do they? Kitchen-sink realism and believable characters are "in" now.' And as they walked over to where Eddy was standing by the car, she pulled her arm sharply away from him and was pleased to see that the puckish smile had left his face.

That night, slipping into Eddy's bed, Vera was warmer and more responsive to him than she had been for years. She whispered, muffled against his neck, 'What would I do without you, Eddy? And I do love you, in my funny way. You know that, don't you? And I am grateful, for everything.'

Yet she could not sleep. The rest and the pills had cleared her throbbing head, but her mind was racing. She prayed that Megan wasn't going to continue to throw these unpleasant little scenes. She was in a position to give her everything, which was what she and Eddy intended to do. Only the past, which was over and of no importance now, would be denied her. Surely it was for the best, for all of them.

Vera sighed as Eddy muttered in his sleep beside her. As she drifted off, at last, she was wondering, as she had so many times before, where Robert had gone from her dressing-room that last time . . .

Cecilia Brandon saw her husband before he was aware of her presence. She was standing at the top of the stairs, one hand on the banister, when she heard the great door pushed open. She stopped and looked down. Pleased, not expecting him back until later, she opened her mouth to call out. Then she saw his face. He looked haggard, as grey and drained as when he had been so ill the summer before they married when his wound wouldn't heal and the fever kept recurring. She started slowly down the stairs.

'Robert? Is that you? I thought you'd be back later. And I didn't hear the car outside. I wondered who it was for a moment.'

He walked heavily into the centre of the hall and looked up at her. His expression hardly changed.

'Ceci – there you are. I didn't see you lurking in the shadows. What's that?' He was like a sleepwalker.

'I said, I didn't hear the car.'

'Oh – I walked from the lodge. I needed some air, after London.'

He looked ghastly. Purely out of instinct, Ceci knew that it was to do with a woman. Her heart raced and her hands were clammy. She had never known why he married her, so impulsively, almost on a whim; and she never wanted to. She forced herself to say cheerfully, 'Was it awful? I can never wait to get away from the place, particularly now. Did you get everything done that you wanted?'

'More or less. The lawyer I hoped to see was tied up, so I came back as early as I could. And what have you been up to?'

He caught up with her on the stairs, put his arm around her and gave her a quick kiss. He was making an effort, looking and sounding more like his normal self.

'Chores, and a marvellous, invigorating ride, like we'll have tomorrow. And I made a very satisfactory arrangement, I think, which I'll tell you about later.' She took his arm. 'I'm on my way to see James in the nursery. Want to come? Nannie says he's a holy terror – he badly needs a brother or sister . . .'

As they walked through the dusky corridors, chatting inconsequentially, Ceci thought, something went badly wrong in London today. Whatever it was, I don't want to know about it. Ever.

When they were changing for dinner, Ceci said casually, 'By the way, your mother's out this evening. She's having dinner with that old general, a friend of Angus's, who's got a fixation on her.'

'Thank God for that,' Robert said quite violently. 'In that case, we'll definitely break out a decent bottle of champagne.'

During dinner, Ceci told him about the arrangements she had made that day.

'It was a brainwave, a positive brainstorm.'

'What was?'

He had mellowed with the wine and the good food and his mind and senses had stilled somewhat. Across the candles and the silver, Ceci was looking very handsome in a black dress that set off her good colour.

'Well, Millie Frampton . . .'

'The schoolteacher? In the village?'

'That's right. There's something special about Millie, I think. She sees right through things, and people. And she's amazingly well read and artistic. She's done it all herself, too. Everyone says she's an excellent teacher.'

'What about her?'

'She's been feeling a bit lonely, since her lovely American went back to the States.'

'Her *what*?'

'Didn't I tell you? I'm sorry, Robert, I do try to keep you up with the local gossip in my letters. Millie Frampton has been living, quite openly, with an absolutely charming American officer from the air base. He's a professor at one of the big universities — Yale, I think.'

'*Millie Frampton*? The one who was a kitchen maid here years ago?' He was staggered.

'That's right.' Ceci laughed delightedly. 'She can't be far off forty and she's never even been known to "walk out" with anyone in her life before. They met at a concert in Glaston and he moved right into her cottage. Millie was so happy and she simply blossomed. They used to read plays and poetry to each other and heaven knows what. He was married — there was no secret about that either — and now he's gone back home to the States. She misses him dreadfully, but she quite understands. Isn't it a lovely story?'

'Good God.' He signalled for more wine and tried to concentrate on what Ceci was saying through the fog that seemed to have settled over his mind.

'It suddenly occurred to me that Millie had the room and she would be the ideal person to have Alain Gesson. They're both very quickminded. So I took him over to the cottage, and I was right. They hit it off at once, I could see.'

'So the boy's going there, is he?' he enquired, distant.

'He's already gone,' Ceci said lightly. 'Once Millie had agreed, he said he would prefer to stay and not come back to Cloverley at all. So we collected his things and I drove them over.'

'Thank God for that, at least.'

Chapter 9

For Megan, the plane trip to Nice – the runway shimmering with heatwaves in the hot sun – was an adventure in itself. As she stepped out of the plane, the light and the sounds and smells were all tantalizingly strange to her. So this was *abroad* ... Outside the airport, they were met by a car and a driver who dealt discreetly with the luggage and wafted them down wide palm-fringed boulevards to a large, very grand hotel. Left alone in her room, Megan flung open the long shutters and stepped out on to the small balcony.

Across the promenade and beyond the line of palm trees was the sea, brilliant blue and glittering in the sunlight. Yachts and sailboats and water skiers skimmed about like exotic sea creatures. The sun beat down on the endless traffic and the swarming holidaymakers, with their tanned limbs and dark glasses and brief, bright clothing. The vibrant scene bore no relation at all to the chilly English beaches Nan had taken her to occasionally as a child. Megan, standing on the balcony – hugging herself, smiling and smiling – was enchanted. She only hoped that her mother would leave her alone as much as possible to enjoy all this warmth and colour and excitement.

And this Vera did. She and Eddy had been visiting the south of France regularly since they were married and their vacation routine was established. Vera's days were tightly organized – just so much sunbathing; lunch by the pool; a little light shopping; the masseuse; the hairdresser. Many of the people they knew, 'café society, so called' as Vera described them, returned, as the Mortimers did, to the same places year after year. Many had villas on the tree-covered peninsulas that jutted out into the Mediterranean or high up in the craggy sun-scorched hills. Almost every night, the Mortimers dined out with acquaintances from London or Geneva or Paris or New York — ending up, often for Eddy's sake, at the Casino.

As long as Megan looked neat and appeared on time for meals, she was left on her own to swim, sunbathe or explore the winding streets of the old town. Sometimes, if he was hanging about or hadn't been invited on somebody's yacht for the day, Eddy would come with her.

After a morning spent poking round one of the open markets, buying bits and pieces off stalls, he surprised Megan by telling her, 'In all the years we've been coming here, I guess this is the first time I've even seen this place. I don't know when I last had more fun.' And he looked a lot happier than he usually did, Megan thought, with a great grin splitting his face from ear to ear, nattily dressed in resort wear, white polo shirt and cotton plaid trousers.

'Let's do it again,' she said, confiding, 'I bought a blouse there the other day, for almost nothing — it's *smashing*.'

But although Megan had a lot of freedom during the days, Vera insisted on one thing — elocution. Every evening, when she was dressing for dinner in the sudden Mediterranean twilight, Megan was expected to come to her bedroom and read aloud from any book or a newspaper or a magazine that happened to be lying about. Vera, who had demonstrated a quick ear for accents herself, corrected Megan's speech constantly; the telltale cockney was to be eliminated once and for all while she was still young and malleable. Each of these sessions invariably ended with several attempts at the hackneyed lines from Pygmalion, and this was the part that Megan dreaded the most, squirming with embarrassment, longing for the phone to ring or for Eddy to wander in from the sitting-room with some message for her mother.

'*Rain* Megan, not *roin*,' Vera said for the umpteenth time, leaning into the mirror to apply more subtle colour to her face. She and Eddy were going to a dinner-party in a private villa a little way along the coast. 'And *Spain*, not *Spoin*. Now read it again – properly this time.'

Wincing, loathing every second, Megan began again, as Eddy, smartly dressed in a white dinner-jacket, wandered in and gave her an encouraging smile behind his wife's back, the ice cubes clinking as he raised his glass.

'*Spain*, Megan, *Spain*, *Spain*, *Spain* ...' Megan hadn't been doing particularly well that night, and Vera whirled round on the stool to look at her, still holding a make-up brush. 'Concentrate, Megan, think what you're saying. It should begin to come naturally now. You've been getting it right for a long time.' Then, a look of horror spreading over her face, 'What on earth have you got on? Where *did* you get that appalling blouse?'

Shocked, Megan scrambled to her feet. 'In – in the market,' she stammered. 'When I was looking round the stalls. Eddy knows where ...' She faced her mother with her chin well raised. 'I used my own pocket money for it – I did ...'

'But it's the colour of a stick of rock! And those silly puffed sleeves and that dreadful floppy bow at the neck! If you *must* wear it – here, where are the scissors?'

Picking the scissors up from her dressing-table, she made straight for Megan. Before she knew what was happening, there was a glint of steel and a sharp cutting sound and the bow – ripped off – fell to Megan's feet.

'That's a bit better.' Vera sounded mollified. 'Fussy things round your neck, Megan, and at your age ... You've got a lot to learn about taste, I must say, so you had better start now ...' As Megan watched, dumbstruck, Vera went back to her dressing-table, sat down, and began calmly putting on her earrings. 'Now let's have "The rain in Spain" one more time – perfectly – and then you can run along.'

Megan's initial shock was replaced by fury. 'How – how – dare you? It's *my* blouse, and I *love* it.' One hand clutched her neck where the offending bow had been cut from. She was outraged by her mother's highhandedness; her voice was trembling and her eyes brimmed with tears. 'It's mine – *mine* ... And you've ruined it.'

Eddy stepped out from behind her. His face had the expression of a worried clown and he was blinking rapidly. 'Now, Vera, dear, I do think ... Poor Megan ...' Nervous grunts came from his throat. 'Now that wasn't very kind, dear, not to a young girl – and your own daughter ...'

Buoyed by even this much feeble support, Megan reached out for the nearest object to hand. It was the hated *Pygmalion* from which she had been reading night after night for nearly two weeks. She grabbed the book and, without thinking, hurled it towards the dressing-table. Grazing Vera's arm – causing her to drop one trembling diamond earring – it crashed among the rows of jars and bottles. One of them, the largest, a bottle of expensive scent, teetered and fell, smashing against the wall. There was a brief, stunned silence as a powerful aroma filled the room. Then Vera whirled round. It was she who was open-mouthed now.

'Megan, what can you be thinking of?'

With a quick movement, Megan bent down to pick up the limp strip of pink cotton which had been the bow and rushed out of the room, slamming the door behind her as hard as she could.

'And what on earth was the meaning of all that, if you please?' Vera inquired icily of her husband. She glanced down at the shattered bottle and the dark stain soaking into the carpet, the diamond earring at its centre. 'Talk about sheer and utter ingratitude ... What did I do to bring that on? I'm only trying to help her.'

Without a word, Eddy walked none too steadily over to the bar and poured himself a full glass of neat whisky. 'She's only a kid, Vera. She's not used to ...' He took a gulp of whisky. 'And I guess everything in her life is starting to change terribly quickly, like leaving Nellie for boarding school, and the blouse ... it was perfectly harmless. You really hurt her feelings badly.'

'*Her* feelings!' Vera almost spat with indignation. 'And what about *my* feelings, if you please? Throwing things at ... her mother ... What kind of manners are those?' As if she hadn't seen that temper before and the wild look about the eyes. Arrogant – a girl like her – just as *he* was, Robert Brandon ... Well, she wasn't about to put up with any of that nonsense. She got up and took off her wrapper, throwing it towards the bed. Her figure was as slim and lithe as it had ever been: long, long legs, taut stomach, small, pointed breasts; she never wore more than scraps of silk for underwear. Eddy watched, leaning against the wall, as she stuck her narrow feet into strappy sandals and stepped into the folds of a pale silk dress. She came and stood with her back to him.

Answering obliquely as he struggled with the zip, he mumbled, 'I thought she looked very cute in that little blouse, myself.'

'It was a cheap bit of rubbish,' Vera responded tartly, holding the sides of her dress together at the back. 'It looked so tacky, so common. And I bought her a wardrobe of nice clothes in London.'

Megan had looked pretty; of course she had. She was – naturally and effortlessly. With Robert's colouring and features and the incomparable freshness of youth, she had no need for make-up and artifice. Envy rose right through her, astonishing her by its power.

'The buttons, too, Eddy,' she said impatiently. 'Hurry up, we're late as it is, and it's at least half an hour's drive to the Hansards on Cap Martin.'

When he had finished, clumsily, he bent to kiss her shoulder. With a hint of disgust, she shrugged and moved away.

'You've had far too much to drink, Eddy,' she said sharply. She picked up her bag and her evening wrap. 'Let's go. At once.'

When they were being driven home from the dinner-party – the lights all along the coast shimmering in the warm night air – Vera felt for Eddy's hand. Although the evening had started badly with Megan's unpleasant little scene, the party had been amusing and stimulating. Vera was inclined to feel touchy and competitive towards Veronica Hansard as a hostess, but even she admitted that nobody could beat the Hansards as collectors of people. Artists, writers, politicians; everyone from the theatre; moneyed men and mistresses; the rich and the nearly rich – sooner or later they all poured through one of the Hansard's residences. And the villa at Cap Martin was a jewel. It was a heady mixture. Tonight had been no exception and Vera was feeling delightfully soothed.

'Eddy,' she said seductively, crossing her slender legs, pressing against his side. 'Help me with Megan, please. You're better with her than I am. Everything I do with her seems to go wrong, get twisted, misunderstood. I've been thinking about it on and off all evening. I'll tell her I'm sorry about the wretched blouse – perhaps I was too hasty. I'll do that, but she must apologize, too – she can't be allowed to get away with that kind of behaviour.' She leant towards him, very close; he could smell the warm, spicy scent she always wore. Her voice dropped to a husky whisper. 'Do that for us – for both of us. Would you, Eddy?'

The following morning, five-year-old Ted Mortimer and his Swiss governess, Marie, flew in from New York. And in the fuss and confusion of settling them in, the incident of the blouse and the broken scent bottle was not referred to by any of them. With Ted jumping about, never still for an instant, to Megan's joy, there was no possibility of any more ridiculous elocution coaching. Apart from a few guilty pangs – she hadn't meant actually to hit her mother or her precious earring – Megan felt rather pleased with herself. Between them, they had created a fine old scene – but she had stood her ground. As soon as she could, she borrowed a needle and thread from the maid, sewed the bow carefully back on, and hid it at the back of a drawer to take home to Trout Lane.

Ted Mortimer, whom she had last seen as a baby, was a trial to them all. No nurse lasted long in the Mortimer household – and Megan quickly saw why, as she told Nellie later. To look at, he was a young version of his father: very tall and skinny for his age with an indiarubber mouth and large ears that stuck out; his brown hair was scalped in the American way. When he didn't get his own way, he fell to the floor, drummed his heels and kicked and yelled. Vera left him almost entirely to the care of the nervous and exhausted Marie. Eddy was patient but overindulgent, giving him anything he wanted for the sake of peace. Most of Ted's sentences started with *'I wanna . . .'* or *'I won't . . .'*

After one embarrassing trip to the beach with Ted and Marie — Teddy chucking pebbles at nearby children — Megan did everything she could to avoid him. A few days later, skulking about in the foyer of the hotel, making sure the coast was clear of Ted and Marie, Megan found herself bumping into Eddy, who was doing much the same thing.

He told her, 'I was going on Dick Hansard's yacht today, but he had a big business merger suddenly turn up. Your mother has an appointment, so why don't we go get a coffee or something in town?'

During the hot, quiet siesta time, they sat under the striped awning of a café, Megan drinking fresh lemonade and Eddy sipping Pernod. There was nobody much about; the waiters were lolling half asleep and a couple of cats sniffed about expectantly between the tables.

'Your mother's really pleased at the way you're coming along, Megan. I know that reading out loud kind of bugs you, but it sure does make a difference to the way you're speaking.'

Megan made a face. 'I suppose so. I suppose I need to for when I go to that school in September.' Her heart sank at the thought of it — only a few weeks away now. 'But she never does seem very pleased, about anything. My mother, I mean. Well — does she?'

Megan swung her bare legs and sucked at her straw. The sun had browned her olive skin, making her alluring green-grey eyes even more vivid. The clothes that Vera had bought for her — simple sleeveless dresses in light colours — made her look older than her years and showed off sexy curves. Her arresting looks were starting to attract a good deal of male interest.

'She's not very good at expressing her feelings,' Eddy said guardedly. 'But that doesn't mean she doesn't care. She's anxious to do the best for you, Megan. You know that.'

'I know,' Megan replied, resigned, squinting across to the sea which had turned a deeper blue now that a slight wind was getting up. She sighed. 'But why doesn't she smile, or laugh, more? She never seems to have much fun.'

Eddy cleared his throat in the way he did when put on the

spot. 'Well . . .' He took a mouthful of Pernod. 'Vera tends to take life seriously, put it like that.'

'I don't know why,' Megan said crossly. 'She's got everything she could possibly want — but she never seems happy, not really. Nan hasn't got anything much, but she always thinks things are going to be all right in the end.'

Eddy flung one long leg across the other.

'You know, Megan, she had it pretty rough when she was a kid, your mother did. Your grandad was gassed in the Great War, and Nellie only just managed to make ends meet.'

'I know that Eddy, but . . .'

'And don't forget, she's been on her own since she was your age, earning her living on the stage as best she could. And that was pretty tough, getting to the top. She was a real star, you know.'

'But I *still* don't see why she's so hard to talk to — about anything important. Nan thinks so, too. I mean, she won't even tell me . . .' She paused and looked straight at Eddy, her lashes swept up, her eyes enormous. 'She won't even tell me or Nan who —'

But Eddy was already on his feet, waving the bill at a waiter. After he had paid, he immediately changed the subject. 'Now what do you say we do some window shopping? You wanted to get something to take back to Nellie, and I think the shops will be opening up again now.'

While they were strolling along the avenue lined with smart shops and awnings, Eddy said casually, 'You know, Megan, your mother is very upset about that scene the other night, the night before Ted got here.'

'I was upset, too,' Megan said airily, stopping to look in a shop window where a red and white pottery jar, with cherries on top, had caught her eye.

'Yes, I can understand that. What's that you're looking at?'

'The little jar, over in the corner. I love the colours. It would look just right on Nan's table in the kitchen.'

'The fact is, Megan,' Eddy said, after they'd bought the jar, 'your mother is truly sorry about the incident the other night.

We discussed it. And she does think she was in the wrong concerning the blouse. It was yours, after all. She didn't have the right . . .'

'No,' said Megan, sauntering on and looking straight ahead. 'No, she didn't.'

'She accepts that. But she thinks that you should apologize to her for what happened after – throwing that book, smashing her things. What I mean is' – he gave one of his frequent nervy coughs – 'she really wants to put things right between the two of you.'

Entering the hotel grounds, they bumped straight into Vera who was coming from the other direction. Crisp and cool in sleeveless pink linen, she was carrying several expensive shopping bags.

Eddy went off to find Ted, so in awkward silence, Megan and her mother walked into the hotel and up in the lift. Standing in the dim corridor outside the door of her room, Vera said coolly,

'I'm sorry if I offended you by what I did to your blouse the other night, Megan.' Her hand, hung with the glossy shopping bags, was already on the doorhandle. Behind the dark glasses, her face was pale and inscrutable.

'That's all right.' Megan stared straight at the shiny black pools covering her mother's eyes. 'And I didn't mean to hurt you or break anything, really I didn't. I'm sorry about that. I was just so cross.' No one would guess how hard her heart was thumping. She took a deep breath and raised her chin. 'I've sewn the bow on again. I borrowed a needle and cotton from the maid. It's exactly like it was before, when I bought it . . .'

Megan couldn't be sure, but before her mother opened the door and vanished inside, she thought she saw the flicker of a smile around her mouth.

On a crisp September morning, Vera Mortimer's car drew up to 5 Trout Lane. Megan heard, and her heart dropped. She had been wide awake, sick with dread, for hours. Anticipating this parting, sewing on nametapes, each trying to cheer the other up, she and Nellie had passed day after miserable day since she had returned from France. Nellie was unusually subdued and frequently snuffled into a hanky; even her lilting singing voice was silenced.

'They're here, Nan,' Megan called from the front room where she had been keeping watch. 'They're here.' There was a convulsive sob in her voice. Nellie hurried out from the kitchen to stand very close, wiping her hands on her apron. Megan's luggage, with the new regulation green winter coat on top of it, was piled at the bottom of the narrow stairs. They could hear Vera's voice and the driver answering, then the sharp rap on the door.

Vera had fully anticipated the sight of two white, stricken faces, but she hadn't counted on her own feelings. She quailed. She saw in a flash that Nellie looked suddenly older and shrunken; as though all the light had gone out of her. Megan, huge-eyed, standing very straight, towered above her. In a painful lurch of memory, Vera had a vivid image of handing the pink bundle that was the infant Megan over to Nellie – and Nellie's immediate, heartfelt response: 'There, now, your Nan's got you.' For the first time, Vera had some inkling of the enormity of what she was doing – to her daughter and to her own mother.

She steeled herself. 'You're looking very smart, Megan,' she said. 'Everything ready, is it? That's good.'

Brisk and businesslike, only minutes later, Vera and the chauffeur had themselves and Megan's belongings neatly stowed into the car. From the moment of Vera's arrival, neither Megan nor Nellie said a word – and neither did they once look at each other. As the car purred back up Trout Lane, Megan sat holding herself very stiff and tense, staring sightless through the windscreen, and even when they turned the corner, she did not look round.

They edged through interminable traffic, at last reaching the open countryside. Megan, in her new green and white uniform, went on sitting bolt upright, looking straight ahead past the driver's cap. Wanting to comfort her, but incapable of finding the words or the gestures, Vera knew that Megan was in no mood for talk. Later, perhaps . . . So she lit a cigarette and stared out at the leafy rolling hills and tried to set her mind on other things which were worrying her.

Eddy's heavy social drinking was beginning to be a serious concern, to her and to others. She knew that the senior people in his firm were alarmed; that their friends were beginning to talk. Twice in the last year he had disappeared for a couple of days at a time on what were apparently drinking sprees. His loyal secretary, her one confidante in this matter, was anxious, too. And Ted's bad behaviour had to be tackled; it was obvious, in France, that he was quite out of hand. Marie had no authority with him; she would have to be replaced, and the wearying round of employment agencies and interviews faced yet again.

She glanced sideways at Megan, feeling ominous flickers of compassion, old memories stirring: *everything to do with Robert — it was so long ago, it was like yesterday* . . . And here she was, removing their daughter from Nellie and Trout Lane, all the familiarity of her upbringing. It was like severing limbs; yet she truly believed that what she was doing was for the best — for Megan.

It was also in September, almost sixteen years ago to the day, that she had handed her, that first time, to Nellie. The siren had gone again while she was still in the taxi on her way home, grieving for Robert, aching for her child, tears pouring down her face, feeling so ill and so weak and so alone that she wondered whether she would ever find the strength to live normally again. Whether any of them would . . .

And yet it ended at last for those who had struggled through preparing to pick up the pieces.

Loyal and dependable Flo, who had seen her through it all, hadn't been one of the lucky ones. She was senselessly killed by a stray bomb while having tea at her sister's house in a leafy street in Purley, only months before the war ended. Coming on top of everything else, it was a loss which Vera felt terribly: it was while they were planning to take the play to New York; Flo, who had settled in confidently as her dresser, would have come too, of course.

On VE day, May 1945, Vera automatically made her way through the crowds to Trout Lane. Ignoring the ugly gaps of bomb craters — Gran Gubbins's cornershop had taken a direct hit the year after she had died, mercifully, of a heart attack — Vera watched the bunting and the trestle tables being dragged out on to the pavements for a victory street party.

She found Nellie trying to tie red, white and blue ribbons in Megan's hair, and Megan hopping about, not sure what was happening, but catching the excitement of the moment for all that. After leaving a bottle of champagne, which Nellie accepted politely — give her a port and lemon any day — she decided to go back to her flat. Nellie wasn't very welcoming, and Megan was shy, clinging tightly to Nellie's hand, begging to be out on the street with her friends, joining in the fun.

When she got out of the lift it was late and she was dog-tired. In the dense crowds there were few buses or taxis about, so she walked most of the way. A long, lean figure materialized from the shadows. It was Eddy Mortimer. He had managed to hitch a ride, he said hesitantly, and he had hoped — if it was all right by her — that they could spend this amazing evening together.

Emotionally numbed, still shocked by Flo's recent death, Vera was grateful for the sight of him. As always, he had brought precious goodies — whisky, ham and tinned fruit. In the quiet, shadowy sitting-room, they sat drinking, eating and talking on and off well into the early hours. And it was then, during a lull in the conversation, that Vera turned to him impulsively and, in a rush, told him about Megan and Nellie in Trout Lane. She did not once mention Robert Brandon's name.

After a long silence, Eddy Mortimer said finally, 'Will you be seeing him again — Megan's father? I'm not asking to know any more than you've told me, and I never would. It's just that I'd like to know what I'm up against.'

Vera thought of New York and Broadway and the possibility of a whole new life, away from all this. And in a split second, she relegated Robert Brandon, as she thought, to her past.

'No, Eddy,' she said, shaking her head. 'No, I won't.'

Tentatively, he touched her cheek.

'Eddy,' she said, passionately, clinging to his hand, 'Oh, Eddy, I'm so glad you're here. I've been so lonely . . .'

*

And so at the height of her post-war New York success in *Partners in Paradise*, the toast of Broadway, where heads craned to get a glimpse when she walked into restaurants, she had married Eddy Mortimer Jr – only son and scion of the 'old money' Wall Street broking family – and renounced show business for ever. She settled in a palatial apartment on Park Avenue, the Connecticut estate, had the influential and very social fund-raising circuit, and at once decided that the rôle of Mrs Edward Mortimer would be her last, and most spectacular.

The elder Mrs Mortimer, since deceased, considered her son 'a darling boy but weak as water', so as she decided to put a good face on his unlikely union – with a hard but decorative English actress who seemed to come from nowhere and have no relatives, with a brief previous wartime marriage – New York society followed suit. Brian Worth, hugely amused at how well Vera had done for herself, gave her away. 'Clever old you, sweetie,' he cooed, eyeing her silly, and very expensive, bit of pale-blue veiling of a hat. 'Fancy landing adorable Eddy Mortimer and all those lovely Mortimer millions . . .' She had reached her limited peak as an actress, thanks to him, and he fancied she was shrewd enough to know it and get out while the going was good. She certainly had the knack of landing on her feet – if one didn't count that ridiculous, all-or-nothing affair with Robert Brandon at the beginning of the war.

Vera Mortimer was not much liked, but she was admired. She had looks and dash and style – plus the Mortimer wealth and name. And her innate professionalism and will to succeed. She watched, and she missed nothing. Soon, she had hooked the best private chef in New York, and invitations to her absurdly formal dinners were rarely refused. Within five years of her marriage she had produced a son, Ted; she had gained a secure place on the best-dressed list; and she was a trustee of a minor, but highly thought of, art museum.

It was mid afternoon by the time Vera and Megan turned in through imposing gates and swept up a long, tree-lined avenue. At the end was the forbidding grey stone mansion that was

Copthorne Hall. The early sunlight had faded, and as they approached, the massive house seemed to glower out of great dark clouds which had rolled down over the hills behind.

At the sight of it Megan's composure crumpled.

'Oh, no,' she moaned, dropping her head into her hands. 'No – no – no –'

It was the first sound she had uttered since her mother's arrival at Trout Lane that morning. With rare impulsiveness, Vera reached out and grasped her shoulder.

'Don't be silly. You're bound to feel a bit strange, but you'll enjoy school once you get used to it, Megan,' she said bracingly. All day, she had been hoping that she wouldn't have to deal with outright rebellion, or a tiring emotional scene. But she couldn't be sure; with Megan, now, she was wary. 'You'll make friends, you'll have opportunities you would never have if you stayed with Nan.' Megan went on cowering with her head somewhere by her knees as the house drew closer. 'You'll be back with her in a few weeks for the half-term holiday – it will be here before you know it, then Christmas,' Vera coaxed. But nothing moved Megan. She was still holding her, half supporting her weight, as they walked past great urns and statuary up the wide stone steps.

At the top, the muddle of beige tweed and old sweaters that was Miss Hopham greeted them effusively. Beside her was a large, slobbering boxer dog. Megan's eyes darted about, terrified, as Miss Hopham – once again disconcerted by Vera Mortimer's formidable chic and self-possession – gabbled inanely. The new girls always came the day before the others, she gushed, so that they had time to settle in and find their way about; and how nice that they had arrived first ...

Megan dragged behind, silent and miserable, as they were shown studies and classrooms and introduced to members of staff. After an hour or so, Vera looked at her watch and decided that it was time she started back for London; they were flying to New York in the morning. She and Megan said their awkward goodbyes in Miss Hopham's study. Waiting to see Vera off, Miss Hopham, noticeably cooler and more shrill once out of

Vera's hearing, showed Megan up to her dormitory and suggested sharply that she began to unpack.

Left alone in the dimly lit, depressing room where there were four iron bedsteads and four chests of drawers and not much else, the bile which she had fought for most of the day began to rise in Megan's throat. And with it, blind panic. Ignoring her trunk which had been dumped beside one of the beds, she went straight to the window. Leaning out, she could just see her mother getting into the back of the car. In an hysterical surge of homesickness, Megan flung open the door and started running wildly through the dark maze of corridors until she came to the main staircase. Aware of Miss Hopham's raised voice in a room close by, Megan flew down the stairs, across the hall – the boxer padding and sniffing behind her – through the front entrance and back down the steps to the drive.

The wind had got up and it was spitting with rain and the light was going fast. Desperate for the sight of her mother, her last chance to get away from this terrible, godforsaken place, she could just make out the red rear lights of the car as it pulled away back down the drive. Her voice spiralling up in the gathering storm, Megan screamed, 'Mother...' – a word she usually avoided at all costs – '*Mother ... please, please, don't leave me, not here, take me back, I hate it, I hate it. I want Nan ... I want ...*' But all the time, the tiny lights, which seemed the only spark of hope still alive to keep her from the horror of Copthorne Hall, got smaller and dimmer, and within seconds, disappeared altogether in the gloom. In despair, Megan gave up, walked slowly back towards the house and sat on the bottom step, head bowed, leaning up against a monstrous stone griffin, crying her eyes out.

This was where Miss Hopham and Matron found her, just as they were preparing to greet other new arrivals. Their voices icy with disapproval, Megan was ordered back to her room by Miss Hopham – '*this instant*,' she barked – and frogmarched inside by Matron just as several more cars appeared. Matron, bristling with indignation, waddling in her starchy uniform, trundled her smartly back to the dormitory and her hated trunk.

The kind of voices Megan had been dreading – loud and confident and plummy – floated up into the cheerless room where Megan, hardly aware of what she was doing, was transferring piles of new green underwear into drawers. She didn't even look up when a large, bouncy fair-haired girl careered through the door and came upon Megan kneeling weeping into her half-empty trunk, thinking that she would, she was sure of it, die of unhappiness in this dreadful place – and away from Nan.

'Hello there,' the girl said, in a light, lilting Welsh accent, plonking herself on Megan's bed and giving her a wide, friendly smile. 'I'm new here, too – and I'm in this dorm. My name's Gillian Thomas – but I'm always called Gill. Do cheer up. Would you like to borrow a handkerchief?'

It was very late when the telephone rang in Miss Hopham's study. Annoyed, she had half a mind not to answer.

'Yes? Who is it?'

There was the sound of something dropping – possibly the receiver at the other end. There were voices – much laughter – a piano thumping in the background. Could it be – perish the thought – a *public house*?

'Yes? Yes? Speak up.' A wrong number surely. She was about to put the phone down when someone spoke.

'Got my Meg there, 'ave you? Well, 'ave you?' It was a woman's voice, not young and certainly not socially acceptable.

'I *beg* your pardon.'

The piano was ripping away now, some common tune. Miss Hopham's nose wrinkled in distaste.

'Meg, I said. You know all right, you got 'er.'

'We do have a new girl called Megan Bowen,' said Miss Hopham, very cold and stiff. 'But I'm afraid . . . I really think . . . you must have the wrong number.'

'No, I 'aven't. That's 'er. Tell 'er Nan wants to 'ave a word.'

'It is much too late for any girl of mine to take a telephone call. In any case, pupils at Copthorne Hall are *only* permitted to speak to *relatives*.'

Part 2

Meetings . . .

Chapter 10

There was Megan, eighteen and a half years old, hanging about in the drawing-room of Copthorne Hall on a hot June day with Gill Thomas, who had been her best friend since that first despairing day as a new girl. With much grumbling, some unhappiness and quite a lot of fun in between, they had survived almost three years of life at the school – which Megan had never stopped thinking of as a sort of middle-class jail.

Nellie was her adored Nan, still. But Megan was a fish out of water back in Trout Lane now. Her old playmates had long left school and taken up jobs; several of the girls had married. Embarrassingly, when they met, they spoke different languages. And although Megan would have died rather than admit it to a soul, the little house did look painfully shabby.

Only Nan's loving heart and endearing ways never changed.

Most of Megan's background was unknown to the people at Copthorne Hall. Vera Mortimer, with Eddy, had visited her there several times, sweeping her off to lunch and bowling an agitated Miss Hopham over yet again. Her stylish clothes, the kind no one thought existed away from the pages of *Vogue*, had caused a lot of excited talk and admiration from staff and girls alike, and Megan's popularity had soared; even outgoing Gill, meeting Vera for the first time, was practically speechless. But it was only Gill, natural and down-to-earth, without a snobbish bone in her body, who also knew all about Nan and her Trout Lane upbringing. She had stayed there once or twice in the holidays, fitting in without a trace of self-consciousness.

It was a Saturday, so as senior pupils, in their last term, they were allowed 'out' in suitable company. Owen Thomas, Gill's older brother, a junior doctor who was training to be a surgeon at a London teaching hospital, was supposed to be taking them out for lunch. Gill had been trying to get him to do this for so long that the outing was a running joke between her and Megan. Time after time it had been postponed or cancelled – until today. It was a quarter past one, and he was already an hour or so late; even Gill was looking nervous.

Dressed alike in crisp green and white cotton dresses and thick brown stockings, they perched on the ancient radiator under the open window, swinging their legs and gazing forlornly down the long, empty drive.

'Perhaps he won't come after all,' Megan said hopefully, wishing she could call the whole thing off. She had met Gill's parents – and taken to them immediately, particularly her mother, Gwen Thomas. Gill talked so much about her family that Megan would sometimes wonder, wistfully, what it must be like to have a normal, secure background where everything was open and where everyone had their say.

Despite her good looks and Vera Mortimer's drilling – nice clothes and holidays in France – Megan was still shy and lacking in confidence and although it had seemed such a good idea when Gill first suggested it – 'You'll like Owen and it'll get us out of this hell hole for a bit' – she now suspected it might be an ordeal. What on earth would she find to talk about to this unknown brother? And he must be clever, like Gill, which would make her feel more inadequate than ever. Anxious, biting her lip and frowning, she was, even so, a beauty – as Nellie Bowen had long been telling everyone around Trout Lane who would listen. Afternoons of tennis and swimming had warmed her skin and her dark, shiny hair curved on to delicate cheekbones; as she got older, her startling eyes were more green than grey.

'Not turn up when he said he would? Our Owen?' In complete contrast to Megan, Gill was a strapping girl, full of bounce, with a mop of fair hair which was close to red. 'Anyhow, I'm sure you'll get on. You're serious types, both of you.'

'I hope he hasn't broken down, or had an accident.'

'There you go, worrying away. Owen's a worrier, too. And precise about everything, except being on time, which he can't help. Pa says that's why he'll make such a good surgeon — nothing's left to chance. If anything had happened, he would have phoned. You can be sure of that.'

'Bashful, that's my Meg,' Nellie Bowen would confide to her cronies in the Mason's Arms. 'Not like 'er Mum. Vera never 'ad a nerve in 'er body. But Meg — she's different. Refined, Meg is.'

Behind them, the door opened and the shaggy grey head of Miss Hopham peered round. Megan and Gill leapt to their feet.

'Still here, girls?' Her eyebrows were raised above the glasses which perched on the tip of her nose and cigarette ash was spilt down the front of her shapeless sweater. The boxer dog padded and snivelled behind.

Despite herself, Miss Hopham couldn't find fault. So she made do with: 'Put your hats on before you leave the house, both of you — and be back at six prompt. Not a moment later, girls.'

'Yes, Miss Hopham,' they chorused.

'Silly old cow,' Gill muttered, pulling a face as the door shut smartly. 'What an example of *womanhood*, for God's sake . . .'

Neither girl could wait to leave Copthorne Hall. The close-knit Thomases took education seriously, and Gill hoped to go on to study languages at university. Megan, who hadn't done well academically — and who had little idea of who she was, let alone what she wanted to do with her life — was starting a secretarial course in London in the autumn, all organized by her mother.

'It's an ideal starting point, Megan,' Vera had said firmly when they were discussing her future earlier in the year. 'You'll have a skill and you can branch out any way you want to. I mean, it's not as if you had any definite career ideas of your own, is it?' And after the course, Vera was determined she should at last come to the States for a long visit. 'Stay with us, and then travel around and see something of the States. We have the best contacts all over. It's crazy not to make the most of them.' Megan felt in her bones, with dread, that her mother intended the visit to be permanent. She was increasingly dismissive of any future she might make for herself in England. 'For heaven's sake,

Megan,' she would say impatiently, 'America is *the* country now — you'd be mad to pass up all the opportunities there.'

But Megan, who sometimes thought that her life was becoming more, not less, mixed up, wasn't in the least sure she wanted them.

'There he is — look.'

Megan saw it first: a battered, low-slung sports car with the top down was cranking up the drive towards them.

'That's him, at last! We're off!'

Ramming on the despised straw hats, they raced down the front steps just as the car, shuddering, pulled up with a final blast from the exhaust. And the first thing Megan noticed about Owen Thomas was a reddish blur — his hair — behind the windscreen.

Gill vaulted into the back seat, breathlessly introducing Megan.

'Hi, Owen, this is Meg. You know, I stayed with her and her gran in London after Easter. And we've got to get a move on, it's almost closing time. Where on earth *were* you?'

Megan found herself shaking hands with a tall, rather grave young man, who resembled Gill in colouring only, although *his* hair, as Megan had seen in a flash, was authentic red. He was quite formally dressed in grey flannels, checked sports jacket and tie. He seemed much older than she had expected.

'We've heard a lot about you in the family,' Owen said quietly, looking directly at her. 'I'm only sorry it's taken these three years before I've managed to get up here to meet you.'

Megan opened her mouth to reply but nothing came — so she smiled and scrambled into the car next to Gill.

After some coaxing, the engine came to life. It had behaved erratically all the way from London, Owen explained — which was why he had turned up late. Gill shouted, 'Here we go!' as the car screeched off, scattering the gravel on the drive. Megan was crouched directly behind Owen. He looked, as Gill said, like someone who took life very seriously indeed. He had a narrow, ascetically handsome face and he gave the impression of having suppressed nervous energy. He held himself ramrod straight, even when he was driving.

Clinging to the side as they swerved into the main road, the breeze whipping through her hair, Megan started to enjoy herself.

Stopping at the nearest pub, strictly out of bounds to girls from Copthorne Hall, they carried drinks and sandwiches out to a shady part of the garden. After he had eaten a sandwich and drunk half his beer, Owen took off his tie, opened his shirt collar and rolled up his sleeves. Megan, looking at him surreptitiously, thought he seemed terribly tired; there were deep bluish shadows under his eyes. He didn't say much, but Gill chattered non-stop about dreaded exams and plans for the summer.

'More cider, Meg? Beer, Owen?'

Owen refused, but when Gill went off, he immediately turned to Megan. She had pushed the short sleeves of her dress right up over her shoulders, which had turned a pale gold, and her hair gleamed like dark silk. Owen seemed to start — then he smiled as though seeing her properly for the first time. This sudden, attractive smile quite took away what Megan had thought was rather a forbidding expression and the tension visibly left his body. He relaxed completely, tipping back his head and folding his arms. His eyes, Megan saw, were very light blue with sandy eyebrows.

'I was on call last night and I hardly got a wink of sleep. I'm whacked. Would you mind terribly, Meg, if I shut my eyes for ten minutes?'

'Of course not.'

'It seems an awful thing to do — and very rude — to an exceptionally pretty girl one has only just met.'

Megan's lashes swept up — and her lips parted. But before she had time to say anything, Owen had closed his eyes. He was asleep in seconds. Neither of them had moved when Gill came back.

'He can sleep anywhere now. He's had to learn to.' Gill handed Megan the cider. She spoke, for her, quite quietly. 'Pa says it's absurd, the hours these young doctors have to work, although he did the same himself. He really hasn't forgiven Owen for not joining him.'

The Thomases' father was a doctor in the Black Mountains in Wales where he had a far-flung general practice in the remote and hilly countryside. Owen and Gillian had grown up there, and their parents and their grandparents before them.

'Why? Didn't he want to?'

Gill shook her head emphatically. 'Not Owen. He thinks Pa's talents are wasted there, driving round the villages, up and down the valleys, in all weathers and at any time of the day or night.'

'Did Owen always want to be a surgeon?'

'Always. Our mother tells the same boring story over and over again — but it's true. When Owen was little, long before I was born, he found a bird with a broken wing and insisted on bringing it home and fixing some kind of a tourniquet. It seemed to do the trick, and it mended. That was when he announced that he was going to be a surgeon — not a doctor, a surgeon. I don't think they thought he knew the difference — but he certainly stuck to it.'

'He must be very dedicated, because it's a very long training, isn't it?' Megan knew he was a lot older than Gill, probably nearly thirty, which seemed to her quite old and experienced.

'Oh, it is, years and years. That's why Owen says he's determined to get to the top of the tree, Harley Street no less. He wants to make money *and* teach *and* do research — everything. The trouble is . . .' Gill looked thoughtful.

'What?'

'I think he does miss our part of Wales a lot. It's in our blood, mine too. He'd never admit it — Owen never wants to talk about feelings, at least not his — but I think he feels a bit cut off in London, even though he's done so well. Cut off from the family, I mean, from Wales, like a foreigner.'

'But it's not all that far away.'

'No, it's not. But it seems as though it is, temperamentally. You'd be surprised. I feel it, too. I was almost as homesick as you when we started at school. I just hid it better. When I saw you sobbing away, that first day, I thought: one of us has got to be brave.'

Megan laughed. 'I don't believe you, Gill.'

'It's true. Look, you really must come to Wales, Meg,' Gill said warmly. 'You've met Ma and Pa and they're very easy and good fun. And the countryside is beautiful, very special, particularly if it's not pouring with rain.'

'I'd love that.'

'We could show you all our favourite places, and walk, and go fishing.' She glanced at their empty glasses on the table. 'That's one of Owen's passions. And we'd take you to the best pub in the world — it's called the Cider Mill. Hello, young Owen's coming back to life, I see.'

Owen opened his eyes and stretched, instantly wide awake. 'Taking my name in vain, are you?' He pushed his fingers through his hair and glanced at his watch. 'Come on, girls, we can't spend the whole afternoon sitting about. I'm programmed for quick reviving snoozes these days.' He stood, full of energy, smiling down at them, looking very much younger and more carefree. 'Let's do some exploring and find a decent place to walk. I could do with some exercise. On your feet, Gill girl. You too, Meg.'

For the first time, Megan caught the sing-song in his voice.

After Owen had done some methodical planning with his map, they drove further out into the countryside, parking the car in a lane beside a pond encircled by trees. There was a stile, and a footpath which seemed to lead through a copse out on to a gentle hill. They followed it, and an hour or so later, taking a semi-circular route, they found themselves back where they had started. All of them were feeling the heat by then.

'That's enough.' Puffed, Gill threw herself down in a shady patch of grass beside the pond. High trees cast shadows across the clear, still surface and a stream trickled in at one end. Owen fetched a rug from the car and lay full length, propped up on his elbow. Megan knelt beside him.

'You'll miss all this nature stuff when you go to New York, Meg,' Gill teased. 'It won't be like this in the Big Apple.'

Owen looked up at Megan. 'Are you going to New York, Meg? When?'

'Oh, not quite yet.' To cover her sudden confusion, Megan

turned to pick a wild daisy growing among the long grasses. Any reference to her mother, and New York, made her immediately self-conscious. She wished Gill hadn't mentioned it; she was enjoying the day so much more than she had expected to. 'I've got to get through that secretarial course first.'

'You remember, Owen. I told you Meg's mother lives in New York. She used to be on the stage — Vera Bowen, the actress. Ma and Pa saw her in the war. She was a famous star in Brian Worth's comedies. Anyhow' — she had kicked off her shoes and was pulling off her stockings — 'she went to New York in one of his plays, was a wild success and married a billionaire . . .'

'*Shut up*, Gill,' Megan interrupted.

'OK, but it's true, ask her, Owen. *I* think it's all fascinating, having such a glamorous background. Ours is so ordinary. I'm honestly quite envious. Meg doesn't, though.' She stood up, hitching her dress, and began picking her way over to the stream. 'I'm off for a cooling paddle.'

Megan and Owen watched as she dodged through rocks and nettles.

'It does sound rather intriguing, your mother's life,' Owen said quietly after a few moments. 'A real fairytale. Vera Bowen . . . I do remember Gill saying something of the sort. I hadn't connected it with you, though.' He had heard, too, of engaging cockney Nellie who served chips with everything and was partial to port, in Trout Lane, the heart of the East End — the last place he would associate Megan with. 'Are you looking forward to it — New York?'

'Not much.' Megan stared down at the white flower she was twirling between her fingers. Her lashes brushed her cheeks and her hair fell forward on to her face. She hadn't once looked at him since Gill mentioned New York. It had unsettled her instantly; Owen was aware of this.

'I know about your grandmother, Nellie, too — Gill said she's a great character. Your stepfather is American, obviously — and your father?' He sounded sympathetic, yet impersonal. He was used to asking probing questions; it was part of his job.

Megan sat very still, her legs tucked beneath her, her arms

bare, slim and graceful in the green cotton dress. Silhouetted there against the sun-splashed water, something about her made Owen think of a mermaid.

She glanced at him sideways, her heart beating very fast, ignoring Gill who was calling for them to come over. 'I don't know who my father is,' she said very softly. 'He and my mother weren't married. That's all I do know.'

She had astonished herself. Except to Nan, she had never uttered these words aloud before. As Nellie and her mother had told her to, she had carried on the fiction of a brief wartime marriage, her father killed, her mother remarried. It was fully accepted, quite commonplace, no further questions asked.

'I see . . .' Owen nodded. 'Do go on — if you want to, that is.'

'Nan — my Gran — doesn't know either who he is. My mother never told her, and she's looked after me since I was a few days old. You won't — you won't . . .' Megan stopped, appalled at her confession. 'I mean, you won't tell anyone — even Gill? I never say, never have before . . .'

So why had she now, to this near stranger? And she had thought he looked so stern when she stood shaking hands with him a few hours ago. Was it because he was a doctor, and older? Was it because she knew, somehow, that he wouldn't be shocked or surprised? Was it because she so badly needed to say it to *someone*?

'Of course not. I would never abuse a confidence.' He looked concerned and attentive. Gill had given up on them and was building a dam across the stream. 'How often do you see your mother, Meg?'

'Once or twice a year. Whenever she and Eddy — he's my stepfather — come to London.'

Owen frowned. His face was angular beneath the thatch of bright hair and he was developing brownish freckles.

'Have you thought of asking her yourself?'

'Oh yes, lots of times. I even work out what I'm going to say. When I was younger it used to worry me dreadfully. I'd lie awake wondering what he does, where he lives, what he looks like. It was a dark secret in my life. I suppose it still is. But it's so difficult with my mother. I did ask her once, just before I came to Copthorne.' Now she had started, it all came tumbling out.

'And what did she say?'

'Only that it was a part of her life that was over. She wouldn't tell me anything.' And how could she even begin to explain Vera Mortimer, now classily American to her fingertips, in her strict couture clothes and pearls, reeking of Chanel; the cold edge to her voice; the next move always planned – a dinner, the theatre, shopping, Eddy trailing behind? And yet – there were such powerful feelings between them, somewhere . . . 'Since then, there just never seems to have been a right time,' she finished helplessly.

'But that can't be reasonable, surely.' He sounded close to anger, on her behalf. 'And it obviously troubles you. You have every right to know the circumstances of your birth and background. Your mother must know this perfectly well, even if she can't bring herself to face it. Which is what it sounds like to me.' He caught sight of the time and jumped up. 'Good God, it's five o'clock already! We can't stay here for ever, peaceful and pleasant though it is.' He put out his hand and helped her to her feet.

Megan noticed that she had been clutching the wilted daisy all the time they had been talking. They both saw this and laughed as she threw it into the pond.

He went on, seriously, 'But if you do want someone to talk to, Meg, come and find me. And I mean what I say.'

'I'll remember. And you promise not to tell – ever?' She hesitated. 'Not to tell anyone?'

'I promise: you have my word. Now let's go and see what Gill has got up to . . .'

After failing to start the engine on his sixth try, Owen gave up.

'We have to make a decision,' he said calmly. 'I think I know what's wrong and I think I can fix it – but it will take time. It's twenty to six now. I'll give myself half an hour. If I haven't got it going by then, we'll have to walk to the nearest farmhouse and get help and phone the school. All right?'

While Owen worked away doggedly at the open bonnet,

Megan and Gill wandered round the pool, not talking much, both anxious. Miss Hopham's wrath was never pleasant. The light lowered softly towards evening: a delicate pink washed the sky and clouds of gnats swarmed about the bushes. Two minutes before the deadline, the car burst into life – and they were chugging up the drive of Copthorne Hall barely half an hour late.

Leaving the engine running, Owen leapt out of the car saying, 'Leave this to me. This was my responsibility, and I'll do the explaining.' Serious, every inch the competent young professional, he took the steps several at a time and disappeared through the wide open front door. The girls stared after him. Megan was secretly relieved at the way Owen had so effortlessly taken charge; and although she knew it would not be mentioned between them, she was fairly sure that Gill felt the same. They had just reached the door, a bedraggled pair in their damp, creased cotton dresses and cock-eyed hats, as Owen swung jauntily out.

'It's all smoothed over, no trouble at all. She couldn't have been more understanding.' He smiled at Megan – friendly and approachable again. And lowering his voice, murmured, 'Although I can quite see why neither of you will be sorry to see the back of this establishment.'

While they were seeing him off, Owen said, turning to Megan, 'I'd like to meet your Nan some time if I could. I miss a bit of home life in London. I'll get your number from Gill and give you a ring. May I do that?'

Megan nodded – and he revved up the engine and zoomed off down the drive, his hand raised in a goodbye salute, the last fingers of sunlight striking his hair.

Later that night, when they were both in bed in the tiny cubicle of a room they shared, Megan said, 'Does Owen have a girlfriend – I mean a steady one?'

'Hmm . . . interested, are you? In an old man like Owen?' Gill teased half-heartedly. She was almost asleep. 'Nobody special that I know of. He had a dreadful tarty girl called Diane for ages. She's a dancer – of sorts. He brought her to Wales once and the parents had a fit. He had a really big thing about her. I don't know what happened. He's had a couple of lady doctors in tow from time to time. He never meets anyone else.' Her voice trailed off. 'And he works so hard.'

Her hands behind her head, Megan stared at the shadowy ceiling. Her mind was crystal clear, very far from sleep. She longed to ask more about this Diane person, but Gill seemed to be asleep, and in any case, she didn't want to appear too inquisitive.

It had been an astonishing day. If anyone had told her, that morning, that she would confide the secret of her background to Gill's doctor brother, she would never have believed it. She remembered the way Owen's nice smile suddenly changed his set and serious expression; she had never felt so safe with anyone. They might have been all by themselves, sitting there at the reedy edge of the pond.

She smiled secretly in the darkness, certain emotions quickening in her for the first time.

School ended, Megan's trunk was packed, and as the taxi taking her to the station trundled down the drive, she turned for one last look at the vast, unadorned grey house. Despite all the heady exhilaration of leaving parties and goodbyes, despite the early memories of deathly homesickness which would stay with her for ever, she did, after all, feel a twinge of regret.

Mooning about Trout Lane, bored and friendless, missing the activity and the company of Copthorne Hall, Megan hardly knew what to do with herself. As usual, she was going to France for a month with her mother and Eddy, early in August. But until then, the days dragged by. Even Nellie noticed.

'I don't like to see you stuck in the 'ouse like this, Meg,' she said, dismayed, after Megan had leapt from the kitchen sofa to answer the telephone – an inquiry about a bill from the gas board – and then curled up in it again, dejected. 'You oughta be gettin' out an' about a bit, at your age.'

'I'm OK, Nan, don't fuss.'

There was no word from Owen Thomas – and she had been so certain that he would get in touch with her. Particularly now, with so little to occupy her time, she had relived those moments when they were alone by the shimmering pond over and over again. She prayed that she wouldn't regret her confidence; she had wanted to tell him that she was illegitimate, she must have, but why had she? He had been so attentive at the time; but perhaps he had forgotten all about her, dismissed her as a mere schoolgirl, Gill's friend, too young to bother about. And perhaps, perhaps — and this was her worst fear — her admission had put him off, been unacceptable. They were both in London, he must have some time off, surely. And he had wanted to meet Nan, he said so. Megan's imagination, romantically stirred for the first time, had raced feverishly ahead.

One evening, when Nellie slipped out to the Mason's Arms, she phoned Gill at home in Wales. She was intending to ask, in the most cunningly casual way, whether she had remembered to give Owen her Trout Lane address which she had written so distinctly, with a brief thank-you message — and which Gill had promised to pass on. But it was Gwen Thomas who answered, warm and friendly, so delighted to hear her voice, she said; unfortunately Gill had left for Spain that morning with a party of friends. Of course — Gill's great summer plans, Megan had quite forgotten. So after a pleasant chat with Gwen, she put down the phone with a resigned sigh thinking: *that's that, then* — and two weeks later, she went off to France, relieved to be out of the claustrophobic atmosphere of Trout Lane.

The Mortimers were having an especially busy and social summer that year, without the distraction of young Ted who had been sent off to a strict summer camp in Vermont. It was as though Vera had decided that she and Eddy mustn't be still, or alone, for an instant. There were no lazy days spent lying about the pool or wandering through the town, in and out of shops and cafés. Sometimes including Megan, sometimes not, if they weren't invited out, Vera frantically organized lunches and dinners or trips up into the hills near Grasse. One scorching midday, waiting for their friends to turn up for lunch, Eddy admitted to Megan, miserably, that he was 'absolutely beat — we don't seem to be having a vacation, it's more like non-stop partying, worse than New York.' And he looked exhausted — much too thin and nervier than ever. Megan, who had found her mother remote and distracted — she didn't even seem particularly interested in the secretarial course she was about to begin or her looming visit to New York — felt, obscurely, that there was a reason behind all this frenetic activity.

They were still there, hard at the social scene, when Megan returned to London. 'We've got the Sporting Club with the Hansards the weekend after next,' Vera told her the morning she left, smoking distractedly and fielding phone calls. Megan, watching dubiously, thought the carefully streaked hair and all the make-up, too heavy for the brilliant light, aged her noticeably. 'Then we're going straight back to New York. Eddy has a lot of business appointments and a thorough medical check-up.'

It was while she and Nellie were having one of Nellie's slap-up suppers, the evening Megan got home, that Nellie suddenly remembered that a man had phoned asking for her the week before.

'Nice voice 'e 'ad, gentlemanlike. I told 'im you was away, in France.'

'*Who* phoned, Nan?'

Megan banged down her cup. 'Owen somebody . . .' Nellie sounded her vaguest. "E give me 'is number . . . 'ere . . .' She felt about in her apron. 'I got it somewhere.'

It took half an hour to find a screwed-up piece of paper, with Owen's phone number scrawled on it, which for some obscure reason Nellie had stowed in a mug at the back of the kitchen dresser. Megan phoned, and left a message, and phoned again the next day. When they finally made contact, several days later, Owen asked her out for supper and they arranged to meet at the main doors of a hotel in Marble Arch. 'And I promise I'll try not to be late, this time,' Owen said hurriedly. 'I've got to dash now, Meg . . .'

*

The weather was in a gloriously settled spell of early autumn — calm and clear and sunny — matching Megan's elated mood. As the sun went down, there was a decided nip in the air and the trees in the park were beginning to turn. Making her way across London by bus and tube, she arrived early for their date. It was what she had been hoping for for weeks, but now that it had happened, she was nervous as a kitten. For a few dreadful seconds, she wondered if they would recognize each other in the endlessly swirling crowds. Then she remembered his bright red hair. It was this that she saw first, moving across traffic-clogged Oxford Street, on the dot of the time they had agreed, seconds before he saw her. He looked casual and jaunty in an open-necked shirt, tall and wiry and straight-backed, dodging between a bus and a taxi. They came together like magnets, both smiling with the relief of having found each other so effortlessly in one of the world's busiest spots.

Owen said, 'I thought on the way what a ridiculous place for us to have arranged. The hotel must have several doors — heaven knows which the main ones are. And all these masses of people. I was furious with myself for having suggested it. Anyhow,' — he was staring at her, lightly touching her arm — 'I've found you — thank God for that.'

Megan's nerves dropped away from her. 'And you're right on time, Owen, not like Copthorne . . .'

'I was determined to be — and I'm not often, ask Gill. Doctoring and punctuality don't go together.' Still holding on to her arm, he steered her purposefully away from the noise and the crowds and the traffic, down a narrow side street. 'All in all,' he said, sounding buoyant and happy, 'I think our getting together like this is something of a miracle.'

They ate in a cheerful, noisy Italian restaurant, forking spaghetti and washing it down with a bottle of rough red wine. Megan, often hesitant and quiet, talked openly and almost without stopping — about Nellie, and Gill in Spain and leaving Copthorne. The mystery of her father — *their* secret now — lay easily between them. She had feared it might be a barrier, embarrassing them both, but it was not; instead, it was a bond. Somehow, Megan had known that the first moment she saw him crossing the street towards her; it was a feeling of absolute trust.

'You're looking wonderful, Meg. When I saw you, I could hardly believe it was the same girl.' Admiring, almost brotherly, Owen looked at her over the rim of his glass. Tanned, her hair cut sleek and short, wearing a chic navy suit that Vera had bought for her, she was hardly recognizable as the uniformed schoolgirl of only a few weeks before. 'My kid sister Gill's friend – and look at her now . . .'

'I'm nearly a year older than Gill,' Megan said defensively. 'They made me stay back a year at Copthorne. They all teased me about it – you know how awful girls can be to each other.'

'That's all behind you now, Meg. You're out in the big, wide world. And you've certainly acquired a great tan.'

'It's all that Mediterranean sun,' Megan murmured, colouring and concentrating on her spaghetti. 'I was in France with my mother. But what about you, Owen? Can't you get a break from the hospital while the weather is still good?'

'I'm hoping for a week in Wales – fishing mostly. Or trekking over the mountains. That suits me better than anything. It's the most marvellous country – wild, empty . . . I can never get enough of it.'

'Gill thinks you miss Wales.'

'Yes, I do. But there's my career to think of, you know.' There was no mistaking the determination in his voice. 'And I see my future here, definitely. Now tell me about what you did in France.'

Unaware of everything that was going on around them in the busy restaurant, Megan told him about the unending social round her mother insisted on – which Eddy, who rarely complained about anything, didn't like.

'It sounds as though your mother wants to keep him distracted from something,' Owen said shrewdly.

'Perhaps.' Megan frowned. 'But I can't think what from.'

'And you like him, don't you?'

'Eddy? Oh yes, he's adorable. I sometimes think my mother is a bit hard on him. She bosses him around a lot.'

'She's a strong personality.' It was a statement, not a question. His intuitive intelligence was wholly concentrated on her. There was something powerful, almost mesmeric, in the way he dealt with people face to face.

'Yes — yes, she is. And she's terribly organized and efficient. And elegant ...' Megan sounded deflated, the way she always did when she spoke about her mother. 'You must meet her, and Eddy, when they're in London next summer. I'd like you to, really.'

The moment she said it, she realized that it was the truth. Close to him in a way she hadn't been to anyone before, she exulted: I'm so glad, after all, that he knows about my father, so glad ...

'I'd enjoy that, Meg,' he said quietly.

While Owen was finishing off the wine, Megan said, 'You sounded frantically busy at the hospital the other night.'

'I always am. It goes with the job.'

'Like often being late?'

They smiled right into each other's eyes.

'Exactly like that. But I honestly wouldn't have it any other way — or do anything else with my life. I've wanted to be a heart specialist for as long as I can remember. I've been lucky. And I do have talent.' He said this matter-of-factly, quite without vanity. 'I've been fortunate. I'm in the right place at the right time in medical history, and I'm doing what I want.'

Megan said wistfully, 'I wish I knew that, about myself.'

Suddenly — and for the first time that evening — she felt a yawning gap open between them: the difference in their ages; his brilliant qualifications; the future he intended which Gill had told her about — Harley Street, teaching, research — and which she didn't in the least understand. The light went out of her face.

'Cheer up, Meg. You've got everything ahead of you, you'll find your way. When does the secretarial course start?'

'Monday week,' she said, looking glum.

'It can't be that bad. And it's a very useful skill to have.'

'That's what my mother says.'

'She's right. And when you've finished she'll whisk you off to

New York and find you a spectacular job. You'll dazzle all the men and you won't have time for your old friends.'

He wasn't taking her seriously; she was a schoolgirl again, his sister's friend.

'I might not go,' she said defiantly, 'to New York.' Her chin came up and her eyes glinted. 'I won't if I don't want to.'

'Of course you will,' Owen soothed. 'You're lucky to have the chance – and you must make the most of it.'

When they were leaving, Owen said, 'I've had a quick look at my diary, and I'm fairly free on Monday week for a change. I've got a lecture in the evening, but not until eight.' He opened the door for her and they went out. It was dark now and all the lights were on. After the fug of the restaurant, it felt pleasantly cool. 'There's a coffee bar near your college.' He mentioned the name and the address. 'I used to go there a lot at one time. Why don't we meet there for a coffee and see how you've survived the first day? You might enjoy seeing a friendly face. About five thirty? And remember what I said about being late. I never know quite what's going to be thrown at me . . .'

Chapter 11

Cecilia Brandon and Alain Gesson were standing in a part of the park of Cloverley Court that had been called New Meadow for centuries. They gazed down across the old apple orchard, past the rather bedraggled gardens, to where the house stood as though rooted in the earth, in timeless, mellowed beauty. The colour of the stone varied with the seasons. And on that particular day, the countryside washed in soft September sunshine, it was a warm terracotta pink.

'I know you love it, Ceci,' Alain said, turning his slow, lazy smile on her. 'But it takes a foreigner like myself to appreciate truly England's great buildings, to have the same feelings of sensuality about them as one would towards a lover.'

Ceci Brandon threw back her head and laughed. The accent he had never lost, his vivid way of expressing himself and those dark, almond eyes always beguiled her. Even in jeans, he looked elegant.

'Nonsense, you're so absurdly extravagant, Alain,' — she sounded amused, affectionate. 'And you exaggerate outrageously, as usual. We adore our heritage, and by and large, we look after it. We just aren't demonstrative. You know that.'

Ever since he had arrived at Cloverley as a young boy, without home or country, Cecilia Brandon had liked, and admired, Alain Gesson. And as the age gap between them lessened, and Alain's engaging personality developed, Ceci's early protectiveness had grown into deep friendship. They enjoyed each other's company; it was as simple as that. Sending him to live with Millie Frampton, largely as a move to placate her husband, had been Ceci's brilliant inspiration. It came about when both Millie and Alain, for different reasons, were desperately in need of human warmth. And despite their disparate backgrounds, the relationship had worked even better than Ceci could have hoped. Ceci sometimes thought it was because they were both, in their way, outsiders, with wide, rather Bohemian interests; and both had a lively intelligence. They had looked each other up and down, liked what they saw, and got on with the business of living together. Since then, Millie Frampton's cottage had meant 'home' to Alain.

Following Millie's lead, Ceci, too, had helped and encouraged Alain through school and university. He was so clever, as Millie said, that he could have done whatever he chose. Anything to do with buildings had always attracted him and he was now a practising architect with a top London firm. But it was the sidelines and the architectural quirks that interested him most. After years of work, he had produced a textbook on architectural follies; and he had just heard that it was to be made into a television series.

'I'm very pleased for you, Alain, of course,' Ceci said when he told her. 'It's terribly exciting. But I hope it's not going to take up too much of your time. You're a first-rate architect, everyone says so. It would be awful not to use your training and talent.'

Alain shrugged. 'There are plenty of competent architects about, Ceci. And it's the foibles and the beauties – like Cloverley – that seduce me and get under my skin. I'm a dilettante at heart, you know that.' He grinned at her. Then, concerned, 'You're tired, I can tell. Let's go back. You shouldn't be overdoing things.'

Ceci was easing herself on to the top of a stone wall. Heavily pregnant, years and years after her second son, Harry, had been born, she had never felt better. Her skin glowed and she exuded happiness and well-being. But she was enormous, and her back ached frequently.

'I'm all right. And I'm pleased about the series – truly. Millie must be so proud. We'll go in a minute.' She settled a shawl round her shoulders above the swathes of rust-coloured smock. 'Robert is working in the estate office today, so he'll be in for lunch. Every waking minute is taken up with politics these days. Now, when the House isn't sitting, is the only chance he gets to see what's going on down here.'

Only someone who knew Alain intimately, as Ceci did, would know that he was instantly on his guard. It was the mention of Robert Brandon and his whereabouts. Whenever he saw Ceci – for lunch or a drink in London, or riding at Cloverley – Robert Brandon was rarely present. This was accepted between them as an unspoken rule of their friendship.

'So I imagine,' Alain said politely, neutral, masking – as he always did to Ceci – his distaste for Robert Brandon's politics. 'He's certainly had a tremendous year as a politician. It's as though he can't do, or say, the wrong thing. And he's an excellent communicator, good on television. He could reach the very top, one hears.'

'Oh, we've got our fingers crossed.' Suddenly, Ceci was fervent, full of suppressed excitement.

Alain thought: she wants this just as much as he does.

'Next summer, perhaps. That would be the moment, if it happens. But it's a long time in politics.'

'Quite. Well, I wish you both luck. But, Ceci, while I've got you, I came down to tell you and Millie about the series – and something else.'

'What's that? Not another young lady?'

'Not exactly.'

'We're still waiting, you know, for the someone special,' Ceci teased. 'I really thought the last one, who you brought to lunch – very blonde and pretty . . . I really thought: this is it. And then when I asked you about her a bit later, you couldn't even remember her name. *Really* Alain . . .'

They laughed, and Alain said: 'Well, we all have our weaknesses . . . No, it was something else I wanted to tell you. Millie already knows. It's this . . .' The exorbitant Gallic charm, which had felled so many women, vanished. 'I'm going to France,' he said abruptly. 'On Monday. To Perpignan first – and then to Paris.'

For one reason or another, principally emotional, he had never once returned. Bitterness for what had been done to him and his family was inevitable; he had no reason to go – and he could not face it. He had known of his mother's appalling death since the end of the war; but no further word had been heard of his father since the day he had left Perpignan for the Spanish frontier, accompanied by two nuns.

'I see . . .'

'Every avenue, official and unofficial, that I have tried has led nowhere – nowhere. In Perpignon, there may be someone who knows, who remembers, who knew the doctor who hid us, who has heard something about what happened to him. I feel I must do it,' he said quietly. 'Now, before it is too late. And then get one more glimpse of the house in Neuilly where I grew up, which was sold before we fled south.' He looked directly at her. 'It's my rubicon, Ceci. And I have to cross it – now.'

She leant forward and put her hand on his arm. 'I understand, Alain.'

Robert Brandon, coming away from the estate office with a mass of papers under his arm, caught up with them in front of the house. The two men shook hands coolly and exchanged a few pleasantries. Then Brandon nodded and went towards the steps as his wife lingered, still talking. Alain bent and kissed her hand and walked off down the drive – as Ceci followed her husband into the house.

She went straight into the drawing-room which was full of sunshine, dancing motes of light, and big, casual arrangements of pale roses and greenery. Every picture and mirror and wood surface seemed to glow with reflected rays, even the dull gold silk curtains which were faded and threadbare – nothing much was ever replaced or redecorated at Cloverley Court. The panelling all round gave warmth and an intimate sense of peacefulness.

Sinking gratefully into the enormous, squashy sofa, gathering up her excited and slavering spaniel, Ceci leant back. She hoped Alain would be all right in France, that it wouldn't be too traumatic an experience for him. She could hear Robert barking orders somewhere to Foster, who was getting more and more decrepit. She supposed it was almost lunchtime. Recently, cocooned in her pregnancy, Ceci, who was always so practical, so vital, had started to lose track of everyday domestic happenings.

Robert came into the room undoing the wire of a champagne bottle. He popped the cork and dealt expertly with the glasses.

'A few sips won't hurt – do you good, Ceci.' He smiled in his racy way, looking every inch the distinguished man in public life caught in an odd private moment for a newspaper or a magazine. Even people who didn't like him – and there were many – thought that Robert Brandon's looks had improved with age. He had lost the slightly raffish film-star image that had cut such a dash in pre-war London society. The moustache was gone and there was a good deal of white in his thick head of hair. His eyes were as penetrating as ever, but the easy, sophisticated charm had given way to seriousness. He had a quick intelligence, sound political acumen – and he had lost none of his arrogance. Anger, as those close to him knew well, was never far from the surface. Loyally backed by Ceci, who was able to laugh off the moods and smooth over the edges, he had become a hardworking and successful politician with firmly held, and ultra right-wing, views.

'Did you get much done this morning?' Ceci asked idly, pushing the spaniel off her lap. She had decided against mentioning Alain and his immediate plans.

'Quite a lot. It's all in a bit of a mess. Thank God my mother still keeps her hand on the tiller.'

Clementine Brandon, well into her eighties, had gone on managing the estate when Robert entered politics. But cancer had been diagnosed earlier in the year – and Nannie, who looked after her ferociously, rarely let her into the office these days.

'I popped up to see her this morning,' Ceci said. 'She looks poorly, I'm afraid, although Nannie shooed me out quickly after telling me I'm much too big.' Robert shot her a keen look. 'Feeling all right? Really and truly?' His hand grasped hers – and Ceci nodded. 'Perhaps it's Cordelia this time . . .' They smiled, suddenly in harmony – as they were, on and off, in the way of rather public relationships with other people always impinging on their privacy. The unexpected pregnancy had surprised, and pleased, them both. James, who had always been a worry, was farming with a second cousin in New Zealand. Harry, at Eton, was a model son, already taking an interest in the estates.

'A girl would be fun for a change – another Cordelia Brandon. Perhaps she would take after the other one in the portrait.' Ceci half yawned. 'I feel so lazy . . .' Nothing relaxed Robert so much as pottering about the grounds or the office at Cloverley. He seemed calm, and he looked rested and well, away from the speeches and the travelling and the constant political round. She always felt happy when she was sure of him emotionally, like this, and she had learnt long ago not to question his movements too closely. She had thought recently that there might be someone rather special who perhaps – perhaps . . .

He got up suddenly and walked over to the windows, standing with his back to her. His bearing was as good as it had ever been. He was wearing a favourite jacket, tweedy and a bit threadbare, which he had had for ever. Tears came to her eyes from nowhere.

'One thing I did decide this morning . . .' He wheeled round. 'The gardens – they're dreadfully run down and the paths are in a terrible state. It's a shame because they're part of the glory of the house. We've got funds and the old plans are still there. Let's go for it – bring it all back, the way it was. What do you say to that, Ceci?'

He looked exceptionally handsome at that moment, smiling brilliantly, his eyes alight. Ceci still thought Robert Brandon was the most attractive man she had ever met.

'Like the old photographs, at the turn of the century?' she said, blinking back the tears.

'Exactly . . .' His expression altered. 'I like your hair like that, pulled up on the top of your head. I just noticed. It suits you.'

A quarter of an hour later, Alain turned left out of the main gates through the village, past the church and the dark spreading yew tree, and into a lane which led down to the river. To one side was a row of five ancient cottages. Bending his head, he entered the last, pulling the door quietly shut behind him.

There was a waterfall of Chopin issuing from the radio in the dark little living-room. Millie Frampton, who was bending down to baste a roasting chicken in the kitchen, didn't hear him until she looked up – and there he was, smiling at her and sniffing appreciatively. She always said he'd make the best cat burglar in the business: he had a quick, quiet way of moving and he was never physically clumsy.

'Not before time, son.' Millie had the lightest of West Country burrs. 'Set the table, now, would you?'

This was a chore which had been Alain's from the April day in 1944 when Cecilia Brandon had brought him over from Cloverley. Alain thought then, as he did now, that the small and cluttered cottage, crammed with books and Millie's 'finds' in country fairs – odds and ends and pieces of Staffordshire and bits of coloured glass, was the cosiest place in the world. It reflected both her deep, self-taught, love of literature and her equally strong magpie instinct.

'See Lady Ceci, then, did you?'

Millie straightened and moved heavily towards the living-room. She had put on a lot of weight in the last couple of years and her arthritis was so bad that she was rarely out of pain. Alain knew this – and worried. But he rarely mentioned it. Millie hated fuss. She turned off the Chopin and came back to watch him neatly placing knives and forks and glasses. Her broad, open face – the ruddy face of a countrywoman – shone with the pleasure of his being there. Behind thick glasses, her brown eyes beamed warmth and intelligence.

'Yes – yes, I did. We went for a bit of a walk, not far. She tires very easily.'

'I've heard Sir Robert's driving them mad at the office now he's here for a few weeks. Changing this and changing that, for no good reason. She's past it now, I know, but old Mrs Brandon kept things going well enough all these years.' From her days as kitchenmaid, before she was put in charge of the village school, Millie Frampton knew something of Robert Brandon's ways.

Alain reached for the salt and pepper, automatically ducking to avoid a low beam. 'And he's determined on high political office too – they both are. I don't know which of them is more ambitious.'

While they were eating Millie's chicken and roast potatoes – and there was no one to touch her for plain English cooking, Alain considered – she said, 'You told Lady Ceci about the television series, then?'

She didn't bother to disguise the pride in her voice.

Alan nodded. 'She thinks I'm wasting my talent as an architect,' he grinned.

'*Pah!* ... She'll be pleased enough when it happens, mark my words.' Millie had no patience with any criticism of Alain – except her own, when it came to the way he trifled with women. He didn't seem to understand the hurt and the havoc he left behind. He couldn't resist it: any attractive female was fair game to Alain. And they went down like ninepins, as Millie well knew. A fine old time she'd had with little Elsie Smith down at the post office when Alain went skipping off to Oxford. The next year, it was Elsie's pretty mother he was courting for a month or two. She didn't care to think about what he got up to in London ...

'And what about the other thing – that you're off to France? Did you tell Lady Ceci that?'

It was Millie who was disapproving now. For the life of her, she couldn't see any good coming of his poking about in that murky bit of history, however important to him personally. It wasn't healthy – and it wasn't right. He must come to terms with his past, not fight it. And she had told him as much in her forthright way.

'She understands, Millie,' Alain said lightly.

Soon after nine o'clock, on a mild September evening, Alain Gesson turned into a quiet, leafy suburban street in Neuilly, just outside Paris. The few days he had spent in Perpignan had led to a wall of silence. Old enmities, he was convinced, still lingered from those troubled times. It was safer to say nothing. All his enquiries – in bars and shops and restaurants, even in the local markets – had been met with shrugs and shaken heads. Nobody knew, or wanted to know, about an unknown man, a Jew from

Paris, who had disappeared on a winter's day in 1942 – or about a doctor, who had been involved with the underground movement. Politely, he was pointed towards official channels, all of which he had long since exhausted. Tired and frustrated, he retraced the steps he had once taken with his parents. He came to Paris – and to Neuilly.

The light was nearly gone now, and the substantial houses, standing behind high walls and hedges, were already hidden in shadows. He stopped. This, now, was the moment. Nerves stretched to the limit, he waited for the memories and emotions that would surely come tumbling vividly back: his mother's voice calling him inside; his father returning home from work; images of the friends he went back and forth to school with . . . Here, on the spot where he was standing, he had catapulted off his first two-wheeler bike . . .

And across the street was the house where he had spent his childhood, before the fall of France and the German occupation and the terror that had blighted the Jewish community. Léah and Pierre Gesson, Alain's parents, were anguished – for themselves and, particularly, for their only child. There were tense family discussions late at night which Alain, crouched on the stairs in darkness, overheard. Then, after anxious telephone calls to friends and underground contacts, the decision was made to close the successful architectural practice founded by Alain's grandfather, to sell the house, and to flee south while there was still time.

His heart was thumping and he was sweating heavily. But far from the consuming emotion he had anticipated, he felt emptiness and a sense of painful anticlimax. He was a stranger in a strange road; he had no place there any more.

He walked slowly across the road. A slight breeze rustled the dry leaves and in a garden somewhere he heard voices and laughter. Standing by the hedge of the house that had once been theirs, Alain could just make out some movement – a child, a boy, was standing on the lawn throwing up a ball and catching it. Light from the house glinted on his fair hair, and the slim silhouette of a woman appeared from the doorway, calling out.

'Jean-Claude, viens ici, il est tard . . .'

Another child; another time; *himself*.

Something touched Alain then. All his passivity vanished and overpowering feeling returned. The futile destruction of his family, and so many others, appalled him afresh. Why had they allowed all that pain to be inflicted? *Why?* His head swam in the darkness; he felt physically sick; helpless fury, so long restrained, shook him to the core and pounded through his being.

He turned – and fled. Racing up the empty road, rounding the corner towards the lighted main thoroughfare, wild-eyed, he stopped at the first café he came to and ordered a cognac. He felt in his pocket for change, found a public phone, banged in the money.

The call went through at once.

Sweating, barely in control, Alain had only one thought: Ceci. Just to hear her voice would be enough, to make some sense of a senseless world as she had done for him once before.

At the exact moment the waiter placed the brandy on his table, the phone rang at Cloverley Court. The ringing stopped and there was a slight pause.

'Brandon here.'

Alain had not, for one second, expected this. Although he knew that Robert Brandon was probably at Cloverley, the phone was invariably answered by a secretary or a private assistant or old Foster. He struggled to pull himself together.

'This is Alain Gesson speaking. I'm so sorry to disturb you, Sir Robert. I'm phoning from France, actually.'

'Gesson? Yes?'

He sounded very curt – and possibly, for some reason, disappointed. Alain had acute instincts.

'I was wondering whether Lady Cecilia . . . there was a question I wanted to ask her, nothing particularly important . . .' He was fully composed now; Robert Brandon always put him on his mettle.

'No, I'm afraid not. My wife is in hospital, in London. She was rushed in two days ago. Twin boys, a great surprise – born more than a month before expected, but healthy.'

'What wonderful news . . . in that case, my congratulations to you both. And Lady Cecilia?'

'My wife is well, thank you.' Alain knew that he couldn't wait to put the phone down; he simply wouldn't consider him worth bothering about or speaking to. 'Anyhow, I'll tell Cecilia that you rang – from France you said? I see. Well, good night to you.'

Slamming down the receiver, Robert Brandon started prowling round the library. What the devil was young Gesson phoning Ceci from France for, at this hour, for God's sake? He was feeling edgy enough as it was. Ceci's dash to hospital had been a close-run thing and the doctors had decided on a Caesarian then and there; the babies were tiny little fellows – but holding their own. It was Ceci who had caused the immediate concern. It had shaken him dreadfully to see her lying there, white and unconscious, hooked up to drips, perfectly still. For one ghastly, heart-stopping moment, it occurred to him that she might be going to die.

But the doctors had reassured him – and the next day she had rallied. Tonight she was almost back to her normal cheerful self – surrounded by flowers, with the telephone ringing incessantly – faintly apprehensive how she and Nannie were going to manage.

After leaving her, he had had a filthy meal at his club, alone, and driven down to Cloverley – much too fast. He hadn't bothered to switch on more than a couple of lamps and the room, which hadn't changed since he was a child, had a fusty, gloomy look. The huge fireplace, so welcoming on winter evenings, gaped blackly.

For once, Sir Robert Brandon MP was virtually alone at Cloverley. He poured himself a whisky, splashed on soda, and stared out at the moonlight dappling the darkness. These days, he was finding it increasingly difficult to relax from the hectic pace of his life, even in the peace of Cloverley, with a drink in his hand. His mind darted restlessly...

He was particularly infuriated at hearing Gesson's voice – of all people, for God's sake; frankly, it irritated him that Ceci had anything to do with the fellow – because he had been expecting to hear from Veronica Hansard. The timing of her call had been pre-arranged, which was why he had belted down from London, breaking the speed limit most of the way. She had been his mistress for some years now, on and off.

Cold, sexually compelling, carrying no emotional baggage, she suited his temperament in many ways. Childless and self-centred, she was married to one of the new breed of tycoons; he was in trade, women's knickers or something of the sort, looking for a knighthood and useful for campaign funds. She and Dick Hansard were an improbable pair, but they seemed to rub along. They had a fabulously beautiful villa at Cap Martin — he had been entertained there several times — which was where Veronica was at that moment. He glanced at his watch. They always had dozens of guests, so perhaps she was finding it difficult to get away.

'Down, Ritchie, down.' Cecilia Brandon's spaniel, missing her spoiling care, pushed through the door and scampered excitedly over the floor at Robert, almost spilling his drink. And although the animal wasn't a favourite of his, he relented and bent down and gave him a rough stroking ... Which was when the telephone rang for the second time.

'But I can't see why on earth all this should stop you coming down here — just for the weekend, after all,' Veronica Hansard said plaintively once he had been through the catalogue of Ceci and the twins and the domestic front. 'Dick's plane is at your disposal. I mean, what are you supposed to do? There are plenty of servants — you'd only be in the way, for God's sake. Please, Robert ...' She was speaking very close to the mouthpiece. Her voice, slightly rasping, was having its galvanizing effect. He could picture her sinuous body, superbly toned and tanned; the narrow bejewelled wrists, those elegant feet in bare thonged sandals. 'And there's a huge gala at the Sporting Club on the Saturday night. We're taking two tables. I've gathered lots of amusing people — the Italian ambassador, a Saudi prince, that novelist who's all the rage and nobody reads. Pretty girls two a penny ... A sweet American stockbroker Dick does business with in New York and his wife — she's a bitch, used to be rather a bad actress, but she's stunning. Aren't I tempting you a little?' She was murmuring now.

'Very much so ...'

It was an attractive prospect, no doubt about it. Could he,

after all, get away with it? God, how he longed for a bit of that light, that sun, those lapping Mediterranean waters; the big white shuttered villa, balconied all round; the Hansard yacht which glided up and down the coast. And Veronica — restless, beautiful, marvellously thin, and with shoulders so eloquent that they sometimes reminded him of . . . But that was what her attraction for him was all about, wasn't it? Vera Bowen . . .

'And there's me — so bored, so wanting. All this heat is very energizing in certain ways, darling Robert . . .'

Amazing how this woman could make love, even over the phone. He had only once known better — and did not expect to experience *that* again.

He took a deep breath. He'd not been the most considerate of husbands, but he couldn't let Ceci down now.

'Sorry. Can't be done. That's all there is to it, my dear.'

After a second's pause, 'Then fuck you, Robert. *Finis.*' She almost spat the words — and hung up.

He poured more whisky and flung himself deep into an armchair, moving his shoulder awkwardly and grimacing. It still gave him considerable pain, particularly when he was tired, although he rarely mentioned this to anyone. And it did nothing to improve his always volatile temper. Ceci knew, of course, and did her best to get him physiotherapy whenever he had a spare moment.

Somewhere out in the blackness an owl hooted, and there were creaks and odd sounds echoing through the house. Cloverley, full of ghosts and sighs and ancient joists, was never totally silent. Physically whacked, he leant his head back and closed his eyes.

So that was that. Pity about Veronica in a way, but she was becoming a nuisance and would soon have begun to bore. There would have been unwelcome calls and letters and ghastly scenes. He didn't have the stomach for these histrionics any more. And for a man in his position, it was unwise. She was expendable, after all; they all were. Only one had got under his skin once, years ago.

But Ceci was such a brick, putting up with him, supporting

him and staying sane. He did realize that, and was grateful, although he never adequately expressed it. Somehow, she kept it all going — the children, the house, the London flat, the ramifications of his career. He wasn't much good as a father — he didn't, frankly, have the time; and he knew he was personally remote. He hardly remembered his own father, so perhaps that had something to do with it. And now, two more children — four sons.

And Vera? She had given up the stage after taking the play to New York and married a wealthy American. That much he knew from the newspapers, although he had heard nothing of her for years now. Attractive, ambitious, worldly women — women like her and Veronica — did these things, he thought cynically.

There was a sharp knock on the open door. He knew that it would be Nannie; nobody else would have dreamt of bothering him unless he had rung. He said, 'Come in, Nannie,' even before he looked.

An elderly female in old-fashioned nurse's uniform was already advancing across the room. 'I thought I heard you, Mr Robert.' He was always that to her. 'And I wondered about Lady Ceci and the babies.'

'They're doing well, Nannie. Jasper and Hugo, we've decided. But we'd so hoped for a girl . . .'

When Ceci's unplanned pregnancy was confirmed, he had been astonished at the excitement that the idea of a daughter aroused in him, even at his advanced age for fatherhood. Perhaps he hoped it would lay the ghost of the one who already was somewhere, an elusive ghost from the past which kept about him like a wraith, troubling him at odd moments. Just the other day, getting off a plane, walking towards his official car, he had seen a girl of about eighteen or so, pretty, leggy, dark-haired, and thought suddenly, it could be, I suppose . . . I wonder . . . Was she adopted? Was she living in the East End, in the same background from which Vera had, astonishingly, emerged? He still thought she had been quite wrong to slam that particular door in his face, whatever his shortcomings. She hadn't the right, despite her bitter feelings at the time. It still rankled in all sorts of ways —

pangs of guilt and, yes, some sense of loss, of what might have been. The truth was that at that time, early 1940, everyone had been slightly mad; he, at least, had badly miscalculated emotionally. He had long accepted this.

'I never did see Lady Ceci with a daughter, myself,' Nannie said briskly. 'She's not the type at all.'

He couldn't sleep, and when the stable clock struck three, he got up and reached for a notepad and pencil. His mind was crystal clear. Politics was his passion now; he had something to say – call it a message if you will – and he knew how to say it. He intended to get to the top of the political tree before long: it was well within his grasp. Concentrating, he worked solidly on an important speech until splinters of light edged through the curtains.

On the day Robert collected her and the twins from hospital, Ceci slept in the afternoon. When she got up, she was still feeling weak and peculiar. She drifted through Robert's dressing-room. There was a note lying carelessly on a bureau, written in a bold, woman's hand. Without touching the paper, Ceci read: 'I meant it – *finis*. V. H.' The address was a villa at Cap Martin.

She stood looking down at the letter until the words misted and blurred. So it was her – not that she knew her well, they had hardly spoken. A hard, skinny, sexy woman, dressed solely for male attention. She had been stuck next to her nice, rich, dull husband at a dinner party last year some time, in London. Well, whatever it was, it was finished. Overwhelming relief blunted the hurt and wounded pride which she could never quite control. Putting it firmly out of her mind, she left the room and made her way gingerly up to the nursery.

Chapter 12

Megan's first day at St George's Secretarial College evoked strong echoes of her arrival at Copthorne Hall — as Owen had suspected it might. Some fifty girls, all talking in loud, assured voices — most, like Megan, wearing plain grey or beige or navy sweaters — gathered in the main hall to be given a brief rundown of what was in store for them in the next nine months: typing, shorthand, book-keeping, elementary accountancy.

Megan supposed she would get used to it, although it sounded depressingly dull work and not particularly easy. At least she would be going home to Nan in Trout Lane every night. And she was — brightening at the thought — meeting Owen at the end of the day.

'You've got to pay attention,' mouthed a petite girl, pretty in a dark, gypsyish way, who was sitting next to Megan in the introductory typing class. Megan, bored, was daydreaming through the window. 'Or you'll get behind, and that's fatal.'

Megan had noticed her first thing that morning. Her bright canary-yellow shirt, cut like a man's, stood out like a beacon in the sea of drab colours. During the midday break, they went out to get a sandwich together. Refreshingly natural and outgoing, she told Megan that her name was Margot Spelling; and she made it clear that she regarded the secretarial course as a first step on the career ladder. Her parents, she said blithely, had had to 'scrape around to find the fees, which are bloody outrageous. We're paying for the name — and it had better be worth it.' She intended to do well and come out at the top. 'It'll make getting a decent first job that much easier,' she said, stabbing a knife fiercely through her sandwich. 'And from then on, it's up to me. I rather fancy advertising – getting a job as a typist in a good agency and working myself up. I know I could do it, probably better than a lot of people who've been to university,' she said confidently. 'Waste of time, that, if you ask me. I'm good with words, and I know what people want.' She gave Megan a dazzling smile. 'I'm going to have a career and make some money. That's for sure. My Dad's a commercial traveller and it's always been jam tomorrow. I'm not slaving away, stuck in some little house in the suburbs like my Mum. Not me. And she's right behind me, Mum is. How about you, Megan?'

Faced with Margot's common sense and determination, Megan mumbled something about 'going to the States next year – and perhaps getting a job there'.

When they reassembled, all of them beginning to regard a typewriter as the enemy to be conquered, she and Margot stuck firmly together. And Megan put her mind to what she was doing.

By six o'clock, she had started to fret; half an hour later, the dregs of a stone-cold cup of coffee in front of her, Megan had virtually given up hope. The place was filling up, and she was having difficulty saving the place at the table for Owen. The relief she had felt that the first day at St George's was over had evaporated. He'd been detained; some emergency had come up. She felt idiotic sitting there, straining anxiously towards the door; but she couldn't pretend that she hadn't been warned.

Pseudo-continental coffee bars had been springing up all over London, sprouting greenery and hissing with various coffee-making machines. This one, in the West End, in Park Lane, was one of the most popular – a well-known meeting place and always crowded, a mecca for foreign students and out-of-work theatrical types. One of the waitresses, who had been eyeing Megan for some time, swept insolently past the table, carrying off her cup with a swish of the hips, making it plain that she was no longer welcome sitting there alone. Just as Megan had given up all hope of Owen turning up, she saw him push through the door, which was jammed with people waiting for tables. She waved at him frantically. It had been drizzling on and off all day and the collar of his raincoat was turned up. Searching the room for her, he looked white and exhausted, barely acknowledging her even when he finally saw her and began to edge his way over.

'Sorry,' he said briefly, pulling out the chair and sitting opposite her. 'I had to cover in the emergency room and there had been a bad car accident. Just my luck.' He looked at her distantly. 'Have you been waiting long?' – swivelling round for someone to take their order.

'Since just before five thirty,' Megan said stiffly. 'But it doesn't matter. Obviously you couldn't help it . . .'

He seemed not to be listening. 'I hadn't realized it would be so damned crowded here. It never used to be as bad as this.' He looked annoyed, and he sounded tense and angry. His face was like a mask, the pallor accentuated by his bright, carroty hair. Megan hardly recognized him as the same man she had spent the evening with a week or so before. A record of a loud, popular vocal group started wailing over the loudspeakers. 'God, as if it wasn't hellish enough here . . .' He waved away a stream of cigarette smoke from the next table. He hadn't bothered to undo his raincoat. 'Let's get something to drink. I'm dying for a decent coffee, and they're good here. What about you?'

'Well – I already . . .'

The waitress, the same one who had snatched away Megan's cup, stood over the table, pad and pencil in hand. She was thin as a rail – not particularly attractive; eyes outlined in kohl and pinky-white lips. Her hair was lacquered into a sticky beehive shape. Megan had taken a dislike to her on sight.

'If it isn't young Dr Kildare himself,' she drawled at Owen in a flattened accent that Megan couldn't place. 'I was wondering when you'd look in again.'

Megan watched, astonished, as she turned her back on her and stood, slouched and posturing, her grubby black sweater almost touching Owen's shoulders. Owen stared at her coldly. He knew her – and well. There was no mistaking the intimacy between them.

140

He said roughly, 'I thought you'd left months ago. I would never have come here otherwise, I assure you. You said that cabaret job had come through. Another lie, I suppose. We'll have two coffees. That's it.'

'OK, sure thing.'

He made no attempt to introduce Megan and the girl sashayed off. Miserably uncomfortable, Megan wished she hadn't come, that he hadn't suggested this meeting in the first place. The noise was appalling, and after the stress of the day her head was starting to throb. Owen was obviously deeply troubled about something – and now this dreadful girl, literally pushing herself between them . . .

'Someone I used to know,' Owen explained briefly.

The coffees were quickly, cheekily slapped down in front of them, with a knowing sideways glance at Owen – which he disregarded. Owen drank his at once; Megan, feeling slightly sick, hardly touched hers. No more than ten minutes after Owen had arrived, they left.

Megan's instinct was to get away, back to Nan, as soon as possible. The meeting had been a fiasco. The long, lonely wait, feeling foolish in front of that sluttish waitress . . . There was no explanation, or apology, for his lateness. She would never have believed it of Owen. They walked silently down Park Lane; Megan, tired and upset, fully intended to hop on the first bus that was going in her direction.

Owen stopped abruptly. 'Meg,' he said humbly. 'I'm really sorry. Honestly.' He sounded it. He put his hands on her shoulders, searching out her eyes. The misty rain had frosted her hair with a halo of lights and dampened her skin. 'This was your day – and I haven't even asked about it, selfish bugger that I am. Please forgive me. How did it go?'

'Not too bad,' she said coldly.

'Meg, please . . .' His voice was gentle now. 'Don't be cross. I've been looking forward to hearing all about it. Really – I have . . .'

The stranger she had hailed across the noisy, smoky room had disappeared. Owen Thomas was back. She could feel her resentment floating away.

'It wasn't too bad,' she said, softening. 'It's very well organized, full of girls exactly like the ones at Copthorne. But I met one who seemed interesting, and a bit different. She's called Margot. She's very keen and she's persuading me I'm going to like it. And it costs so much — I hadn't realized — that I've got to try to do reasonably well.'

'There, you see, taking plunges is never as bad as we imagine. It's all the anticipating.'

Talking away easily, they walked slowly on — interrupting, turning eagerly towards one another. He waited with her by the bus stop at Hyde Park Corner, asking sensible questions about the work. And when she asked, straight out, about the unnamed waitress, he thought for a moment before he said, 'There are some people one shouldn't see. Ever. For me, she's one of them' — and promptly changed the subject. 'I'm free next Saturday, Meg. I thought it would feel good to get out of London, into the country, for a few hours. Is there any chance I can drag you with me — and make up for this evening?'

'I'd like that.'

'I wanted to give you a bit of moral support tonight.' He grinned ruefully. 'But I didn't half make a mess of it, and I've got that damned lecture that I can't get out of.'

As the bus loomed into sight, Owen said very quietly — Megan could hardly hear him over London's roar, 'There was a child in the car this afternoon. And there was nothing we could do, we tried everything. We lost her. It never gets any easier. If anything, it's harder.'

The accidental death of a child was one of the saddest things in the world. To Owen, expecting so much of himself as a physician, impressionable in a way no one could guess, it was scarcely bearable. It tore him to pieces inside. Megan understood this instantly.

As the people in front of her started shuffling towards the heaving bus, she turned and grabbed his arm. She had to say something, to help him.

'You're blaming yourself, Owen. You mustn't, really you mustn't. Of course you feel terrible, but it wasn't your fault.'

Someone jostled from behind, pushing her forward, dragging them apart. She called back over her shoulder, 'See you on Saturday — and thanks for coming.'

She went on watching him, standing very straight, his hand raised towards her, as the bus carried her away into the darkness.

Owen's car roared off the steep Cotswold ridge and down Burford High Street. It wasn't Wales, but it was very pretty all the same, wasn't it? he yelled at Megan, sitting beside him, late the following Saturday morning. The top had been down all the way from London and the rushing air had exhilarated them both, sweeping away all the gritty urban tensions. Brilliant autumn sunshine warmed the solid stone walls of the houses and dazzled tubs of late-flowering plants. After dawdling up and down, in and out of shops and hidden alleyways, they had lunch in the White Bear in Sheep Street. Coming in out of the brightness, they settled in a dark, comfortable corner, by an old inglenook fireplace. Owen had been in high spirits all morning: when they started out, he said he felt as though he'd had enough of that hospital for a lifetime. And Megan was equally delighted to be away from her hours spent in front of the typewriter. Released from the constraints of their everyday world, they both felt light-headed.

'That sweater you've got on is a knockout.' Owen was wolfing down his bread and cheese. He looked relaxed, and there was colour in his face. There was no sign of the inner anguish he had attempted to express the other night — and Megan had no intention of mentioning it, unless he did.

'I blew most of this month's allowance on it.' Surreptitiously, she forked pickled onions from her plate on to his. 'Margot Spelling says everyone at St George's wears the most boring things, and colours, she's ever seen. And she's right — except for her. We saw this in the window of a Bond Street shop last week.' It was deep purple cashmere, ribbed, with a high, rolled collar. 'We both thought, how wonderful, and she dared me to go in and ask how much it was. And then I really couldn't get out without buying it — which I wanted to do anyway.'

'There's a girl, this Margot ...' He was amused, eating her onions – the Welsh lilt creeping back into his voice. Megan had noticed that this tended to happen when he was natural, at ease, not putting on his professional front. He even looked younger today. As she chattered on Owen was studying her, his head on one side.

'That purple makes your eyes look like – I don't know – green apples perhaps. Granny Smith's ...'

'*Apples?* Why not emeralds? Purple is a royal colour, after all. And does it?'

'Indeed to goodness it does, as we say in Wales. All right, emeralds then. Now there's a daft conversation for you ...'

But he was smiling, catching her giddyness.

'Listen Owen Thomas – *Doctor* Thomas – if you're going to be personal, I might as well tell you that the first thing I noticed about you, at Copthorne, was your hair. I saw the red first – and then you. It looks like – I don't know – carrots? Pumpkins?'

'Look you, young lady, I've been teased about it mercilessly all my life. And that's enough personal remarks ... pax?'

'Peace.'

They put their elbows on the table and laughed and laughed as though they were the funniest people in the world.

In the afternoon, they tramped through woods that were turning copper and gold. Megan said that she had heard from Gill. She had started at her university, plunging into classes and activities with the enthusiasm she brought to everything.

'She was always like that, even as a child,' Owen said. 'Acting first, then thinking. That's Gill. I remember in the war our father telling her never, never to pick up any strange object in the road or the garden in case it was some dangerous object dropped by the Germans. It sounds mad now. But it was serious then. And if anyone was going to pick up anything like that, it was Gill.'

Megan laughed, shuffling through the carpet of leaves. 'And where were you then? Still at home?'

'Only some of the time. There was no petrol to take me to school, so I was evacuated to a boarding school in North Wales.'

'I hardly remember the war at all. But I do remember my mother coming to see me once. I can see her now . . . she had on a hat that was made out of foxes' heads. I was petrified and I screamed and screamed . . .'

'But she never brought your father?' He dropped a hand on her shoulder, steering her on to a smoother path. 'Or not that you remember?'

'Never.' She shook her head emphatically. 'If she had, Nan would have told me. And a year or two after, she married Eddy.'

Megan could hardly believe she was speaking so naturally — to Owen — on this of all subjects.

'Are they back in New York now, then?'

'Yes. I had a letter from my mother this week. Apparently Eddy hasn't been feeling too good, so he's going to have a thorough check-up.' She frowned. 'I didn't think he looked well in France.'

'I expect it's all that heavy socializing they do. Bad for the liver. Seriously.'

On the way back to London, changing gears while they stopped at a traffic light, Owen shot her a look.

'You helped me a lot the other night, Meg,' he said quietly. 'I was in a bad way.'

'I know you were. Can't you talk to your father, Owen? He must go through it all the time. All doctors must.'

'Not about this, I can't. He did a lot for me once, when I was pretty desperate. I admire him as much as I do anyone. But he really wanted me to work with him, or in the district. And when I decided to go my own way, it set up tensions.' He was driving fast, weaving in and out of traffic. 'It's hard to talk to anyone about — feelings . . .'

But you did to me, Megan thought, you did to me . . .

After a silence, he said, 'Most of the time I can handle the difficult situations, talk to the families and so on. But occasionally it gets to you. And you have to deal with it' — he shrugged, grinding the gears — 'as best you can. However unsatisfactorily. I think we all feel that, it's only human. That night was one of those bad times.'

With a wisdom she didn't know she had, she said, 'You take too much on yourself, Owen.'

'That's what my mother thinks.'

They were inching through Central London, when inspiration came to Megan. She wondered why on earth she hadn't tumbled to it before. The girl in the coffee bar, the one Owen had reacted to so violently, was she a dancer 'of sorts'? Was her name Diane? And why was a trollop like that someone he, Owen Thomas, should never see?

When she came to again, Owen was saying, 'I haven't had a home cooked meal for months. Now when am I going to meet that Nan of yours?'

With Owen's heavy schedule and Megan's long days at St George's, it was late in November before they settled on a suitable evening for Owen to come to Trout Lane. Since the outing to the Cotswolds, they had had several quick meetings, for a drink or a coffee or a walk through the park, but both of them – Owen particularly – had been working very hard with little spare time. And when at last it happened, Megan leading him into the warm fug of the kitchen on a freezing cold night, Owen Thomas and Nellie Bowen fell for each other on sight.

'Nan,' she said, squeezing in ahead of Owen, as Nellie was fussing round the stove. 'This is Owen, Gill's brother. Sorry we're late.' She unwound her muffler and started to unbutton her camelhair coat. Owen stood behind her – reserved, watchful, holding back, and physically exhausted after an unexpectedly long stint on duty.

'Oh, there you are then. Wh's that?' Nellie turned, wiping her hands on her apron.

'This is Owen,' Megan yelled. The television was on, loudly, in the corner – and Nellie's hearing was getting worse. 'Gill's brother – you remember. I told you I was meeting him at the hospital and bringing him back here for something to eat.' You never knew what Nellie did or did not remember.

'Well, come on in now, the pair of you. No need to shout,

Meg. I know, I know, I've been waitin' for you, both of you.' She went over to Owen and peered up at him, holding out both hands – which he took. A nice-looking young fellow, she was thinking, a bit peaky with that pale skin that always came with red hair – dark circles under the eyes, too – but something about him: held himself well, distinguished, that was it – or would be ... Her eyes were still china-blue and her cheeks were flushed from bending over the cooking pans; and when she smiled, her whole face lit up. 'Gracious, but you've got cold 'ands – take yer coat off an' come an' sit by the fire an' 'ave a drop of somethin' while I dish up. Now make yerself useful, Meg. It's cod 'n chips 'n peas. You looks like you could do wiv a good meal.'

'It sounds absolutely marvellous to me,' Owen said, already half charmed, as Nellie pulled him further into the room. 'Smells good, too.' He was dead on his feet and couldn't remember when he'd last had something decent to eat. There was a nasty flu going round and lots of the staff were down with it so they were terribly pushed. He had kept Megan waiting for over an hour tonight in the dismal waiting-room, staring at peeling paint and ancient magazines while he dealt with some crisis. And driving here through the freezing mist, he'd had a hard time keeping his eyes open. All the way through the crawling traffic of the East End he'd been wondering what on earth he'd let himself in for, despite Gill and Megan's glowing reports of this cockney sparrow of a Nellie who had so improbably brought Megan up. Now he thought he understood.

Megan hung up his coat and found the gin which was all the booze Nellie kept in the house these days; she'd 'gone off' port, she claimed. There was the remains of a bottle of tonic, so Megan poured drinks for them both, not bothering about Nellie who had probably been at it already. Owen, feeling immediately at home, sat on top of the fire, sipping his drink, warming his hands and letting himself unwind, while Nellie chattered away non-stop, never pausing for an answer, as the fat sizzled and the kettle whistled and the television blared. Megan, polishing up the cutlery which was none too clean, thought how right she had been to get the two of them together.

The old kitchen table was covered, as always, in a shiny plastic red and white checked cloth. Owen ate ravenously as Nellie shovelled extra chips on to his plate. Megan had managed to reduce the volume of the television, so as they washed the meal down with cups of Nellie's strong, bitter tea, conversation – of a kind – took place.

'Owen's a doctor, Nan, he works in St James's hospital. He's training to be a surgeon.'

'Fancy that,' Nellie said. 'The knife, Gawd 'elp us . . .' Owen choked over his cod and Megan laughed. 'Well, I suppose someone 'as to. Not been near a doctor since my Vera, Meg's Mum, was born, I 'aven't, an' that was a year or two ago . . .'

Owen passed his cup for a refill. 'You keep it that way. But if everyone was as healthy as you, Mrs Bowen, we wouldn't have any work to do. Actually, we're worked off our feet.'

''Ere – 'oo's this Mrs Bowen, then?' She winked broadly. 'Never 'eard of 'er . . .'

'Nellie.'

'Tha's better . . . Well, you looks like it,' Nellie said. 'More dead than alive when you walked in, you were. Better now though. Fetch a drop more water from the kettle, would you, Meg, luv?'

'That's because you're looking after me so nicely,' Owen said. When Megan got up, they exchanged amused looks and smiles. 'And it feels just like home here already.'

'You're welcome any time, I'm sure. Any friend of Meg's . . . 'Ow's that sister of your's gettin' along?'

Nellie wasn't sure about Gill, who had stayed with them at Trout Lane several times. She thought her a big, noisy girl – goodhearted, but inclined to bossiness. She liked this quiet, older brother much better. Quite a gentleman – *and* educated, *and* a doctor. And she hadn't missed the way Meg looked at him either: she was prettier than ever, bless her. She was only nineteen, that's true, but she could do worse for herself than a lad like this.

'She's at university and I think she enjoys it. By the way, I've got some time off in the spring – Gill has too – and we're hoping to get Megan up to stay with us in Wales, right, Meg?'

148

'That's all right, isn't it, Nan?'

'I'll say. Lucky girl – I like to see 'er enjoyin' 'erself. I've 'ad 'er since she were days old, I 'ave.'

'Owen knows, Nan,' Megan said quickly. 'About my mother, too ...'

'About Vera?'

'Yes.' Megan flushed.

'That Vera,' Nellie cackled, slapping her hands on her knees. 'You waits till you meets 'er ... Mrs 'igh and mighty 'erself, an' she no better 'n she ought to be, years ago, neither.'

Mortified, Megan held her breath.

'Well, she's a real credit to you, your granddaughter, Nellie,' Owen said, covering Megan's embarrassment – and thinking that Nellie Bowen was an amusing old girl, a real character. 'And I can see where she gets her smile from, too.'

Megan cleared the table and Nellie nodded off while they were watching the news. Soon, Owen indicated to Megan, in sign language, that it was time he went. While he was putting on his coat, he looked down at Nellie who was sleeping like a baby – and for a moment, Megan thought he was going to plant a kiss on her cheek. But he just put his hand on her shoulder and they tiptoed out of the room.

The front door opened on to a blanket of icy fog.

Owen said quietly, 'You can't stand here, you'll catch your death of cold, and I'd be responsible. Now nip into the car for a minute or two.'

They sat in the near darkness while Owen coaxed the engine and managed to produce a few gusts of heat. Megan – hugging herself, shivering – tried not to laugh.

'Owen, this car should end up in some museum.'

'You're right. When I've finished this hospital stint and got a decent job, the first thing I'll do is buy a new one.'

'I'll miss it,' Megan said softly. She had been in it many times since the day last June, when she spotted it chugging up the drive. It started to get warmer and she stopped shivering. Owen turned to her. They were sitting very close in the low-slung bucket seats. Lights from the houses wavered in the mist which clung to the windows, heightening their sense of isolation. The ease which they had felt with each other from their first meeting had grown in the past months — and Megan knew instinctively that for all his brilliance, away from his work Owen Thomas was not at ease with many people.

'I expect I will, too. It's been a good friend.' Owen smiled, normally tired now, not exhausted as he had been, the strain gone from his face. His arm slid across the top of her seat. 'And it was such a good evening.'

'You didn't want to come . . .'

'But I was glad as soon as we got there,' he said quickly. 'Your Nan's a marvel.'

'Isn't she just? And she's always the same. If the Queen, her idol, happened to stop by she'd just put on the kettle and sit her by the fire, or offer her a "drop" of something. I don't expect she'd even turn the telly lower.'

They laughed and Owen's hand slipped down on to her shoulder. Very gently, he tipped her face towards him. Megan closed her eyes — waiting, expectant, hardly breathing. He brushed her lips very lightly, very softly with his. He had never kissed her before. Then, 'You're such a knowing innocent, Meg. Now off you go.' He leant across her and pushed open the door. Startled, Megan emerged into the cold, two steps across the pavement and into the doorway of number five. 'It was a lovely supper,' he called. 'Thank Nellie for me, will you? I'll be in touch soon.'

The door slammed and the car lurched off into the fog and Megan let herself into the house. She stood in the hall with her back pressed against the door, letting her pleasure flow through her — not thinking about anything very much. Some American heartthrob was crooning loudly on the television. Soon, she went into the kitchen, where Nellie was snoring softly, her head on one side, put on an apron and rolled up her sleeves and started on the dishes.

The next day, Margot shot her a suspicious sideways look across her typewriter.

'What's been going on in your life, may I ask? You're looking very pleased with yourself.' And when Megan smiled and said nothing, she shook her head and tut-tutted. 'I can see I'll have to keep a sharp eye on you, young lady. By the by, my boyfriend's friend is at a loose end on Saturday night and I thought we could make up a foursome ...' Megan made some feeble excuse – and Margot looked knowing. 'OK, OK, I understand. But you're going to have to get your speed up faster than that or you'll never get a job.'

Chapter 13

Alain Gesson swept aside the debris of last night's dinner – two wine glasses, two plates and two knives and forks – and poured cereal into a bowl. As there was no chair in the small galley kitchen, he ate standing up. His airy studio flat was bare of all but the essentials – white sofa, a couple of chairs, functional lights and bookcases. A curving iron staircase led up to an attic bedroom. His few private possessions, which included the satchel he had brought from France years ago, were stored in drawers beneath the wide divan bed. A large Kilim rug, of subdued blues and reds, was the only decorative object visible.

Pouring coffee, he glanced at the newspaper which was propped against the refrigerator. Halfway down the front page, a short article caught his eye. Skimming the piece, he read: 'MP's flight to Washington returned to Heathrow with engine trouble ...' The politician was Sir Robert Brandon, who was heading a trade delegation from the Foreign Office. After a tense landing – the emergency services alerted and foam on the runway – the party was immediately transferred to another flight and continued on to Washington, several hours behind schedule. Sabotage was not suspected but could not be entirely ruled out etc. Sir Robert, the article went on, was now considered 'the front runner' to be named as new Foreign Minister in the cabinet reshuffle which was expected in a couple of months' time. 'Sir Robert's particular interest has always been foreign affairs, his speciality being the question of immigration to this country ...' The copy, which used words like 'charismatic' and 'authoritative', ended by saying that 'Sir Robert has always been ably supported by his popular wife, Lady Cecilia, a noted hostess, whose lunches are a regular part of the London social scene.'

'Well, now,' Alain said aloud. 'Well, well ...' It looked as though he'd got it, after all. Millie wouldn't be pleased, and neither was he — except for Ceci's sake. Acres of newsprint had been devoted to analysing why 'a toff' like Robert Brandon should have his finger on the pulse of the working man and woman — as he seemed to. Alain believed it could be summed up in one word: prejudice.

Later that morning, absorbed at his drawing board, he did not immediately hear the shout: 'Telephone, Alain.' It was only when it was repeated, loudly, that he started and straightened. He put down his pencils and instruments, slowly and precisely, and went into the outer office.

'Hullo? Gesson here.'

'Alain? Alain, it's Ceci.'

'Good heavens!' His pleasure at hearing her sang down the wires, although she had never before phoned him at his office; this was another of the many unspoken rules of their friendship. She had been vaguely in his mind since reading the piece about Robert Brandon earlier. He said so.

'I was going to phone you at home tonight, Alain, but I decided not to wait.'

'I saw the paper this morning,' he said. 'It sounds as though they had a near miss there with the plane.'

'Oh, yes, really very worrying. But nothing sinister has turned up.' They were always circumspect on the phone.

'And it's looking good — for Robert, I mean.'

'Yes — at long last. But there are difficulties.'

She sounded badly stressed, as though something had severely shaken her usual confidence. And she had recovered her energy quickly after the twins' birth eight months ago.

'Difficulties? Of what sort?'

'Not here — I really can't. Is there any chance you could come down to Cloverley? We could talk over dinner. I'm not going to be in London at all this week, with Robert away. And I really do need to see you — to ask your help, Alain. Could you come down?'

'Perhaps.' He sounded doubtful. And he was wondering how on earth he was in a position to offer Cecilia Brandon help. 'I'm pretty pushed at work, Ceci. If we could have a drink . . .'

'Cloverley would be best. We can talk properly here.' She was insistent.

'Let me think . . .' Alain looked at his watch. In less than half an hour, he had an important presentation to give to a valuable client; he had been concentrating on the final, crucial details when she rang. 'Listen, Ceci, I'll drive down tonight. After work.' It was late spring and the evenings were light and long. 'I should be with you by seven or so. And would you tell Millie I'll look in on her after dinner?'

He got away from the office earlier than he had anticipated, firmly shelving a clutch of messages to be dealt with. The client had taken on the presentation virtually at a glance, delighted by the concept. That was enough for today. So he slid out of the office, blowing a kiss as he went to the attractive receptionist who had shared his dinner, and his bed, the night before. He retrieved his car, which had acquired several expensive parking tickets, and headed out of London. He was puzzled, and a little disturbed, by Ceci's phone call. He could only think – *Robert* . . .

Turning off the motorway and driving along quiet roads in the golden evening light, he came upon a countryside dense with dappled green foliage. Reaching Cloverley, he drove past the gatehouse and up the curving drive, delighted as always by the first sight of the mullioned windows and weathered stone. Restoration work had already begun on the gardens and the areas of paved courtyard which surrounded the house. Now, early honeysuckle and pale mauve clematis softened the old walls.

As usual, the door was open – so he went in and stood in the centre of the great, shadowy hall, which was full of ghosts and echoes from the past. White lilac in two huge bowls, set on dark oak chests, wafted perfume. Foster shuffled out of the gloom, peering about. Alain was well aware that he, like Nannie, had never approved of him and what they considered his 'foreignness'.

He said pleasantly, 'Hello, Foster, would you tell Lady Cecilia . . .'

At that moment Ceci appeared, running full tilt down the stairs, calling out, 'Alain, I'm so glad you're here – and long before I expected.' They touched cheeks as Foster slunk away. Alain, watching her carefully, saw that she was looking fresh and well. She had slimmed down after the twins were born, and she was always at her best in the country – clear-eyed, her cheeks a vivid pink.

'I came as soon as I could.'

'I've been helping bath the babies.' She was wearing a simple blue cotton dress and the pearls she was never without. 'We'll go outside, it's warm enough. And I'll tell them that we want to eat fairly soon. I saw Millie, Alain, she's expecting you later.'

Relieved, Alain thought, whatever's worrying her can't be so desperate after all.

During dinner in the small family dining-room, Ceci was once called away to the phone. 'Robert,' she explained when she came back. 'Sorry . . .'

Although she said nothing further, Alain sensed something altered about her, an excitement which she hadn't shown before.

'These are stirring times for him, Ceci, for you both.'

'Oh *yes*,' she agreed, turning to him quickly – passionate, her eyes alight. 'Oh *yes* . . .' She picked up her fork and toyed with the food on her plate. Whatever vision she was seeing, Alain thought, it had nothing to do with him, or Cloverley, or even her children.

At last, they were left alone in the drawing-room, the door shut behind Foster who had lumbered unsteadily after them with coffee and brandy.

Ceci warmed her brandy glass between her hands and faced him, squaring up, lifting her chin slightly, more serious than he had ever seen her.

'It's a strange request I'm going to make of you,' she said quietly, 'And you may not like me for it.'

'No? Try me, Ceci.'

'You know what you said just now, at dinner, about these being stirring times for Robert?'

He nodded.

'Well, they are.' She picked up a cigarette – and immediately put it down. 'Tonight . . . his call from Washington . . . we've got a code, a very simple one, so when something important happens I'll know instantly, nothing actually said. We've been hoping for this for weeks. Well, it's happened, or will soon.' She sat on the edge of the sofa – straight, tense, worried.

'The Foreign Office?'

'Yes.'

Alain inclined his head. As if from another world, faint noises could be heard in other parts of the house. It occurred to Alain how simply, almost casually great power was conferred and the knowledge of it passed on.

'Well done.'

He meant: to both of you. It was Ceci's back-up and her popularity, just as much as Robert Brandon's competence, which had brought it off.

'It's what he's always wanted, always.' She was like a coiled spring, ready to burst out with – something. Alain, always subtly attuned to other people's emotions, searched about in his mind. 'It won't be announced yet,' she said quickly. 'It won't happen until July. *Nobody* else knows, you understand; nothing must be said or implied to anyone.'

'Of course not.' Her words of this morning came back to him: *there are problems* . . .

'Ceci, the difficulties you spoke of . . . are they to do with this new office?' She got up and walked over to the windows, her arms tightly folded. 'Are they, Ceci?'

She turned. 'Yes.'

She came slowly back and sat opposite him.

'Unless you tell me, I won't know if I can do anything to help – which seems unlikely – now, will I? So, out with it, Ceci.' He was beginning to feel uneasy. Everyone in London knew, or said they knew, that Robert Brandon had mistresses. Alain had the unpleasant feeling that something of this – some liaison or other – was about to be revealed. And he would hate to see Ceci humiliated.

'All right. I've warned you, Alain.' She took a sip of brandy, stubbed out the cigarette, and leant towards him.

'In the late 1930s, and in the very early weeks of the war, there was a group of people, influential people, in this country who believed that war was still avoidable.' She spoke fast. 'They wanted to put out feelers and negotiate, if possible, a settlement with Germany.'

'Even after war was declared?'

'In the end, yes, some of them.'

'So – with the Nazis?'

She nodded.

'I had heard something of the sort.' Alain shrugged. 'It's very likely, after all. But whatever may have transpired came to nothing and has been forgotten, surely?'

'Not quite.'

'In what way?'

'There are files – under lock and key but existing: documents, records, minutes of meetings. And names are named.'

Alain leant back and finished his brandy. There was no need to ask whose name was among them. So it wasn't to do with a woman after all. Thank God for that.

'Robert's,' he said. It all fitted; he wasn't even slightly surprised. 'But Ceci, he was in the army throughout. He fought for his country. He was decorated, he was badly wounded. He showed great bravery.'

'Oh, he *did*, Alain, he *did*,' she cried out. 'He changed his mind completely once he realized it was inevitable, and that the war against Fascism was one that had to be fought. He could so easily have died in France in 1940. The whole idea of appeasement was' – she flung her hands wide, searching for the word – 'an aberration, no more.'

'I can understand that,' Alain said evenly. An echo of the despair he had felt in Perpignan last year touched him. Ceci pushed the brandy towards him but he shook his head.

She went on, 'And he had, remember this, lost his father and two uncles in the Great War, when he was a schoolboy. All his generation was scarred for ever by the horror of that slaughter. Then, twenty years later, it was starting again. Imagine how all those who had lived through it must have felt.'

Alain took a deep breath, he was prepared to be fair.

'Look, Ceci, Robert is an admired and respected politician, even if I don't, as you know, agree with his views. If he was caught up in this movement, let's say that Robert, fallible like the rest of us, more than made up for a lapse of judgement, or a failed vision, or whatever it was.'

She poured herself another brandy, interrupting, without looking at him, *'Which has come back to haunt him.'*

'Go on, Ceci.'

'There is a man called Amos Werner. Have you heard of him?'

'Yes. The Banque de Werner?'

'That's right. A German Jewish banking family from Berlin. He came out in the early 1930s and started a branch of the bank here, which has been quietly but brilliantly successful. He is extremely well thought of, a considerable philanthropist — and an ardent Zionist.'

Alain picked up his coffee cup, wondering where these astonishing twists and turns were leading.

'I know this. I haven't met Werner, but I know something about him. And I'm trying, Ceci, to discern what possible link he can have with Robert Brandon.' He did not bother to keep the irony out of his voice, but Ceci was too intent to notice.

'I'll tell you. A letter came for Robert this morning, marked "private and confidential". I open mail like this when he's away, I always have done. It was from Amos Werner.' She paused.

'Is he a personal friend of Robert's, then?'

She shook her head. 'Not at all. They've been on a couple of committees together and met socially, but Robert never liked him.'

'And what did it say — the letter?'

'It said that he was in possession of a document dated 1939, signed by Robert — among others — which convinced him that he was a person morally unfit for high office.'

'Strong words. What exactly was the document?'

'It was a resolution to begin secret negotiations with Nazi contacts and to try to persuade the British government into a last-ditch agreement, with Hitler, to avert war.'

'I see.'

'And there was more. Werner, like everyone else, knows that Robert is in line for the Foreign Office. He says that if he accepts, he will see to it that the document is made public.'

Ceci lit another cigarette without once taking her eyes off Alain's face.

'Poor Ceci, what an awful shock you must have had! No wonder you sounded so distraught this morning. Have you told anyone else? Robert?'

'I couldn't, not on the phone. I've told Dick Loveday — he's our friend as well as Robert's agent. And Peggy. There's no one more loyal than those two. Because I must stop this happening, Alain, I must.' Her eyes were suddenly too bright. 'It's so wrong,' she burst out. 'It's so unfair. Robert doesn't deserve it, he doesn't.'

'Then why not "publish and be damned"? It would all be over and forgotten in a few days.'

'*Never.* Dick Loveday agrees with me. Can't you imagine what the left-wing press would do with this? Can't you see how his political opinions — and they're strong ones — would be re-interpreted, slanted, through this? No, Werner must be stopped, once and for all.'

'How, Ceci?'

She looked straight at him, her head thrown back.

'By you,' she said boldly.

Alain was relieved that the atmosphere was altered, at that moment, by a knock on the door and the re-entry of Foster to take the coffee tray and enquire about drawing the curtains. While Ceci answered impatiently, dispatching him as quickly as possible, Alain marshalled some thoughts and questions. He wasn't in the least sure that he wanted to be drawn into this potentially sticky situation — even for Ceci. And he was uncomfortable about her fighting Robert's political battles for him.

When they were alone again he said, 'He — Amos Werner — must be fairly sure that Robert is going to be appointed. He moves in informed circles, he knows what's going on all right. It's a daring move, that letter, and one must assume he means what he says, Ceci, and feels strongly about it. He's a much respected man, and not just in the City.'

'I know that. He's very powerful, very clever. His wife died years ago, tragically young I believe, and he never remarried; but he goes out a good deal. We see him all over the place. And he knows everyone. He's considered to have a lot of influence behind the scenes — and I expect he does. Anyhow,' she said confidently, 'you'll see for yourself soon.'

'Yes?' Alain was guarded.

'He's coming to a lunch I'm giving next Friday, in London.' Her chin rose defiantly. 'I telephoned him this morning at his office. His secretary put me through to him straight away. He was very courteous. He would be delighted, he said, absolutely delighted. Nothing else was mentioned, of course. And you're to come too, Alain, to meet him.' He had rarely heard Ceci speak so peremptorily. 'You will, won't you?'

'Of course.'

It was all quite clear to him now — amusing in a bleak sort of way.

'And I want . . .'

'I know what you want of me, Ceci.' He leant towards her. 'You want me to call up ancient depths, to speak to him as one Jew to another, to tell him that you and Robert took me in as a Jewish refugee child, to assure him that Robert Brandon is not a racist or an appeaser or an anti-Semite. To persuade him, once and for all, that he is an honourable man who would not abuse power. And that whatever mysterious document suggesting otherwise is in his possession should be destroyed forthwith. That's right, isn't it, Ceci?'

Her eyes did not flinch. 'Yes, Alain, that is exactly what I want.'

He parked the car in the darkened lane, making as little noise as possible, and walked over to the cottage. Tapping on the lighted window, he saw Millie heave herself out of her chair. The latch squeaked and the door shuddered open.

'Sorry I'm late, Millie,' he said, stooping to avoid the lintel and kiss her cheek.

'Never too late for me, my boy. I was just reading and listening to a bit of music.'

She settled herself back on the big, overstuffed armchair and Alain sat in the rocking chair to one side of the small fire which she kept going most of the time.

'So what did her Ladyship want with you all of a sudden, then?' She looked at him keenly, full of lively curiosity.

'Oh, this and that, Millie.'

He was evasive, and he sounded tired, and she accepted this. She gave him her broadest smile.

'Now, listen, young man, I've left the coffee out ready to be ground. The kettle's on the boil and there's new shortbread in the tin — don't forget to take it with you when you go. We'll have a better cup of coffee here than you're ever likely to get up at the Court.'

When he brought the steaming coffee in, Millie bantered, 'With you coming down so sudden like, I thought Lady Ceci had performed a miracle — found the right girl for you or some such thing.'

Alain shook his head. 'No such luck, Millie.' He gave a wry smile. 'But it would be nice, now ... Funny thing, coming from me, isn't it?'

Millie leant forward and put her hand on his knee. 'These things happen when you least expect them, son. Look at me and Joe here in the war, loving to our hearts' content and the world well lost for it. And whoever would have believed it? Now you remember that.'

He patted her hand affectionately. 'I'll remember.'

On Friday morning, Alain left his office and took a taxi to Eaton Square. It was a glorious May day, the greyness of London banished by warmth and sunlight and flowery blossoms.

Ceci had telephoned his flat the evening before – brisk, assured and a little cool.

'Don't be late, Alain, you're such a useful guest. I'll introduce you to Amos Werner – after lunch, I expect.' Then, lowering her voice, 'Robert's back and I've told him what we discussed. I know I can rely on you.'

If he was in any way disillusioned by Ceci's ruthless manipulation of their friendship, as he was, Alain told himself that it was understandable and he must accept it. Even Millie, who adored Ceci, thought her hard as nails; Alain believed she was what her husband had made her – and a survivor, as he was himself. He had thought through Brandon's political situation, and his record, very carefully indeed; assuming Ceci's assessment was accurate, he would do whatever he reasonably could – but he was decidedly apprehensive.

He was not the first to arrive at the Brandons' large, high-ceilinged flat. The routine of these lunches hadn't varied since Ceci first started giving them, soon after Robert was elected to parliament. The idea was to mix people from all spheres of life, throw them together, and let them get on with it. It usually succeeded brilliantly. Cecilia Brandon always greeted her guests, some of whom she scarcely knew, in the hall. A drink was immediately thrust into their hands and they were sent straight into the dining-room. Nobody bothered much about introductions. Everyone was expected to fend for themselves socially, and those who didn't measure up weren't invited again. The first twenty minutes or so were spent standing squashed uncomfortably around the long table, making conversation, while the rest of the guests turned up. After an experienced scan of the room, Alain made a beeline for a young actress who was hovering near the door.

Just before one o'clock, Robert Brandon swept in and heads automatically turned towards him. His presence caused a small buzz of excitement; he already exuded the aura of power. He was taller than photographs in the press implied, totally at ease – his hand outstretched, a word in someone's ear; a kiss on both cheeks for an ambassador's wife. After a momentary lull, conversation resumed. And at the last possible moment, a very large man of about seventy, heavy and impressive in a dark-blue suit and leaning on a stick, appeared. He surveyed the room briefly, his heavy-lidded eyes flickering about as though taking in every detail. Alain, who was watching discreetly over the actress's shoulder, saw him bend with immense courtesy to kiss Ceci's hand. This, without doubt, was Amos Werner.

On the dot of one, lunch was served. There were always placements, carefully thought out by Cecilia, but otherwise there was no formality. Long before it was fashionable, Ceci had organized idle daughters of friends to help out with the service and she still called on them in relays. Food and drink was placed on the table: casseroles and salads brought up from Cloverley and bottles of very ordinary wine. Guests helped themselves to whatever was nearest and plates were cleared by such girls as Ceci had managed to collect. Fruit and cheeses followed; the menus never varied. Once coffee was brought, it was perfectly acceptable to leave; but Ceci was equally happy if guests stayed on for the rest of the afternoon, drinking brandy and talking. Over the years, deals and relationships of all kinds had been started round that table.

Seated that day between a publisher and an artist, Alain, as usual, found himself caught up in the moment – listening to a conversation across the table as well as talking hard to the artist beside him. Looking up from time to time, he noticed that Ceci seemed to be paying a lot of attention to Amos Werner, who was sitting on her right.

When he got up to leave, reluctantly, Alain made his way into the hall where he came face to face with Ceci and Amos Werner. Ceci introduced them, turning away immediately – and Alain was left confronting Amos Werner. There was something about his appearance and bearing that put him in mind of a Roman senator. Shrewd dark eyes weighed Alain up.

'I must be on my way – an appointment. You, too, evidently, Mr Gesson?' He spoke with a guttural German accent.

'Yes.' Alain's eyes held his. 'Time always flies at these lunches.'

People were pushing past them, shouting goodbyes, exchanging addresses and calling for Ceci.

'You have known the Brandons for some time, I gather. 1943 . . .'

'1942. I came out of France across the Spanish border.'

Amos Werner held up his hand, silencing Alain instantly. There was no mistaking his compelling personality.

'Lady Cecilia has told me. Mr Gesson, I would be most interested to have a discussion with you, on that and other matters. Would you by any chance be free to come for a drink at my house on Sunday evening?'

'Yes – yes, certainly.'

'In that case . . .' He handed Alain his card. 'Six thirty, shall we say?'

He half bowed, turned, and moved away, again using his stick.

Soon after, Alain also left, running lightly down the stairs and out through the wide porticoed door. Walking up the square, past trees and bushes heavy with blossoms, a perfumed breeze blowing in his face, it seemed as though it would be May for ever. He had the heightened sense of well-being that he always felt after Ceci's lunches. But this one had been extraordinary in a way he couldn't yet fathom. He was intrigued to have met Amos Werner, who, despite his wealth and connections, had always avoided personal publicity and who was thought of as a slightly mysterious power broker. And it amused Alain, who had a detached way of looking at things, to think that they had been brought together, by Ceci, to consider the future of Robert Brandon.

Once Alain had started speaking, he went on for some time. Amos Werner's study, at the back of the house, was dim and quiet. A huge desk to one side was piled with papers; the windows were draped in heavy, dark curtains and the oriental rugs on the floor were worn, almost threadbare. Werner, an immense, brooding presence, sat in a wing chair smoking a cigar. He watched Alain as he spoke – urgent, sitting forward on the edge of the sofa, without once taking his eyes off his face. Occasionally he nodded, or asked a brief, pertinent question. Glasses of Krug champagne at both men's elbows were untouched.

When at last he had finished, there was a long, full silence. It was the first time Alain had let go the emotional dam and spoken with complete frankness, step by painful step, of the years from the late 1930s to the present day.

'I assumed most of this,' Werner said at last. 'Certain details, of course . . .' He waved his cigar. 'But yes, most of this is as I had imagined. It is a story all too familiar to me, alas.'

'A story of our time.'

'Unfortunately so. Yes, my late wife . . .' He stopped and looked away, his expression inscrutable. 'Hungary, Budapest . . . her father, a lawyer, died young. Her mother refused to leave. We did everything we could, when the worst happened, but by then it was too late. My wife never got over it, never . . .' He seemed to retreat into a sombre, private world.

Another silence, then: 'Bitterness, too, destroys, Alain. But you have not permitted this. You have grasped opportunities and made the most of them. I admire that. And an adventurous social life . . .' The hint of a smile, his r's rolling heavily. 'I understand that you will soon become a partner in your firm.'

'Who told you this?' Alain asked quickly.

'Our mutual friend suggested as much, and I also thought it prudent to make one or two enquiries after I knew we were to meet.' He smiled and raised his glass. 'A connection I have. And I heard, as I had expected, precisely the same things as from Lady Cecilia.' He replaced his glass very deliberately. 'Which brings us to the reason for which we have been brought together.'

'Robert Brandon.'

'Precisely.' He looked at Alain sharply. 'How much did Lady Cecilia tell you?'

'She gave me the gist of your letter to Robert.'

Amos Werner placed his fingertips together. 'I must say to you that I have the gravest doubts concerning Brandon's moral judgement.'

Alain waited.

'The proof of this previous commitment is irrefutable. It was deemed politic by the Government at the time to let the thing – the *cabal* let us say – die a natural death. But nothing was destroyed and all the files are still in existence, locked up in some dusty filing cabinet in a lawyer's office.'

'You've seen them?'

'I have. There are a number of us who have made it our business to keep track of these things against any possible recurrence of Fascism. There were others involved, of course — well-known names, many of them: wealthy men, landowners — all with a great deal to lose in case of war or occupation. And all, I don't doubt, sincere in their beliefs at the time, however self-interested; but unpleasantly tainted with pro-Nazi sympathies. None has sought power or public position since. Except for Robert Brandon.'

Amos Werner's forcefulness, matching his physique, was formidable.

'And you believe that this disqualifies him — from top political office?'

'I'm not absolutely certain.' He ruminated, blowing cigar smoke towards the ceiling. 'In his political life, he has flirted, to say the least, with causes too far to the right for my comfort. Combined with this former débâcle. Frankly, I do not think his close involvement in this group can be said to become the man. At the very least his judgement is called into question.'

The house was silent around them. Even the distant traffic was only a faint rumble.

'Enough to destroy his career?' Alain asked quietly. 'Because it would, without doubt, if it ever came out.'

Werner heaved himself out of his chair and refilled their glasses.

'Continue.'

'And I am not convinced that he deserves this, not convinced at all. His politics are not mine, nor ever would be. But you must remember' — he looked squarely at Werner — 'that the Brandons took me in, a Jewish refugee child, gave me a roof when I had none, and supported me through my education.'

'If I may correct you, Lady Cecilia Brandon was responsible for all this, not, I believe, her husband. And she has recently been reminding you of her kindnesses, of course.' He was on the verge of chuckling.

This touched a raw nerve in Alain. He stood, suddenly furious. 'Every word of this is the truth: as true as everything else about my background I have told you tonight. What the Brandons did for me — was that the action of racists, of bigots? Was it?'

'No, no.' Werner soothed, motioning him to sit. 'You are much too sensitive, Alain. And Lady Cecilia is a splendid woman — no one questions that.'

'I would do anything for her — *anything*,' Alain said emotionally.

'So I see.'

Alain thought, fuming, he believes I'm her lover. Well, let him.

'And I do not consider that anything I have known of Robert Brandon, and for years I lived in his house, justifies your action of releasing these papers which belong to a time and a particular situation no longer relevant. To do so would be in itself a nasty, malicious kind of blackmail. And I would condemn it outright,' he finished abruptly. It wasn't pleasant to be in the position of defending Robert Brandon, but he believed in what he said.

'And any moment now you are going to tell me of his most excellent war record, his conscientiousness as a politician.'

'All true.'

Amos Werner inclined his head. 'Indeed. Although my intuition tells me that despite your admirable loyalty — to Lady Cecilia *and* to Robert Brandon — your feelings about him are not dissimilar to my own.' Alain did not answer, so he went on, 'However, I am of the mind to let sleeping dogs lie. He has had, as they say, a warning shot over the bows. This should do no harm.'

Just then, a heavy door slammed, the sound reverberating through the house. Somewhere outside the room — in the hall perhaps — a girl's voice, half laughing, half sobbing, curiously out of control, called: 'Papa, Papa — where are you?'

The study door burst open. A young woman, dressed entirely in white, stood looking in. She was thin to the point of fragility and her long dark curly hair rippled in waves, like a huge, bushy halo, making her pale, delicate face appear even smaller than it was. Her eyes and her smile were scintillating. Alain felt as though he had been jolted by an electric current. His first reaction

— she's not normal — was superseded by: *she's astonishing . . . she's strangely beautiful . . .*

She came in and sat on the arm of Amos Werner's chair, her hand resting lightly on his shoulder, one leg swinging, a strappy white sandal suspended on her toe. She did not once take her glittering eyes off Alain.

He saw that she was all three of those things . . .

'My darling, where have you been? Wearing yourself out, dragging all those paintings about? This is Alain Gesson . . . my daughter, Zillah. Now fetch yourself a glass, my love, and come and entertain us — do.' He shifted his bulk in the chair, leaning slightly towards Alain. 'Zillah,' he said, with a superb pride, 'Zillah is an artist.'

After some stilted, formal conversation, during which Zillah went on staring at Alain over her father's head, Werner was called to a phone in another part of the house. Zillah drew up a chair close to Alain's.

'So tell me, Alain . . .' Her voice was light and gay and full of exaggerated syllables; and her eyes, heavily outlined in kohl, still hadn't left him. Hand on her chin, intense, her astonishing hair billowing away from its centre parting, she questioned him closely — about his profession, where he lived, what he most enjoyed — wanting to know this, sharply challenging that. And in the space of a few minutes, she prised from him some of what he had already told her father, and more besides, even the forthcoming television series. She gave another luminous smile. 'Follies? Funny, eccentric bits of buildings? This is *so* fascinating. I knew it would be, I expected it.'

'Why?'

Alain, still pinned in her gaze, was mesmerized by this gamine young woman who had suddenly erupted in these staid, rather old-fashioned surroundings. Accustomed to generating the chemistry in his relationships with women himself, her bravado amazed him. It was he, not she, who was effortlessly exerting her sexuality between them.

'Oh,' — Zillah got up restlessly and started moving about the room — 'I don't know — the way my father spoke of you after you met at Ceci Brandon's. We're very alike. We always take to the same people, always.'

'But . . .' Alain was giving her his wholehearted attention.

'Here, have some.' She thrust a tray of sandwiches at him that the butler, who had called Werner away, had brought in. 'I'm starving, aren't you?' She looked as though she never ate a morsel, but she began stuffing a sandwich into her mouth, still talking. 'I'm an artist, my father told you.'

'He seemed very proud of you.'

'Did you think so?' Alain noticed that she had a slight speech defect, the trace of a lisp. 'He believes in me,' she said simply. 'He always has. Have some more sandwiches, do. And you've nothing to drink . . .'

She went on talking — and he couldn't take his eyes off her. He had never met anyone remotely like her. She was standing in the middle of the room, unselfconscious, her skinny arms and legs sticking out from the starched white cotton, like a child in a party dress; she had the body of a nubile young boy. Alain's senses stirred.

'We have things in common, Alain, apart from our Jewish European background.' She dropped back gracefully into the chair beside him.

'What is that?'

'Our mothers both died, very young,' she said softly. 'But I have my father — and you?'

He shook his head. 'I don't know anything — anything whatsoever of what happened to him. He disappeared, in France, during the Occupation.'

With the barest touch, her fingers drew a line down the back of his hand. The door opened.

'There you are, Papa. We've been having a good, long talk. Alain and I.' Only then did she raise her hand from his. 'We've got things in common, we're discovering.'

'I thought that might be so.' He did not look displeased, or surprised, but neither did he go back to the expansive wing chair. Alain had the feeling that the interview was over. He stood. 'Zillah, my darling, have you told Mr Gesson about the show you are having, your first, in the gallery?' He bowed very slightly towards Alain. 'If you leave your address, Mr Gesson, I shall arrange to have an invitation sent round.'

Alain walked back to his flat – close on three miles – even though he didn't have an overcoat and the night was chilly. He strode along, hardly aware of his surroundings, the image of Zillah in her white dress, her hair massed about her face, dancing in front of him. The reason for his visit to Amos Werner's house had been wiped clean from his mind.

Chapter 14

Megan took the train to Wales one promising Saturday morning in May. Owen, who had just finished his long surgical job at St James's, was expected home later that day; so it was Gill, back from university for the weekend, who met Megan at Abergavenny Station.

In the best part of the year since they had left the cloistered life of Copthorne Hall, the appearances of both girls had changed dramatically. Gill, big and busty, her wild fair hair all over the place, had thrown herself into the more Bohemian aspects of university life and lived in tight black trousers topped by an untidy assortment of baggy shirts. Megan, taken in hand by the stylish and determined Margot, looked neat – and quietly sophisticated.

Gill had borrowed her mother's car, and all the way to the Thomases' house – through the bustling market town and out into the countryside which was frosted in white-flowering blackthorn – she gabbled non-stop, telling Megan everything she could think of about college: the classes, the blessed freedom, the men . . .

'And you've been seeing quite a bit of Owen in London, haven't you?' Gill asked, as they sped down a perilously narrow road into a deep valley. And before Megan could reply, 'I'm so glad Meg, really. You know the saying, all work and no play etc. – that certainly applies to Owen these days.'

'We do meet sometimes, when he can get off,' Megan said carefully. 'He comes to Nan for a meal now and then. She thinks he needs feeding up and spoils him dreadfully.'

'I bet she does.' Gill laughed.

'He does work tremendously long hours – I don't know how he keeps it up. But if he wants to get to the top of his profession there's no other way, is there?'

'Hmm – Owen's staying on in London is a bit of a sore point in the family just now. I don't expect you know, but he's been offered a job in general surgery at the hospital near here, the one Dad uses. An opening came up unexpectedly. It's either that, or struggling on in London, as you say. The parents, naturally, are dead keen that he comes back here for good. He'll have to make the decision very soon, this weekend I should think.'

'But I thought . . .' Megan stopped. Owen had told her, only last week, that he was in line for a job in London, at yet another teaching hospital; he was delighted, praying that he'd got it. This was a definite move up the career ladder, he'd said.

'I don't have to tell you what the parents are hoping,' Gill went on as they bounced over a stone bridge and came upon a pretty village. 'And they're prepared to put pressure on Owen at this point. They both think he'd have a much better life up here and – well . . .' She frowned. 'I haven't told you, but he had a bad go a few years ago, a bit of a crack-up. It wasn't just the work – but I don't think either of them, Pa particularly, are sure he can stand all the strain a consultancy job in London would mean. He bottles things up. He's not outgoing like the rest of us. Now, here we are . . .'

The car swung into a drive halfway up a steep hill just outside the village, and they stopped in front of a big square white house, its plainness relieved by an elegant portico. It had breath-taking views right down the valley, across a wide river at the bottom and over to the mountains beyond. The lawns and garden were immaculately kept, and a row of pink blossoming cherry trees shimmered in the sunlight.

The door opened wide and Gwen Thomas swept out to meet them, arms outstretched in welcome. Megan had always admired her when she came to the school – secretly envying Gill for having a mother who was charming to everyone and could never be an embarrassment; who wasn't an exotic creature who people stared at, who you could never really talk to, like hers. She just had time to take in the warm smile and the white hair which still retained a touch of red before she was gathered in a warm and friendly hug.

'Meg, dear, how wonderful to see you again! Alec and I have been really looking forward to this weekend, having you young people round us.' She held Megan at arms' length. 'And what an attractive young lady this is ... I see you've made the most of being finally out of the green Copthorne uniform, Meg. And I hope you'll try to use your influence on my harum-scarum Gill.'

'Here we go,' Gill grumbled cheerfully behind them, heaving Megan's case while Gwen Thomas led her indoors, past a clutter of gum boots and macs and an assortment of fishing tackle. 'I hope this isn't going to become the theme song of the weekend ...'

'We'll have better things to talk about, won't we, Meg?' Gwen kept her arm round Megan's shoulder. But Megan was already looking about her with pleasure. Light poured in from tall windows, splashing the beautifully polished wood floors. The rooms were simply, almost sparsely, furnished: bleached linen curtains, rugs, some good pieces of dark oak furniture. It was obvious that everything — every chair and picture and ornament — had been chosen to create a harmony: to give the impression of space and comfort and tranquillity. A large black cat, ignoring their arrival, lay curled in a pool of sunlight.

'Oh, what a lovely house this is,' Megan said, ecstatic. 'It's wonderful — and it feels exactly the way a real home should.'

In the afternoon, Gill and Megan walked down to the shops and poked around the village; and when they got back, Owen had arrived. When they strolled up the hill in the warm sunshine he was standing by the gate talking to the old man who helped with the garden. Even though he had his back to them, Megan could tell from the way he stood, his hands thrust deep into the pockets of an old anorak, that he was subtly changed from the tense, overworked young doctor she had been seeing all these months in London. Forgetting all about Gill, she had begun hurrying towards him, when he turned and saw them. He was fresh-faced and carefree; the anxious expression Megan was used to, some worry or other never far from his mind, was wiped clean away.

'Hello there, you two,' he called out gaily, starting down the hill. 'I was on my way to find you.' As he came closer, his eyes never left Megan's; they were both smiling and eager. Neither was aware of Gill, huffing and puffing just behind. Sunlight dappled the mountains on either side and larks rose and fell high in the soft spring air. An overwhelming sense of peacefulness and security came upon Megan. And when Owen held out his arms towards her, she walked straight into them – as though it were the most natural thing in the world for her to do.

Domesticity of any kind was an anathema to Gill, so it was Megan who found herself helping Gwen prepare dinner that night in the big, friendly country kitchen. Unlike the rest of the house, it was comfortably cluttered. A huge Welsh dresser, covered in plates and pots of dried flowers and piles of scribbled notes, took up most of one wall.

'Here's an apron, Meg, and this is a good knife. You're an angel to give me a hand.'

The phone rang constantly, usually for Gwen. From the bits of conversation she overheard – a jumble sale, a coffee morning, Mrs so-an-so's arthritis – Megan gathered that in her competent, friendly way, Gwen Thomas ran the village. Both Owen and Gill had a high opinion of their mother's judgement. 'Our Welsh witch', they called her. 'I'll have a word with the doctor,' Megan heard her say at one point. 'And I'll pop in and see you tomorrow, Mrs Jones.' She had a part-time teaching job in the local high school and she was now involved in reviving an old spinning mill in the next valley.

Alec Thomas, a big bear of a man with shrewd blue eyes beneath bushy brows, put his head round the door to offer gin or sherry.

'Sherry, Alec, please. What about you, Meg? The same?'

He brought the drinks to the steamy kitchen saying, 'I'm sorry we're being anti-social, but Owen and I are having a deep discussion in the sitting-room. You won't be surprised what about, my love.' He winked at Megan good-humouredly.

Gwen said briskly, 'I thought you might be. We'll leave you to it. Who's winning?' Megan could tell from the easy shorthand between them that they were a very close couple indeed.

'Not me, I'm afraid. At least, not so far.' He went out and shut the door.

With the vegetables done and the lamb roasting, Megan and Gwen sat opposite each other at the huge kitchen table. Even when she was cooking, flushed by the heat and wisps of hair escaping from the knot at the nape of her neck, Gwen Thomas was still a handsome woman.

'You know what all this is about, do you, Meg? The job that has just come up at the hospital here. It's perfect for Owen – and although Alec would never admit it, he'd so love to have him back here working. It's a dream of his – and he's coming up for retirement soon.'

Gwen sat very straight. Her heart skipping a beat, Megan thought, he gets his bearing, as well as his red hair, from his mother.

She said tentatively, 'But I thought, for Owen, that London was what he wanted. Private practice as well as research, teaching.'

'We don't think it's right for him, Meg,' she said quietly. Beneath the bright overhead light, Megan could see the web of fine lines around her eyes even when she wasn't smiling. She looked suddenly tired. 'We both think it's too pressured for him, for his temperament. He's a clever young man, and ambitious, but . . .'

Megan looked down at the pale sherry in her glass. She longed to ask, did Owen once have, or nearly have, some kind of a breakdown, as Gill had implied? And was it to do with more than just his work – with that girl, Diane, for example? She had wanted, desperately, to ask Gill that afternoon when they were in the village. But somehow, the opportunity never came. And they had both changed in this past year; their lives had taken different paths. They no longer had the closeness they did when they shared that tiny room at Copthorne.

She found herself saying, 'I'm sure Owen is doing what's right for him, Gwen. He must make his own decision. I know he misses all this, his home and his family, when he's away.' Gwen was watching her closely. Megan saw this — and it gave her confidence. 'But he needs to feel whatever he decides, you're all backing him. Otherwise, it's just another anxiety. And what he wants is to get on with his career in London — and take it as far as he possibly can. I'm certain of that.'

Megan didn't know where the words, or the sentiments, were coming from. But she knew they were right. Gwen leant forward and put her hand over hers.

'Well done, Meg,' she said, 'Well done — and thank you.' Megan saw she meant it; she respected her opinion. 'And now we're going to talk about *you*. Tell me how the course is going. Gill says you're liking it more than you thought you would.' She was smiling at her affectionately.

Megan nodded. 'That's true. It's a challenge, and I like the idea of getting a job, although I'm not sure where I'd begin. I'd do almost anything to get some experience first of all, then try to latch on to an interesting company and work my way up.' She was parroting what Margot had been drilling into her all these months.

'And you're going to the States, to be with your mother and stepfather — at least for a while. That's right, isn't it?'

Just the thought of it, while she was sitting so contentedly in the Thomases' kitchen, made Megan's spirits drop. 'I suppose so,' she agreed listlessly. 'I haven't really thought that far ahead.'

'Gill has told us about your mother. She really was spectacular, marvellous-looking. Alec and I saw her, in the war, in *Partners in Paradise*. Did Gill tell you?'

'Yes — yes, she did.'

'It must be — well, a bit difficult — having a mother who lives in such a very different world.' Gwen chose her words carefully. She and Alec had discussed Megan's unusual background, torn between Vera Mortimer, living in the whirl of New York, and Nellie Bowen in Trout Lane. And her father, they had wondered? They knew Megan had a stepfather but they couldn't recall Vera

Bowen marrying earlier, and surely there would have been publicity?

Lulled by her sympathy and obvious interest, Megan burst out unhappily, 'Oh, it's *impossible*. There's just such a huge gap between us.' She was no longer the mature young woman but a vulnerable girl again. 'We never seem to be able to talk properly, not like this. And we've had some awful scenes. I know I've got a quick temper, but ...'

Gradually, as the old clock ticked away and the vegetables began to bubble, Gwen Thomas drew her out. And Megan talked — willingly. Gwen heard about the elocution lessons and the blouse with the bow cut off and the dreadful day her mother took her to Copthorne Hall.

'Gill was homesick, too,' Gwen said gently. She waited. Suddenly, Megan was on the verge of telling her what she had already told Owen, about her father. She looked across at her — eyes wide and green and penetrating.

'But about my mother ... The real problem is ... and it's always, always there ... I don't know, she won't tell me ...'

The kitchen door opened, and Alec Thomas reappeared. 'The coast's clear,' he boomed. 'You can come out of here now. We've had our discussion and I put up my side of the argument. But it's to be London after all for Owen. And we've shaken hands on it and it won't be mentioned again. We've closed ranks, and he'll have our backing.' He placed a large hand on his wife's shoulder. 'Fair's fair — that's right, isn't it, Gwen?'

Megan and Gwen exchanged looks.

'Of course it is,' Gwen agreed wholeheartedly.

Behind them, Megan saw Owen standing in the doorway, smiling straight at her above his parents' heads.

When she and Gill were dragging up to bed, much later, tired out from playing Scrabble in front of the smoky fire, Megan said innocently, 'Did Owen ever feel he didn't want to carry on being a doctor in London, then?'

'Oh, all that was ages ago.' Gill yawned. 'Soon after he was qualified. I didn't really know what was going on — and he was mixed up with that Diane at the time. I overheard Pa telling Mum that he was "obsessive" about her, and that she was very bad news.'

'How?'

'Drink, drugs, bad company ... the usual things. She *looked* like something the cat brought in – really freaky; God knows what he saw in her. I think she came from Australia – or was it South Africa?'

'So what happened?'

'Nothing much. They never told me, thought I was too young. He wasn't coping and he must have rung here. The next thing I knew, Pa had jumped into the car, just like that, and driven through the night down to London to collect him. He brought him back and I suppose he had a good rest and they banged some sense in his head because he carried on quite soon after. Diane disappeared, or seemed to, about that time too.' Gill yawned again. 'It's all old history now. 'Night, Meg.'

Cloud and drizzle draped the mountains the next day, so they hung about the house waiting for it to clear. Fitful sunshine broke through after lunch. Gill disappeared, mumbling something about visiting an old friend, and Gwen Thomas set off to the village with a dark glance in her husband's direction.

'Gwen sometimes thinks I neglect my patients,' Alec Thomas remarked to Megan, amused, watching her march off, head held high, a cape tossed round her shoulders. 'That's right, isn't it, Owen? They know she's a softie and they try to get at me through her. I'll bet she's off to see that wily Phyllis Jones.'

Owen, who had been scanning the mountains through binoculars, turned sharply.

'There's no one more conscientious than you, Dad, as a GP. If you ask me, you've wasted your gifts and training acting as midwife and physician to the folk in this valley, out at all hours, in all weathers.'

There was a silence while Alec Thomas lit his pipe. Still put-putting away, he looked his son straight in the eye. 'That depends on what your values are, doesn't it?' he asked quietly. 'Now why don't you two go off for your hike while the weather holds. I've got mounds of paperwork waiting in my study.'

They left the winding main road and walked in a wide swathe across the foothills of the mountains, through fields, up and down stony paths, clambering over gates and stiles. There were sheep all around them, bleating noisily, some crowding together, others scattered about the fields; little black lambs on unsteady legs made Megan smile. Remembering their sedate strolls in London parks all through last autumn and winter, she was silently grateful to Gill who had tipped her off on Owen's passion for walking and advised her to bring sturdy shoes. Owen, his long legs in old corduroys and scuffed boots, strode easily; unused to this kind of tramping, Megan had to work hard to keep up with him. Cheerful, exhilarated by these wild, familiar surroundings which he loved and the invigorating mountain air, he talked eagerly.

'The old canal runs up there, Meg,' he said, taking her arm and pointing halfway up the mountainside. 'Look – can you see?' And: 'There's an ancient church up there in among a maze of winding roads. It's so hard to find that even we get lost. It's got some perfectly preserved wall paintings. Perhaps there'll be time to take you there tomorrow.'

Gradually, they made their way back down to the river which ran, wide and majestic, at the bottom of the valley. After a dry spring, it was low and calm, eddying shallows rushing on to little falls and flat, bleached stones disturbing the surface. Huge trees, ash and oak and alder, grew along the banks, overhanging the dark water. Megan was beginning to flag, so Owen slowed and took her hand and led her along the narrow towpath. They could still hear the cries of the sheep in the distance and birdsong filled the air all around them. Mist had blocked out the pale sun and it was coming down again, creeping off the mountain and hanging in the tops of the trees. When they came to an old wooden fishing hut which Owen said he and his father had used for as long as he could remember, they decided to stop for a rest. They sat, legs swinging, on the side of the open verandah.

'We used to play down here, on the banks, when we were kids. Not too whacked?' Owen asked. 'I didn't mean to walk you off your feet.'

Megan shook her head. 'I've got my second wind now – and I'm loving it. And this afternoon – *here, now*. I can see what you mean about this part of Wales being so special. It is beautiful and it's – Oh . . .' She tried to find the words. 'Remote, full of peace, like going back years and years in time. I feel as though we're the only people in the whole of nature,' she ended in a rush, turning to him impulsively.

'I hoped you'd feel that way. I thought you might.'

He looked at her gravely – a little uncertain. For once, his face had a high colour, his cheeks clashing with his red hair above an open-necked shirt and old navy sweater. Megan suddenly understood what Gill meant about him: he *was* cooler, more introverted than the rest of them. She had a sudden urge to reach out to him, so she put her hand on his arm.

'Oh, I do,' she said passionately, 'I *do*.'

The moisture had beaded her hair and her lashes; her eyes were alight and her lips parted. Owen's expression was one of great longing. Understanding came to her: he's shy, that's what it is, the reserve; he hides it, the shyness, underneath the professional exterior. So it was Megan who reached up and pulled him to her, his arms coming round her at once, holding her so tightly that she thought he would never let go – until she managed to turn slightly and his mouth left the soft dampness of her hair and moved slowly, slowly down her cheek . . .

They walked back to the village, arms round each other, not talking much, both very happy. Although it was only early evening, it was dark and overcast and beginning to drizzle.

'Typical Welsh weather this is,' Owen told her. 'Yesterday was far too good to be true. This is much more like it.' Then he said, 'That's the sort of place I'd like to own one day, over there.' He pointed towards a whitewashed cottage, set back from the road, at the end of a path which ran up the middle of a tangled garden. There were lights on inside and they could see dark beams and a low ceiling. 'In the early spring, that pear tree is a mass of white blossom right against the house. I've thought about it, in London, quite often.'

'You'll never get this Welshness out of your system, whatever happens, will you?'

He squeezed her shoulder. 'I don't suppose I will.'

They went into the pub, the Cider Mill, because it was on their way back to the house.

'Gill won't like missing this,' Owen said, ducking as they went into the long, low building which was painted pink with a mossed slate roof. 'It's her favourite.'

Inside, a small fire flickered in the huge hearth and there was a cosy assortment of chairs, sporting prints and gleaming brasses. Owen went over to the bar and Megan sat in a wooden settle to one side of the fire, rubbing her hands, glad of its warmth. After some cheerful joshing, Owen came back with their drinks.

'They'll be sending out the search party if we don't get back soon,' Megan said. They sat side by side, shoulders touching.

'Oh, the family is used to me and my walks. Meg . . .'

Her eyes were wide and bright and the cap of dark hair, wet from the rain, clung to her head. Like his, her cheeks were flushed with the fresh air and the strenuous exercise. 'What?'

'I think you're beautiful.' He touched her face. 'I thought so last summer, when I came to the school, when you came running down the steps with Gill.'

Did he? And he had seemed so stiff and formal – she the shy one then. Something caught in her throat and her breath came fast.

'Owen . . .'

He silenced her with his fingers lightly over her lips. 'Don't – you'll break the spell, and I've never said these things – to anyone – before.' She knew, somehow, that he had not. Her heart thumped suffocatingly. 'And you're so young, Meg, a kid, and me an old man past thirty.'

'Twenty in September, older than Gill,' she murmured into his fingers, talking to him with her expressive eyes. He kept his fingers there.

'I'm taking the job in the London hospital. I've told Dad.'

She nodded. 'I know. And they understand, they're right behind you. Your mother said.'

'Yes, they are now. We talked it through, Pa and I. Gwen told me that you stood up for me.' He sounded amused. 'And you'll go to New York, Meg? You must, it's important.'

She sighed. 'For a bit.'

'But you'll remember this, today?'

The happiness rose like an immense bubble and broke right through her. 'I'll remember.'

Only then did he take his fingers away.

Owen saw her off at the station early on Monday morning. After their long walk, they had spent little time alone together during the rest of the busy weekend. Driving to the station, they were both subdued and not quite at ease with each other. The magic of their mountain hike was obscured in the realities of every day – train times and tickets and roadworks. Shooting a sideways look, Megan quailed. Owen's expression was closed, almost stern; stirred by his tenderness in those enchanted moments by the river, she had a dismal sense of emotional let-down.

When she had found a seat, she leant out of the carriage window and looked down at him, standing with his arms crossed, squinting in the sunlight which turned his hair to orange.

'Thank you, Owen, for everything.'

He reached up and grasped her hand. 'You were a big hit with the family.'

'I loved them. They made me feel so welcome.'

'Meg ...' He took her other hand and feeling welled up between them. 'I'll phone when I get back down to London – in a couple of weeks. I'll have to fix up the new job and find a nice cheap flat to rent.'

'You'll enjoy this time at home with them.'

'Fishing.' They laughed – and the whistle blew. 'Here – give me a kiss ...'

She bent down as the train started to move. Owen walked along the platform, still holding on to her hand as it gathered speed ... and Megan went on leaning out, waving and waving, until he disappeared from her sight.

The telephone rang the next evening, just as Megan got in from posting a note to Gwen Thomas. Nellie was out the back, planting the geraniums she had bought off a barrow up the street, so Megan rushed to answer it. Was it the secretarial college investigating her non-appearance that day? The final tests were coming up in a few weeks, as Margot kept reminding her. Or was it ...? Could it be ...?

It was Vera Mortimer, speaking from New York.

'Megan — is that you?'

Coming from giddy heights, she was plunged into acute disappointment. 'Yes,' Megan said, wondering glumly what had made her phone, because she rarely did.

'Megan? Speak up, I can't hear. Is that you?'

'Yes,' Megan shouted impatiently. 'Yes, of course it is.'

It was a bad line, full of echoes and crackling. Nellie, thinking she heard Megan calling, poked her head round the kitchen door, but Megan shooed her irritably away, thanking God that for once, the television was turned off.

'I tried to get you at the weekend. Where were you? Nellie said you had gone away.' Nellie didn't remember much now, particularly telephone messages. 'Where were you?'

'Oh, staying with friends in Wales,' Megan mumbled.

'I see.' She hesitated as though she wanted to ask more. 'Well, there's been a slight change in our plans for the summer.'

'In what way?' Megan sounded, and felt, sullen. She would have given anything in the world to be back in Gwen Thomas's kitchen at that moment. After walking through the wild Welsh countryside with Owen, the rest of the world seemed intolerably dull and drab.

'Eddy hasn't been at all well recently.'

'Eddy? I'm so sorry.' Jerked out of her self absorption, Megan was genuinely upset. 'It's nothing serious, is it?'

'Nothing that can't be fixed.' The brittleness survived even the bad trans-Atlantic connection. 'He's been overdoing things in the office, the doctor says, letting things get on top of him, and he needs a complete break. He's having a rest in a nursing home in the country, quite near us.'

'Eddy is? I do hope he gets better soon — give him my love, won't you?'

Megan was mystified. This didn't sound like the Eddy she knew, although he hadn't looked good last summer.

'Because of this we'll only be spending a short time in France this year. We want to see you, of course, so I'm arranging for you to visit for a week. Then Eddy's going home and I'm planning to come to London — and we'll travel back to New York together.'

'All right.'

'You don't sound very thrilled,' Vera said huffily. 'Is Nan well?'

'She's fine — we both are.'

'That's good. Well, I just wanted to let you know.'

When she had hung up, Megan went out into the narrow back yard. Nellie was bent over her pots, watering can in hand, wheezing away as she packed tea leaves round the new plants.

'That was my mother,' she told her. 'She tried to get me last weekend, she said. It was a terrible line, I could hardly hear. She's coming to London in July and taking me back with her. Only for a visit,' she added quickly. Nellie went on tending the plants.

'Vera, was it?' She didn't sound much interested. That daughter of hers could be living on the moon instead of New York City for all it meant to Nellie Bowen. 'What's she up to, then?'

'I told you. And Eddy's not well so they can only go to France for a bit. He's been packed off to a nursing home. Poor old Eddy . . .'

'To get 'im off the bottle, I shouldn't wonder. I always said there'd be trouble between 'im an' 'er.' Megan pondered this as Nellie stomped back into the kitchen. 'And I thought for a minute when the bell rang it were your young man.'

Part 3

. . . and Marriages

Chapter 15

Three days after his meeting with Amos Werner, coming home from work, Alain found a large, stiff white envelope, addressed to him, on the mat inside the front door. It had been hand-delivered. He stood looking at the bold handwriting, accentuated by black ink and a thick nib, and he knew, without a shadow of a doubt, that it was Zillah's.

He tore at the envelope on his way up to his flat. The invitation was to a private preview of the paintings of Zillah Werner at an established Chelsea art gallery, the following week. The same round hand that had written his name at the top had also written 'over' along the bottom. There he read: 'Help! I'm still trying to decide which pictures are best for the show — come to the studio and give your advice. Nerves, nerves. This weekend? Do ring — please.'

He leapt at the phone and began to dial. 'Zillah?'

'Alain, I'm so glad you called. I'm in an agony over these wretched pictures, agony — and you seemed such a strong, calming influence.' Her voice came over sweet and musical. She should see him now — sweating, gripping the receiver, curiously elated.

'I don't know what help I can possibly be, but I would be delighted to come.'

'Lovely. Would Saturday be all right? We're starting to hang on Sunday.'

'Saturday's fine. Where shall I come to?'

'Come to?' She sounded surprised. 'Why, the house of course.'

'But you said your studio, I thought . . .'

Her laughter bubbled in his ear. 'You didn't see my nest, did you? Just ring and they'll send you up. About five.'

After pacing up and down the room for several minutes, feverish, still holding on to the card, he got in touch with the office receptionist — an on-and-off girlfriend — and deliberately charmed her into having dinner with him. He couldn't stay there alone, not in that excitable state. Just as he was going out, the phone rang.

'It's Ceci, Alain, I've been trying to reach you.'

'Oh, Ceci . . .'

'You seem *such* a long way away.' She sounded full-voiced and confident. 'Listen, we won't say anything specific, but whatever it was you did or said the other night worked brilliantly — absolutely brilliantly.'

It took Alain several seconds to comprehend what on earth she was talking about. Then he remembered — Amos Werner and Robert Brandon's curious political proclivities at the beginning of the war. He had given in on this evidently — or, as was more likely, decided that it was not really a very serious matter. As if Alain gave a fig for any of it; but if Ceci was pleased, that was fine. He said so.

'You do sound odd, Alain. Nothing the matter, is there? You got on with *him* — no names — very well, I gather?'

'You've spoken?'

'Yes. He phoned today. He just said a few words in that funny, rolling accent. But it was enough. He won't act on it. We're very grateful; Robert is, too. He said to tell you particularly.'

'So when . . .?'

'Early July, we think. But what did you make of him — A.W.?'

Amos Werner and his daughter Zillah, who he had met purely by chance, through this curious Brandon connection . . .

'I liked him. Look Ceci, I'm glad it turned out well, but I'm a bit rushed just now . . .'

At the Werner house in the imposing London Square, the same silent butler directed him through the hall and up the stairs. He came to a landing, more stairs, and a second front door. It was open.

'Keep climbing.' Zillah's voice floated down from somewhere high above his head. 'Right up.' Alain saw that the top floors of the house had been made into a separate flat. 'You're nearly there.'

Hair spread wildly, she peered down as he pulled himself up the last steep spiral stairs, emerging into the brilliant light of a studio, roofed and walled entirely in glass, running along the back of the house.

'I was *terrified* you wouldn't come after all.' The urchin smile seemed to break her face in two. 'I thought I might have imagined coming upon you in Papa's study.' It was she, not he, who was breathless. Her eyes were heavily outlined as before, but she wore no other make-up. She was barefoot, in tight white trousers and smock, both splashed with paint. 'All mine.' She flung her arms wide.

'My God – but it's magnificent, and so unexpected.' He walked into the centre of the room taking in the light, the space, the ingenuity of design.

'It is, isn't it? You can't imagine the problems with the planning. But we got it right in the end. Papa's very persistent.'

The studio gave the effect of an island, floating in space above the narrow London gardens far below. It reeked of turpentine and oil paints; there were rags and palettes and pots of dirty brushes on every surface. Canvasses were stacked against all the walls; a very large one, full of bright blues and reds, still gleaming wet, was propped on an easel.

Now that he was with her, the turmoil he had felt since meeting her vanished, leaving him profoundly tranquil.

'Thank you for the invitation,' he said, peering at the painting.

'Oh, *that*.' She drooped. '*How* I wish I'd never got into it in the first place. I dread it, absolutely dread it. I feel so – so vulnerable.'

He noticed a smear of blue paint on the side of her cheek.

'They wouldn't have asked you if they hadn't liked your work.'

'I suppose not.' The smock, which was much too big, emphasized the too-thin body beneath. 'But Papa, of course, has invited half the world, those wicked art critics included. Anyhow, they're over there, the ones the gallery has chosen, if you want to look.'

One by one, they examined each picture – exclaiming, pointing things out to each other, arguing over a line or a colour or a perspective, totally absorbed in each other's reactions. Alain, who knew something about drawing and how to look at a painting, was suprised by her talent. Zillah painted as she did everything – intensely. She had a good sense of colour and design, and a bold, fresh way with paint. Her best work looked as though it could be licked right off the canvas. There were still lifes – flowers in a pot, a view of a London park in winter, a cyclamen on a shelf by a window, pear blossom against a terracotta wall.

It was only when they came to the last few paintings that Zillah said suddenly, 'I'm being appallingly rude, taking advantage.' They were crouched on the floor, each holding a picture. Alain had long since taken off his coat and tie and rolled up his sleeves. 'I shouldn't be keeping you here like this.'

The spring sunset had streaked the skies all around them in glowing blues and pinks and purples; they might have been alone at the top of the world.

'I'm a very willing captive.' He touched her face; she looked like a tomboyish kid – there was no hint of the demure sophistication that he remembered from the other night. 'You've got paint, here . . .'

She rubbed at it. 'I always do. It's a messy business.'

'And your feet are dirty, Zillah,' he said gently, amused. She looked at them – long and narrow, skeletal ankles beneath her trouser legs. 'The soles –' She turned them up. They were grey with dust and spattered in paint.

'Quite right,' she said obediently, like a little girl. 'So they are.'

Alain carefully replaced the picture he was holding and took the other from her hand. As they bent towards each other, Zillah's hair ballooned against his chest, and his arms wrapped easily round her.

'I think,' he said, his chin resting on the top of her head, rather as though he was talking to himself. 'I think that in some part of myself I have known and loved you for ever.'

When they finally came down from the studio he caught up with her from behind, holding her gently as though any force would crush her delicate frame. She responded instantly, like a tiger. Minutes later, shaken to his core, he unwound her skinny arms from round his neck.

When he could he said, 'What about a good drink?'

'I was so afraid I had dreamt you,' she whispered. 'I didn't, did I?'

When the lights came on in Zillah's living room, Alain blinked. It was so astonishingly full of things that he wondered how on earth she, or anyone else, moved around it. The long, double room, which included a dining table, ran the depth of the house. Books, boxes, papers, magazines, ornaments, pottery, sculpture silted up every corner and spilled over on to tables and chairs. A large, rather elegant sofa, covered in maroon velvet and piled with cushions, faced the fireplace with a mirror above. Looking up, Alain saw that brightly coloured party streamers curled like tentacles round the elaborate chandelier.

'I'm in here, Alain,' Zillah called. 'Open the champagne, will you?'

The kitchen was entirely black and white, clinical and immaculate. Taking the bottle from her, Alain said, 'This room looks as though it's never been used.'

'Oh, I *never* cook. I'm funny about food – sometimes I like it, sometimes I don't.'

'Is this the drink of the house?' he asked, after a quick look at the label. 'Vintage stuff.'

'Papa's. I'm very spoilt,' she said gravely. 'You know that, do you?' Under the bright kitchen light, she looked younger and paler than ever with her black smudged eyes. She reached for a glass as the cork popped. 'Do you, Alain?'

'It can't have done you too much harm,' he said eventually. 'Otherwise you wouldn't be such a disciplined artist.'

'That is one of the nicest things anyone has *ever* said to me.'

They wandered back to the living-room and picked their way over to the sofa.

'Don't you ever throw anything away?'

'Not much. I'm a hoarder.' Zillah flung some cushions over the side and curled up with her feet tucked under her.

'We must get some food,' Alain said. 'Any ideas?'

'There's a Greek place round the corner, very small and simple — I love it.'

'That's fine, then. What about your father?'

'Oh no, we live *absolutely* separately,' she said quickly. 'He's very good about that. In any case, he's going to some great fund-raising concert for Israel. That's his cause: he's raised literally millions. He offered tickets but I declined — for both of us.'

She put down her glass and turned and lay with her feet up on the arm of the sofa, her head in his lap.

'You did right.'

'He's very grand, Papa.'

Alain laughed.

'Oh, but he is. Very clever, very manipulative, very secretive — a lot of people are afraid of him.'

'I liked him. He has a very subtle, perceptive mind.'

'That's funny. He used the same word about you — *subtle*. Tell me, do you often think about France, and your parents, when you were young, before the war?'

'Not so much now. I went back there last year and since then it has been different. It didn't lay all the ghosts, it couldn't — but I think I've accepted, once and for all, that it has happened. To me.'

'I remember my mother in flashes — a particular dress she wore, something she said. I was eight when she died. I think of her as laughing, always laughing, and my father, who was so much older, always so solemn. She was terribly extravagant, but Papa didn't mind. He adored her. But she was sad at the end,' she said, looking up at him, her face stricken. 'When she got ill, and I was sent away to the country.'

Alain stroked her wild hair. 'Where did you get your wonderful name from?'

'My grandmother. She was Zillah, too; my mother was Magda. They were Hungarians, from Budapest. The other Zillah refused to move when the war came. She wouldn't leave her beautiful home, she wouldn't believe what was happening, not even when my father begged and pleaded.'

'Hush, hush . . .'

'What happened to her was insupportable to my mother.' She was staring up at the ceiling. *'Insupportable,'* she repeated fiercely.

'I understand, Zillah.'

She insisted that he came upstairs with her when she changed. Her bedroom, conventionally decorated in soft blues and whites, was only slightly less jumbled than the sitting-room. The bed had not been made, a quilted silk spread was crushed in a heap and clothes were strewn carelessly everywhere. Unconcerned, she removed her smock and her trousers, leaving them where she dropped them; slim as a boy, wearing only the skimpiest of bikini pants, she disappeared into the bathroom. The chairs were piled high, so Alain sat on the bottom of the bed.

'I've done my best with my feet, but I really need turps,' she called through the half-open door. He caught sight of her reflection in the mirrored bathroom wall. She had a foot in the bidet and was scrubbing around her heel. Her hair fell forward like a great bush; beneath it was her androgynous body — narrow hips and thighs, breasts that were nothing more than tiny mounds with dark nipples.

'I forgive you — hurry up, or we'll never get out to eat.'

He wasn't at all sure, at that moment, that they ever would. He was usually so cool and guarded, but this zany girl made all his senses spin out of control.

Back in the bedroom, still nearly naked, she sorted through a crush of garments and pulled out a creamy shift dress.

'I'm dreadfully untidy,' she said unnecessarily, dropping the shift over her head. 'They do their best, the servants, but I'm beyond their powers.'

She sat at her dressing-table and brushed at her hair, swiped on pale lipstick and dabbed some scent. Then she stuck her feet into flat shoes and grabbed a jacket and a small bag.

'Ready . . .'

'What a *wonderful* night,' Zillah said, sniffing the blossomy spring air as they strolled to the restaurant. 'I feel *marvellous*, don't you? And I don't always – feel so well . . .'

He took her arm as they crossed the road. At a mere touch, the emotional intensity in that childish body sent the electricity charging through him. The hair bobbed along somewhere by his shoulder.

'In what way?'

'Oh, I have my lows, like my mother did. Don't let's talk about it. And I feel better now that you've gone through the pictures with me. The opening is a horror, but you'll be there, won't you? You'd *never* let me down, would you Alain?'

And yet, by a freak of chance, he did.

That morning, the morning of Zillah's show, his office had arranged for the first on-site meeting of the projected factory, which Alain had designed, some fifty miles north of London. This was followed by lunch, and the first serious costings meeting.

So far, so good, Alain thought, looking at his watch while one of the accountants droned on incomprehensibly. He was keeping an eye on the gathering black clouds through the window – and thinking about Zillah, worrying about the state of her nerves.

The meeting ran on later than expected, and by the time they left, it was five o'clock and the rain was teeming down. The next hour and a half was spent in solid traffic. Alain, tense and silent, sat in the back and fumed. On this of all days . . . Then the car broke down in a spume of steam erupting from under the bonnet – and he knew that the game was up.

When they limped back to London at around ten o'clock, he went straight along to the gallery anyway. There was no point in trying to get in touch with Zillah on the phone. No doubt the show was long since over, and the dinner arranged by Amos Werner at a nearby restaurant in full swing. Alain couldn't remember ever feeling quite so dejected as he walked along the gleaming wet pavements of Chelsea.

He got to the gallery and stood outside, his hands stuck deep in his trenchcoat, the collar turned up, his briefcase under his arm. Although the rain had stopped at last, water still ran down the high windows, shimmering over a large flower painting of Zillah's which was being displayed. Alain could just make out a red sold dot beneath it.

Inside, a few lights were still on. He tried the door and went in, avoiding the empty wine glasses and ashtrays littered about. It smelled of smoke and heated bodies and the sweet perfumed lillies that had been arranged in the centre. Somewhere in the back, a waiter was clearing up; the pictures hung blankly on the walls. As he was turning to go, he caught sight of a pale heap, curled up by the staircase. It was Zillah, fast asleep, in a white silk dress. When he touched her lightly on the shoulder, she opened her eyes at once and smiled at him, perfectly serene.

'I knew you'd come,' she said.

He pushed her into a taxi and brought her back to his flat. They couldn't find her shawl, so Alain took off his damp raincoat and draped it round her shoulders. They both talked continuously, interrupting each other, huddled close as the taxi rumbled through empty streets. The pictures were almost all sold, she said. The evening had been a noisy, nerveracking blurr, so she was quite glad to be left there in peace for a bit. Was his meeting a success? Did they appreciate him properly? She didn't in the least mind missing the dinner her father was at that moment hosting – he wouldn't mind either. They both thought, in retrospect – and Alain in huge relief – that the broken-down car was really rather a good joke.

He made coffee and they devoured half a tin of Millie's shortbread. All the time, he was itching to get his hands on that silky smooth skin that sent shock waves rocketing through him. He couldn't wait, not any longer ... Zillah still had crumbs round her mouth when he started to make love to her. He had deliberately resisted on Saturday night when she had all but fallen asleep in the restaurant and he had practically carried her back to the house, leaving her in bed with the quilt drawn up to her chin like a child. Now, blowing away the crumbs, he was kissing her everywhere.

'Wait,' she commanded.

She wriggled away from him, stood up and lifted the white dress clear over her head: a topless ballerina, with breasts that hardly counted and yet were curiously erotic, in white stockings, suspenders and high satin shoes. Alain watched from the sofa, tantalizingly aroused.

'Zillah . . .'

He caught her and led her up to the bedroom, yanking at his tie, undoing belt and buttons as they went. She sat on the bed, arched on her elbows, legs crossed, her head thrown back. Very carefully, he peeled down one stocking. She lifted her bare foot as he pulled off the other one. His hand wasn't steady then – she was very knowing. Her fierceness and her uninhibitedness astonished him and lifted him to great heights. After, she lay across him, hardly any weight at all, her hair, messier than ever, brittle against his face. A burnt-out candle, she was, still quivering. They were both, briefly, exhausted – glowing in sweat, elated. But a nagging insight pulled him down.

He said quietly, 'There have been a lot of men, Zillah.'

'Oh yes,' she agreed readily. 'Lots and lots. Like you, Alain – all those women . . .'

When his laughter, which seemed to sweep away emotional cobwebs from long, long ago, had finished, she raised her head and looked at him. Her eyes were black as soot from all the make-up. 'It started when I was an art student, at college,' she said. 'And finished with a friend of my father's. I had come straight from him that night I found you in the study with Papa.'

Alain winced visibly. He had never before felt physically possessive about a woman.

She rolled over and up and sat astride him, very straight, now an artless, woolly-haired Joan of Arc.

'It wasn't much different from you – one after the other, not meaning very much. Perverse . . . proving . . . I know. Papa told me. But, Alain, it's *finished*, for me – don't you see? Now that I have you. There will never, *never* be anyone else now. There couldn't be.'

'Promise, Zillah?'

She lifted his hands, lovingly licked each finger, and placed them over her breasts. 'Cross my heart. And you, Alain?'

'Bien sûr.'

Some time later he asked, 'Won't your father worry if I don't get you home?'

'Of course not. He will know that I'm with you and that we'll be together always now.'

'How is that?'

'He told me he'd met you at that lunch. He knew what would happen then.'

Later still — it was nearly morning and they had slept in snatches — Alain used a torch to show Zillah two dog-eared snapshots of his parents that he had brought from France in the canvas satchel, his single possession then. He had never shown them to anyone before — not to Millie, not even to Ceci. After they had pored over them for a long time, they lay together under the covers and talked until it was time to get up.

Alain rang Millie while they were having tea, nicely brewed by Alain, in the living-room. Zillah's dress lay where she had dropped it and Alain had fixed her up with a pair of his jeans, rolled up and belted, and a V-necked sweater over a white shirt. She had put on the high-heeled satin shoes and outlined her eyes in the dark pencil she took with her everywhere.

'I've got someone very special for you to meet, Millie,' Alain said into the receiver, his eyes on Zillah. 'A very extraordinary and talented young lady whom I'm intending to tie down in matrimony as soon as possible.'

Zillah, who was heaping sugar into her tea, and finishing off the shortbread, made no sign that she had heard this.

Millie said that it was about time, she had been expecting something of the sort — quick, sure-fire things sometimes did happen between people, she knew that herself. And could Alain please remember to bring the biscuit tin back with him?

'I will do that, Millie — it's empty anyhow, or almost. We'll pick you up at about twelve on Saturday and whisk you off to lunch.'

Zillah lay on the sofa reading the outline of the 'Follies' script while Alain showered and shaved and got ready for work.

'Darling Alain, it's not fair, you're so sleek, like a seal.' She put down the script when he came back, looking his normal, professional self in a dark suit and a sober tie and precisely fitting blue shirt. 'How I wish I could look like that,' she said despondently. 'But it's my mad hair that does me in. It's only fit for a sort of stylish eccentricity.'

Alain laughed. 'Your hair is an entirely separate being,' he said. 'It has a life of its own — and I love it, too.' He kissed the tip of her nose. 'Is it too early for me to phone your father, do you think?'

Showering briskly, going entirely on instinct, he had come to some definite conclusions.

'I shouldn't think so.' She looked surprised. 'But why? This is *very* interesting, Alain.' She picked up the script again and went on reading as Alain dialled. He caught Amos Werner just as he was leaving his house for the City and the two men agreed to meet for lunch that day quite as though it were a routine occurrence.

Chapter 16

The Mortimers' suite in the quietly grand hotel in the south of France overlooked the sea and a dramatic swathe of coastline. They took the same suite, with the same view — Vera Mortimer insisted — year after year, and Eddy's New York staff dealt with all the arrangements behind the scenes. They had arrived some days earlier for their shortened stay, and Megan had flown out to join them for her week's holiday.

It was a blazing hot day. They had no other plans, so Vera had decided that the three of them would lunch out on the terrace. The Mediterranean was dead calm and azure blue, yachts gliding about as if on glass. Waves of purple bougainvillaea cascaded over the terrace walls and the pristine furniture glistened beneath a yellow and white striped canopy. Cicadas clicked over in the pine woods near by and a lizard or two darted about. The lazy midday hush had settled.

Megan was sitting in the shade, staring moodily out towards the hazy skyline, thinking what a waste this was without Owen; although since Wales, their meetings had been brief and casual, not at all what she had anticipated. Owen was deeply involved in his new job, working harder than ever. She caught her lip, frowning. Eddy Mortimer sat opposite her, holding a newspaper, which he seemed not to be reading. He had a glass and a large bottle of mineral water at his elbow. They were both cocooned in private, separate worlds, still as figures caught on camera.

Vera stepped out into the heat and the silence. 'I must say, you're very poor company, you two,' she complained, swirling the ice cubes in her aperitif. Long tanned legs flashed beneath her crisp white skirt as she sat next to Megan and reached for a cigarette. 'Heavens above, what long faces! I've been doing some telephoning, but I can't seem to get hold of anyone.' There was a discontented look about her mouth. 'And I haven't heard yet how the business course finished up, Megan — except that you passed.'

'I was in the top five per cent, in everything.' Megan went on scanning the horizon. That she had passed at all, let alone near the top, was largely due to Margot's influence. Owen had been impressed, and said so. She and Margot had had several intensive swotting sessions in Trout Lane just before the final exams. Margot even persuaded Nellie to turn the television off altogether for hours at a time. And Nellie had taken to Margot. 'Sparky', she had called her, 'a nice, sparky little thing. She'll go far, that one will.'

'That's good,' Vera said, only half listening. Ever since Megan's arrival she had been thinking, pleased, how attractive she looked — and what a pleasing manner she had developed. 'We'll have to put our heads together and see what we can come up with in the way of an interesting job for you in New York — the United Nations, or an embassy perhaps — won't we, Eddy?' But Eddy, still staring vacantly at his newspaper, didn't appear to have heard. 'I said, won't we, Eddy?' his wife said sharply, for a second time. Eddy started, and the paper fell into his lap.

'Oh yes, dear. That's right, dear, we certainly will.'

Megan, who had given up on the horizon, watched him in alarm. He had developed a nervous twitch in his cheek and he looked shaky. He was very pale, and what hair he still had had gone white.

'I don't know where on earth our lunch is,' Vera said petulantly. 'Go in and phone down, would you, Eddy?'

He got up, very slowly, and shuffled into the sitting-room, bent like an old man.

Looking after him, Megan said quietly, worried, 'Is Eddy all right? He doesn't seem like himself at all. What did the doctors say?'

'Nervous trouble,' Vera said decisively. 'That's all. He's had a lot of business worries and so forth. He seems a bit slow because of the medication. They've prescribed quite strong tranquillizers, so he can't touch a drop of alcohol. It's nothing to be concerned about, it's all under control. Now, tell me more about what you've been doing with yourself this past year.'

But while Megan was dutifully going through the catalogue of college, Nan, Margot and the Thomases — purposely not mentioning Owen at that point — Vera's thoughts were wandering.

They'd been there almost a week, and so far, there had been one brief phone call, from Veronica Hansard, and not a single invitation. Not one. Not even for a drink or a swim off someone's yacht. And they were all here, all the old crowd they'd been seeing for years, happy enough to accept the Mortimer hospitality before word got round of Eddy's pitiful fiasco — there was nothing else you could call it . . .

There had been a reception at the small, prestigious museum, in a manorial townhouse on the upper East side, of which she was a trustee, in the spring. Everyone was there, the old guard, stolid and sedate in evening dress; the glitz had been kept very firmly away — they didn't need their money or the splashy publicity seekers. Eddy had come home from the office looking, well, peculiar as he so often did, reeking of whisky, his speech slurred. Vera decided on the spot that he should stay at home that night: she would go to the reception alone. She had attended more and more functions without him in recent years; nobody would think twice about it. Much later, some time after ten, when the party was in full decorous swing in the pillared gallery with its priceless fountain and potted palms, a loud commotion came from the entrance hall. Conversations stopped in mid sentence, heads turned, expressions froze. Because there, making his way into the throng, despite the best efforts of the guards to restrain him, was Eddy Mortimer — roaring like a lion, shouting God knows what, without a shadow of a doubt drunk and disorderly. And evidently hugely enjoying every second.

They had forgiven him, of course, Vera thought bitterly, because he was one of them. Poor dear old Eddy, always a bit weak and unstable ... There was that fabulous clinic in Connecticut; they'd have him right as rain in no time, although they didn't want any more public embarrassments. And it was *she* who had to bear the brunt of the ghastly scene, braving stares and snickering, somehow dragging him home ... *she*, who didn't belong to the gilded circle despite the Mortimer name, who hadn't been to the right schools and grown up knowing everyone else's cousin, who had no known background at all, *she* who was asked the following day — with the utmost discretion — to resign her trusteeship, which had been the one symbol of 'belonging' that she had really valued ...

While Eddy was in the nursing home, she had carried on as usual, held her head high, ignored the amused gossip, dealt with the camp for Ted and his faithful secretary at the office. She had stuck Eddy on the wagon, pulled him through the crisis, got him — somehow — on the plane for France. And for what? To be shunned by all their former so-called friends, even Veronica Hansard, the two-faced bitch ...

Vera forced herself to pay attention. Megan was rounding on her, looking, really, almost beautiful — and older, more mature, in some subtle way.

She was saying, '... so you see I'm really not sure I want a job in New York after all.'

'Not want a job in New York?' Vera looked bewildered. 'Most young people would give their eye teeth. Why on earth do you say that?'

'I've told you, if only you'd listen.' Vera stared at her daughter. She had seen those smouldering eyes before. 'I've already put out some feelers for a job in London.' It was Margot who had done this for both of them. 'Of course I want to come to New York for a visit. But I might not want to stay on. That's what I'm saying.'

'We'll see about that, Megan, when the time comes. And that reminds me,' looking at her critically, her head on one side, 'we must get your hair cut here, by that marvellous man. It looks so cute when it's short and perfectly shaped. Now what can have happened to Eddy — and our lunch?' She stubbed out her cigarette, swivelling right round in her chair.

Megan said very clearly, to the spotted silk T-shirt that was her mother's back, 'When you're in London, I'd like to bring someone for dinner one evening – someone I want you to meet. A man. Is that all right?'

The day before Alain Gesson and Zillah Werner were married, in July, Robert Brandon was named as the new Foreign Secretary. It was announced from Downing Street in time for the late afternoon news bulletins; and the following day, the papers were full of it, the consensus being that this was a suitable reward for a loyal and long-serving political career. Brandon was experienced, he looked the part, and he was considered 'a safe pair of hands'. The grumbles on the left were forestalled on account of this being the tail end of what was seen to be a lame-duck government, and he was unlikely to serve more than eighteen months. The press photographers were mildly interested because both he and his wife were well known socially – and photogenic. About the only excitement attached to the appointment was heard in the clubs and across buzzing telephone wires in London: how the hell had this fellow, whose steamy affairs and dubious, right-wing views were well known, managed to get away with it – and end up with a red dispatch box, smelling like a rose?

Alain, buying his morning paper on the street corner, saw the Brandons smiling out at him from the sunlit white stucco of Eaton Square. Feeling extremely merry himself, he smiled right back at them. Robert looked very good: suave and handsome with a touch of gravitas. Beside him, her arm possessively through his, stood Ceci: large and comely and wearing her best family pearls. Even in grey newsprint, she glowed, the matter which had seemed so devastating to her that May night at Cloverley long since forgotten. He stuck the paper under his arm, hailed a taxi, and gave the address of Amos Werner's house.

Vera Mortimer had been holed up in Claridge's for days – meals sent up to her room and a fire lit on the grey summer evenings. Eddy, in custody of a nurse, had flown straight back to New York; she and Megan were following by boat. On her last morning, a cigarette and a cup of coffee in one hand, she picked up the newspaper and took it to the window – and after a moment of appalled disbelief, she was faced by the picture of Robert Brandon, handsome and assured, photographed in yesterday's London sunshine: the apex of the country's establishment.

Seconds passed and the cigarette burned nearly down to her fingers. It wasn't fair, she thought bitterly, once the shocking recognition which had knocked her sideways had stilled; it wasn't fair that men, certain men, improved as they aged. He looked so like Megan that her heart turned over. He was twenty years older and at the peak of a consuming political career, buttressed by a large and attractive wife whose smile dazzled above an impressive pearl choker. Images of Robert, so long suppressed, flickered in front of her eyes. And as the awful desolation of what might have been swept over her, one thought hammered triumphantly through her mind: Megan – I have Megan . . .

Zillah opened the front door before Alain had time to ring.

'I was talking to Papa in the study, I heard you arrive,' she said, kissing him demurely, her hands behind her back. 'He's waiting for you.'

With marriage pending, she had taken on a slight air of mystery which amused Alain. She had also reverted, curiously, to sexual puritanism, which Alain trusted was no more than a bit of temporary rôle-playing.

'You look like a beautiful waif,' he said, kissing her back. 'Very fetching. Can I see you later? The office is safely packed in for the next two weeks. So could we not, for example, spend the afternoon in bed?'

'*Certainly* not.' Standing there in the gloomy hall in a pale linen shift dress, she looked about seventeen; she sounded like an outraged duchess. 'That would be *most* unsuitable. I've got things to do. I am a *bride*, you know.'

'But aren't there things we ought to arrange?' he asked hopefully. 'Plans for the future? The state of the nation?'

She shook her enormous head of hair. 'Not a thing. It's *all* done. You know Papa by now.'

Since Alain had asked Amos Werner's permission for his daughter's hand in marriage, there was hardly a day the two men had not seen each other. Werner was profoundly satisfied with the turn of events. He had a high regard for Alain; this was the son-in-law he would have chosen – and in a way, he had. He made only one stipulation: for the time being, they would continue to live in the flat upstairs. He and Zillah could make any alterations they thought suitable; but this was his wish. Alain, slightly taken aback, agreed. In any case, Zillah refused to be parted from the studio.

The marriage ceremony had been agreed to by Alain, Zillah and her father during the evening following the first luncheon, hours after Alain had proposed. It was to take place, very quietly, in a synagogue near the house. Amos Werner, who was a member there, had effortlessly smoothed the way. The only other participants would be a few elderly Werner cousins, and Millie Frampton.

As Zillah slipped away up the stairs, the study door opened. Werner stood there, filling the entire doorway. His usually impassive face creased in a smile, he held out his arm, head inclined, courteous as ever. 'Come in, come in.' And as the door closed behind Alain, 'I see our friend has succeeded in his ambition.' Gesturing towards a pile of legal documents on his desk, he turned his mind to other matters.

Superficially composed, her mind carefully blank, Vera went out into the busy street, sheltering behind large dark glasses and enveloped in a light wool coat. Purposely avoiding a newsstand, she turned into Bond Street. The long day that stretched ahead had to be filled somehow. She had already made a brief, dutiful trip to Trout Lane, she and Nellie shouting at each other at cross purposes above the television – which gave no pleasure to either of them. Megan had told her, in no uncertain terms, that she had things to do all day. She was showing a worrying lack of enthusiasm for her forthcoming trip to the States; she had been moody and offhand in France, too. And Vera was apprehensive about this young man she was bringing to dinner that night –

the brother of a school friend, apparently, a young doctor. 'He's absolutely brilliant, and he's got bright red hair,' Megan had confided eagerly. Something about the way she said it — and her suddenly glowing expression — had made Vera uneasy. She fancied she might be getting her away from London in the nick of time. With her looks and the Mortimer background, she had the world at her feet: all the opportunities *she* had never had in those long-ago days in the East End; before she clawed her way to stardom; before Robert . . .

Vera took a deep breath, which caught in her throat. Robert Brandon, in charge of the Foreign Office . . . But what did it matter to her? Those grainy, black and white pictures plastered all over the morning papers had nothing whatsoever to do with what had happened between the two of them years ago.

And what, in the rare, quiet moments when she was honest with herself, she knew she couldn't forgive or forget or recover from . . .

It was a mild day, the sun filtering through high cloud cover and splashing on to crowded pavements. There was no point in bothering with Nellie again. She couldn't get a word of sense out of her nowadays — and they'd never had much to say to each other, even when she'd been a sullen child, slouching through her first dance routines in Nellie's front room. Although she'd been good with Megan: rock solid, better than she could possibly have imagined in those desperate days with the war ahead and Robert lost to her, when she had so painfully deposited her baby into Nellie's waiting arms.

Vera walked swiftly on, down Bond Street into Piccadilly: a very tall, elegant woman with the aura of wealth about her and a chilly, unsatisfied expression. Her height and her stage training had given her presence; heads turned everywhere she went.

And Robert . . . ?

She had sent him away that last time, sixteen long years ago, hardly knowing what she was doing — which had given her some bleak satisfaction. It was too late; there was no point in prolonging the agony, for either of them. And as for telling him about Megan, nothing on earth would have made her tell him anything more, although he had wanted to know, to help, desperately in the end; but he had forfeited his right absolutely — and she had kept her pride over that, too, although it was cold, bitter comfort.

Past Fortnum & Mason's, she swung on down towards Eros. During the last week — and for the first time since she had married Eddy and assumed her American persona — London had belonged to her again, odd snatches of the past vividly and unexpectedly resurfacing.

One morning, she had stood for the best part of an hour looking up at the flat that had once been Jim's, then hers.

She had sold the lease, practically given it away, when the cast of *Partners in Paradise* left for New York and the bright lights of Broadway. Kind, decent, rich Eddy was on the scene by then, and it was part of distancing herself from England — and from Robert.

Only yesterday, gliding through the food halls of Harrods, past the expensive fish counters, she had caught a whiff of something — cockles? mussels? — and she was transported back, horror of horrors, to the Great Kiddies Talent Competition, to Nellie and Gran Gubbins and the amusement arcades and the appearance of Ben Maynard, who had died of a heart attack soon after the war.

She turned smartly into Regent Street, heading back to the hotel. No one could say she had had it easy, she thought resentfully, no one who really knew, however luxurious and cosseted her life might appear on the outside. Whatever else, she had never lacked guts. It hadn't been much joy grimly hanging on in the theatre — and knowing that if she failed, there was nowhere else to go except back to the poverty and the boredom of Trout Lane.

Ben had given her her first chance; then Jim; then Brian Worth — who had led to Robert Brandon, and her daughter.

She remembered those icy winter days, one after the next; the helpless longing for Robert; the clammy panic which she had somehow fought down; and the makeshift surgery in the suburban house. She had prevailed there — and she was proud of it: Megan was the pride of her life, although she had never been able to show it. She would do anything for Megan, anything at all, except share the knowledge of her father with her; the agony of all that was still too great; and there was nothing, for Megan, to be gained from it.

As for Eddy, she had been fervently grateful for his gentleness and protection in the beginning, and during the brief, heady excitement of New York and her Broadway success and the glamorous marriage. Despite what everyone thought, and she knew well enough what was said behind her back, it wasn't just his money she had been after.

But now there was the drinking – and she knew what people thought of that, too: that it was largely due to all their socializing, which Eddy didn't much like, and her reputed coldness towards him. All jealous rubbish, Vera thought angrily. For all his goodness, she understood Eddy's weakness, his fatal lack of assertiveness, better than anyone. She had worked hard at being a suitable consort for Eddy Mortimer, the kind of wife he should have; bent over backwards to be accepted by the Mortimer family and their circle. Let their so-called friends like the Hansards call her a jumped-up go-getter coming from nowhere ... And she was counting on Megan's visit to New York more than she cared to admit. It was coming at a time when her nerves were in tatters, when she needed all the support she could get. She had never had a talent for friendship; she was tolerated because of who she was. A pretty, well-brought-up young English daughter of a brief wartime marriage, arriving fresh on the New York scene, could do much to mend fences with people who had been stiff, if not cold, since what she made herself think of as Eddy's 'illness' had become so publicly known.

Crossing against a red light, she pulled back quickly as a horn blared close by her elbow, bringing her sharply back to the present – and the fact of Robert being at the centre of the affairs of state. He had always hankered after power; now he had it. She felt, to her horror, a spasm of sexual longing, remembering how he would appear from the country, late on summer Sunday afternoons – nut brown, his hair all over the place from driving with the top down – throwing her into bed, time and place lost to both of them; and how the following December, he had casually dragged the small jewellers' box out of his pocket. Since then, passion or emotion or whatever it was called had lain like a dead thing inside her: a cancer, blighting everything, even her relationship with her daughter. It was only with Robert that she had ever felt a whole person – confident, pulsing with life force – and that was no more than the truth.

The traffic streamed past – shiny black taxis, scarlet buses and cars dodging; there was a bit of sun struggling through a patch of blue high above the congested streets.

When she got back to the hotel, she asked for the fire to be lit. Huddled over it, despite the warm, humid day, she went back to the morning paper, drawn to it like a magnet. Blood drumming at her temples, she read right through the comment and background information on Robert Brandon, which included the fact that he had four sons, two of whom were twins.

At the very end, there was a small addition, barely half a paragraph. It said: 'Owing to the death of Sir Robert's mother, Mrs Clementine Brandon, widow of Captain Charles Brandon DSO, the cabinet announcement was delayed by two days. The funeral will be held next Wednesday at the parish church of Cloverley.'

Vera heard, as clearly as if it were yesterday, the chilling voice which seemed to be coming from a long way away, from the inner sanctum of that breathtaking country house; the decisive click as the phone was put down. It was Clementine Brandon who had intercepted her letters, who shielded Robert at that moment. That was when Vera finally accepted defeat, calling for Nellie Bowen's help. But she knew, even then, that it wasn't Clementine who had sabotaged her hopes. It was she, Vera, who hadn't mattered enough in the end to him.

She kicked off her shoes and went blindly into the bedroom and flung herself on to the slippery satin spread.

At ten minutes past two, Nellie Bowen, who rarely knew, or cared about, the time, peered at the clock on the shelf in the kitchen. Tripping into the front room where Megan was standing looking out of the window she said, ''E's late, that young man.'

'I know, Nan.' She didn't move or turn round.

Nellie hesitated, thinking how small her waist looked, clasped in that funny, wide belt that seemed to be made of string. 'Jus' so long as you knows, Meg, luv.' She hovered uncertainly and went back into the kitchen.

In the dark little hallway, Megan's cases for America were packed and labelled, ready for the morning. It was her last day in London for goodness only knew how long, and beneath the surface, her senses were in turmoil. On the one hand, she couldn't help but be excited at the prospect of New York and the voyage with her mother; on the other, the thought of leaving all she had ever known — and Owen in particular — filled her with despair.

They had both been working flat out. Megan's exams hadn't finished until the end of June, and then there was France and the preparation that her trip to America involved. Owen was still living in digs; he hadn't been able to find a flat that he could afford. They had seen each other most weeks, but never for long. Coming for a quick supper at Trout Lane, pulling Nellie's leg, bringing her plants for her window box — always ravenous — he would soon look at his watch and dash off again. He would tell her about a particular patient, or something funny that had happened on the wards, and Megan would glimpse his caring, professional side; but to her, he was distant, almost brotherly. To Megan's bewilderment and dismay, he talked enthusiastically about all the opportunites she would have in New York — the very last thing she wanted to hear.

If only she could say, or do, something that would bring back the effortless magic of Wales; it had evaporated like the mist on the mountains when the sun got up. Sometimes, Megan had to relive those moments in her imagination to convince herself that it had happened at all. It was as if he had decided, clinically, deliberately, to draw back from the brink of commitment.

Yet when they arranged the dinner with Vera Mortimer for that evening, it was Owen who had insisted that he would take the afternoon off as well. He would make a point of it. He would pick her up at two o'clock, look in on Nellie, and they would go off by themselves, do whatever she felt like, make an occasion of it. Megan, living on dreams since their heady walk in Wales, aching for Owen's affection, was counting on this to settle things between them.

The night before, she had phoned Gwen Thomas to say goodbye.

'I hope you have a wonderful time, Meg. But don't forget us, will you? You're very special, you know, to all of us.' She seemed to want to say something else; Megan had felt particularly close to her since their long conversation at the kitchen table. 'We do need you, you know.'

And did they? Did Owen? Or had the attraction she had been so sure was mutual simply passed?

She hadn't moved a muscle when the phone rang twenty minutes later. It was Owen, from a phone box.

'Owen?' she said. 'Owen . . .?'

'Meg, it's me . . .' And after a silent second or two, 'Please forgive me, or try to, on this, of all days, but an old friend has asked a special favour . . . I can't explain, but I felt I couldn't refuse.' His voice sounded heavy and flat.

'But we're going out, Owen. By ourselves . . . It's my last day . . .' Her voice was rising in disbelief. It was like a rerun of the evening of her first day at St George's. 'And then we're going to the hotel, to meet my mother . . .'

'I'll be there, I promise. Seven thirty, you said. I'm looking forward to it. But this afternoon . . .'

'But – but – I wanted us to be together,' Megan burst out, on the verge of tears, her voice trembling. After the weeks of uncertainty and disappointment, she couldn't hold back any longer. 'You said, Owen, you had some free time, it was your idea . . .'

'Meg, I can't help myself . . . I'll see you this evening.'

Megan was still sitting on the rickety stool holding the receiver when Nellie came out of the kitchen with a strong cup of tea. She gave it to Megan without asking a single question. All she said as Megan took the tea and replaced the receiver was, 'You look prettier 'n ever when you bin cryin', Meg. Now you run along upstairs an' 'ave a bit of shut-eye. You's goin' out tonight, remember.'

With Megan in her room and the television going full blast, Nellie repeated furiously, out loud, 'If I 'ad my 'ands on 'is neck, I'd strangle 'im, I would, wiv' my bare 'ands.'

The moment Megan walked into her room that evening, Vera thought, Good God, she's in love with him, this Owen Thomas. She's serious. And she's not happy, either.

'Owen's waiting downstairs,' Megan told her, standing by the door, her silk skirt swishing round her knees. 'I said we'd join him when you're ready. D'you want any help?'

Vera turned back to the mirror where she was putting on a gold necklace. After a day of raw, churning emotions culminating in an uncontrollable outburst, she was pale, on the verge of a migraine. But the sight of Megan transfixed her. She couldn't put her finger on it exactly, but there was an aura about her and her eyes were luminous – just like Robert when he was passionately involved.

Fumbling with the clasp, she said, 'Do this for me, would you?'

She had assumed that it was a casual boy-and-girl relationship; or that Megan had a youthful crush on a rather older man. But not this. She hoped to God she was wrong, but all her antennae were out; and the degree of protectiveness she felt towards her daughter, which was almost primitive, astonished her. She was dimly aware that this had something to do with her own tumultuous feelings and the memories which had emerged that day. Robert's exhilarated smile flashed from the morning's newspapers; a few quick years – and now the cycle was beginning again. With Megan. She had never imagined that she would feel so vulnerable.

Vera's hair was already sleeked into a high chignon. And when the necklace was in place, it was Megan who fastened the diamond bracelet and fetched a black evening bag and high-heeled shoes. When Vera put down her scent bottle, Megan picked it up and sniffed and dabbed, fidgeting impatiently.

'I'm ready, Megan. Let's go down.'

Vera's room was on the first floor, so they came down the graceful stairs together, appearing to float into the marbled hall below. Owen was waiting to one side, immaculate in a dark suit, his hair slicked down. It was perhaps his particular way of standing, of holding his head up high, which gave him an air of apparent superiority. He had already been there when Megan arrived a quarter of an hour before. Showing some of her mother's steel, she had washed her hair, put on make-up and dressed in the clothes she liked best – the swirling skirt and a new silk shirt. And when Owen had stepped forward to meet her, she had given her brightest smile, told him that this afternoon's change of plans was just as well because she had all sorts of last-minute things to see to, and gone straight up to fetch her mother.

The picture of sophistication, Vera crossed the floor, her arm, tightly encased in black silk, extended.

'Owen, how nice to meet you. I remember your sister, of course, at Copthorne. Shall we go straight in and have a drink at the table?' And as they were ushered towards a discreet corner, 'Megan told me to expect a redhead . . .'

As the meal proceeded – the food and the wine already chosen by Vera – the talk went smoothly. Megan, hiding the upset of the afternoon, spoke a little too gaily, as her mother noticed. Excitability was always a sign of temper in her – as it had been with Robert. Vera concentrated on Owen. It was those prominent cheekbones and the pale eyes that made him look hard. He had an interesting, but immobile, face, which just missed being truly handsome. She probed – and he parried: his work, his parents, his ideas for the future, the field of medicine he had chosen and why. He was amusing, and slightly ironic. Megan had spoken so little about him that she hadn't known what to expect, except that he was an able young doctor. Despite his fluent conversation and his obviously high intelligence, she wasn't sure that she liked him. His composure impressed her; or was it a front, for something else? She suspected hidden depths, she didn't know what . . . And there *was* some constraint between him and Megan, despite the ordinary, bantering conversation they kept up: Vera sensed this, too. Megan had looked on edge the moment she arrived.

After the coffee, Vera rose, pushing back her chair – 'We have an early start tomorrow, Megan' — signalling that the evening was over. Vera walked with them out on to the pavement. It was still quite light, the street clogged with taxis. His car was parked round the corner, Owen said, looking quickly at Megan. And of course he would see her home. After an almost imperceptible silence, the thanks and the goodnights began. As Megan and Owen began to edge away, after the plan for the morning had again been rehearsed, Vera put out her hand to Owen. He took it, and held it, and their eyes met directly.

'Get Megan home safely, won't you?' Vera said lightly, with the trace of a smile.

And Owen, still grasping her hand, said, 'Yes.'

Manoeuvring the car clear of the West End crowds, Owen spoke first.

'That was a splendid evening — what a dinner — and I liked your mother,' he said. 'She's very impressive indeed. I can believe what my parents said about seeing her on stage years ago.' And when Megan, head averted, staring unseeing out of the window, didn't reply: 'Meg?' His hand left the steering wheel and found hers.

'Oh, I suppose so.'

She didn't turn, or react, and he withdrew his hand. The car sputtered on . . .

After some long, silent minutes, he said soberly, 'I'm sorry about this afternoon, Meg. Do believe me, please.'

There was so much hanging, unsaid, between them in the enclosed darkness.

'I told you — I had lots of things to do. It didn't matter.' Her voice was tight with misery. Then, dropping the vivacious front she had kept up all evening, she exploded furiously, 'Where were you?' — searching out his profile which was etched against the blackness and the garish neon lights.

'Someone I've known for a long time was in a bad way. I considered it would be dangerous not to see her.' He stared ahead, not meeting her eyes for a second, concentrating on the driving.

The anger that had been building all day dissolved in hurt. She wanted, and she didn't want, to ask, *But who?* Wretched, almost in a whisper, she said, 'And this was more important than me, on my last day?' Just as he was the only person she had ever told about the father she had no knowledge of, she wondered how many people had glimpsed, as she had, what lay behind Owen's impassive façade – a man who was driven, over-sensitive, a lot less confident than he appeared. 'Was it, Owen?'

'I can't explain. Don't ask me to, Meg,' he said, stubborn.

'But I'm going, *tomorrow* . . .' She was in anguish, her hands clenched.

'Meg – wait . . .'

He slowed and turned the car into a side street, drew up and turned off the engine. His arm around her shoulders, he pulled her to him. She murmured helplessly, 'And I thought – I thought – we were so happy together – in Wales . . .'

She had broken through his defences at last. They clung together. For whatever reasons, reasons that she didn't understand, Megan knew that he was as unhappy as she. When she drew back a little and saw his face, it was as pale and haunted as it had been the night he had told her about the child who had died in the accident.

He said, with an intensity that shook her, 'I didn't know there was happiness like that anywhere.'

The rest of the way to Trout Lane, they spoke on and off like old friends. Holding the wheel with one hand, he gripped hers tightly with the other. They would write often – and yes, she would really try to get on well with her mother. She hadn't seemed as definite about everything that summer as she usually was; Megan said she thought she had sensed a change in her; perhaps she was mellowing. And now that she was an adult, away from England and the past, she might, she might . . .

'Your father, you mean? It will happen, Meg, some time,' Owen said quietly. 'It must. There can't be this secret territory between you for ever. It isn't right. One day, something will happen and she'll tell you. As much as she can.'

While she was away, he might even find the perfect flat,

within his means. And he would definitely get a new car. There was no mention by either of them of her settling in New York and finding a job there. And when she at last crept up the creaky stairs, past Nellie's half-open door, she was drained, but comforted.

She was almost asleep when a name leapt out of her subconsciousness. *Diane* . . . her mind still active, Megan flung herself restlessly about the narrow bed. Did she still have some hold on him? Even though she lied and his parents disapproved and he knew himself that she was someone he should never see? Why was there something 'dangerous' about her – and why wouldn't he tell her?

But there were no answers, and soon she slept.

Vera walked into Megan's cabin the following afternoon and found her with her head buried in a bunch of long-stemmed yellow roses. Seeing her expression when she raised her head, Vera's heart dropped. So she had been right after all. She mustn't cut herself off from everything *she* could offer her; but was it already too late?

She said briskly, 'Are those from Owen? How nice of him. He's an impressive young man, I thought, and he's obviously got a great future ahead of him. We'll be sailing soon, so let's go up on deck, shall we? You mustn't miss all the excitement.'

Looking up at the towering bulk of the great liner – the funnel blowing, gulls wheeling, wind and sunlight whipping the water – all Megan could think of was Owen's message. He had written, unsigned, 'To happiness'.

Chapter 17

'New York, New York – it's a fabulous place . . . New York, New York – it's a helluva town . . .'

When Megan arrived, slap in the middle of the torrid summer heat, the city was at the zenith of its new world power and prosperity and best-of-everything post-war dazzle. Even the raw, tacky glitter of Broadway, with the lights and the neon and the smoking Camel cigarette advertisement, had about it a gorgeous honky-tonk innocence.

'. . . it's a helluva town, the Bronx is up and the Battery down.'

So it seemed to Megan that July morning, standing on the deck of the liner – Owen's last yellow rose wilting in the lapel of her suit – and catching her first glimpse of that famous skyline. Struck by the early morning sunlight, the skyscrapers rose like great silver shafts high into the clear blue sky; on their right, the towering Statue of Liberty was encircled by gulls and bobbing craft. Nothing had prepared Megan for the sheer exhilaration of this arrival. Hugging the rail, watching the spume and the green water and the tug boats far below, she gave herself up to thrill of it all.

Once they had docked, Vera took charge. She was taller than most people, effortlessly chic, totally in control; Megan, bewildered by the frenetic scene, clobbered by the heat, followed in a daze. There was no sign of Eddy. During the voyage, Vera had broken the news that after returning from France, the nurse and their doctor had decided that he would benefit from another short stay in the clinic. 'He worries too much, lets things get on top of him,' she explained vaguely.

On a magic carpet of monied privilege, they were wafted through customs and immigration. Their luggage materialized; and so, as if on cue, did the Mortimer chauffeur. They were driven uptown, through the clogged and hooting traffic, edging past yellow taxis and monstrous cars with tails like fins and across gaudy thoroughfares, until they reached a wide, sedate avenue. The car rolled on, past lines of brilliant flowerbeds and high, forbidding grey buildings and deposited them outside a canopied foyer.

Uniformed doormen came running. 'Welcome back, Mrs Mortimer, Miss . . .' A nod in Megan's direction, a white-gloved hand touching his cap. The sun caught her fiercely as she crossed the sidewalk. Then Vera swept ahead, through the dark, cavernous hall, into the lift and the blissful coolness. Once they were inside the apartment, all sense of place fell away. They happened to be high above Park Avenue in Manhattan; but the Mortimer apartment could have been any supremely elegant dwelling place of the very rich, in any world capital. There was room after room — quiet, restrained, filled with just the right amount of carpets and furniture and pictures and objects, all of the highest quality. Everything was polished and immaculately kept. Plants and flowers, trailing from impressive containers, looked morning fresh. Heavy silk curtains and the hum of air-conditioning almost obliterated the sound of traffic far below.

There was a maid and a butler — obsequious, answering Vera's quick questions, over-eager to oblige. She ordered a light lunch, and they ended up in a pleasant study, which was obviously Vera's. Stripping off her gloves, she began to flip through a pile of mail on the desk. Then she glanced over at Megan, who was hovering by the window, staring down, mesmerized, at the cars below that looked like moving toys.

'We're home now. Come with me, Megan, and I'll show you your room. I had it done over in the spring: I hope you like it. It's marvellous for me that you're here — at last.'

And Megan believed she meant it.

It was heady stuff; impossible for Megan not to be caught up in the verve and the glamour, the colour and the excitement, and the steamy, drenching heat. She was stunned by everything she was experiencing; England and Nan — even Owen — seemed more than an ocean away. All along Fifth Avenue, where she walked with Vera, there were women dressed as if in uniform: in chic little black linen dresses, patent pumps and white gloves and tiny veils wrapped across their eyes. Vera, stepping from the car, her long legs as slim as ever, was easily the best-dressed woman around. Wherever they went, people turned to look at her, as Megan noticed. In the icy cold fairylands of the shops, Saks and Bergdorf's and Bonwit's, Vera bought Megan pastel shirtwaist dresses and flat matching shoes like a ballet dancer's; Bermuda shorts and shirts; and a flouncy, off-the-shoulder cocktail dress.

'And is Eddy getting better?' Megan asked. She was missing his amiable presence, and she had overheard bits of the long phone calls Vera made each morning to staff at the clinic.

'He's coming along fine,' Vera told her, 'just fine. The doctors don't want him to have visitors. He needs to be completely quiet. He'll be home soon.' And the conversation was abruptly changed.

At the weekend, they were driven to the Mortimer estate in Connecticut: a sprawling old New England-style house painted white with green shutters and surrounded by acres of wooded countryside. Ted Mortimer, now ten, was unrecognizable as the spoiled brat of Megan's first visit to France: he was dogged, quiet and unnaturally subdued for a child his age. He was clearly going to be very tall and he seemed to be perpetually trying to twist his long, skinny body into knots. Finished with his summer camp, he hung about the place, alone, often bored. He and Megan became friends, despite the gap in their ages, hitting tennis balls at each other and splashing around in the pool. He didn't seem to have any friends of his own age, and Vera was continually preoccupied. To Megan, he seemed almost neglected; he had none of the warmth and cosiness of home life which she had known with Nan in Trout Lane.

'Ted,' Megan said awkwardly, as they were wandering about one hot afternoon, 'what's wrong with Eddy — with your Dad?'

She felt that she shouldn't be asking such questions of a ten-year-old; but he seemed so worldly wise, like a little old man.

'It's the drink,' he said casually, chewing gum and kicking at a stone. 'Gee, Megan, didn't you know?'

'Not really,' Megan said unhappily. 'I knew he liked a few drinks, but . . .'

'I've seen them all – and Mom – pouring bottles of it down the sink. It's OK – it's no secret.'

'Poor Eddy, it's so sad.' Nan had been right all along; so much for her mother's explanation of 'nerves'. 'It's an illness. But they can cure it, can't they?'

'Sometimes they can, sometimes they can't,' Ted replied sagely. 'I guess it kind of depends on the person.'

Now that they were in the country, acquaintances of Vera's and Eddy's dropped by – smartly groomed, confident women who easily dazzled Megan. Sometimes they brought their children who were Megan's age or a little older, to swim in the pool or play tennis with a sullen Ted acting as ballboy.

'It's great that you're meeting some young people,' Vera would say, svelte in sleeveless linen, reaching for another cigarette. 'They're all well connected – the kind of people you should be meeting. Chuck Winston is an adorable boy, everybody says so. And wildly eligible. Eddy practically grew up with his father.'

Megan, thinking of Owen in his white coat somewhere thousands of miles across the blue grey ocean, didn't reply. She felt a sudden surge of homesickness.

But Chuck, a tall, blond young man with a crew cut who went to Yale and drove a snazzy red convertible, was soon asking her out on dates. He thought Megan was 'neat', and he was 'crazy' about her. Megan, who was looking very pretty – suntanned and wearing the casual, expensive American clothing bought by Vera – couldn't help but be flattered. He would drive her fast through the hot nights with the top down, and take her to smart restaurants in picture-book towns which were dotted about the craggy Connecticut countryside. They drank Martinis or Scotch on the rocks, and ate steaks larger than anything Megan had ever seen on a plate. Afterwards, he fumbled around with her in the back seat of his expensive car. And Megan, embarrassed and uncomfortable, ached for Owen – who seemed to her more than ever like a knight in shining armour, a serious man doing serious work, compared to this amusing, good-time boy who appeared to have inherited the earth, or believed he soon would. And later, restless and lonely, watching the moonlight silver her room, she would lie awake and think about Owen and wonder where he was, what he was doing and who he was seeing.

She wrote to Nan, and Owen, and Gill. And she sent cards to the Thomases and Margot. Airmail letters from Owen arrived weekly: short, scrappy letters written hurriedly and which never said very much – but which made Megan come alive. Vera noticed those envelopes on the breakfast table, and the way Megan floated through the rest of the day. He was working hard, he wrote, totally absorbed by his work, at last feeling confident of his skill; Gill was hiking through Europe on her long vacation and Alec Thomas was seriously considering retiring into full-time fishing. In her long, detailed screeds back, almost apologetically Megan tried to explain how easy, how seductive this new life she had fallen into was: a never-never land of long, lazy days with nothing pressing to do. If Megan ever mentioned her future or going back to England, Vera would put her off with: 'I've got too much to think about now, Megan. Later, when Eddy's back. Surely you've got enough to do with yourself? Don't you have a date with Chuck Winston in New York on Saturday night?'

Once, Megan and her mother spent a whole day together, driving in bright autumn sunshine to the north of the state, stopping at antique barns and warehouses, trying to find a desk for Eddy's study. 'He'll be back any day now,' Vera explained. 'He'll want to spend a couple of weeks in the country, just to get on his feet, and there's so much stuff piled up from the office.' So they plunged from town to town, stopping where they felt like it, poking about in grimy storerooms, hilariously pointing out ugly objects to each other, both knowing that they would never find anything remotely suitable – both suddenly, and unexpectedly, enjoying the outing. Off on this wild-goose chase, by themselves, it was as though they had thrown off the constraints of their normal rôles.

Megan, watching her mother drive for the first time, realized that she had never seen her like this before: relaxed, almost without make-up, her hair – showing lots of grey – blowing loose around her shoulders. The sleeves of her shirt pushed up casually. Feeling obscurely happy, she wanted to tell her that she liked the way she looked; that it was the way a middle-aged woman should do. But she couldn't find the right time or the right words.

And Vera was calling over the noise of the engine, 'When we get back to the city, we'll start doing a bit of entertaining. I'd like to get the Winstons, I haven't seen them in a while.' Pillars of New York society, they had been distinctly cool after Eddy's drunken foray into the museum party. 'We'll ask them one night when Chuck can come too.'

'OK.'

But Megan wasn't sure that it was. Chuck had gone back to Yale, and she had been discouraging his pleas for her to come up and see him. Although nothing on earth would induce her to tell her mother, after tossing back Martinis he had once made a number of snide remarks about her. 'Lady Muck,' he drawled, grinning foolishly. 'That's what my parents call her, and so do half the people in town. And everyone knows Eddy's a lush.' He thought it all a great joke, but Megan was furious, demanding to be taken home at once.

'You don't sound very enthusiastic.' Vera glanced at her sideways.

'He's terribly immature.'

'Listen, Megan, the Winstons are about the most prominent family in the whole of New York.'

'Big deal . . .'

One crisp late September day, Eddy Mortimer came home. He was helped from the car by the chauffeur and a nurse; Vera, carrying a rug, followed them into the house. Watching from an upstairs room, Megan thought he hadn't changed much, except he looked older. He welcomed her warmly and said how good it was to be home and how he would soon get back 'into the groove'. He was quieter than ever, almost withdrawn, pathetically dependent on Vera for every move. After two weeks of gentle recuperation, Vera decided that he was well enough to come to New York. He wasn't jaunty and joky like the old Eddy, but a good-enough imitation. The nurse departed — leaving a quantity of pills for Vera to administer — and they made the move back to the city apartment. Vera lost no time in mending social fences and doing some serious shopping. Aimless, bored with hanging around in her mother's life, missing Nan and everything about England, panicky that Owen could be getting involved with someone else, Megan made tentative suggestions to her mother about going back.

'Oh no,' Vera would say every time, looking stricken. 'You've hardly got here. And we haven't even thought about a job. And Megan, you can't leave, not with Eddy like this. I need you, I really do.'

And Megan, gracelessly, acquiesced.

Once they were settled in, Eddy started to go down to his office on Wall Street for a short time each day, his schedule kept light by his efficient secretary. He was looking, and sounding, so much better that even Vera started to breathe more easily. One afternoon, the day that the Winstons were coming for dinner, Megan was about to set out for a stroll when she was called to the phone.

'Hullo,' expecting Chuck, or one of his cliquey friends.

'Meg.'

She gasped; she almost dropped the receiver, her cheeks going pink. It was Owen, from Wales, from his parents' kitchen.

'I've been having a heart-to-heart with my mother, Meg, and she's just gone out and shut the door.'

He sounded so close, so intimate, that he might have been in the next room.

'Owen ... I didn't think ... I'm so surprised ...' Megan felt dizzy at the sound of his voice, tremulous with excitement.

'It's late here, Meg, after supper. I'm only up for a few days, but I'm missing you terribly.'

'Me too,' she breathed.

'And I was wondering, Meg . . .'

Closing her eyes, she could picture the warm, untidy kitchen exactly. He would be standing by the dresser where the phone was, wearing a tatty old sweater, totally at ease.

'I was wondering, and it's probably the most massive impertinence on my part – my mother has told me I can only ask – I was wondering . . .' And the words came out in a rush. 'Would you please come back – and marry me? Or consider it . . . Would you, Meg?'

Tearing out of the room some ten minutes later, Megan almost collided with a maid who was carrying her newly pressed cocktail dress over her arm. She flew on, past the butler who was assembling glasses for the party . . . Hardly aware of her surroundings, she raced into the bedroom wing. And there she came face to face with her mother.

'You're back from the hairdresser's – I'm so glad. Can I come and talk to you, now?' Breathless, her voice so high and light that it was almost as though she was singing. She didn't notice that Vera, her hair elaborately piled up, was white as a sheet. She said tonelessly,

'Eddy – has – gone – missing . . .'

The alarm had been raised by his vigilant secretary when he failed to return from a lunch appointment. On checking, she found that he hadn't even kept it. He had left his office at twelve-thirty. It was now four o'clock, and nothing had been heard of him. Vera, and the secretary, feared the worst. The police were alerted, and the family doctor. Bars and restaurants and hotels were contacted. Details were given to the emergency rooms of several hospitals. 'It's not only the drink,' Vera said tersely to Megan, who never left her side as she made call after call. 'He's heavily sedated also, he has been for months. The combination could be lethal.'

The Winstons were put off with an excuse that Vera knew

wouldn't fool them for a moment; beside herself with anxiety, she hardly cared. She paced up and down, smoking one cigarette after the other, waiting for news. Megan, bursting with her secret excitement, longing to pour her heart out, waited with her.

It was after two the next morning when Eddy finally staggered in, smiling foolishly, his hat on the back of head. He reeked of alcohol and his speech was slurred, but he was otherwise none the worse for wear. His demeanour was gentle and docile; his manners as impeccable as ever. Megan thought he looked happier than she had seen him for ages. The doctor, who had been keeping vigil with them through the interminable night, called a private ambulance and Eddy was whisked away, past the dozing night porter, back to the nursing home.

Vera then allowed herself a first stiff brandy and walked shakily into the study. Megan followed.

Unable to contain her feelings for one moment longer, not bothering to shut the door, she burst out: 'Owen phoned, late this afternoon, just before I heard about Eddy. He – he asked me to marry him.' She didn't have to say any more; her face said it for her.

Vera, who had collapsed in an armchair, shut her eyes. She had known since London, of course, that Megan was mad about him. And she had also known that she was hurting, deep down, that night; which had put her instantly on her guard with Owen. And she had hoped – getting her right away, meeting other people, that she would outgrow this youthful passion.

'Please, Megan,' she said faintly. 'In the morning. We'll discuss it then. I've had about as much as I can take for one day.'

'But I'm so happy, don't you see?' Megan slipped down on to her knees, imploring. 'It's what I've longed for. I thought he cared, I was sure of it, but he seemed to get cold – I couldn't reach him. I know there was an old girlfriend, something very complicated, that went on for years, and I thought he might have gone back to her. I was so miserable . . .'

'I said: in the morning, Megan.' Vera's eyes were still shut against her daughter's passion.

Megan ignored this — if she heard it at all. 'And I want to go back to London as soon as I can. It's not that I haven't enjoyed being here, or that I'm ungrateful or anything, but I can't bear being away from him a moment longer than I must. Not now.'

'I do think, Megan,' Vera said quietly, 'that whatever your feelings concerning Owen Thomas are, you might, just this once, consider mine.'

'But . . .'

Vera's pale, prominent eyes stared and the heavily lacquered hair was oddly lopsided. 'You are quite adult enough to know the ordeal I have just been through. After years of this, the drinking getting worse and worse, I thought we had faced the problem and overcome it. After what happened today, I think perhaps we never will. You have just witnessed your father carried off to an extremely expensive asylum.'

'He — is — not — my — father . . .'

In an instant, the dim, quiet room was rocketing with the powerful, unresolved feelings between them. All around, heightening the tension, the great vibrant machine that was New York City had slowed, but not quite stilled. Dizzy from a few sips of brandy after the hours of anxiety, Vera had the eerie sensation of Robert Brandon's hovering presence, an unsurmountable barrier irreparably dividing them. She could feel her heart palpitating violently; her skin was burning hot. She was facing middle age, and Eddy's crisis, in a gilded cage in which she didn't quite belong; while Megan, haloed in her youth, her beauty and her happiness, was on the verge of . . .

Icily calm, she said, 'I'll make a pact with you, Megan. That subject is never to be mentioned between us — unless, and until, I choose. I regard that as my right. And that is my final word. Promise me this, and you may go back to London, and do what you will: I'll put nothing in your way.'

Torn, hot-tempered, Megan blurted out, 'Then I've got no choice, and it's so unfair. Don't I have rights, too?' In a supple movement, she was on her feet, her back to her mother, standing in the doorway, silhouetted by the single lamp at the far end of the corridor. 'Don't I?' her body was rigid with long-suppressed hurt and anger. And when Vera didn't answer, she willed herself not to turn round, even when she heard a quickly muffled gasp.

'Please don't leave, Megan.' Vera's voice was hoarse. 'Not now . . . a couple of weeks, a month . . . Owen will still be there, it won't make any difference. And you're far too young to rush into marriage . . .' There was a note of helpless panic. Tears were welling up in Megan's eyes. 'I need you here, I must have someone — someone that I love.' She didn't even try to disguise a sob.

'Of course I'll stay on for a bit, if you want me to,' Megan said, unyielding; each wanting desperately the unstinting love and approval only the other could, and would not, give.

When Vera didn't reply, very slowly — and thinking hard of Owen — Megan began to move towards the beacon of the lamp, shining at the end of the corridor. Her mother was crying quietly and openly behind her now.

It was the longest walk of her life.

Chapter 18

'Tell me again, Owen,' Megan said for at least the tenth time. 'Tell me what it was Gwen said that made you realize, that made you pick up the phone and call me in New York.'

On a winter afternoon, weeks after she had returned to London, Megan was lying in the lumpy double bed in the attic flat near the hospital, which Owen had rented. It was dark and poky with sloping ceilings; one side overlooked a light well, the other a slummy, run-down street. To Megan, who was determined to make it into some semblance of a home, who had already brightened it up with bits and pieces from Trout Lane and various market stalls, it was a corner of paradise.

Owen shifted on to his side and his hand began tracing the curvy outline of her body – smooth, naked, warm – from her thighs, past her waist, up to her breast.

'She sat me down in the kitchen and said, "Come on, out with it." Apparently, I was looking like a lovesick calf – Gwen's words. Then she said, is it the work, is it getting to you? And when I said no, she gave me one of her most witch-like stares.'

He bent his mouth to between her breasts.

'Go on . . .'

Her arms, which were thrown up above her head, came down around his neck and shoulders.

'What with?'

She stirred beneath him and his mouth moved slowly up her neck.

'This . . .'

*

Later, when they were lying very close, in each other's arms, Megan murmured into his hair, 'What did she say then — after the witchy look?'

'She said: you love her, she's the one for you — why don't you try telling her?'

'And then she left you alone?'

Despite the mattress's lumps and bumps, which they were starting to get used to, and even like, Megan felt blissful.

'I had your last letter, with the telephone number, in my pocket.'

He was drowsy. He had come in very early that morning, quietly elated after a long emergency operation which had gone well, and they had spent the day together pottering about the flat. He would be going back to the hospital later. She watched his face, inches away from hers — young, clean cut, all the tension gone.

'And I was just about to go out. If it had been five minutes later, I would have been window-shopping on Madison Avenue. Isn't that amazing?'

'Mmm . . .'

While he slept, she lay without moving, his head somewhere by her chin. And as the room darkened around them, she contemplated the future. There was unspoken understanding between her and Gwen Thomas. Each knew what the other was about. In her own way, as Gwen had divined, she would provide the stable background Owen craved as the foundation on which to build his medical career. She would be the kind of wife — and mother — that hers had never been: warm, open, loving.

Owen sighed and turned in her arms and she pulled the covers up around them.

The coldness of the parting with her mother still rankled painfully; leaving her — troubled, unhappy — had been a cruel wrench. Megan closed her eyes and felt herself drifting into sleep; she wouldn't let herself think about Vera, not now.

As the weeks fled past, it seemed as though they had been together always. They bought a Victorian ring, a wide gold band with rubies, on a Saturday afternoon in the Portobello Road, and decided that they would call themselves 'engaged'. They were like kids acting as a pair of adults. It was a wild, grey afternoon in February, but they didn't particularly notice; on that crowded, raffish London street, it was Wales all over again. Owen, who had been singled out from among many for a job as senior registrar — which would surely lead to a consultancy — was robustly cheerful. Whipped by the wind, his cheeks were a red which sat oddly with his hair — as they rarely were in London. When Megan remarked on this, he pulled her into a doorway and told her, mock severe, that he'd had quite enough impertinence from her, and enveloped her in his coat — she was chilled and shivering — and kissed her for a very long time. Everything they said that day seemed gay and amusing. And all the way back to Trout Lane, where they were going to have supper with Nan, Megan couldn't stop staring at her ring.

The first person they told was Nellie, who was already frying the fish when they arrived.

'You see's you looks after 'er, young man.' She gave Owen a sharp look. She had taken to him the moment she set eyes on him but she hadn't forgotten the way he'd not turned up right before Meg went away — or Meg's tears; because of this, never mind he was clever as a monkey and a doctor, she had her reservations. Moody, he was; she'd seen that for herself. All over her one day, didn't want to know the next, although Meg said his mind was taken up with his work, she shouldn't take it personally.

'I'm the luckiest man alive, Nellie,' he told her, looking as though he could take over the world. 'I don't deserve her, but I'll do my best to make her happy.'

'That's more like it.' Nellie broke into a smile despite herself, wiped her hands on her apron and went to inspect the hand Megan was holding out so proudly.

'Look, Nan, isn't it pretty?'

'Smashin'.' And she thought to herself that if Meg went on like this — those eyes like greeny marbles, a decent colour and a real beauty of a smile — she couldn't complain, she really couldn't.

When they phoned the Thomases, Gwen enthused, 'There's wonderful news, Meg. Any nonsense from him and you come straight to me, mind. You'll be the saving of him, I know so.'

Alec Thomas, in his turn, boomed much the same, adding that he must give Megan his standard five-minute pep talk on what a doctor's wife should expect. 'A pity you won't be living up here, the two of you. But we'll feel happier, Meg, now that he's got you to keep him in line in London.'

'What did Gwen mean?' Megan asked, bewildered, when they'd finished speaking. 'Who am I supposed to be saving you from?'

'Myself, of course,' Owen answered lightly. 'Now come here and give me a kiss.'

Vera was polite but restrained. The suddenness of Megan's leaving, at such a difficult time, had been a bitter blow to her pride. And she fancied, from their single meeting, that Owen Thomas was not an easy personality — which was another worry she turned over in her mind during long, sleepless nights. Since Eddy's temporary disappearance and Owen's telephoned proposal, there had been no meaningful communication between her and Megan. Neither had once referred to the searing conversation in the early hours, in the darkened study.

Five days later, Megan had left for London. It was Ted, back from afternoon classes at his day school, who had watched as she and her luggage piled into the car; he who had waved, crestfallen, as she disappeared into the traffic. Their mother, after distant and edgy goodbyes, had stayed upstairs in the apartment.

Whatever her reservations, Vera had resigned herself to an engagement. 'But you can't surely be considering getting married any time soon,' she countered, when Megan made a brief, dutiful phone call to New York. 'Owen hasn't finished the last part of his training yet. So shouldn't you start thinking about a job, Megan?' she shrilled. 'I meant to tell you before — I've decided to go into partnership with a young man from Sotheby's. We're starting a very small, very select, fine arts business, scouting for serious collectors. All the girls have jobs in New York — it's *the* chic thing.' There was a discontented note in her voice. 'And I'd hate to think that your course was a complete waste of time and money.'

Stung, Megan replied stiffly, 'I'm already looking.'

She had been, after a fashion, when she could tear herself away from playing house in the gloomy little flat. But after Vera's angry dig, it was Nellie who got her going. While they were chatting over a cup of tea, Nellie's cloudy mind suddenly focused. ''Ere, that funny little thing you was at college with, lots of go about 'er ... Margot someone — she'll 'ave some ideas about jobs, bet you.' Megan had been so preoccupied with Owen and their flood of romantic feelings that she hadn't even had time for Margot. From one brief phone call she knew that she was working like a mad thing and still living at home to save money.

Megan got in touch with her again the next day. She was working in a small new advertising agency, full, she said, of talented young people, mostly female, 'with lots and lots of buzz'. When they met for lunch, Megan sounded her out, very tentatively, about a possible job. But Margot looked doubtful. She knew about Owen and their wedding plans, and she made it clear that she didn't approve. She was much too young for all that stuff, in Margot's opinion — housework and screaming babies, just like her Mum — and there was no point in Megan starting out on a serious job or career if she didn't mean to carry it through.

'We're all very dedicated in the office,' Margot said righteously, looking severe. Attractive and bright, she had already been promoted, and was helping to run a couple of accounts as well as doing secretarial work. 'We don't want anyone who's only whiling away some time before they walk up the aisle. It's the group enthusiasm of the company that's starting to bring in some good work.'

'But I am serious,' Megan insisted. 'I do want to work, at least until we have children. And we don't even know when we're going to get married yet. It really depends on Owen's job. And it's all happened so quickly.'

'Well ...'

Megan grabbed the offensive. 'After all, Margot, *you* didn't know you'd be any good at the advertising business when you started. Perhaps I will be, too. And I'd do anything,' she pleaded, 'anything.'

Margot took her back and introduced her to one of the partners, who told Megan, with an encouraging smile, to have a seat in her office; she would be with her soon. The small set of offices was like a beehive – phones ringing non-stop, typewriters going at full stretch, lots of shrieks and noise and comings and goings. But after an hour of looking at a wall which was plastered in slogans and artwork, Megan decided that there wasn't much point in waiting around any longer. She was just leaving when the partner, a young woman in her early thirties, returned. Mortified at having forgotten all about Megan, she didn't bother to ask about her experience or expect her to take a test, both of which Megan had been dreading. She told her that they were absurdly short-handed, as she could see for herself, and if Megan would like to come in on Monday, and didn't mind being a general dogsbody, she could have a temporary job, and they would take it from there; the money was the standard basic rate. Elated, hardly able to believe her luck, Megan walked out past Margot's desk, pulling a face at her as she went.

When Owen picked her up on Saturday afternoon, he said, 'I've got a surprise for you.'

'You're getting a new car.'

Owen gave a shout of laughter. 'As a matter of fact I am. Next week. I'd meant to keep it a secret. How on earth did you guess, Meg?'

'Woman's intuition,' she said primly. 'Or perhaps I'm a witch, like Gwen.'

When she was boiling the kettle to make tea, she told him about her job, expecting him to be as excited about it as she was. The laughter – and they had been laughing for most of the afternoon about something or other – left his face and his cold, professional expression slipped on like a mask.

'But aren't you pleased, Owen? I thought you would be. You encouraged me all the way through that wretched course. You said it was a good training. And Gwen has always worked.'

'That's different,' Owen said quickly, standing rigid in front of the battered electric fire. 'Everything's different in the country — slower, less competitive. I'm counting on you to make a home, Meg. I don't want some pushy career woman for a wife.' To her amazement, Megan saw that he was serious. As though any job *she* could do would threaten *him* . . . 'I hope that friend of yours, Margot, hasn't been getting at you with all her feminist ideas.'

Shaken, Megan said, 'But what on earth am I going to do if I don't have a job? In the first place, I need the money. And we're not married yet, and you work such long hours. If we had children' — her cheeks went pink — 'it would be different.'

As quickly as he had taken up this quirky stance, he relaxed. The tension went out of him and he put his arms around her and held her so tightly that she could hardly breathe.

'I'm sorry, I'm sorry. I'm a selfish so-and-so, Meg. I want every bit of you, just for me, all the time. Of course you must have a job — and I'm very proud of you. We'll take everything as it comes. OK?' Megan nodded. These lightning mood changes could still knock the stuffing out of her. 'And I'm going to take you out to dinner to celebrate.'

But although they both tried their hardest, the evening somehow lacked gaiety. They went to the Italian restaurant where they had had their first date — ordering their favourite food and a bottle of wine. And perhaps unfortunately — Megan was still trying to make sense of his unexpected reaction to her job — Owen chose that night to bring up what Megan hoped had been forgotten: his non-appearance at Trout Lane the afternoon before she sailed to New York.

'I want to make a clean breast of that, Meg.' He looked at her seriously across the little table with its checked tablecloth, the candle and the wineglasses. 'It's something that disturbs me very much.'

'Owen, please . . . it's all over, it doesn't matter.'

He touched her hand. Whatever it was he was about to say

was of urgent importance to him. 'Yes, it is now,' he said quietly. 'But you should know this. I want you to. For a long time, there was a girl I was involved with . . .'

'Owen – no . . .' She winced.

'I must, Meg, I must. She was no good, particularly for me. I knew that even at the time – and yet I couldn't seem to help myself. I was hopelessly weak.'

Already overwrought, Megan had a feeling of dread; she was suddenly afraid that she was going to break down in tears. She wanted to shout that she knew, that it was part of his past, that she couldn't bear . . .

He gripped her fingers. 'She used drugs, and drink – addictively. She's a talented actress and dancer, but totally self-destructive. That particular day, and I hadn't seen her for months and months, even casually, she left a message to say that she was going to do something drastic if she didn't see me. I fell for it. One look and I was out of there. It was the daftest thing I've ever done in my life. And on that, of all days. I hurt you. I can't forgive myself that.'

Diane. That girl in the coffee bar. She was sure of it . . . everything Gill had said fitted.

Her voice was a whisper. 'Have you seen her since?'

'Yes. But I won't again. It's over for good now. I can promise you that – on my life.'

'While I was in New York . . .'

He nodded.

'You told Gwen all about it, right before you phoned the apartment . . .' It was like reading a book inside her head. 'Why are you telling me this, Owen?'

'Because I love you.' He smoothed her damp cheek very gently with his fingers. 'And because you've made me strong.'

It took Margot weeks before she could bring herself to say 'well done'. But she did in the end, when they were having lunch at their local café. Megan's temporary weeks had stretched and stretched, into the spring and summer and beyond. Megan was now a permanent member of the staff, and she seemed to have a natural flair for copywriting. 'They call you my protégée,' Margot giggled.

Although Megan was still nominally living in Trout Lane, she and Owen spent most of their time away from work in the flat, which Megan had succeeded in making into a comfortable home. Nellie, in a haze of cigarette smoke and non-stop television, sensibly didn't ask questions. 'If 'e makes you look like that, 'e must 'ave somethin' about 'im,' she would say as Megan dashed in and out. Owen, who was steadily gaining recognition and had been recommended for a job as a consultant physician, told her that this was the first time he hadn't felt like a foreigner in London.

Getting some time off together, they drove up to Wales to spend a week with the Thomases. Gill was there, cramming for her finals.

'Owen's looking a lot easier these days,' she told Megan cheerfully. 'You're the only one who can take him out of himself, loosen him up a bit. Wasn't it lucky for him that we were put in the same dorm that awful first night at Copthorne?'

One evening, when they were strolling round Gwen's vegetable garden, admiring the results of all her hard work, Megan said, 'Owen and I were talking on the way up in the car. We'd both love to be married in the village church, we've decided that . . .'

'Go on, Meg,' Gwen said.

'And perhaps have a small reception here in the house. We could get Nan up with my mother and Eddy – and perhaps Ted – and put them up at the pub for a couple of nights. And a few of our friends from London, people we work with. Owen feels so strongly about his Welsh roots and all the locals he's known since he was a boy. You know I'd help with everything – but would it all be too much trouble for you and Alec, do you think?'

Gwen took Megan's face between her hands.

'You lovely, silly child. It's the nicest thing I've ever been asked. Now when your mother comes over next month, why don't you name the day? We often have a glorious bout of weather early in September when the trees are beginning to change and the berries ripen.'

The Mortimers arrived in London towards the end of June, and late one soft, sunny afternoon, Megan left her chaotic desk and hopped on a bus which deposited her round the corner from their hotel. Although she couldn't match Margot, who was devoting most of her life to the agency and making rapid advances, Megan had quickly got the hang of the business. She dealt well with clients; she had the knack of smoothing over whatever it was that hadn't gone right — bad printing or ruffled feelings or a missed deadline. The agency was a small, tight-knit group and she was regarded as one of the team.

This was the first time that Megan and her mother had been together since Megan's visit to the States — and since her hasty and emotional departure. Megan saw at once, her heart plummeting, that since then, much had changed in Vera's life, as well as in hers.

'We're giving France a miss this year,' Vera said breezily, after some stilted greetings. 'My partner, Carl, and I want to look round the galleries here, and there's a very interesting sale on at Sotheby's this week.' She looked her daughter up and down. In her neat grey working suit and ivory shirt, Megan was every inch the young career woman — slim, svelte and attractive. 'In any case, we wanted to meet the Thomases, of course — and see Owen again.' She was being formal, far from enthusiastic, with a hard edge to her voice.

And as Megan saw with dismay, she had taken to wearing dark glasses, even indoors, and had drastically shortened her skirts. A skinny, shiny high-necked sweater clung unbecomingly. She had always stuck to stunningly simple styles — leaving the effect to her height and her figure — that she had worked out for herself, years ago; Megan had never seen her dressed in any other way. And now this.

Trying not to stare at the outsize white enamelled earrings, Megan said, 'Gwen and Alec are coming down to London on Friday. Alec has a meeting in the afternoon — and Owen won't be working late. They're longing to meet you both. So I thought we could all have dinner that night.'

Once that was settled, Megan felt more relaxed. She and Gwen had already put a good deal of thought into the wedding, and she wanted to break the plans to her mother as tactfully as possible. Tea was ordered and the gaping chasm between them papered over. After some perfunctory questions about Nellie, Owen's work and Megan's job, Vera returned obsessively to the arts business in which, thanks to Eddy's money – as Megan well knew – she was now apparently deeply involved.

'We go to all the sales, Carl and I, every single one,' Vera explained fervently. 'I'm getting really quite knowledgeable. And of course I know so many people who are dying for someone with a cultivated eye, like Carl, to tell them what to buy. We've had some marvellous publicity recently – *Woman's Wear Daily* did a whole piece. I don't know what on earth I did with my time before . . .'

'That's good,' Megan said politely, thinking, Owen has to stay at the hospital until eight tonight, so I'll have time to dash to the shops after this.

When Megan enquired, she was told that Eddy had gone for a stroll round the block.

'You'll find he's gone quite deaf,' Vera said, pouring the tea. 'It happened with his illness. Oh, here he is now,' as Eddy came through the door, a bit bent, but with his old, warm grin, making a beeline for Megan. 'Owen and his parents are coming for dinner on Friday night, Eddy,' she said brightly, raising her voice. 'If your mind's made up, Megan, I suppose we'll have to start thinking about a wedding.'

'My mother has turned into a freak,' Megan said glumly, wrestling with lamb chops under the grill.

'What do you mean by that?' Unwinding with a beer after a long day, Owen was sprawled in front of the television. 'I thought she was an amazingly elegant woman, very much in control.' He yawned. 'Any sign of some food? Sorry I'm not helping you, Meg, lazy bastard that I am.'

'It won't be long. I couldn't get the flame to catch – the potatoes are ready . . . Just wait until you see her hair.'

'What? Oh, your mother's.' He was paying attention to the news. 'What about it?'

'She's dyed it black as coal and it looks dreadful, terribly hard. And she's wearing skirts up to her knickers. She's become obsessed with some kind of art business in New York with a partner called Carl.' She forked the chops on to plates and carried the potatoes to the table. She sat down – drooping, dejected. 'When I saw her like that, today, I could have cried.'

Owen came and stood behind her chair and put his arms around her, resting his chin on the top of her head. He said gently, 'That's because she's your mother, and you love her, despite your differences – and one day, you'll believe me.'

Friday night's dinner was a strain all round. Although Eddy was a lavish and generous host, his deafness was socially isolating. Owen said to Megan later that he was certain he would benefit from a hearing aid; couldn't she hint as much to her mother? Vera Mortimer and Gwen Thomas hadn't taken to each other on sight. Immediately sensing Megan's rapport with Gwen, Vera was like a cat with an arched back, ready to spit with jealousy. Gwen, who had plenty of spirit and a forceful personality, had no intention of being overwhelmed by the Mortimer style; Vera played it cool and casual, giving the impression that this meeting, of families soon to be joined by marriage, was something she had just managed to fit in between appointments. Megan hovered nervously between them, while Alec and Owen, downing a couple of strong drinks, did their best to make conversation with Eddy.

As Owen's consultancy, making him one of the youngest cardiac specialists in the country, had only that day been confirmed, the evening started off gaily. But this soon wore off as it became apparent to Vera that the wedding was to be in Wales, not in London as she had supposed, and that most of the arrangements had already been made.

'We feel so close to Meg, as though she's family already,'

Gwen said fondly, her hand on Megan's arm. 'We know — we have from the first — that Meg is exactly what Owen needs.'

'And that he will make *her* happy, I trust,' Vera shot back frostily. 'Whatever his needs may be.'

'Of course.' Their eyes met, unblinking. 'It's their big day after all, and they must do as they choose.'

'Owen really does want us to be married in Wales,' Megan cut in, on tenterhooks, looking at her mother directly.

'That's that, then,' said Vera, shrugging. And with a glacial smile from one to the other, she went on, 'Suppose you both tell me exactly what it is that you've planned for the wedding. Just to put me in the picture, as it were.'

When Megan told Owen that Eddy, who she had lunched with alone that day, was insisting on buying them a house for a wedding present, Owen's face tightened, the way it did when he was bottling up strong feelings. 'There's no need for it, Meg. We'll buy our own house.' He looked like thunder.

'But if my mother and Eddy want to do this for us, why not let them?'

'Look, Meg, we're both earning. I'm making a good basic income and working my way into private practice as well. It's all going as I'd hoped. We can do it on our own. We don't need their help.'

'Leave this to me, Owen, *please* . . .'

Megan came upon the house in Somerset Crescent a couple of weeks later. She had taken the afternoon off and set out with an estate agent — and the period terraced house was the last on the list. It was cloudy and beginning to rain by the time they arrived; empty and rundown, the house could not have looked less welcoming. But Megan saw that beneath the neglect and the broken plasterwork, the rooms were well proportioned and light. It had the central location that was essential for Owen's work; and unlike most London houses she had seen, it wasn't too big and it wasn't too small. Also, peering through grimy windows, Megan spotted two very old, gnarled apple trees in the garden.

Owen came the following day and saw its possibilities. 'Almost everything needs doing,' he grumbled, still bristling with stiff-necked pride. 'If we got something already modernized . . .'

By-passing her mother, Megan spoke directly to Eddy in his office in New York, bawling into the phone. Eddy insisted on a professional inspection by a surveyor. He wanted her to have what she liked, he told her, but he didn't want her to make a mistake. If it passed muster, the house, which sounded like a bargain to Eddy who hadn't seen it, would be bought outright in their joint names.

'Eddy, you're a wonder. We can never thank you enough,' Megan yelled. 'I'll do everything you say.'

Within a month, the house was theirs and the builders took over.

Three weeks before the wedding, Megan and Owen turned up very late one evening to inspect the day's work, as they had on most days during the long renovation. Owen was by now as absorbed in every detail of what would soon be their home as Megan was. After they had spent an hour or so poring over the half-built kitchen, they locked up and went back to the car.

'Meg.' He turned to her. 'Do you mind very much if I drop by the hospital on the way home?' He looked drawn and serious. Megan had known all evening that his mind was only half concentrated on the house.

'Of course not. I've got to get used to this, haven't I?'

He squeezed her hand. 'I shan't be long.'

He parked, and disappeared behind swing doors. An hour later, when Megan was thinking of abandoning the car and jumping in a taxi, he came out. He muttered, 'Sorry', and started the car. They had almost reached the flat before another word was said.

'Was it something very bad?' Megan asked hesitantly.

'It will be.' He went on looking straight ahead. 'He's only forty. Two young kids, a good job. He's not going to make it. And there's nothing we can do about it. In ten years' time, perhaps we'll have progressed — things will be different. His wife was there, so I took her out into the waiting-room and sat her down and got her a cup of coffee and we talked — or rather, I did . . .' His voice tailed off. He slammed his hand hard against the wheel.

He went straight to bed and was asleep the moment his head hit the pillow. I might not have existed for him after he left the hospital, Megan thought, lying there — stiff and resentful. She hated the coldness that came upon him, excluding her utterly, whenever he thought he had failed or proved in some way inadequate. Still nursing her resentment, she turned on her side, away from him.

In the morning, he made love to her — so delicately that afterwards, still drowsy, Megan wondered if it had been part of a dream. She was asleep when he brought her a cup of tea, dropping a kiss on her forehead, shaking her shoulder and telling her that she had ten more minutes in bed and not a second longer. He was fully dressed, ready for work. Leaning back against the pillows, sipping the tea, she watched as he stuffed some journals into his briefcase. Happiness had narrowed her world down to that one small room.

'Owen . . .'

He looked up. His expression was tender — and vulnerable.

'What, my love?'

'I'm sure that you did help the lady last night, the one whose husband is so ill, that you did find the right words. I think it's because you care so much — about people and suffering — that makes you such a wonderful doctor.'

Late on their wedding night, as they were speeding down to London on the way to a honeymoon in France, exchanging notes on the day, Megan remarked, giggling, that it was too bad that Gwen and Vera had both been wearing outsize navy straw hats. Owen immediately saw the joke.

'I really should have tipped one of them off,' Megan said, when the fits of laughter had subsided. 'The trouble is, I only knew about Gwen's, but perhaps I should have dropped a hint to my mother. The hats kept clashing every time they got within a few feet of each other. Did you notice?'

He had – and they both started laughing helplessly again.

Gwen's promise of fine, warm autumn weather had held. That afternoon, the small church was packed with the locals and friends from London, smothered in beams of sunshine which slanted through high windows, and decorated with great drifts of wild flowers and berries from the hedgerows. Arriving on the dot, tight-lipped, holding Nellie by one arm, and Ted by the other, Vera swept them through to the front pew, looking neither left nor right. The tube of slithery navy crêpe that was her suit was topped by an enormous matching cartwheel hat. The Thomases were already seated; out of the corner of her eye, Vera could just glimpse the outline of Gwen's hat, so uncomfortably like her own. Owen was waiting a few feet away, standing very straight, no sign of nerves, the sun burnishing his hair. Nellie, who had looked out a mothy blue velvet dress left over from her days at the Mason's Arms, was in a daze, and none too steady on her feet. Her only concession to a new outfit was some full-blown pink silk roses, which she had seen in a shop window and thought just the thing to trim her old black hat.

There was an expectant hush, the whispering stopped, and the congregation rose. Like everyone else, Vera had half turned towards the aisle. Ted was fidgeting and craning to one side of her; on the other, Nellie mopped her cheeks and blew her nose. Then Megan, in airy white organza, appeared at the church door with Eddy, and as the organ swelled, they started slowly up the aisle.

Beneath the elegant exterior, Vera dissolved. Beyond her control, the feeling came in waves – unexpected, raw, as real as any physical pain. Megan was her daughter and she loved her; that was what this agony was about. Her gloved hands gripped the ancient polished wood. She was so young, so sure, so confident of the future; wholeheartedly in love – as she had been once. Would he be good to her, Owen? For all his brains and ambition, was he kind? Even Nellie thought him moody. There was some unsavoury liaison in his past, Megan had hinted. And was it enough, as Gwen Thomas thought, that Owen needed her so badly?

Vera watched stonily as Megan took her arm from Eddy's, handed her bouquet to Gill, her only bridesmaid, and moved to stand next to Owen. Nellie was sniffing openly then – and even Ted was still for a moment. Megan and Owen turned to each other, their profiles caught in the golden light, Megan's veil frosting her dark hair and cascading down into her train which spread behind; Owen's expression was rapt, as though in all that congregation only Megan existed for him. As Eddy turned back and edged into the seat beside her, next to Nellie, Vera's anguish stilled as suddenly as it had assaulted her.

Part 4

Friends and Neighbours

Chapter 19

Early one misty February afternoon, Megan Thomas sat in the kitchen of her Victorian terraced house in a leafy London crescent and wrote one word – 'Gin' – at the top of a list, then stopped and bit her pencil. Their new next-door neighbours were coming in for a drink that night and Megan, who had watched the comings and goings during the past months – a procession of workmen and decorators and much banging and crashing – with intense curiosity, was looking forward to it. She had caught glimpses of the husband, Alain Gesson, many times; she had recognized him at once from various television series he had presented, all to do with unusual homes and gardens and architectural features. But she had never once seen his wife, which struck her – domesticated and totally wrapped up in her home and family as she was – as decidedly peculiar.

It was to Alain Gesson that she had spoken when she phoned two days ago with the casual invitation.

'But we would be delighted.' There was an intriguing hint of an accent, certainly French. 'My wife is an artist and she has been working crazy hours changing her studio recently, which is why I've been dealing with all the moving. But we will both be installed here permanently as of tomorrow, with our son, Peter.'

'I believe he's about the same age as our Harriet – Daisy's younger. Do bring him, won't you? We'll expect you at about seven, then.'

That night, after they had checked that even Harriet, who would read by torchlight under the bed-clothes until any hour, was asleep, Megan said to Owen, 'I'm longing to meet them properly – the Gessons, I mean. It's nice to think that there will be a child living next door. And Harriet's so ahead of herself for her age that she and Peter will probably get on. Do you suppose it's because she's an artist that Mrs Gesson, whatever her name is, doesn't bother with the house – even the decorating?' She stared at her reflection in the oval dressing-table mirror. 'I've never seen her around, so she can't have had much to do with the renovation. And we know that it was in quite a bad condition – it hadn't been touched for years.'

Owen, who had been riffling through a pile of medical journals which inevitably, and to Megan's irritation, found their way from his study to their bedroom, came over and dropped a kiss on the top of her head.

'Not everyone is the dedicated homemaker you are, and one of nature's born mothers,' he said affectionately, teasingly. 'We can't all be alike, now can we?'

Their eyes met in the mirror. Even now, something happened to Megan's heart when she knew that she had his full and undivided attention. With growing professional pressures and demands on his time – and he was rapidly gaining recognition in his field – he was so often harried and remote. Megan never knew how he kept up the hours he did – ward rounds at the crack of dawn, the operating theatre, teaching, private practice; he would often slip back to the hospital to see a patient after they had eaten or been out to a party. But now, for these seconds in the dusky mirror, he was hers, completely. Her smile, so like Nellie Bowen's, lit up her eyes.

Megan occasionally said, in fanciful moments, that Owen had the look of a medieval knight minus the armour: there was something in his bearing, his watchfulness and his still remarkably red hair that reminded her of some painting she had seen long ago in a museum and only half forgotten. Nellie had always said that he looked 'distinguished', even as a young man; now an eminent cardiac surgeon, sure of his skill, pushing back medical frontiers, he had grown into her description.

Megan leant back against him and took his hands, holding

them tightly under her chin, her face tipped towards him above the blue and white stripes of his pyjama sleeves.

'But *you* like me as I am — as a homemaker — don't you?'

She had gone on working at the agency until just before Harriet was born. And now that Daisy was at school, she did sometimes think about picking up the threads of her old job in the dizzy, competitive world of advertising. Her mother, who was still roaming the world with Carl, picking up esoteric artefacts for their astonishingly successful business in New York, made no bones about what she thought. 'What on earth do you find to do all day, Megan, hanging about that little house? Surely a man like Owen expects a more interesting type of wife?' she would say, exasperated, before dashing off, much too thin in her funky, fashionable clothes and expensive accessories, to meet the unctuous Carl at some gallery or other. But it was Owen who had wanted a full-time wife and had never liked the idea of her working in the first place; who had blamed Margot for filling her head with odd ideas.

'But don't you, Owen?' she insisted, squeezing his wrists more tightly. 'Truly?'

'Truly.' He began kissing her neck, nudging the strap of her nightdress off her shoulder with his chin. 'And now come to bed, my pretty one, at once, before I go right off to sleep . . .'

Later, Megan lay awake watching the soft play of the street light against the drawn curtains. She always treasured these quiet moments — warm, loved, drowsy, the children asleep upstairs. Safe. It was when she let her mind wander freely where it would; on important things that somehow got lost in the press of her daily routine.

On the nigglings she had begun to feel, but stifled, about getting another job; on her mother, and the brittle coldness between them. Essentially, nothing had changed since the pact Vera had forced on her in New York; however Megan manipulated a conversation, even when they were alone, she had never managed to reopen the scorching, dangerous topic of her father. Whenever she tried to talk to Vera, intimately, she came up against a stone wall: an impasse that Vera deliberately maintained. Aware of time passing, the panicky desire to know who her father was now, before it was too late, haunted Megan increasingly, more than even Owen knew, coming upon her at odd moments when she was driving the children to school or shopping in the supermarket.

She sighed and moved closer to Owen.

'Don't forget that the Gessons are coming for a drink tomorrow,' she whispered into his naked back. 'Will you check before you go in the morning? Leave me a note if there's anything I need to get.'

And Owen, who through years of habit had perfected the technique of simultaneous sleeping and waking, muttered that he would, turned over and gave her a last, quick kiss.

He was up early, soon after six, instantly clear-minded, moving deftly in the greyness of the murky February morning. Megan hardly stirred. When he had dressed, he ran down to the kitchen, collecting the papers from the hall on the way, and made himself a cup of coffee. He then went into the dining-room to check on the drink supplies.

Crouching by the sideboard, he heard, as he had expected, a thud at the bottom of the stairs. Seconds after, Harriet's wiry body was beside him.

'What are you doing?'

'Seeing what we've got to drink. Mum has asked the Gessons in tonight.' He turned, pleased and amused that she was with him; obscurely glad that they were the only ones awake in the household. She had outgrown the pink flannel pyjamas and her skinny arms and legs protruded. Beneath the carroty hair, her face – the greeny-grey eyes under well marked, upswept eyebrows – was so like Megan's. But her incisive mind and her impatience with social niceties were, Owen hazarded, entirely after his own heart. 'You're up very early, young lady.'

'They've got a boy, the Gessons have. I've seen him. He's always chucking a ball about. I think I've seen his mother too. Just once. If it *was* her I saw, she's potty.'

'Harry...' This was his pet name for her; nobody else ever used it. 'You can't possibly know anything of the sort. Look — it's a cold morning and you've got nothing on your feet.'

'Potty,' she repeated. 'How much will you bet me?'

'Nothing at all. It's against my Welsh nonconformist principles, and it should be against yours too.'

They went back to the kitchen where Harriet took out the cereal, and for a few minutes they sat companionably. A large and dignified black cat stalked around the russet tiled floor, hoping for breakfast but too proud to make a fuss.

'Who are you cutting up today, then?' Harriet asked conversationally through a mouthful. 'Anything particularly interesting?'

'Well, I've got a very full schedule...' Owen's mind was already beginning to focus on the problems of the day ahead.

'I hope you don't find something nasty that you hadn't expected or get a real bleeder.' Harriet already had a rudimentary grasp of modern surgical methods. 'We've got a maths test today — easy-peasy. Any chance of more pocket money if I come top?' She splashed on more milk and Owen consulted his watch.

'I'll think about it. Oops — time I was off.' He got up and pushed his chair in. 'I'll be late for my rounds and Sister will have the hide off me.'

'Ha, ha, ha.' Harriet was well aware of the aura of power, almost deification, which surrounded eminent consultants in London teaching hospitals, particularly if they were relatively young and personable. 'Anyhow, don't be late for the Gessons.'

'Which reminds me...' Owen stopped at the door, briefcase in hand, and turned back to Harriet. 'Tell Mum "gin" — don't forget. Have a good day in school, and good luck in the maths test.'

While Harriet moved competently about the kitchen, Megan went up to the floor above and tiptoed into Daisy's room. For almost a minute, she stood looking down at her — smiling indulgently, knowing she had to wake her, yet loath to disturb the sweetly sleeping cherub that was Daisy Thomas. She was lying on her back, open-mouthed, pink-cheeked, her fists clasped somewhere near her silky hair which was yellow as butter.

'Daisy,' Megan said softly, bending over her. 'Wake up. It's time to get up.'

Eyes like blue moons opened slowly.

'No,' whimpered Daisy. 'Please no.' She turned on her side, closed her eyes and stuck her thumb in her mouth. Megan opened the curtains as noisily as possible.

'Yes,' she said, with a briskness she didn't feel. 'Up you get. Harriet is ready and unless we get a move on we're going to be late. We have to pick up the others today.' Daisy snuggled further into the bedclothes, and Megan could feel the resolve, which she frequently summoned when dealing with her younger daughter, begin to crumble. In addition to her not having a career, her mollycoddling of Daisy was her mother's most frequent — and shrill — criticism; Owen, too, was disapproving. She whispered, 'If you get up this minute, Daisy, I'll help you.'

By the time Daisy was dressed and stumbled into the kitchen behind Megan, Harriet was buttoning up her coat.

'I'm off. Hi Daisy — late again ...' Harriet, after years of pleading, now took the bus to school and back. Daisy shot her sister a baleful look and rubbed her eyes. 'Coffee's on the table ... and the post has come. There's a letter from Vera,' she said importantly. Harriet idolized her grandmother, who treated her as an intelligent adult of much her own age. 'Are you going to open it?'

She stood, challenging, agog to hear any snippet of news. But Megan, who was increasingly out of sympathy with her mother, thinking that she should chuck Carl and the globe-trotting/antiques nonsense and stay put in New York with nice, dear, neglected Eddy, snapped, 'Later, Harriet,' and stuffed it in her pocket.

Harriet put her head in the air and threw her scarf over her shoulder. 'I'm off,' she said, shooting up the stairs and banging out of the front door.

Megan immediately remembered, guiltily, that Harriet had a

difficult test today, and that she should have wished her good luck.

'What kind of cereal do you want, Daisy?' she asked irritably.

'Don't know.' Daisy was slumped at the table, still half asleep, in her regulation navy skirt and sweater and crisp white blouse. Megan had brushed her hair and pushed it back in a navy headband above the soft blonde fringe.

'Well, make up your mind,' Megan said sharply, glancing at the clock on the dresser. 'We're late enough as it is.'

Daisy blinked, removed her thumb from her mouth, sat up straight and smiled angelically across at her mother.

'I'll have whatever you're having,' she lisped.

By two o'clock, Megan had finished her chores and was back in her big, homely kitchen – and paused, wondering whether to give Nan a ring now or wait until the children were back from school. Nellie was still living alone in Trout Lane, and although she lied cannily about how she spent her days – 'off to the shops, I were, this mornin'' – Owen was getting worried about her. Megan trekked over regularly once or twice a week, bringing food and staying to chat, but Nellie was terribly confused, living more and more in the past. Frowning, Megan got up to go to the phone – when it rang.

'Mrs Thomas?' Megan immediately recognized the flat tones of the secretary/receptionist in Owen's Harley Street consulting rooms.

'Oh, hello, Iris.'

Megan could never put her finger on why this should be, but whenever Iris phoned, she invariably felt a frisson of dismay and the desire to cease speaking to her as soon as possible. She often thought lovingly of Mrs Butter, who had been with Owen from his first days as a junior consultant. Since Iris's arrival about two years ago, introduced by an acquaintance – Megan never bothered to find out who – just as Owen's patience with Mrs Butter was running out, his schedule ran like clockwork. And because of this, he accomplished a good deal more every day. But Megan still missed Mrs Butter: appointments may have occasionally been muddled, and Owen wasn't certain of being in the right place at the right time; but Mrs Butter would always manage to tip Megan off, tactfully, if something had gone wrong and he was in a bad mood; and she was invariably cheerful and sympathetic. As a young woman, learning to be the wife of a much-sought-after doctor, coping with two demanding children, Megan had good reason to be grateful to the motherly Mrs Butter, whatever her secretarial shortcomings. Now there was the saintly Iris . . .

Iris was always polite, always calm; controlled even when she had to relay the inevitable news of emergencies. The perfect receptionist, admirably efficient, but wholly unmemorable: nice-looking but inclined to be sallow, her face was devoid of any expression. Even over the obligatory Christmas drink, Megan found it impossible to get to know her any better. She seemed to have no personality whatsoever. She came from South Africa and was separated from her husband who had returned to Cape Town. She had no children and she lived alone: that was all Megan knew about her. But without her, and with important commitments all over London, Owen would be lost. Megan told herself this often, yet she could never prevent her instinctive, negative reaction.

'We have guests this evening, Iris, at about seven.'

'Which is why I wanted to have a word,' Iris interjected smoothly. Megan drooped. 'Mr Thomas is running a little late, nothing out of the ordinary, and he hopes to be back by eight.'

'I see.' However many times this happened, Megan was never able to keep the disappointment out of her voice. 'Well, thanks for letting me know.'

Megan sighed. She would phone Nan when the girls were home after all.

'Damn, damn, damn,' she said aloud to the ticking clock and the gently purring machinery. '*Damn.*' Resentment pricked uncomfortably as it did more and more often nowadays. Owen's absences at crucial times were something, she frequently told herself, that she must be grown-up enough to accept. He was achieving everything he set out to do long before she met him —

his students, his patients and his nursing staff would follow him anywhere; and she had been under no illusions about the life of a doctor's wife, a doctor like Owen, when they married. But on that hazy, chilly afternoon, she thought, a trifle sourly, that while Owen Thomas might be 'God' in his operating room, it was a very good thing that he had a wife willing to keep the earthly home fires burning for the sake of everything — and everyone — else in his life. Gwen, she knew, would agree.

Remembering the gin and Daisy's car run, she grabbed her anorak and car keys and she was slinging her bag over her shoulder, when something smacked — hard — into the kitchen window, at semi-basement height. Reeling back, Megan thought it must have been a ball. Seconds later, a dark head and a boy's face, large-eyed and serious, appeared, looking down to where she was standing. Recognizing the Gessons' son, Megan smiled up at him and opened the window.

'I'm most terribly sorry,' the boy said. 'I was mucking about. I get home from school early on Wednesdays.'

'Don't worry,' Megan told him warmly. 'No harm done. Jump down and get it. I was just going out, so I'll come and see if you've found it.'

He was waiting by the front steps.

'Hello, I'm Megan Thomas.' She held out a hand, holding her anorak closed with the other. 'And you must be Peter.'

'Peter Werner-Gesson.'

'Hello, Peter.' Megan made a mental note of the double surname as they shook hands solemnly. He was a sturdy, almost stocky, boy and his straight hair was long, cut in a fringe. 'Did you find the ball?'

'Easily — sorry about that.' He shifted awkwardly from one foot to the next. 'I'm not doing games for a few weeks because I was ill after Christmas and my mother fusses dreadfully. And it gets so boring.'

'I'm sure it does. You'll have to meet my Harriet. She's very athletic, a real tomboy. Are you getting settled in the house?'

'Sort of.' He looked glum. 'We'd got everything the way we wanted, me and Papa and Bertha. But Mama's here now, so everything's a mess.' Suddenly looking more cheerful, he continued, 'I say, why don't you come in and meet Mama now? Oh do, – she'd love it.'

'Actually, your parents are coming over to see us tonight.'

'I know. I'm coming too. But do come in for a minute, please. I insist that you do.'

'I really can't stay long,' Megan told Peter, reluctantly following him up the path to their front door. She had wanted to look her best when she met the Gessons, not wearing grubby jeans and a sweater. And she would never have time to get the gin. As they passed, she saw that the almond tree by the gate was already in flower despite the freezing cold. 'I'm on my way to pick up Daisy from school.'

Peter leapt up the steps and pushed open the door. 'Mama,' he called. 'I've brought Mrs Thomas to meet you, from next door. Where are you?'

Wondering why on earth she had allowed this self-possessed young person to push her into such an embarrassing situation, Megan hesitated in the doorway. She looked inside – and took a step backwards. A woman with olive skin and a lined face and the figure of a teenager was crouched among the astonishing chaos which almost completely choked the hall right up to the high ceiling, flowed up the stairs and into the living-room on the right. There were crates and more crates, paintings, bronzes, chairs and tables, clothes bags and cases; an ornate chandelier was perched dangerously halfway up the stairs. Blinking dizzily, Megan saw that whatever way there might be through to the kitchen and the rooms downstairs was blocked by a huge, haphazard pile of women's shoes, perhaps fifty pairs. These were all a very small size – and extremely expensive.

'This is my mother,' Peter said. He sounded totally resigned in a manner far beyond his years.

The crouching woman rose at once in a fluid movement of considerable grace. She was wearing very tight white trousers and a large, pale shapeless sweater. Her tight curly hair, coarsely streaked with grey, stood right out from her head.

'Megan Thomas . . . how clever of Peter to have captured you.

I've been longing to meet you. Alain spied you the other day – and you're even prettier than he said.' She almost danced towards Megan, her arms outstretched, a radiant smile lighting up her face. 'Take no notice of all this. Peter bothers so. You see, I've never moved before, except to the place in France which doesn't count. Alain has been organizing – he's such a perfectionist – with Bertha, our housekeeper, who's visiting her sister in Germany. And now I've come and upset everything.' She started to laugh, peal after peal. 'Oh dear, oh dear, oh dear.'

Still standing by the door, Megan reached out and took her hands and began to laugh with her – happily, helplessly.

'I'm Zillah Gesson. But of course you know that, don't you?'

There was no need for Megan to have bothered about the gin in any case, as Alain Gesson arrived that evening carrying two chilled bottles of excellent champagne. He led the way through the creaking iron gate; like some curious sprite, cloaked in white velvet, Zillah darted up the path at his side; Peter followed doggedly. Within seconds of the bell ringing, Megan had thrown open the door and stood with the warm, lighted hall behind her – welcoming, ushering them in out of the bitter cold night. Daisy, bathed and rosy and ready for bed, was pressed close to Megan, clutching her hand, prepared for admiration. Harriet watched guardedly from the bottom of the stairs.

Alain deposited the bottles, gave Megan one of his most alluring smiles and bent and kissed her hand. 'This is such a happy occasion for us.'

'Like this afternoon,' Zillah interrupted breathlessly. 'Megan found me in all my stupendous mess – and we just laughed and laughed. I knew we were going to be friends from that second – and what an utterly divine child, *so* beautiful.' She lunged at Daisy, who raised her head against the silky black folds of Megan's dress. Her limpid eyes rounded. 'Daisy, I really *must* paint you – may I?' She crouched beside her.

'Yeth,' whispered Daisy.

'Hello, Harriet,' Alain said over Zillah's head. 'Have you met Peter yet?'

Peter, looking owlish, emerged from behind his parents and he and Harriet shook hands solemnly. Daisy, satisfied that she had made her intended effect, went sweetly off to bed; Harriet led Peter down to the kitchen; and Megan, still pleasantly flustered by Alain's gallant greeting, took the Gessons into the drawing-room.

'But what a perfectly charming room,' Alain said at once, looking round. 'Look, Zillah.' Pale coral walls blended with the chintzy polished cotton curtains, which were drawn against the cold and the darkness. The fire leapt, bathing the room in flickering shadows. Above it was an enormous, ornamentally carved and gilded mirror, found by Gwen in a house sale soon after they were married, and now the dramatic highlight of the room; pictures and ornaments that Megan – and Gwen – had collected over the years added warmth and colour. It was an attractive room by any standards – and even Vera Mortimer grudgingly approved. 'It's very ordinary, of course,' she had said on her last visit, swaying about on teetering heels, peering at a picture and looking hard at a chair. 'But the colour does help against London's awful greyness.' She was, Megan knew, itching to get her hands on it. Believing herself – and the idolized Carl – to be the last word in house decoration, Megan could tell that she was dying to do some drastic rearranging. But she gritted her teeth over that, muttering to herself, Not in my house, over my dead body you will.

'I must apologize for Owen,' Megan was saying as Alain began opening the champagne. 'His secretary phoned this afternoon to say he'd been delayed.' She looked disconcerted. 'He's usually on time these days, so something exceptional must have happened.' She accepted a glass from Alain. 'Anyhow, he won't be long, and I can't tell you how delighted we are that you've moved in next door.'

Alain turned towards her, his back to Zillah – who was now draped full length on the Victorian chaise longue. He raised his glass, his eyes, above the rim, never leaving Megan's.

'We also ... And what extraordinary luck to have acquired such a very pretty neighbour. Such an aesthetic sight to watch you coming and going. Estate agents never tell one important things like that.'

Colour crept into Megan's cheeks. He was a charming man, this Alain Gesson – he had a way with him all right; she had read something of the sort in the papers when his television shows were running. Bending very slightly towards her, holding her look almost mesmerically, he made her feel, at that exact moment, that she was the only other person in the world as far as he was concerned. It was his being French, Megan supposed vaguely, smiling back at him, the champagne bubbles tickling her throat.

'Alain, come back here,' Zillah called imperiously behind him. 'There's so much I want to know – and we must tell you about *us*, Megan, *everything*,' she continued, shaking her head, and her hair, from side to side.

Accustoming herself to Zillah's exaggerated manner of talking – which Alain would temper from time to time – Megan learnt quickly that they had lived at the top of a very large London house, her father's; and when he died, quite recently, they decided that it was unmanageable. Hence the move to Somerset Crescent, now a much more fashionable residential neighbourhood than when Megan first saw it. 'We have the place in France as well,' Zillah said, waving an arm, 'near Perpignan. That's what Alain wanted, and my father quite understood. So he and Alain found it, and dealt with everything.'

'I see,' said Megan, looking blank.

Alain, who was now sitting close to Zillah, shot her an amused look.

'We have been spending a lot of time there since my father-in-law's death. When he was ill, he naturally depended on having us around all the time,' he explained. 'The French house is a manor farm, terribly romantic, and it's the most fantastic toy for me, of course. I've adored all the renovation. And Zillah has a studio set up now. You feel well there, Zillah, don't you?'

'Oh yes,' she agreed, her face radiant. 'Wonderfully, marvellously well. And I can paint like a dream. The light, the light ... Otherwise I can't always, can I?' Her voice rose unnaturally high

– and Megan caught a note of hysteria. Zillah clutched at Alain with childish fingers, bitten to the quick, as though begging for reassurance. It occurred to Megan that Alain's demeanour towards his wife was one of patient parent to a wilful, highly strung child.

'All artists work well in good strong light, Zillah,' Alain said pleasantly and firmly. 'You're no different from any of the others in that respect.' Then he deftly changed the subject to Owen's work.

'They're performing miracles on the human heart these days,' Megan said simply. 'Owen says that himself – as though even he can't quite believe how fast they're progressing.'

Zillah's hand was still locked on to Alain's arm. 'It's that light in France, I must have it,' she exclaimed feverishly. 'You know that, Alain, don't take me away from it, don't . . .'

Megan watched uncertainly.

Zillah had begun to tremble and as Alain put his arms around her and held her briefly, he and Megan exchanged looks above the tawny grey bush of her hair. Megan was astonished to feel a jolt of sexual energy. Then, as quickly as it had erupted, Zillah's capricious mood evaporated. She lay back, perfectly calm, as Alain got up to refill their glasses. And the talk among the three of them turned to schools and the theatre and the most convenient shops in the neighbourhood. Zillah was speaking quietly and sensibly; sitting across the fire from them, Megan fancied that Alain was breathing easier. He was relieved – about something. She also noticed that there was a good deal of white in his coal black hair.

Harriet, drinking squash and playing patience with Peter in the kitchen, was the only person in the house to hear Owen's car pull up. She had been listening, bored, to Peter droning on about his grandfather.

'He had his own bank, the Banque de Werner, and he was brilliantly successful. He knew everyone, even royalty. But he didn't have anyone to carry on after him – only my mother – so I took his family name as well. I'm his heir.' He added, 'So I suppose I'll have to be a banker, too.'

That's Dad, Harriet thought, hearing his key in the lock. Not to be outdone, she said airily, 'I've got the most amazing grandmother called Vera. She lives in New York. She used to be an actress and she looks a bit weird. She's married to a nice man, Eddy, who's got lots of money. But she's got a partner, a creep called Carl, and they run an art business. They go round the world, buying up hideous things which they sell on to other rich people.'

'I know the type,' said Peter respectfully.

Even Megan, deeply engrossed in a discussion about a play they had all seen, was taken by surprise when the door opened and Owen appeared. She jumped up, pulled him in and introduced him rather too gushingly; Alain poured him a glass of wine. Megan saw at once that Owen looked white and strained – and made a mental note to ask what had gone amiss. He never, or rarely, felt himself quite good enough professionally – no matter what he was doing. Megan was always amazed at this bottomless insecurity under the controlled and competent exterior, despite the reputation he was establishing.

He sat in his usual chair, a little way away from the rest of them. For some reason, his presence jarred. Although Alain, backed up by Zillah, made considerable efforts to draw him out and ask pertinent questions, Owen didn't give very much of himself that night. Megan believed that he was profoundly upset and went over in her mind, beneath the bright conversation, why this should be. His brooding presence swamped the gaiety that had sprung up between the three of them, and soon, with promises of meeting again shortly, the Gessons collected Peter and went home.

Megan marched Harriet firmly off to bed, collected some glasses and went down to the kitchen. Her head was still whirling from the encounter with their exotic new neighbours and the vintage champagne. Owen was making a couple of important phone calls, so she laid the table and took the baked potatoes from the oven and set out the cold meat and salad. He hung up and immediately started dialling again. He looked over at her. 'This one will be quick, Meg. Owen Thomas here . . .'

From long experience, Megan wisely decided not to ask why

he was so late tonight, when he knew that they had guests they both wanted to meet. The reason would come out during the evening, naturally — or not at all. He had looked dreadful, standing there by the drawing-room door; she hadn't seen him so white, or so rigid — a sure sign of unresolved tension in Owen — for a long time. She must get him back to Wales, perhaps for the children's spring holidays, for as long as possible. He was always at peace with himself when he could look up and see his beloved Black Mountains.

When they at last sat down to eat, she said cheerfully, 'They're charming, the Gessons, aren't they?'

'Alain seemed pleasant enough. A bit of a dilettante, I thought, despite his television success and his architectural training. I suppose it's marrying into all that money.'

He slashed at the meat and helped himself to salad.

'Zillah's father, you mean?'

'That's right, I remember hearing about him. I believe he headed a big fundraising appeal at one of the hospitals here. A Jewish family — bankers . . .'

'I suppose Alain is Jewish, too. And Zillah's a very serious artist. I think I've read about her having exhibitions. She's amusing in a zany way, a bit odd.'

'She didn't look an entirely well woman to me,' Owen said heavily. 'What did Harriet make of young Peter?'

'I think she was impressed that he's going to inherit a bank. She said he wasn't too bad, considering he was a boy.'

But nothing lightened Owen's mood, or expression. So Megan got up and began clearing away, leaving him to the papers.

Just before the television news, Megan said, 'By the way, I had a letter from my mother this morning. Typed, and signed, by her assistant. And very maddening she sounded, too. It's Nan's eighty-fifth birthday in September, and she's making plans to come over for it. Eddy doesn't feel up to making the trip — he's been having some dizzy spells recently — so she's threatening to bring the ghastly Carl. Ted is stagestruck, apparently, and he's got a job in Summer Stock at the Cape which goes on until

October. All this was followed by a long list of instructions of exactly what I'm supposed to do – no please or thanks or anything like that.'

Megan didn't add, as she might have, that the innuendo was: underachieving housewife that you are, deal with this minor matter, so that the rest of us are free for weightier things. It occurred to Megan, when she first read it, that it was exactly the kind of letter you would dictate to an employee – never a daughter. And although she didn't feel like admitting it to Owen, at least not in his present frame of mind, this rankled badly.

After a moment or two, Owen said brusquely, 'Oh, do grow up, Meg. I'm sick and tired of hearing you carp about your mother. She's a busy woman, leads an active life.' He rustled the paper irritably. Megan turned and stared at the thatch of red, duller now, that was all that was visible of his head. 'It's the least you can do to make a bit of an occasion of Nellie's birthday. God knows if she'll twig what it's all about, but at least she'll enjoy the fuss.'

Megan bit her lip just in time to stop herself retorting that if anyone loved Nan – and looked after her well-being – it was she, and that she had always counted on his absolute support in her volatile dealings with her mother. It was one of the basic tenets of her life, going back to their beginnings. Owen's steadfastness, more than anything else, had made it possible for her to live with the dark mystery of her fatherless background which went on and on and on; and which she sometimes felt, in moments of extreme bleakness, would one day swallow her completely. Opening drawers and banging cupboards shut, she could feel tears pricking. After the exhilaration of the Gessons' company, she was finding Owen's unapproachable gloom, for whatever reason, particularly exasperating. And she saw his trivial championing of her mother's chilly letter, which he had not yet read, as a kind of personal betrayal.

Keeping a tight rein on her charging emotions, she came and sat on the big, comforting old sofa which had straddled part of the kitchen all the time they had lived there. Occasionally, they made half-hearted efforts to move it upstairs, but the television was on the shelf opposite — and it was so warm and familiar — that it stayed exactly where it was.

Leaning back into the shabby cushions, Megan said, deliberately casual, 'I never asked about your day. Did everything go all right? It was good of Iris to let me know you'd be a bit late. Because you hadn't expected to be, today, had you?'

Owen's whole body, which had been quite relaxed, tautened. He said tersely, 'For Christ's sake, Meg, surely you know by now that I can't be tied to times? Things happen that have to be attended to. An appointment in my rooms overran.' There was no explanation of the patient, or the type of problem, as there would have been once. 'It's in the nature of the job. And don't ever say you weren't warned.'

Stung by his vehemence, Megan caught her breath.'Owen, I only asked . . .'

For some moments, they stared at the television screen. An American president was making a speech at the United Nations; neither were aware of this or took in a single word. Then Owen's capable hand edged around her shoulders and pulled her towards him. He half fell against her.

'I do love you, Meg. You must believe that. I know I can be bloody difficult.' He was muttering desperately against her shoulder, the words torn out of him, as though in some private pain. And although she held him tightly, out of long habit, above him, Megan stared, unsmiling, into space.

It was when she was calling the cat in — catching her breath against the sharp night air — that Megan's thoughts turned from the unhappiness of Owen's mood and her mother's letter, back to Zillah and Alain Gesson. They were a charming, stimulating couple; she and Owen were extremely lucky to have them as neighbours. And she remembered, with a warm and pleasurable sexual thrill, the unexpected sensation of Alain's long, dark look.

Chapter 20

'Don't you ever miss it, the work?' Zillah asked, turning her intense stare on Megan. 'I mean, I wouldn't *exist* without being a painter – even with Alain and Peter. It's what makes me *me*, don't you see?'

Megan threw back her head and laughed. 'And there could only possibly be one Zillah,' she said affectionately.

It was a warm and sunny afternoon in early May, the beginning of the Gessons' first summer in Somerset Crescent, and they were sitting on the small patch of grass in Megan's pretty garden, waiting for Harriet and Peter to come home from school. Daisy had made the most of a snuffly cold and was kneeling a little way off, stringing blossoms into a crown, and Zillah had taken one of her rare days away from her studio.

Megan had been telling her, lightheartedly, about some of the campaigns she had worked on at the advertising agency, before Harriet was born, in what seemed to her now a different life. The agency had prospered and had been in the news recently when a large American firm had tried to take it over. Margot Spelling had succeeded in her career beyond what even she could have hoped when they were starting out together at St George's. She had been appointed to the main board, and Owen had seen an article recently referring to her as one of the most creative women in advertising in the country.

'I suppose I do miss it – sometimes,' Megan said, pushing her hair back with her hand and squinting over at Daisy. 'A lot of it was tremendously exciting – and the people were fun. I loved feeling that I was part of a group, all dedicated to doing the same sort of thing well. I suppose it's the people I miss most. My mother can't understand why I haven't got a job – she's always needling me about it'.

But what she couldn't very well tell Zillah, whose own mother had died young and who was the most undomesticated creature in the world, was that above all else she wanted to be everything that Vera Mortimer had not been: she wanted to create a happy home with the man she loved and raise their children. That, to Megan Thomas, was a fulfilled existence.

Despite their very different lives and outlooks, she had kept up her friendship with Margot Spelling, inviting her for dinner when they had a spare man, usually a doctor; despite a string of boyfriends, she had never married. And Margot, too, seemed to regard her as a relic from a bygone age, amazed that she wasn't itching to be back in the thick of things. They had lunched together a month ago, Margot dressed to the nines in a strict suit and a silk blouse, very assured, flying off to Chicago on business the next day, bursting with plans.

But it was Megan who had to rush off and pick Daisy up from somewhere, leaving Margot to finish her coffee alone, shaking her head. She had always thought Owen, however brilliant, a dry stick – although Megan seemed as keen on him as ever. It was Owen this, Owen that, quite as though she never had an original thought in her head. Knowing her capabilities, this infuriated Margot. Talk about lack of self-esteem ... And she was ruining that child Daisy, who could wind her round her little finger, in Margot's view.

Megan, happy in the warmth, in the garden which she loved, with Daisy playing placidly near by, stretched out luxuriously. She was used to Zillah and her intensity by now. They had immediately become close friends – available, never intrusive. Megan was positive that despite hundreds of acquaintances – and the Gessons were always out at the opera or the ballet or a series of parties in a single evening – Zillah had no close friends. For all her strange attraction, she was too eccentric.

She pulled her flowered cotton skirt up above her knees, kicked off her sandals and felt the warm new grass sliding between her toes. Zillah was dressed, as she usually was, in skin-tight white trousers and an oversize shirt. The lined, weathered little face – that looked as though it had lived through so much – always surprised Megan; it was as though it didn't belong to that lithe, small-boned body.

After a while, unknowingly echoing Vera and Margot, Zillah said, 'Perhaps you ought to go back to work – get in the swing of it again. You were obviously good at it – and talented.'

'I don't know about that – but I might, some time . . .' Megan was thinking what a picture Daisy looked by the trunk of the old apple tree. Delicate pink roses climbed up and round and through it, tumbling among the fresh green leaves. That had been one of her small gardening successes; even Owen, walking round one evening last week, had noticed. 'But I always seem to be busy with the house and the children. Honestly, I'm never bored.'

'You're perfect, Megan,' Zillah said simply. 'So calm, so good. It sounds mad, but I mean it. I admire you *totally* – so does Alain. Your house is lovely, so are the children. You can cook divine meals. You understand about gardens. You're incredibly pretty – more than that, beautiful, with those wonderful eyes and brows and skin: look, you're getting tanned already, a lovely olive, the way Alain does. Lucky Owen . . .'

There were times when Zillah was so unrestrained in what she said that it was embarrassing; Megan felt her a little out of control now.

'We're different, Zillah,' she said briskly. 'And we do different things. And you've got the treasured Bertha, remember.'

Bertha was an inheritance from the stately Werner household, who now took charge of all the Gessons – particularly Zillah. Because, to Megan's amazement, Zillah, who was incapable of being anything other than open and direct, did exactly as she claimed: she never lifted a finger in the house to do anything. Harriet, who was fascinated by Zillah, told Megan that Peter had never seen his mother make a cup of tea. He didn't think she knew where anything in the kitchen was kept. If she wanted a spoon, Harriet had continued, she simply waited until someone got it for her. Bertha dealt with everything – cleaning and shopping and catering and laundry and making some sense of Zillah's clothes, which she changed several times a day. Everything she took off, she left exactly where she was standing; several times, Megan had seen trails of shoes and shirts and underwear throughout the house, awaiting Bertha's care.

'Thank God for Bertha, as you say. Papa spoiled me rotten — but I expect you gathered all that. Alain looks after me now,' she said, like a confiding child. 'He and my father bought the place in France together. I was working on an exhibition at the time. I didn't even see it until they had decided on everything. It's not far from Perpignan, up in the hills. Alain has a great thing about that part of France because his father disappeared there in the war, just as Alain escaped to England. They had left their home in Paris, you see. His mother was killed in one of the camps, but his father . . .' She shivered. 'There's no trace. Alain has done everything, my father did too. But terrible things happened in those times . . .'

'Oh, Zillah, how dreadful, I'm so sorry.' Megan, appalled, turned from contemplating Daisy, who was growing restless. 'Poor Alain, I didn't know.'

'He doesn't talk about it much, not any more, not even to me. But my father understood. Alain's father was Pierre; we named Peter after him. And Alain hopes that some day he may discover something, or someone, in the district who knows *something*.'

'How lucky that your father . . .'

'That Papa was so rich? Oh, yes, but I've never known anything else, so I've never really thought about it.' She sat there like an urchin, with her boyish figure and her plain little face and her arms hugging her knees. 'Peter will inherit everything. He's such a serious little boy. We think he takes after my father in lots of ways.'

'But what I meant about your father, Zillah, was how lucky for Alain, for them both, that they were such good friends.'

'That's so true. They were like father and son from the first time they met, almost. And you could say that Papa found Alain for me — and that was as much as giving me my life.'

While Megan was trying to digest all this Zillah burst out

excitedly, 'I must tell you, I've got an amazing commission. Well, I suppose you could call it a commission.'

'Zillah, that's wonderful. Is it another portrait?'

'Not this time — it's something quite different from anything I've ever done before.' Her eyes were glittering. 'I've been asked to paint the gardens of a wonderfully special house.'

'That sounds interesting, particularly at this time of year when there's so much colour. It's a challenge, Zillah.'

'Yes, yes it is. I expect I'll be terribly nervous. I always am when I'm not very sure about something. And Alain can't come, he's working on a new television project here.' She sounded terribly tense. 'He says I'll be all right, with friends.'

'Where is the house?'

'It's called Cloverley Court — in the West Country. It's a divine house, turreted, perfectly sited, Jacobean.'

'I've heard of it, I'm sure.'

'It belongs to the Brandon family. Now that Robert Brandon has been put out to grass politically, he's there all the time. His wife, Ceci, has done so much to restore the gardens. They're heavenly now — it was her project for years. And they fancy having some paintings done . . .' Her voice trailed off.

'Robert Brandon? Heavens, I am impressed. I must tell Owen.'

'We know them well, the Brandons, because Alain stayed there in the war, when he first came out of France. Afterwards, he lived with a marvellous woman called Millie Frampton, in her cottage. We both love Millie. Alain adores Ceci, but he's not so keen on Robert. I don't think I am either.' She rested her chin on her knees and gazed, brooding, across the garden. 'I've been getting wicked vibes ever since I agreed to do it. And I'm jittery, jittery . . .'

They were sitting like that, not speaking, when the kitchen door banged open and Harriet and Peter, coming home from school on the same bus, came bounding down the steps.

Having dinner with Owen that night at a local restaurant — her skin golden against a bright pink dress — Megan was vivacious and talkative, full of interesting bits and pieces she wanted to share with him. First, she told him about Zillah's commission to paint Sir Robert Brandon's gardens; then something of Alain's tragic background, which Zillah had disclosed during the afternoon.

'She implied that her father had found Alain for her — "and that was as much as giving me my life," she said. What on earth could she have meant by that?'

'What was that?' Owen, who had been studying the menu, looked round for the waiter. 'Zillah is given to exaggeration,' he said, smiling. 'I think we all know that by now. She doesn't seem very stable. I've no idea how she copes with all this socializing they do, let alone her work. Now what are you going to eat? Getting out to a restaurant on a week night must be some sort of a record for us.'

Once they had ordered, they conjectured about Alain's life, and his past, on and off through the meal . . . As well as Gill, who couldn't settle at anything for long, and was now teaching in Thailand . . .

They had spent several weeks in Wales in the late spring; since then Owen had looked a different man. His haggard expression had disappeared. He was calmer — and gentler. Certainly he had difficult days when appointments went wrong or he was futilely angry with himself. But in general, he was happier with his work — and more optimistic. Megan, too, had revelled in their time away. Her mother would never understand, not in a million years; but chatting with Gwen in her kitchen, the children tearing around outside, Owen putting his head round the door asking if there was a cup of tea going . . . This was the happiest holiday Megan remembered. It was all she ever wanted, really.

'You look as though you've just come back from the south of France, Meg — not two weeks in the Black Mountains.' Her hand was lying on the table and Owen covered it with his. 'Deliciously toasted — and pretty — and the pink with the eyes . . .'

Smiling, remembering how red his hair had been when she first got to know him, Megan moved her hand and twisted her fingers, hard, through his.

They walked home in the warm, sweet-scented dusk. Owen was talking unusually freely about his recent work: an article he had had accepted in a top medical journal; a paper he was giving at a conference in Boston, later in the month.

'This research I've been doing is being taken up, Meg. It could change my career structure considerably,' he said seriously. 'Heart by-pass surgery will be standard practice in a few years, we're all convinced of that...'

Contented, only half listening, Megan murmured something noncommittal. Because a thought that had been forming in her mind for hours had suddenly surfaced: she and Alain Gesson had something profoundly important in common — their fathers. Both of them were missing, or unknown. This seemed a quite extraordinary fact to Megan. She thought about mentioning this to Owen — but obscurely, decided against it. Hugging the knowledge to her, she shivered, pleasurably.

They walked on, Owen's mind still on his work. Turning into the crescent, Megan said, 'I was wondering, Owen. You're so dependent on Iris these days to keep everything running smoothly: don't you think we ought to ask her for dinner one evening?' She remembered, almost guiltily, her lovely afternoon in the garden with Zillah and the children. 'Her family is in South Africa — perhaps she's lonely in London.'

'Look, Meg,' Owen said forcibly, holding her arm more tightly. 'She's my secretary-cum-receptionist. She's good at her job. I'm lucky to have her. There's no need whatsoever to start inviting her to the house. All right?'

'I only thought...'

'Meg — don't.'

When they had finally seen the last of Bertha, who was baby-sitting, they went upstairs. Owen came very close behind her, his arms around her waist. Not even bothering to look in on the children, they went straight to their bedroom. They were standing in the semi-darkness, Owen kissing her neck, Megan pressed against him, when his bleeper went off. Reluctantly, they pulled apart. Owen muttered 'Goddamn' and automatically reached for the phone by the bed. He spoke a couple of brief sentences, grabbed his keys and blew her a kiss.

'Don't run away before I get back.'

Chapter 21

Megan was never sure afterwards why, but the moment she saw Alain standing on the doorstep at ten o'clock one morning some two weeks later, she knew it had something to do with Zillah. And she knew that it was serious.

'Megan,' he said, those dark eyes on her. 'Megan, I need your help.'

He was as elegantly dressed as ever; he was perfectly calm; yet she knew he was afraid.

'Zillah?'

'Yes. She's unwell. I have to go and get her, and I may not be able to manage alone. She may get hysterical – out of control. I won't know until I see her. Anyone strange would derange her. Can you come please, Megan?'

That word – 'derange'.

'Of course.'

A few days after their pleasantly idle afternoon in the garden, Zillah had disappeared down to the country. When Peter had wandered into the house the day before and was squabbling amicably with Harriet, Megan had asked when she was expected back. 'Soon,' he said. 'Papa says it depends how well her work goes. I think he's worried. You never do know with *her* ...' Megan had gone about making supper without giving it a second thought – except that she was vaguely conscious of missing Zillah's electric presence near by.

'Bertha will look after the children. Is that all right?' Alain asked quietly. Megan, who had just returned from dropping

Daisy at school, was already halfway up the stairs to collect her bag and a sweater.

'Of course.'

'Good – I'll explain when we're on the way.'

They slid out of London in Alain's powerful car. Manoeuvring through traffic, desperately agitated beneath despite his surface control, he hardly spoke. When they were clear of the worst hold-ups, he turned quickly to Megan.

'I'm terribly grateful for this.'

'You know I'll do anything I can. Zillah's having some kind of emotional crisis – is that it?'

The intensity of the moment and the confined space of the car seemed to draw them closer.

'Yes. We thought – we hoped – that she was stabilized for good.' He looked grim. Megan had never seen him devoid of gaiety before. 'But apparently that is not so. I'll tell you a bit about the background in a minute.' As they stopped at traffic lights, his fingers drummed impatiently on the wheel. 'She's down at Cloverley Court, you know, doing paintings of the gardens for the Brandons. That's where we're going.'

'She told me. I think she was rather afraid of it – of failing. She said it was a new direction for her as a professional painter.'

'She was excited. She felt it was an honour – particularly as we know the family so well. I spoke to her last night and she thought her work was good; she was pleased, she said. I admit I had been uneasy; I don't know why. I shouldn't have left her there by herself, I can't leave her – ever.' It was as though he was talking to himself, and his accent was more pronounced than usual. The strain of caring for Zillah, which Megan had suspected all along, was plain to see. The lines around his eyes cut deep. 'Ceci phoned this morning – Ceci Brandon. She had come down to breakfast and found Zillah sitting in that hall, staring into space. She wouldn't speak and she wouldn't move and she was holding ... but I'll come to that later.' His pain was almost physical. 'Ceci knows ... the history, so she phoned at once. And Millie Frampton is with Zillah now, thank God.'

'This has happened before?'

'Yes — very seriously, a few months after Peter was born. She had been terribly up and down — high one moment, weepy the next. The doctors said this was nothing very unusual. She had always been highly strung since she was a child. This was a continual worry to Amos, her father.' The car leapt down the empty motorway, eating up the miles. He glanced at his watch. 'We should be at Cloverley in a little over an hour.'

'It's not unusual, Alain, post-partum depression. I was very blue and mopey after Harriet, for absolutely no reason at all.'

'This was what we hoped for Zillah. But we were wrong.' Alain had gone very white and Megan had an imminent sense of dread.

'It's so terrible, I can hardly bear to think about it. But I believe I must tell you. You see, we know masses of people, but Zillah has never really had a woman friend — except you . . .'

It was an April evening, twelve years before. The beginning of spring at last, Alain had thought walking home from work and stopping to buy an armful of white, scented flowers for Zillah. Crossing into the square, he let out a huge intake of breath, releasing all his pent-up tensions . . . Zillah. She was getting a little better each day, please God. She had had a difficult pregnancy and a long, exhausting labour. But Peter Amos Werner Gesson, on arrival, had turned out to be large and sound and lusty. From the first, he ate well, slept well and thrived. Those dark winter months afterwards, when Zillah had cried for hours at a time, then rushed out on a crazy buying spree — only to come home and start crying again — were receding into the past. She was a lot brighter, funnier: more like her usual gamine self. On good days, she was even talking about starting to paint again.

Amos Werner had watched his daughter's condition over the months with despair. Active, powerful and agile-minded, over this — his daughter — he was helpless. Doctors were consulted, and an experienced nurse engaged to look after Zillah and the baby, who was already the apple of his grandfather's eye. Alain, deeply fond of his father-in-law, delighted in this.

'He's growing up into such a nice young man,' Megan said quietly as Alain stopped talking to concentrate on the driving. He smiled at her quickly, warmly – and continued . . .

That morning, before he left for work, when Zillah was looking out of the window at the row of pink blossoming trees and drifts of daffodils, she had suddenly spun round.

'What a perfectly wonderful day,' she breathed, her hands clasped beneath her chin and her eyes brilliant. 'I feel really well again. Oh, the bliss of it . . . I can't tell you, Alain. I'm going to give Nurse the afternoon off. I'll take the baby to the park and give him his bath – and stop being a hopeless, weepy nuisance of a mother. I'm well, Alain, whole and well.'

She ran over to him and twined her arms around his neck. Her body had quickly regained its suppleness and she was thinner than ever. She looked like a teenager, far too young for motherhood.

'You're absolutely sure, Zillah?'

He was dizzy with joy and relief, wanting so much to believe her – and that his world was righting itself. So the doctors had been correct after all. It would pass, they said; it was not uncommon, this depression following childbirth, and given Zillah's nervy, artistic temperament, something of the sort might have been anticipated.

'All right then,' Alain agreed, smiling at the radiance her enthusiasm always generated – like the halo round a burning candle. Zillah's intensity, combined with her ethereal looks, always had the power to move him.

So Nurse was summoned and given an unexpected afternoon off. And Alain left the flat with Zillah's laughter floating out behind him. She was giving Peter his bottle, enjoying holding her son and watching him smile; and for days on end she hadn't even wanted to see him.

During an early afternoon meeting, Alain slipped back to his office and phoned his father-in-law. Soon after their marriage, Amos Werner had suffered a severe heart attack and although he was making a good recovery, he spent more and more time in his study at home these days, minions from the bank arriving in relays. Yes, indeed, he soothed, Zillah had taken Peter out for an airing. He had watched her through the window, pushing him in the big dark-blue pram up the square in the direction of the park. She had run down to see him earlier in high spirits and promised to bring Peter to visit after she had given him his bath, at about five o'clock. So perhaps Alain could get back from work earlier this evening and join them?

It was soon after five when Alain let himself in the front door. Hearing no sounds in the bottom part of the house, he climbed the stairs to the flat above.

'Zillah,' he called. 'Zillah, I'm back. Where are you?'

Silence.

'Zillah?'

Puzzled, he glanced around the living-room, then the dining-room; put his head into the kitchen — nobody there. He went on up the curving stairs to the bedrooms. He was sweating now and his mouth was dry. On the top landing, the carpet was wet. He followed the dark, widening stain to where water was seeping out from under the bathroom door. He banged it open.

'Zillah . . . Oh my God . . .'

She was lying naked in the bath, which was gently overflowing. Her eyes were closed. Her head, slumped sideways, was bobbing just above the water line and her hair floated, soaking wet, in water that was a faint, but deepening, rust colour.

In one moment of absolute horror, all feeling left Alain. He reacted instantaneously. He lifted her out and laid her on the floor and bit and tore at pieces of towelling, kneeling, clumsily binding her wrists. He pulled at another towel, covering her up to her chin; the white flowers he had dropped scattered around her among the crimson splashes. Near her head, something glinted on the white-tiled floor. Racing to the phone, his whole being pounding and pounding, he glanced in at the nursery. Peter was tucked in his cot, turned on his side, sleeping peacefully. Seconds later, an ambulance was on its way to the house.

*

She would live; she was in no physical danger. They were told that at once. The wound on one wrist was relatively superficial; the other, severing an artery, more serious. If Alain had not arrived when he did, it might have been another story. But the underlying problem, the terrifyingly destructive depression, was what had to be tackled. And this would take time, perhaps a lot of time, once the first shock of Zillah's attempt to take her life had worn off.

Until late into the night, Alain and Amos Werner – who had insisted on coming with them to the clinic in the ambulance – sat on either side of her bed, not talking, not taking their eyes off Zillah's closed, white face. Her wrists, now expertly bandaged, lay still on the sheets. When at last they left, driven back to the house, they went straight to the study, to the room where they had held their first lengthy conversation and where Zillah had burst into Alain's life. It was then that Amos Werner told Alain what he had long suspected. Zillah's mother had not died tragically young of a cerebral haemorrhage as he had implied; Magda Werner had killed herself at the beginning of the war, separated from her family in Hungary, unable to face the future.

'But how dreadful, and how terribly sad, for *all* of you – Zillah, her mother . . . it's as if she's living under her shadow,' Megan breathed.

'Exactly.'

'Does she know – that her mother killed herself?'

'We're not sure, not even the doctors. She was sent to the country the week before it happened. Her father did everything he could to keep it from her. But I think she knows – and Amos did, too.'

Megan could hardly take in everything Alain had told her – the drama, the heartbreak, the poignancy. She longed for Owen and his calm professionalism. 'You can never really tell about people,' he said sometimes, when he was lying awake in bed very late, worried about some diagnosis. 'You can never get inside their heads, however well you know them. Sometimes it's the same with bodies, even now. We never really know until we get inside.'

Alain continued, 'The worst of it is: where do we go from here? We've tried it all – drugs, talking, electric shock, more drugs. It's all taken the hell out of her physically – you can see that – but we've been able to contain the mood swings since. And here we are again, suddenly, after all that, back where we started.' Despair ran through his voice like a thread. 'I've already spoken to the psychiatrist. We'll get her back, if we can, and take her to the clinic and they'll admit her straight away. Peter will have to be told.'

'He can stay with us, for as long as he wants.'

Alain took his hand off the wheel, picked up her hand and kissed it very quickly. Caught unawares by his touch, Megan drew in her breath. For the first time since she had seen him on her doorstep, he smiled. And there was a glint back in those deep dark eyes.

The countryside flashed past in a blur of leaves and ripening fields of corn and wheat. They had left the motorway and were on the edge of a market town.

'Cloverley – the village – is just a few miles on.'

They drove the last part without speaking. Megan was acutely aware of Alain's hands tight on the wheel. Pulling the car round, his shoulder brushed hers.

'Here we are.' The car nosed through wide gates and into open parkland. 'You'll see the house in a moment.'

They rounded a curve and there it was, Cloverley Court, with its turrets and pinkish weathered stone and oriel windows and intricate maze of gardens, all framed in the soft brilliance of the summer greenery.

Megan forgot the reason why she was here. She even forgot Alain, sitting so close beside her. She leant forward, her cheeks deepened to a wild rose colour.

'It seems to grow right out of the ground,' she exclaimed. 'As though it's part of nature, not man-made at all. It's the most enchanting house I've ever seen.'

Cecilia Brandon met them as they walked into the great, dark hall. There were at least three dogs yapping behind her. She came towards them, arms outstretched to Alain, and they embraced.

'Millie came at once. She talked to her, and she took away the kitchen knife,' Ceci said in a hushed voice when they pulled apart. 'There was no problem about that. Millie's been superb.'

It wasn't that she ignored Megan, standing just behind; but totally absorbed as she was by Alain and the drama with Zillah, she simply did not see her. Megan, in any case, was looking about her, entranced — at the minstrels' gallery, the wide, shallow staircase, the intricately carved woodwork and the tiers of bosky family portraits.

'Forgive me.' Alain turned swiftly. The dogs were nuzzling around their ankles. 'Ceci, this is our friend and neighbour, Megan Thomas, who kindly agreed to come with me.'

'How very good of you.' Ceci turned her blaze of warmth and good looks on Megan, holding out both hands. She had put on weight again, and in middle age it became her; her face was remarkably unlined. Milky ropes of pearls were draped casually across her bosom; and in her long denim skirt and plain white blouse, she carried herself like an empress. 'Zillah spoke so much about you last week. She said that moving to the house next door to you, your doctor husband and your two little girls, had been such a pleasure. You particularly.' She went on holding Megan's hand. '"My friend Megan," she said, many times. And Zillah never has had friends in the ordinary sense, has she, Alain?'

'Zillah always exaggerates,' Megan said quietly, unconsciously echoing Owen. 'But we're all terribly fond of her. I was so shocked to hear . . . I had absolutely no idea . . .'

'But how could you have? And she's been fairly well for years, hasn't she, Alain? Come . . .' She began moving them forward with her effortless authority. 'Zillah is in the little study, with Millie. Why don't you go in — she's quiet as a mouse — and I'll get them to bring you coffee.'

'We won't stay long, Ceci,' Alain said quickly. 'The sooner we can get her medical care at the clinic, the better.'

'I understand.' She left them by a closed door in a pitch-dark corridor just off the hall. 'Just knock and go in.'

Zillah was curled into a lifeless heap in the corner of a deep sofa, her face hidden, the mass of her hair spread out. A very stout elderly woman sat on a straight-backed chair beside her, gripping a walking stick, swathed in a colourful cotton tent. Alain gave her an affectionate pat on the shoulder as he went to Zillah and put his arms around her.

Megan hung back.

'Come along in, my dear,' the older woman said in a warm country voice. She had a wonderful smile, radiating serenity and good humour. Despite the bizarre circumstances, her voice naturally hinted at laughter. *These things happen in life and we've got to make the best of it*, she seemed to be saying. Her grey hair was neatly waved and she wore thick glasses. Megan liked her instantly. 'Bring up a chair, do. I'm Millie Frampton and you must be Megan. I expect Lady Ceci's gone for coffee – or what they *call* coffee up here.' She sniffed. 'I daresay you could both do with a cup.'

'I honestly could,' said Megan, gone suddenly weak. She forced herself to look over at the limp, doll-like bundle that was Zillah. Alain was holding her like a child, but she had not moved or looked up or showed any sign that she was aware of their presence.

'Watch out for the dogs' hairs, dear, or you'll get covered. They're over everything in this house,' Millie Frampton warned cheerfully. The small room with mullioned windows was very untidy, all the furniture was dilapidated and shabby, and piles of country magazines and horsy memorabilia were flung about haphazardly. 'There now, she'll be better for having Alain close,' she said comfortably, 'Even if she doesn't show it.'

'I've never seen her – like this,' Megan whispered.

Millie Frampton put her hand on Megan's arm.

'The poor soul, she does suffer. Weeks and weeks she spent with me at the cottage while they were trying to get her right after Peter's birth. But you can't let it upset you too much: it does no good, least of all to her.'

Megan nodded and Millie went on in her friendly way, 'You must get Alain to bring you down some time, with Peter and your girls. Zillah was full of you all when she walked over to the cottage to see me the other day, before she took ill.'

'I'd like that,' Megan said, meaning it. Then, 'Was it so sudden – this, with Zillah?'

'Right out of the blue it was. She'd been nervous about the pictures, I know that, whether they'd approve of them and such like. I told her not to think twice about it. Lady Ceci thought them wonderful, she said so. And they're her gardens that Zillah painted —she's been the making of them, bringing them back to life, I can tell you. I'm not sure about Sir Robert. Modern art isn't his line. And he can be difficult – although she knew to take no notice.'

'But it was waiting to happen again,' Megan said softly.

'That's right – its the temperament. And it's a mysterious ailment.' On the sofa, Zillah was still curled against Alain, totally unresponsive. 'There are those who think it's a payment for Parnassus – the price of talent, you might say. But if you ask me, it's part of the whole person – like blue eyes or being able to carry a tune.'

A young woman arrived with a tray of coffee. Millie Frampton poured, looking thoroughly disapproving – and soon, Cecilia Brandon returned. It seemed that when Ceci came upon Zillah that morning, she had been holding a knife that she had taken from the kitchen. Her bed was undisturbed; she had clearly been sitting there all night. Millie Frampton, who had gone through much of the last depression with her, was there within half an hour. Nothing unusual had happened the previous evening, Ceci said; in fact, Zillah had been rather gay and talkative during dinner. Robert, it was true, had thought the paintings 'a bit messy and too modern', he said. 'But we all know Robert and his ways by now, don't we?' she asked, looking from Alain to Millie and back with some amusement.

It was decided that Alain would pack up a few of Zillah's things while Millie stayed with her, and then they would go straight back to London.

'And you come with me, Megan,' Cecilia Brandon said. 'Let me look after you and show you round.'

*

The morning was almost gone. Sun had broken through the haziness, and the house and grounds were flooded with delicate light.

'It's sad about poor Zillah, isn't it?' Ceci said, leading Megan back down the sun-dappled staircase. 'Ghastly for Alain, too. He has to bear the brunt of it. And he's looking wretched. It's a continual strain. Personally, I think he copes with it amazingly well.'

'I had no idea, before this morning.'

'Oh yes, she had a terrible breakdown after Peter was born. Between you and me, I think it's always a bit touch and go with her.' Ceci pushed her heavy hair back with her fingers. 'I always thought Zillah was too arty and ethereal a creature for Alain. But I suppose it was a suitable match in many ways, with their similar backgrounds. That sly old Amos Werner certainly thought so. It settled Alain down — he was quite a wicked lad . . .' Ceci laughed. 'And it seems to have been a happy marriage, in its way,' she added magnanimously. 'Although frankly, I think it's a pity that Alain has had to devote his life to being Zillah's minder.'

'He's working on another television series, I believe,' Megan said quickly.

Ceci raised her eyebrows. 'Really? He should really have been one of the best working architects in the country, if not Europe. He had it all — talent, charm, ambition . . .' She seemed to want to go on — but she stopped herself. She took Megan's arm. 'My dear, I'm not doing my stuff over the house. Robert would be furious: he's positively steeped in the place. Now up here . . .' And she pointed out a large portrait which dominated the panelled wall overlooking the stairs and the great hall. 'That's my husband's American grandmother, Cordelia. She's a beauty, isn't she? I'm wearing those pearls now.' Ceci gave her deep, throaty laugh. 'I expect she'd have a fit if she could see me like this, in my gardening clothes. But we're all rather fond of her, even the boys, who never notice much.'

When Megan asked, Ceci told her that their eldest son, James, was in Australia. 'He's mad about boats and he's started up his own business. Hiring out canoes and dinghies, we think. He was always tiresome, even as a child, so we're quite glad he's off there doing his own thing.' The second, Harry, was 'a tremendous help, especially to my husband, learning the estates'. And her youngest, the twins, were at university — one at Oxford and one at Cambridge, both scholars.

'Imagine,' she said to Megan, who was beginning to see why everyone always spoke so warmly of Cecilia Brandon. 'Imagine *me* having two brainy sons . . .' She gave a burst of laughter, thoroughly enjoying the joke. 'I'm almost completely uneducated; my parents never bothered, not with the girls. It was just dogs and horses and finding a husband. Honestly, I can hardly write my own name. And the twins are absolute brainboxes.'

After a leisurely walk through the gardens — which Ceci had restocked and replanned, and which Zillah had been painting — they came back to the drawing-room. The long, panelled room was filled with sunlight and gleaming patinas and great vases of brilliant spring flowers. Alain put his head round the door.

'I've got a couple of phone calls to make — one to Bertha, Megan, to keep in touch. And then we're off.'

'You won't stay for lunch, Alain? We would be delighted to have both of you.'

'Thank you, Ceci, but I think not.' He seemed less anxious. 'We should be on our way. Is that all right with you, Megan?'

'Of course. Let me know if there's anything I can do.'

'I will. But Millie's coping for the moment. And she's utterly passive this time, as you saw.' And he vanished.

Moments later, Robert Brandon strode in. After so many years of managing virtually on her own while he was totally immersed in politics, Ceci had never got used to having Robert continually about the place, poking his nose in where he wasn't wanted, always demanding, always on the edge of boredom.

'Oh, Robert, there you are.' She didn't sound particularly welcoming. 'This is Megan Thomas, Zillah's friend. Megan — my husband.'

Robert Brandon put out his hand. 'How do you do? But

haven't we . . .' He hesitated – quizzical, his head turned a fraction sideways. 'Surely we've met?'

'No, I'm certain not,' Megan smiled, taking his hand. A strikingly pretty young woman, poised and charming in a summery cotton dress. 'I know I would have remembered,' she said flatteringly.

He looked older than she recalled from photographs in the papers and on television. But he was still an exceptionally handsome man in his early seventies: vibrant, only a little stooped, with white hair springing back from his forehead. It seemed strange, to Megan, to see this public figure in domestic surroundings, however imposing.

'No? With your husband perhaps, somewhere?'

There was still something dashing about the way his mouth curved; an hypnotic look in his eye, the politician's glitter. Anyone, anywhere in the world, would take Robert Brandon, correctly, as an Englishman to the manner born; and as a man used to exercising power.

'I'm sure not.' Megan went on smiling, shaking her head.

'Your husband is a doctor?' Robert frowned. His instincts were still working away furiously. Some breakthrough, somewhere, refused to come. He was feeling unpleasantly breathless, too.

'He's a consultant surgeon at St James's.'

'Ah, yes, so Zillah told us. And a top man in his field. Heart, is it?'

'That's right.'

'I'll have to consult him,' Robert said, straightening, allowing a small, ironic smile. 'I've been having trouble with my ticker.' He patted his chest. 'Can't say I took to any of the fellows I saw – although I've been given the all-clear for the moment.'

'You should, Robert,' Ceci interrupted. 'We've heard marvellous things from the Gessons about Owen Thomas. I know he's a top man. I'm going to hold him to that, Megan.'

'Oh, you must,' Megan said, her face alight with warmth and sincerity. 'He's the best there is, really.' There was no mistaking her pride. 'He's giving a paper in Boston next week – and he's always having things published here. His patients would follow him anywhere. He has rooms in Harley Street, number twenty-seven.'

'I've gone one better,' Ceci said. 'I've already prised the phone number out of Alain, and I fully intend making an appointment. Leave it to me.' She smiled at Megan. 'They won't stay for lunch, Robert. Megan is going to sit with Zillah while Alain drives her to the clinic. But I'm sure we could all do with a drink.'

They sat in the large and beautiful room, sipping gin and tonics and making idle conversation about children and the weather and going abroad, waiting for Alain to reappear. Only Robert Brandon was aware of ghostly emanations hovering among them, just eluding his consciousness. Puzzled — feeling oddly disturbed — he stood in front of the mantelpiece which was crammed with an arrangement of pale, overblown tulips and a flurry of stiff white invitation cards. The cravat he was wearing instead of a tie gave him an elegant, slightly old-fashioned look. Megan sat on one of the large, formal sofas; and Ceci straddled the arm of an overstuffed brocaded chair, holding an excited dog with floppy ears on her broad lap, nuzzling its chin.

Robert Brandon's eyes returned to Megan's face and lingered . . . Thousands of people had passed through the kaleidoscope of his busy public life. And yet — no, that wasn't it.

When Alain came back, saying that Zillah and Millie were in the car and they were ready to go, they all stood awkwardly, in a group. Then Ceci took Alain's arm and walked with him into the hall, speaking to him intimately. Robert Brandon stood aside as Megan followed — and caught up with her.

'It's an extraordinary thing, Mrs Thomas . . .'

'Oh, Megan, please.'

'It's quite astonishing — Megan — how you remind me of someone, yet I can't quite place . . .'

'Perhaps you'll remember later, somewhere totally unexpected, in the bath or somewhere. That's what usually happens.'

They laughed easily and he touched her elbow as they came to the door, flung open on to the sunshine and the broad green spaces of the park.

'Perhaps . . .'

When they shook hands, Robert Brandon held on to Megan's just a shade longer than was necessary. He straightened and beamed the full force of his considerable charm right at her. 'And if I remember, as I expect I shall, I'll let you know — Megan.'

'Is there any particular reason, Ceci, why these potatoes are rock hard? Can no one in the kitchen even cook a potato any longer?' They were lunching alone in the huge dining-room, sitting at one corner of the table that had been known to seat eighteen. Robert Brandon, helping himself to more salad, sounded exasperated. Ceci took no notice and stifled a yawn with the back of her hand.

'Sorry,' she said briefly. 'Yes, they're almost inedible, aren't they? I must have a word with our present cook,' she said vaguely. 'The twins are coming down for the weekend with a couple of girls. And they're fussy about what they eat.'

Since Robert Brandon had left politics in a burst of valedictions, domestic duties had become largely unimportant to his wife. When people came to Cloverley, as they did — friends, journalists, television reporters, assorted statesmen — the place looked a dream and the drink was first-rate and plentiful. The food depended largely on the mood and inclination on whoever had been persuaded to do a stint of cooking. Ceci rarely bothered to supervise much, because it had dawned on her, in her early fifties, that it was no longer essential to devote her life entirely to Robert and his career. She had done that — and it had worked: the children, the two homes, the entertaining, the dutiful politician's wife. But she was still young enough and vital enough to want other things — for *herself* now. So while Robert charmed and pontificated — and at last put his mind to running the estates — Ceci spent a good deal of time up in London. It was an open secret in the county that she was having an affair with a farmer she had hunted with for years: Bert Woods, a sixty-year-old widower, with no pretentions of gentrification, who had farmed all his life and was well liked locally. Millie was all for it. 'Sir Robert's in a fury, so they tell me,' she had chuckled to Alain recently. 'Lady Ceci makes no bones about it, comes and goes from the farmhouse as and when she pleases. There's nothing to it, of course, just a bit of sex and good fun – and Bert's a decent man. It does his lordship good to have a taste of his own medicine for a change.'

'I wish you'd do something about it anyhow – the food.' Robert glared. 'I've got my agent coming tomorrow and I trust we'll rise to something better than this.'

'There's some marvellous cheese,' Ceci said, looking hopefully towards the sideboard. 'But I'll have a word with her about tomorrow. I shan't be here myself, I'm afraid.'

'London again?'

'That's right.' Sensing he was on the warpath, she reached for an apple. He was a dear thing, Robert, the only man in her life to count for anything. And he'd been divine, of course, years ago – madly attractive; lots of the young still thought he was. But he had hardly been a saint, and after all the years of loyalty and devotion, not to mention anguish, she had no intention of giving up Bert's bed simply because Robert objected. Tomorrow, they had planned to take in an agricultural show, have a good late lunch and who knew what the afternoon would bring . . .

'Pity. We're going over the details of a lecture tour in the States for the autumn. Mostly colleges, and in all the nicest places – New York, Washington, Boston.'

'The States? But I'd no idea.' Ceci put down her apple. 'That's splendid, Robert. But what do the doctors say?'

'Nothing – as long as I don't overdo things.'

'How absolutely marvellous. I'll come with you – may I? You always enjoy lecturing. It should be exciting, I adore New York – and we can see lots of old friends.'

It was the first time for several years that she had sounded genuinely pleased to be doing anything with him.

'I'd hoped you would, Ceci. I wasn't sure.' It was absurd to be relieved, almost humble – but he was. He loved her dearly, in his selfish way; he had depended on her greatly and still did. And he was starting to realize that even though he found the situation faintly humiliating, he would simply have to sit out the ridiculous Bert Woods affair and put up with her wanderings.

'Silly Robert...' She got up, stood behind his chair and put her hands lightly on his shoulders.

He found her later doing some weeding under the eagle-eyed supervision of one of the old gardeners.

'I remembered,' he called over to her. 'It suddenly came to me, Ceci, just like that.' He sounded elated, like a young man, and there was a spring in his step.

'What are you talking about?' Kneeling, Ceci stopped what she was doing and shaded her eyes with her hand. Earth from the flowerbeds had smudged her skirt; her splendid neck and arms were brown as berries. 'I simply don't understand, Robert.'

He strode around the paths towards her, his shoulders back and his head held high. 'Didn't I tell you? That young woman, Zillah's neighbour, reminded me of someone. I told her so, but I couldn't think who it was.'

'Megan? She's a remarkably attractive girl, I thought. Well, who was it?' He was standing directly above her.

'Cordelia Brandon.' He almost shouted it, triumphant. 'Don't you see?'

Ceci considered. 'That's funny, I pointed out her portrait to Megan this morning. It didn't strike me then.' She thought for a moment. 'But yes – yes, I think you may be right.'

When Alain dropped Millie at her cottage and sped off towards London, she went straight to the kitchen. Humming, she moved stiffly about preparing some lunch, trying to ignore the sharp twinges round her hips. In Millie's experience, any sort of human drama soon made for hunger. A pity, she thought regretfully, that Alain couldn't have stayed – and that nice, pretty Megan Thomas. But the sooner Zillah was back with the doctors who understood her illness the better. It often pained Millie to think what Alain went through with all her ups and downs, treating it like his destiny. Millie had a gut feeling that with prompt treatment, she was going to recover from this bout a lot quicker than the last. But with acute mental instability, it didn't pay to go looking too far ahead into the future.

Twenty minutes later, she sat down to a perfect cheese soufflé, fresh brown bread and a glass of dry, local cider.

Alain had arranged to deliver Zillah straight to the clinic. Utterly passive, like a sleepwalker, she gave no resistance; all the way up, she had sat in the car staring and wringing her hands, not saying a word. Once they had reached central London, Alain dropped Megan off at a convenient corner and she grabbed a taxi.

Unusually — it was only five o'clock — Owen was already home when she arrived. She saw his car parked outside the gate and moments later, he opened the door. Megan sensed, as she had so many times before, the particular qualities he had which made him special to many people — if they were in pain, or troubled, or performing some excruciatingly difficult task, like painstaking surgery. It was only at home, when he was worried or physically exhausted, that he shut himself up inside himself — unreachable, even by her.

'I heard from Bertha and I was able to get away early. I wanted to be here when you got back,' he said as he helped her inside and sat her down in the sitting-room, firmly shutting the door against Daisy's pathetic cries.

'The children can wait,' he said, sitting beside her. 'Bertha is in charge. Now tell me all about it, from the beginning.'

When she had finished, he said quietly, 'Poor Zillah, poor Alain, poor Peter.'

'But they'll get her better?' Megan asked anxiously. 'Won't they?'

'It's likely — this time. But not without cost. It's particularly draining for Alain, of course.'

They sat leaning against each other, not speaking.

'I liked Robert Brandon,' Megan said eventually, her head on his shoulder. 'He's charming — very attentive and natural. He didn't seem at all arrogant and hard, like people say he is. And I think I've got you a patient — as if they weren't queuing up already. He's had heart trouble, and Ceci, his wife, is going to make an appointment. He didn't like whoever it was he saw.'

'I wonder who that was?'

But she wasn't listening. Suddenly remembering something, Megan turned to him, the trauma of the day banished, her face alight. 'And Owen, Cloverley Court is – is – pure magic.'

Three days later, a letter arrived for Megan. It was a short handwritten note from Robert Brandon, from Cloverley Court. He wrote that he had indeed remembered who it was he thought she so resembled: his American grandmother, Cordelia Brandon, whose portrait by Toldini was on the stairs. Because it was such an attractive picture, it had been placed in a prominent position – and she might remember his wife pointing it out. The likeness was uncanny, his wife agreed. He remembered her from when he was a boy, a long time ago now. She was very popular and very beautiful; and he would like, if he might, to pass that compliment on to Megan. It was a strange coincidence, wasn't it? And she must come again to Cloverley and see for herself. There were two lines, as an afterthought, scrawled beneath his signature. 'It came to me after lunch when I was reading *The Times* in the library, not in my bath!'

Pleased and rather flattered, Megan was impressed that he had bothered to write at all. Then, her head filled with Zillah – and coping now with the three children as Peter had decided he would rather like to spend a few nights with them, if that was all right – she stuffed it into one of her desk drawers. And almost forgot about it.

Chapter 22

The paper Owen delivered in Boston in May was received better than even he could have hoped. The following day, parts of it, with his picture above, were reported on the front page of the *New York Times*. In recent years, he and his team in London had been developing techniques in heart surgery that were now being closely monitored, and emulated, throughout the world. And Owen Thomas – still relatively young; of good appearance; an excellent public speaker – had made a profound impression on the audience of his most respected peers. His doggedness, his talent, and his ability to inspire had succeeded. Overnight, his international reputation was assured and the scope of his career widened immeasurably.

A string of lecture offers followed at once – mostly abroad. Putting as many of his immediate commitments as possible on hold, he accepted what he believed were the most valuable, and embarked on an ambitious and frenetic schedule. Hopping back and forth to Europe or across the Atlantic, he often went straight from the airport to the hospital or Harley Street. All the correspondence – tickets, connections, acceptances, schedules – were seamlessly co-ordinated by Iris. Able to sleep anywhere, even on planes, Owen somehow found adrenalin enough to keep it all going. Several of his colleagues told Megan that it was possible that his name would one day be mentioned as a candidate for the Nobel prize.

Hearing this, Megan managed only a small, tight smile; because as the weeks and months passed, her initial pride gave way to disbelief, then resentment, then anger. Owen's sudden eminence stunned her. Was this the way their lives were to be from now on — for Owen, for herself, for the children? After the brief regeneration in Wales in the spring, when Owen had again become the warm and human man she had married, sensitive to a fault, when he was at home — and this was rare enough now — he had reverted to his emotionally introverted self. For weeks at a time, Megan couldn't reach him — sexually or in feeling. She would lie tense and sleepless beside him as he made up for bouts of jet lag or sheer physical and mental exhaustion. When she tried to talk to him, Owen faced her pleasantly — but coolly. This was what he had been aiming for all these years; surely she understood that? This was what he had been after when he had decided against taking the job in Wales that his parents had advised years ago. He was at the top of the tree: he had no option but to grasp, now, what opportunities were offered. For the moment, at least, he and his team were 'a hot ticket'. They were doing brilliant, vital work: work that had the potential to affect thousands and thousands of lives — and generations beyond. He was away a good deal, he realized that, which was difficult for her and the children, and he was terribly stretched, working as a pure scientist and a clinical doctor at the same time, but that was the way it had to be.

'But what about me?' Megan was all eyes. 'I was finding all the ramifications of your career hard enough to cope with before this,' she said unsteadily.

'Look, Meg,' he said wearily. 'I'm dealing with life-and-death situations every day. You know that perfectly well. On the research side, we're making great strides. And this is enormously satisfying. I need your understanding — please. And never say you weren't warned.'

Megan left the room.

On a Saturday afternoon in September, the date that Vera had designated as suitable for Nellie's eighty-fifth birthday party, Megan opened the cupboard in her bedroom and pulled out a navy and white dress that she hadn't worn before. She held it up against her, critically, in the mirror. Still having a bit of a tan left over from the summer helped everything – her complexion, and even her depressed spirits. It wasn't a distinguished garment, but it would do. And she had better hurry; Vera would be arriving at any moment. She started hunting around in the bottom of the cupboard for a pair of matching shoes.

The actual birthday had been nearly a month before; but that week there had been a big art sale in New York and a party at the Museum of Modern Art. The quick trip to London had been planned far in advance to fit in with Vera's busy life – the typed, crisply worded letter winging its way over to Megan, many months before, in wintry London.

'Like royalty,' Megan had grumbled that morning, depressed that her mother was bothering to come at all, wishing it was all over, hoping it wouldn't be too much for Nan – who had been particularly confused lately. The one blessing was that the egregious Carl had been left behind, manning the business in New York. Also, astonishingly, Owen had juggled his schedule sufficiently to take the whole day off.

Everything was ready for the small family party. Harriet and Daisy had spent the morning decorating the kitchen with balloons and coloured streamers; the pink and white birthday cake, made by Megan and decorated by Harriet, was in the middle of the table – a tactful assortment of candles waiting to be lit. Owen had put the champagne in the refrigerator before leaving with the girls – all dressed up in new shoes and frocks – for the drive to the East End to pick up Nellie from Trout Lane.

Megan had only just finished dressing when she heard a taxi idling outside the gate. She rushed down the stairs and opened the door in time to see Vera sashaying up the path, a small, expensively wrapped package dangling from one finger.

'Concorde is the only way to do it,' she said, stripping off buff-coloured gloves and checking her face in the hall mirror. The odd, extravagant clothes of a few years ago had given way to simple – and very expensive – elegance, usually silk; her hair had been cut short and was now a skilfully managed greyish blonde. 'There's no problem with the time change, and one gets so much more accomplished. You must tell Owen – surely it's all part of his expenses.' She looked Megan's dress up and down. 'It's all very quiet here – where is everybody?'

Megan had just finished explaining that Owen and the children were fetching Nan, when the phone rang down in the kitchen. 'I won't be a moment,' she said. Vera went into the sitting-room. Noticing the package her mother had left on the hall table as she passed, recognizing the wrapping paper, Megan wondered what on earth Nan was going to do with an object from Tiffany's. But she was glad, at least, that her mother had made the effort to attend the birthday party.

She picked up the phone.

'Am I interrupting? Has the party begun yet?'

'Alain!' She was surprised and delighted to hear his voice. 'When did you get back from Switzerland? Is Peter all right?'

During the summer, with Zillah still in the clinic, her health uncertain, Alain had decided to send Peter to boarding school. If he was to go into the family bank, languages were essential; and after much consideration, he had settled on a well-known school near Zurich.

'Peter was very brave, very stoic. And I shall be going over to see him next month.' As always with Alain, the words lightly caressed. Through all the worry over Zillah, Alain had lost none of his innate charm. After the initial shock of her illness, Megan thought that he even felt a certain relief, knowing that, for the moment, the full responsibility for her well-being was not his. 'And I have other news. I've just come back from a quick visit to the clinic. Zillah has made great progress, even since you saw her last week. I spoke to the doctors – and she's being allowed out, on condition that she goes straight to France. With a nurse, of course. And I will follow as soon as I've dealt with the house and my work here.'

'Alain, that's wonderful news. I'm so pleased – for all of you. And as you're home, won't you come over this afternoon? It's only ourselves, as you know. But my mother is here – and it would help enormously.'

'Of course I shall,' he said gaily. 'With pleasure. But for one reason only.'

'What's that?'

'Now that Zillah is truly better, to thank you, properly, for coming down to Cloverley with me that day. I don't believe I ever did.'

Smiling the way a woman does when she feels appreciated by an attractive man, Megan reached the door of the sitting-room. And there she stopped. In the short while she had been in the kitchen, Vera had swopped about small chairs and tables, subtly altering the whole layout of the room. She was in the process of taking down a pair of gilt-framed watercolours. Megan's anger flared; she could feel herself shaking.

'What the hell do you think you're doing?' she bawled at her mother's beautifully clothed silken back. A small, still part of her was aghast. Was this she, Megan Thomas, shouting these words — crude screaming, with decided cockney overtones, that she hadn't heard since Trout Lane, before her Copthorne days? 'I never asked you to decorate this house. And I damn well never will. You put every single thing back in the same place you took it from. And be quick about it.'

Her head was high and her colour had come up. She was beside herself with fury, inhibition and manners thrown to the wind. Her mother, still with her back to her, shrugged — and took a simple Staffordshire figure from a side table and replaced it on the mantelpiece where it belonged. She then blew delicately and ostentatiously on her fingertips, apparently to remove any trace of defiling dust. This infuriated Megan still further.

'And the rest,' she said roughly, breathing hard. 'If you think you can come in here and start messing my life up — the way you always have, right from the beginning — you can bloody well think again.' Her chest was heaving and her eyes flashed dangerously.

One by one, Vera — with matchless aplomb — restored the small chairs, pictures and a side table to their usual places, in total silence. They could have heard a pin drop in that room. When she had finished, Vera turned slowly, and surveyed her daughter — the actress again — haughty, disdainful, knowing just how to play the role.

'Allowing for your insulting language, Megan,' she drawled, 'what exactly do you mean?'

'My father — that's what I mean.'

The whole episode had taken perhaps four or five minutes. In that time, all the deep and twisted feelings that existed between them had finally surfaced and exploded; the social veneer that had papered them over since Megan walked out on her mother in the New York apartment was ripped to smithereens. The pretence was over. Without this single, simple truth — the identity of Megan's father — no further relationship was possible between them. They both knew this.

Vera's eyes narrowed; her hands gripped the back of a chair. Across the bright and airy room, which Megan had so lovingly and painstakingly furnished, they were like a pair of alley cats: fierce, intent, squaring up for a fight to the finish.

'If it's so important to you — a name . . .' Vera hissed.

'Yes . . .'

'Then you may have it . . .'

Megan's hand covered her mouth. She waited . . . and she waited . . .

Noises came from somewhere — the front gate scraping, voices, commotion, the door pushed open, Harriet calling out — high, fluting, 'Vera, Vera, I know you're here, I can smell you, it's Chanel. We've got Nan . . .'

Neither Megan nor Vera had even heard Owen's car.

It was while they were all milling about in the kitchen — Megan and her mother ignoring each other as much as possible; Megan and Owen still emotionally strained beneath a layer of politeness — that Nellie dropped her bombshell.

'A slum, 'e says, that man from the council. *Trout Lane a slum* . . . well I ask you . . . I was quite shocked, meself, I don't mind tellin' you.' She was installed in a highbacked chair, stuffed into the dress she had worn at Megan's and Owen's wedding, her hat crammed on her hair and her carpet slippers flapping. She wasn't entirely sure what all this party fuss was about, but it was nice to be with Meg and see the kiddies running about. 'I'm only glad my Alf didn't live to 'ear 'im say it. Why, when we bought number five, we thought it were grander than Buckingham Palace.' She set her teacup on the table and sat back. She'd got their attention all right – and Nellie always had enjoyed the limelight.

'What man was this, Nan?' Megan asked, worried. It was the first she had heard of it – and Nellie Bowen mixed fact and fiction a good deal now.

'Is it to do with relocation? Did he say you might have to move?' Owen asked attentively.

'Tha's right.' Beneath the battered hat, her face still had an innocent prettiness. 'Talkin' about some 'igh rise flats wiv lifts an' heatin' – stuck up in the sky like a bird, I ask you. As if I ever would . . .'

Megan and Owen exchanged glances.

'When did he come, Nan?' Megan asked. 'This man, whoever he is, from the council.'

'A day or so ago,' mumbled Nellie. 'Nosy 'e were. I knows the sort.'

Just then, Alain poked his head in through the garden door and the adults' attention was diverted. Alain kissed Nan's hand and made a fuss of Harriet and Daisy, took a cup of tea from Megan and half knelt beside Vera. Not having met him before, Vera was pleasantly intrigued. Dashing in an elegant designer sweater, he gave her his complete attention – sounding knowledgeable, asking all the right questions. Soon afterwards, Daisy, looking angelic in a frilly pink dress, and feeling ignored, decided to make a scene – deliberately popping a balloon as noisily as possible and bursting into tears. Wise to Daisy's ways, Alain immediately broke off his animated conversation with Vera. Passing Megan, who was looking – and feeling – fraught, he gave her a wink and a smile, scooped Daisy up and took her off into the garden, followed by Harriet. Relieved, the adults returned to the topic of Trout Lane.

'Tear it down? If you ask me,' said Vera crisply, 'it's about time. The street isn't fit for humans. It should have been gutted years ago. And there's not the slightest need to worry,' she told her mother, crossing her excellent legs. 'We'll fix you up somewhere much more suitable. Owen must have contacts. I wouldn't give it another thought.'

'Wha's that?' yelled Nellie Bowen after a moment's shock while the penny dropped. 'Me – move from Trout Lane? Not bleedin' loikely I won't.'

'You may have to. I can't see what all the bother's about,' Vera said impatiently.

'*Bover* . . . I'll give you bover, my girl. You never did know nothin' about nothin', did you, Vera?' Nellie shouted. She was red in the face and getting puffed, and the roses on her hat bobbed crazily. 'Too uppity for the likes of us, me an' Nan Gubbins, you was, from the moment you got on the stage, so-called, some tuppenny-'a'penny sing-song down at the seaside . . . But we was good enough when you got yourself into trouble, in the family way.'

'Look, isn't it time we cut the cake?' Owen asked, stepping forward purposefully. 'Meg, get them in from the garden – and we'll light the candles.'

But Nellie Bowen wasn't finished with her daughter yet. Megan, riveted, hovered by the door.

'An' there's another fing, Vera,' she said venomously, wagging a finger. 'I never did tell you before – all them nights in the war when the Blitz were so bad, we wasn't under them stairs, me and Meg, we wasn't that daft. We was in the cellar at the Arms – ha, ha, ha,' she cackled. 'Ha, ha, ha . . .'

And to Megan's amazement, Vera started to laugh, too – at deep private memories of her own. Because it seemed to her – at last, at last – a marvellous joke that Robert Brandon's daughter had spent much of her infancy in the cellar of an East End pub.

For whatever reasons, sudden gaiety lifted the small party. Megan called them in, and despite the tensions swirling ominously beneath the surface, everyone started smiling and talking animatedly. Standing with Megan, a little to one side, Alain murmured, 'Only you, Megan. I couldn't have borne anyone else that day. Nobody else could have been so – so – *sympathique*.' Megan flushed and handed the matches to Harriet.

When the cake was cut, Owen opened the champagne and they toasted Nellie and gave her her presents. She was thrilled to bits with the silver bangle from Tiffany's, which Owen just managed to work over her knuckles; she swore they'd ''ave to cut me 'and off to get it, they would'. Well away, she pulled herself to her feet. All this jollity put her in mind of other merry times. Clinging on to Owen's arm, she shushed the lot of them and started singing, quavery but still sweetly, as she had so many times before in the beery, smoky sing-alongs on Saturday nights at the Arms,

>'Tiptoe ... through the tulips ...
>Da, da, da, da ... da, da, da-da, da-da ...
>Tiptoe ... through the tulips with me ...'

Once the impromptu singsong, in which they all joined, had died down, Vera left as soon as she decently could. The confrontation with Megan in the sitting-room had agitated her profoundly; she must find the courage to tell her everything, and soon. However much she might dread it, she had no alternative. It was that — or the loss of her daughter. She accepted that, now; the question was, when?

On her way out, calling her goodbyes, she made a point of speaking to Alain Gesson. 'Come and see us in New York — do, please. My husband would be delighted.' She waved an arm. 'Megan will tell you how to get in touch with us.' She swept on out of the house — Harriet following closely — down to the gate and straight into a waiting taxi. That night, she was going to a dinner party the Hansards were giving in their Chelsea home for Brian Worth. And after the shattering scene with Megan, she wanted some time to compose herself before facing that foxy, inquisitive Veronica.

It was after nine o'clock before they sat down.

'And my darlings,' said Brian Worth, looking around the Hansards' dinner table with satisfaction — pink-cheeked, garrulous, filled to the brim with booze. 'Just think of it, *Partners in Paradise* coming back to the West End after all these years positively gathering dust on the shelves . . .' He helped himself to whatever it was that was being handed round; Veronica never had had any idea about food, he recalled. 'I must say, it's all rather a thrill.'

Sitting diagonally across from him, on Dick Hansard's right, Vera said, 'That brings back some memories' – and immediately wished she hadn't. Nothing much escaped Veronica Hansard.

'I'll bet it does, darling,' she screeched from the top of the table. 'I mean, wasn't it your finest hour? Such fun we had in the war, let's be honest, sweetie. The Café de Paris and the doodlebugs and the brass hats on the bedposts . . . Looking back, wasn't it all grand?'

'I meant Brian's production,' Vera said icily, sending a chilly stare over the gleaming silver and glass and the flickering candles. 'I did create the role of Gina, after all.'

'With a little help, dearest,' cooed Brian Worth. 'But you *were* divine – utterly, utterly. I don't know who they've cast as Gina, but nobody will *ever* come down those stairs in that slinky white dress like Vera Bowen.'

'I did see you, actually,' Dick Hansard said gruffly, leaning confidentially towards Vera. 'Twice . . .'

'Twice?'

'Two performances in the same day. I was hanging around London on my own, miserable as hell. The winter of '43/'44 it must have been . . .'

'Good heavens, Dick, we've known each other all these years and you never said.'

'Never dared, my dear.'

Privately, Vera had always scared the hell out of him. She was looking her stunning best tonight – wonderfully garbed, jewels in all the right places – and there was something about her: star quality – whatever that was. She'd got Eddy off the hard stuff, he'd give her that. Not that he didn't look a sad old sack these days, poor chap. Pity about her running round with that ghastly dago fellow, Carl somebody. Bad show that, he felt for Eddy there.

'I suppose I should be flattered.'

'It's what I intended.'

When they were toying with the pallid fruit salad, Dick said, 'I know Veronica will tell you all about this, but our old friends the Brandons – he was the UK Foreign Minister a few years back – are coming to New York in October. Robert's doing a lecture tour and Ceci is coming with him. Veronica spoke to them today down at Cloverley and we've arranged to give a cocktail party for them in New York. You and Eddy will be sure to come, won't you?'

In the middle of chasing the children into bed that night, Megan took a long phone call from Gwen Thomas. And much later, when she had finally cleared the party debris, she went into Owen's study. He looked up from his desk. He was wearing glasses – which he did more and more frequently now. She could tell at once that he had been fully absorbed in whatever he was doing. He was working on an important paper that he was to deliver in San Francisco towards the end of November. Megan knew that of all the encomiums that had been heaped upon him this year, this was the one he most prized.

'I think Nan enjoyed it, don't you?' she asked, curling up on a chair in a dark corner; she hadn't realized how tired she was.

'I'm sure of it. By the way ...' He pulled out a sheet of paper. 'I've already made some inquiries, and got some recommendations about homes for Nellie. You may want to follow them up.' He might have been talking to one of his staff.

Megan reached over and took it. 'I'll make a start. Fortunately, these great social ideas usually take ages, or never come to anything. I just hope, for Nan, that it won't be necessary.'

'Quite.'

It was then that she told him about Pear Cottage; it was coming on the market – and Gwen had rung to tell her, beside herself with excitement. She didn't know the price, but she thought it would be reasonable. Owen looked at her – uncomprehending.

'But Owen, you know ...' She leant forward, blinking in surprise. Surely he remembered; surely he hadn't moved so totally away from his Welsh roots and his background, from her ...

'The cottage in the village — with the path leading up the hill. You've always loved it, said it was the sort of place you'd like to own one day. When I first came to Wales, you told me that the pear tree was a vision of white blossom in the spring.'

'Oh, that one.'

'And we thought that one day, if we could possibly buy it . . .'

'But we can't, Meg, now, can we?' He shifted around in his chair, on the verge of irritation. She must have disturbed him at a crucial time — as usual. 'Be reasonable. It looks as though I'm going to be spending a considerable amount of time in the States for the next year or so. And much as I would love having our own place there, when would we use it? It just doesn't make sense.'

Megan could feel her pleasure and her hopefulness draining away. It had seemed to her, briefly, that Pear Cottage represented the possibility of restoring the closeness which she felt, increasingly, was slipping away from their marriage. And Gwen's call had also done much to obliterate the hateful scene with her mother that afternoon. She had no intention of telling Owen about that, as she would have once. The very thought of their raw anger appalled her; it had left an unpleasant taste in her mouth. She still couldn't bring herself to imagine what she might have learnt if Harriet hadn't come bursting in, if they had been a few minutes later, if the car had broken down.

'But Owen,' she began steadily, determined to fight, to make her point at least; and for more than the cottage — for values that she sensed were vital to their future. 'Even if we couldn't get there very often, we'd know we had it. And it would be so good for us; it's what we need so badly — a bit of peace, by ourselves. It's never been more important for us — it never will be. *Because* of the work you're doing. Don't you understand?' Her eyes had grown into great green pools in her small, pale face.

'It's no good, Meg,' he said tersely, looking away from her, fiddling with something on his desk. 'Right idea; wrong timing.'

Megan got up very slowly and walked to the door. Owen made no move to follow her. He was still sitting there, staring down at his desk, when he heard the door close softly behind her.

Chapter 23

In the middle of October, Megan came back from visiting a possible nursing home for Nellie to hear the phone ringing. It rang all the time she was walking up the path, finding her key, opening the front door; whoever it was, was extremely persistent. Harriet and Daisy were spending the half-term break from school with the Thomases in Wales; Megan experienced a quick spasm of parental fear.

'Hello . . .'

It was Margot Spelling. Megan relaxed, kicked off her shoes, and prepared for a good chat.

'Margot! What a nice surprise, I was just coming in.'

With the children away, Megan was enjoying her freedom, catching up with galleries and meeting friends. She made a mental note to pin Margot down to lunch or dinner this week, if possible. But Margot was in no mood for chit-chat. Intense, with a voice that seemed much too deep for a woman her size, she was telling Megan, with the crisp authority she had had since she was a girl, that she had left the agency, taken several of the plum accounts with her and was setting up on her own.

'Margot, that's great news. It's what you've always aimed for. Well done you.'

Margot then rapped out, 'And I want you to get off your backside and come to work with me. I know you're good. And I know I can trust you. It's time you got away from the domestic front, particularly that naughty, spoilt Daisy of yours. I've got ten million things to do – this instant. So make up your mind within the week and let me know. And we'll discuss the details. Ciao, ciao.' And she rang off, leaving Megan open-mouthed.

'Iris,' Megan said, trying to sound as confident on the phone as Margot did, 'I'd like to speak to Mr Thomas, please. I won't keep him long.'

'I'm afraid that won't be possible, Mrs Thomas, he's with a patient at the moment.' She sounded bland, a bit nasal.

'In that case,' keeping her voice strong, 'could he please give me a quick ring before he sees the next? I won't keep him a moment.'

'He's running behind, Mrs Thomas. He has three more patients to see yet. And he's expected at the hospital at one o'clock.'

Megan counted silently to five. 'Iris, are you telling me that it is impossible for me to communicate with my husband at any time during the next hour?'

'That's right, Mrs Thomas.'

After sitting there for a few minutes, steaming, a name that had been floating about in Megan's head materialized. *Alain* ... She knew he was in London. Owen had spoken to him, briefly, in the street last night when he was parking the car. Peter had settled down nicely in school, he told him; and Zillah was stable, thanks to a battery of drugs, but lacked the will or the inclination to paint — which Owen, privately, put down to the side-effects of her medication. Alain was tying up a new series and expected to be hopping back and forth from France for a while.

When Megan phoned, it was as though he had been standing there waiting for her call: he picked up the receiver on the first ring. Megan began burbling something about not being able to get through to Owen and heartily loathing his secretary ... Even to her own ears she sounded confused. After a few minutes of this, Alain came smoothly to the rescue by inviting her for lunch at his favourite Knightsbridge restaurant. She would be doing him the most tremendous favour, he said persuasively. He would make the reservation and pick her up in twenty minutes flat. As she flew upstairs, wondering what to wear, pleased that she had washed her hair last night, Megan felt as ardent as a young girl going out on her first date.

By the time they were settled at a choice table in one of the most fashionable restaurants in London, all the ordering effortlessly dispatched by Alain, Megan had quite forgotten the reason for her getting in touch with him in the first place. The female proprietor had fallen on Alain with cries of delight — and a crafty look at Megan — when they walked in. Glasses of fizzy pink wine arrived instantaneously. Surrounded by what Megan took, correctly, to be mostly rich and/or famous people, discreetly hidden by banks of greenery, she mentally parked her present dissatisfactions and abandoned herself to enjoyment.

In the first place, it pleased her simply to watch Alain, immaculate in his expertly tailored suit, with exactly the right amount of cuff extended, his hair attractively touched with white. There were deep creases round his eyes when he smiled now. Everything he did had a deft elegance: raising a glass or cutting a roll. He emanated a sense of controlled energy. Even sitting in the chair, opposite her, it was as though he was slightly on the alert — for something. Totally at ease in these sybaritic surroundings, he was amusing company: he had a neat touch in the gossipy stories of the day, pointing out an actress here and a minor royal there, telling her outrageous tales of a soon-to-be prime minister.

And of course, Alain agreed, inspecting his seafood pasta closely, of course Megan must take the job she had been offered — if she thought it would enhance her life, and be fun. That was the important point, wasn't it? They had already eaten figs and ham and drunk more than half a bottle of icy white wine, and Megan was feeling agreeably heady. The restaurant was full, setting up an exciting buzz. Above them, the sun streamed through the high windows, dazzling the silverware and the spotless white cloth. 'Fun is so important — and I think perhaps you don't get quite enough of it. At least not at the present time.'

Megan stuck her fork in the pasta and dropped her eyes. She had dragged out a cream tailored suit, much more expensive than her usual clothes, that she had bought for a wedding two years ago and never worn since. And she knew that her face looked good, her faintly olive skin enhanced by brilliant pink lipstick. She looked up quickly. 'How did you know, Alain?'

'My darling girl . . .' He gestured helplessly with his hands. 'How could I not?'

Megan concentrated on her food without replying. Her cheeks were hot and her heart was racing. Those dark, almond eyes that saw through her clothes, her skin, to her essence as a woman; the smile that made her smile right back at him . . . Beneath the table his hand, which had touched hers briefly, was smooth, almost soft. Alain Gesson, Zillah's husband and protector . . . Zillah, her friend . . .

'Eat up your lunch, there's a good girl.'

When she asked, later, he told her, lightly and vividly, about why they had chosen the part of France they had; of his father's mysterious disappearance; of his deep friendship with his late father-in-law which he had so valued. And when Megan asked if he thought they would settle there for good one day, he said, 'Of course. Now that Peter is in school in Switzerland, we're no longer tied to London. And much depends on Zillah's health; France seems to suit her temperament better. You – and the children – must come and see us.'

'I'd like that. Perhaps I will one day. Who knows?' She picked up her glass. 'Tell me about the Brandons. I thought he was remarkable, very dashing still. He said he was going to consult Owen.'

'I hope he does. He's been very unwell in the last couple of years. Ceci was extremely worried.'

'I adored *her*.'

'We all love Ceci – although she's quite a tough lady in her way. And you made a big hit with my Millie. "Now there's a young woman for you, that nice Megan Thomas," she said. *That's what I call a real cracker* . . .' He imitated her country burr to perfection – and Megan laughed.

'I liked her, too,' she agreed. 'I thought she was a marvellous character.'

'She is indeed. I've always been ambivalent about Robert for various reasons.' He shrugged. 'In my opinion, Millie's the best of the lot of them down at Cloverley.'

'Better than Ceci?'

'Even Ceci.'

When they were drinking black coffee – and the place was

starting to empty — Alain said, looking at Megan thoughtfully, 'You know, if you do start working, I'm sure Bertha would help with the children. She's very fond of them. We're hardly there now; she misses Peter badly and she really doesn't have enough to do.'

And after several more cups of coffee, when they were almost the last people there, Alain took her hand across the table and said gently, 'I am wondering, darling Megan, if you are grown up enough to understand when I say that I want very much to make love to you — and that I believe that you feel the same.'

Outside in the late autumn sunshine, Megan's senses whirling, Alain grabbed her hand, signalled a cab and dived in after her neat, flashing legs. Graceful as a pair of sleek screen lovers, hands entwined, they were whisked to the secret loft which Alain had never given up. And in that simple room, dim after all the brightness, their physical absorption in each other blotted out every other single thing in their lives; it was a shared language they had known for ever — totally absorbing, totally familiar — concerning lust and pleasure and honest liking. Hers and his equally.

Clothing flew about, landing where it may. Moving together — hands, legs, tongues, senses — to a peak that left them giddy and gasping.

Lying half across her — and his body was as smooth and compact as Megan had anticipated — he whispered into the hollow at the base of her throat, 'Beautiful Megan ... We are loving, loyal friends who need each other. No regrets. Remember.'

Still smiling, eyes still closed, she gave a tiny nod.

As they were leaving, smoothed and groomed, looking much as they did when they walked into the restaurant hours before — except for a dewy glow that had fallen upon Megan — Alain pulled out his diary.

'Dear one, a moment ... wait ...'
'What?'

'Don't disappear, not yet, not before . . .' He lightly kissed her mouth, drew back. If only she could stop looking at him the way she knew she was. Whatever would become of her, later, in that other world that lay in wait somewhere outside this hallowed room, down all those stairs, beyond the imposing yellow door?

'I am leaving for France tomorrow,' he said gently. 'She doesn't like me to be away when she's sad and she can't paint.'

'I understand.'

'You do, don't you? Listen — in two weeks, I'm coming back for a day or so. Could we . . .' His head turned very slightly sideways. 'Could we say' — he already had a pen in his hand — 'Wednesday the 7th? Lunch at San Lorenzo, one o'clock. And after . . .'

Megan tried to concentrate, to think ahead: Harriet's coaching; Daisy's dancing lessons; Owen . . . Owen; the job she might be starting. Usually so organized, her domestic life appeared, at that moment, an incomprehensible muddle. Out of it, she said, 'Yes.' Quite certain, smiling like a creamy cat. 'Yes, Alain, of course.'

When Owen came home that evening, Megan met him at the door. Poised and attractive, offering her cheek to be kissed — not quite meeting his eyes — she asked him about his day before dashing down to the kitchen to turn the oven on. Once Owen had glanced at a couple of messages, quickly deciding there was nothing urgent, they went into the sitting-room. The last of the sun touched the warm greens and corals of the room with gold; and the huge mirror blazed in the red, reflected sunset. Megan poured them both a glass of sherry. Smiling a bit too warmly, she commiserated on new developments at the hospital which were adding to his load of paperwork and asked how the vital paper he was writing — whenever he could find the time — was progressing; he was off to Munich for a seminar in the morning.

When they had both commented, laughing, on how peaceful and tidy the house was without the children, Megan came and sat facing him on the chintz-covered sofa. She was wearing a vivid blue dress she knew he liked — and she felt lighter and happier than she had for a long time; perfectly in control of her life and her emotions. She would broach Margot's whirlwind job offer – and, possibly, the bloody-minded Iris – later.

Leaving Alain, floating home in a trance, she had half expected some ghastly catastrophe to have struck while she had been gone, in those other-worldly, lost hours which already seemed to be spinning away from her. Surely, effortlessly, Alain had unlocked in her physical sensations that she had never dreamed of before. Her body still tantalizingly stirred, she felt herself blushing at the memory ... But her face in the hall mirror was the same as it had always been; all the normal struts of her life – the house around her, the cat prowling, piles of laundry waiting to be ironed – were reassuringly in place. Bending down to feed Soots, she thought, It is only I, in my innermost being, who have changed one iota.

'There was nothing really wrong with that nursing home,' she said, offering Owen a dish of olives. 'I couldn't put my finger on it, but there was something about the atmosphere. I thought it was cold – efficient but cold. It wouldn't do for Nan at all.'

'I'd always hoped she would be able to live out her life in Trout Lane. She's a bit wandery – but otherwise, she doesn't seem in bad shape.'

Owen leant back. With his clean-cut features and clear eyes, he was distinguished in looks as well as reputation. Nan, bless her, had always said he'd make his mark. Nobody would guess the prickly sensitivity, or the insecurity, that lurked beneath the competent professional exterior. Megan sensed that part of his mind, at least, was elsewhere at that moment – probably worrying away at that paper.

'I pray she can stay in Trout Lane,' she agreed. 'Nobody I spoke to in the planning office seems quite sure what's happening. But the whole area around the house is being redeveloped; they've already started a couple of streets away. I'll have to contact the next home on the list you gave me. Shall we phone the children before supper?'

After a gossipy chat with Gwen, Alec and Harriet spoke simultaneously, on different extensions. Alec had taken Harriet fishing in the afternoon and he thought she might have a bent for it. She certainly sounded excited enough.

'What a nice idea,' Owen commented, as he and Megan sat at

the kitchen table. He looked genuinely pleased. 'Perhaps I'll have some company down on the river in my old age.'

Megan thought, with a twinge of regret, of Pear Cottage. It had not been mentioned between them since the night of Nan's party. Like so much in their life, recently, it was buried – ready to burst out – beneath a civilized surface layer.

'You'd enjoy that,' she said evenly, jabbing a spoon into the casserole. 'Teaching Harriet all the lore of fishing – wouldn't you?'

'What's that?' He was smiling to himself, perhaps imagining Harriet, her legs stuck into waders, walking with him along that magic river path. Something like jealousy – some avid, unsatisfied longing – flared in Megan. And my own daughter, she thought; for shame ... Picking up her fork, she looked down at her plate. An unbidden memory of that afternoon came to her, and with it, a hot spasm of desire.

'By the way,' she said brightly. 'I've been longing to tell you, but I wanted to get the children and the nursing home over first. I was offered a job today. By Margot Spelling. She's starting her own agency and she's taken several good accounts with her. I think she wants me to manage the office for her, to start with at least, so that she can concentrate on the creative side.'

'Good heavens, Meg.' Owen put down his knife and fork. 'Why didn't you say this before? When did she phone?'

'I told you, today. When I got back from the nursing home.'

She had his full attention at last. This was how he must look – alert, watchful, utterly committed – when he spoke to patients across that massive desk in his big, formal consulting room. Here, he only lacked the aura of his white coat.

'But this is important – why didn't you let me know at once?'

Megan waited for a few seconds, then she said, 'I tried to get through to you the moment after she phoned. I was informed by Iris' – and she didn't bother to keep the sarcasm out of her voice – 'that you had patients waiting and that there was no way I could speak to you for at least an hour – if then. After that put-down, frankly, I gave up.'

His expression changed. This was noticeable. Megan, startled, thought he looked as though he was in pain.

'Are you going to take the job?'

'Yes.' This was the first time she was really aware of the decision that she had made at some point during the day. Enormous pleasure, and relief, broke through her. 'Yes, Owen, I am.'

'I've never been keen on your working. You know that.' He looked wretched. Did he mind so much? As their lives had silted up with busyness and day-to-day responsibilities, it took something like this – a call from Margot, out of the blue – to make Megan realize how little her personal needs had been addressed in their marriage. It was her fault, perhaps, but did Owen even know?

'The children are older now. It's been in my mind for some time. I'd like to accomplish something outside the home, to do something for myself.' She could feel the inner steel stiffening her resolve. 'I always expected to go back sooner or later. Then this happened. Salad?' Even to herself, she sounded flippant – and hard.

'But Meg, shouldn't you think this through a bit more carefully? For one thing, what about Daisy? How's she going to accept your not being at her beck and call all the time?'

'Daisy . . .' Megan said briskly, getting up to fetch some plates. 'Daisy will just have to learn to do without me. And I suspect she'll be all the better for it.'

For the rest of the meal they talked, rather stiffly, about practicalities: Bertha and the children and the school run for Daisy. 'I'll speak to Margot tomorrow,' Megan said. 'I'll know more about the hours, and what she really has in mind for me, then; and as I've decided, I might as well start at once.' They skirted round the fact that Megan's working would radically change their lives. And at no point did Owen inquire what this sudden opportunity – if indeed it was – meant to Megan, and what she wanted for herself.

Later, Owen went into his study to work on his paper. For some time after she heard the study door pulled nearly shut, Megan sat curled in the corner of the kitchen sofa, staring at a newspaper, deliberately thinking of nothing in particular. It was not until she had tidied up and was pushing the cat out that she glanced next door. There were one or two lights on; so Alain was in. She was breathing faster, glad that the mothy darkness hid her high colour, even from herself. Tomorrow, he was off to France. But he would be back soon; she had watched him write their date, the 7th, in his diary — a capital M with a circle drawn round it. And it also occurred to Megan, that in addition to a lot of hard work, a job would give her greater personal freedom . . .

On her way up to bed, Megan looked in on Owen, still hard at it at his desk. His face looked washed out in the harsh pool of light. Megan thought, He's overdoing it; he can't keep it up; he really mustn't . . .

He said awkwardly, 'Meg, I feel dreadful about the way Iris shut you out today — when you wanted to talk. It was unforgivable.' He repeated the word, a tremor in his voice.

'Don't worry about it,' she told him lightly, wondering why he so obviously did. She grinned. 'I'm getting used to Iris and her coldness. It's a sort of Berlin wall she's thrown up round you. I know she's tremendously efficient, which helps you get through the amount you do, but I still miss dear old Mrs Butter, and I expect I always will.'

He was stricken, sitting there with his books and his papers, looking at her over his glasses. Even the mention of Mrs Butter, always an affectionate joke between them, didn't raise the trace of a smile. For the first time, Megan felt the sickening twinges of guilt, as she thought of Owen working here until midnight after a long day; Zillah downcast and angry, unable to summon up her talent, her lined little face looking much older than it should — while she and Alain, moving in perfect time, like dancers, skin sliding on skin, were lost in their private, blissful world.

'Don't stay up too late.' Standing behind him, Megan slipped her hands round his neck. He reached up and held them. She could see his skin pulled taut over his cheekbones. He sounded weary.

'I'll try not to. I'm starting to think, Meg, that I can't do everything,' he muttered. 'Perhaps my father was right after all . . .'

*

An hour or so after, he came into the bedroom, pulling off his tie, ruffling that red hair she loved. Megan was already sleepy, only pretending to read. Snapping off the light, he leant over and kissed her.

'I'm a rotten, boring excuse for a husband these days, aren't I? Don't know how you put up with me . . .'

But there was no need for Megan to reply, because by the time she had thought of something that was both meaningful and neutral, he was asleep. So she lay there, with her hands behind her head, watching the familiar dappled curtains, thinking that she would phone Margot first thing in the morning. The die was cast now.

And another thought crept into her mind: why, she wondered, hadn't she told Alain about her own father, at lunch – the father whose name, whose looks, whose very existence, were denied her? She had sometimes thought about this curious similarity in their pasts. Today, in the restaurant, it had been on the tip of her tongue; it would have been so easy, so seductive, to confide in Alain. But something had stopped her.

She turned on her side, towards Owen. And her last thought before she slept was: I'm glad I didn't. I'm glad I held back – my father – even from Alain. That's always been our secret – Owen's and mine.

Chapter 24

By design, Vera was one of the last of the hundred or so guests to arrive at the Hansards' luxurious apartment building on the upper East Side of Manhattan. She was alone. Darkness had already fallen and the lights were on. There was a crisp tang of autumn in the air and the sky was streaked with the dying pinks and purples of a luminous sunset. Vera always thought that October was the best time in New York: the heat and the humidity were over, the tourists had left and there was a sense of new beginnings after the summer lull. Sitting in the back of the long, sleek Cadillac, she felt a chill tremor of anticipation.

Eddy had disappeared to his club for a hand of bridge with some old cronies. Carl had made his own arrangements for the evening; his homosexuality was a part of his private life that was entirely closed to Vera — and she respected this. For all their busy-busy, non-stop togetherness, the gossip and the clothes and the travelling and the business deals, she knew little of this half world he slipped in and out of.

As the car drew up, uniformed flunkies rushed to open doors. Vera swept on through, past the gleaming chrome and a forest of foliage, tall and slim, straight-backed and elegant, dressed from top to toe in black silk, with diamonds trembling at her ears.

The elevator was waiting; the noise from the party in the penthouse, now in full swing, got louder.

She threw her wrap towards a maid at the door and, lifting her head high, walked into the vast, L-shaped drawing-room, now packed, which overlooked on two sides the dizzying, glittering spectacle of night-time New York. She looked simple and sensational — and she had always known how to move. No one who saw her snaking her way through the laughing, chattering crowd towards her hostess — and there were many who looked — would have guessed the nerves beneath the poise.

All day she had dithered about coming; it would have been so easy to phone Veronica Hansard or send round a note. Wrung out with nervous strain, it had seemed to her, finally, a bore — this evening and what it might bring, not worth the effort and the energy and the possible consequences. But it was too late now.

She took a glass from a tray and turned, deliberately avoiding a couple she knew well. Cecilia Brandon was standing in a group quite near, shepherded by Dick Hansard. You couldn't miss her — Vera picked her out instantly — large and rather lovely in her way, fresh-faced, talking loudly and amusingly in the unmistakable accents of the British upper classes.

Someone clawed at her arm.

'*Darling*, where have you been? I thought you'd *never* come. And you're looking too dramatic for words.' It was Veronica Hansard, shrieking her loudest. 'Come and meet the guest of honour. I'm going to drag you over to Robert at once.' Pushing towards the edge of the room, screeching at this one, waving at that, she was in her element, loving the brittle artificiality, the noise and the brightness, that was entirely her own creation.

Vera saw the back of his head first as he bent down to catch what someone was saying. He was turned sideways to her, a glass in his hand; his dark suit, which he'd probably had for years, looked as though it was part of him. She could feel some inward sinking. Oh God, here we go, why have I . . .?

When Veronica reached him and whispered something, he excused himself, straightened — and looked right at Vera. They shook hands as their hostess moved off, still twittering. He didn't recognize her; he had not the slightest inkling. He was smiling with the practice of a successful politician, a gentleman born, totally at ease in the sophisticated, admiring crowd, ready — and expecting — to charm every last one of them.

'Mrs Mortimer?'

He had always been good with names, she remembered.

'Yes, I ...'

Instantly arrested, his eyes bored into her. She was an older woman, but she was certainly something to look at, and he'd always had an eye for that. Her figure was a slender black column; and her skin was still smooth and unlined. The large diamond earrings that she had hunted down at a sale in Geneva glinted. And at the neck of her dress was a diamond star.

Suddenly rocked by powerful emotion that he had thought long lost, he exclaimed, 'Vera!'

'Hello, Robert,' she said quietly.

He was so very different; he was exactly the same. The feeling that came to her then was mostly regret — and thankfulness that she had come that night after all. She must give him time.

Expression was wiped clean off his face — and she could swear that he went pale. She thought very fast: *I knew; I had all the advantages; I shouldn't be doing this to him* ... minding about him — even then.

He pulled a handkerchief out of his pocket and drew it quickly across his mouth. He recovered.

'You've changed something, your hair ...'

'More than thirty years, Robert.'

'And the American accent.'

'I live here, in New York.'

He was making some rapid calculations, breathing hard. 'Vera — listen — we can't talk here. When can I see you?' He was in charge again — and she was ready for this. He always had to keep control.

'Lunch? Tomorrow?'

He nodded.

She took a card out of her bag and handed it to him. 'It's written down. One o'clock. Yes?'

'Yes — I ...' The meeting had shaken him badly. He looked his age: handsome and urbane, with a gleam in his eye, but an elderly man, all the same. He looked at her hard, searching her out. Apart from the white hair, his features were not much changed. The people all around them, the cacophony of voices, and the white-coated waiters receded. They might have been alone, high above Manhattan, his head and shoulders outlined against the great black starry expanse of sky. He said, 'I always wondered, I thought some time, somewhere, and I hoped . . .'

'That we would – bump into each other?'

'Yes.'

'And so we have,' she said lightly. Then, 'I'm going to leave now.'

His hand was on her arm. 'But we'll meet tomorrow – that's definite?' he said urgently.

'Yes.' After one long look, she turned abruptly back into the crowd – it was all over in a matter of minutes – just as Veronica arrived with yet another clutch of guests to be introduced.

As she passed, on her way to the door, Vera heard Cecilia Brandon braying to someone, 'But *of course* I remember – you came to Cloverley, didn't you? It must have been when my husband was still in office.'

When Dick Hansard started edging round the room looking for her, wanting to introduce her to Cecilia Brandon, he was told to his surprise that she had already left.

She arrived early at the discreet Italian restaurant, not far from the Hansards' apartment, which she had deliberately chosen over more obviously fashionable places. She and Carl frequently lunched there, often bringing clients, so she was well known to the staff. Several days before, she had booked a particular table in an alcove at the back, where they would be undisturbed; and she had consulted with the chef and chosen the menu. There was to be no mistaking the fact that this was *her* luncheon in what was now *her* territory. A bottle of champagne, Pol Roger as it happened, would be chilled and waiting.

She had been sitting there for a good quarter of an hour when Robert came in out of the bright fall sunshine, said something to a waiter and was brought through to her table. She thought, with a shock, When Megan is Robert's age, that is exactly how she will look.

Without moving a muscle, she watched him walking towards the table – as assured and distinguished as ever, raise his hand and smile in recognition and take his seat across from her. The wine was poured. Robert lifted his glass as they were left in peace; at that secluded table, slightly apart from the rest of the room which was starting to fill up, it was tolerably quiet.

'This is a very great – and I may say unexpected – pleasure.'

'For you, not me,' she said quickly. 'Not unexpected. I'd known for weeks that the Hansards were giving the party. And Veronica said you were staying on in New York for a day or two. So I gambled on your being free for lunch today.'

He hadn't been, of course. But it was the easiest thing in the world to make up some excuse and cancel – which he would have done a thousand times over, although her dramatic appearance last night had, frankly, knocked him for six. Steadying, he watched her appreciatively. He was learning that when American women look good, they look better than anyone else. And Vera was a case in point: her hair was shaped and lightened, the grey softened to silvery blonde, but not hidden; she wore a simple suit the colour of violets and some expensive jewellery. The indestructible elegance, which he had worshipped, had acquired the stamp of wealth and security. There was a tight feeling round his heart which was close to pain. It was the way she turned her head, her shoulders; the long expressive hands holding the stem of the wine glass. She had never been a beauty. It was her body, and the way she used it, that had driven him mad. That – and the vulnerability underneath, although God knows she'd done her best to hide it.

'I'm delighted that you did. And you are' – he glanced at the bottle in the ice bucket between them, his eyes crinkling – 'certainly doing me proud.'

The Pol Roger . . . he'd remembered, and he probably drank it still – with someone. She felt a drop of black depression.

'It's been a long time, Robert.'

'Your choice, my dear.'

Stung, sparks suddenly flaring between them, she shot back, 'Only at the end – and that was no choice at all.'

After that, both a bit shaken, aware of the vital electricity that still sparked between them, they drew back into banalities. And as the meal progressed from pasta to veal, they skirted carefully round certain parts of their lives — his political career, her thriving arts business; living in the States; the colleges at which he would be lecturing. There was no mention of husband or wife or children; it wasn't safe, not after that quick bit of flame had erupted.

When they had ordered coffee and brandies Robert said, 'We might have met again at any time, I suppose, with the Hansards. Strange, isn't it?' And then, relaxed, mellowed, through a whiff of cigar smoke, he said, 'I don't know why — it's all right if I tell you this, is it? — but years ago, something about Veronica faintly reminded me of you.'

So he had felt as deeply as she, after all; she had known it all along really. It was a weak triumph, tainted with bitterness. All she could think of was the waste of it, all those arid years, however it had turned out eventually.

It was when they were almost alone in the restaurant that he said quietly, 'You must know what I want to ask you more than anything.'

She looked down at the pristine pale-pink tablecloth; she did, of course — and she was ready for this, too.

'Yes.' She met his eyes, very cool, giving nothing away. 'Well?'

His elbows slid across the table towards her. 'Where is she? What is she doing?'

'She's married, to a professional man, who happens to be extremely successful.'

'Living in this country?'

'In London.'

'And — children?'

'Two girls.'

'Is she happy?'

After some seconds, Vera said, 'I don't know.'

'I see. I assume you're not going to tell me anything more?' And when she didn't reply. 'Do you see her?'

'Yes, when I can. I can't say we're close, or ever have been.

But I keep an eye on her, very much so. And I think, perhaps, that now...' She stopped, and bit the corner of her lip.

'I always wanted a daughter. I've thought... wondered about her... so many times.'

'She's beautiful,' Vera said, with pride. 'And she works. I think she may have talent.'

'Does she know about me – who I am?'

'Nothing. And she only will – if I decide to tell her!'

'Vera.' His voice was getting so low that she had to lean closer to hear him. His eyes bored into her. 'I must tell you, I have always felt bitter that however strong your reasons at the time, you denied me access to, and knowledge of, our child.'

The air sizzled between them.

'Bitter, Robert?' She spat. They were like two live wires ready to explode. 'Then that, let me tell you, makes two of us.'

Standing outside at last in brilliant sunshine under a garishly blue sky, they were controlled – almost strangers again. They lingered, both wanting to leave, yet both reluctant, making meaningless conversation. It was Robert in the end who found some grace. He straightened, as though shaking off the painful passage that had just passed between them, and grasped her arm.

One touch – and he was unerringly sure of her, as he always had been, the old, essential something crackling between them. The world, their lives, had changed and moved on – but not that. He'd grilled Veronica, who thought his interest curious, although he hadn't cared. And he'd found out what he was after. There was a rich husband everyone spoke well of. A drink problem in the past. A marriage that kept going, not much more. For years, Vera had been running round with some pansy, a lot younger than she, her so-called business partner. There hadn't, he suspected, been anyone else, not importantly – for either of them.

'Listen, Vera, if I had to do it all over again,' he said recklessly, smiling in a way she'd never been able to resist, still holding her by the arm, 'I would have done it very differently. And I fancy you would, too. It might, or it might not, have worked. But oh, my dear, how we would have enjoyed finding out...'

It was only when he finally turned away that he noticed – and his eyes weren't so good now – the diamond star in her lapel.

She strolled back to her apartment, all the way up Park Avenue, past the streaming traffic and vivid flowerbeds in the centre – uplifted. That afternoon, one of New York's rare and perfect days, the world was her oyster. Something important had at last been put right between her and Robert; for her and for him. She did not expect to see him again – and that, too, was right. When the time came, as she accepted now that it would, she must convey this, somehow, to Megan. Arriving at the canopied entrance, she heard herself murmur, 'Not bitter – *bittersweet*, that's it.'

Eddy was standing in the doorway of the library as she let herself in, looking right at the door as though he had been waiting for her. Something was badly wrong. His face was contorted in distress. He managed one word – 'Vera' – before he crumpled sideways and started to fall. He was unconscious when she got to him, on her knees, cradling his head, screaming for help.

For the following day and night, Vera scarcely left his side. She came in the ambulance to the hospital; sat up with him through the first critical night; snatched a few hours' rest on a cot in his room. He had suffered a serious stroke – but he was lucky. As soon as he regained consciousness, his speech started to come back; only his left arm and hand were limp. He had no memory of what had happened.

When, exhausted, Vera was finally persuaded that he was out of immediate danger and she could go home, Ted was waiting. Megan had reached him at Yale and he had rushed down at once. He looked white and worried. 'How's Dad doing? He really is coming along, like the doctor told me? Megan feels just dreadful. You see, she had just told him about Nan . . .'

'Told him what?' Vera asked faintly.

Ted took her by the shoulders – she was still wearing the violet suit she had put on to lunch with Robert – and gave her the message he and Megan had rehearsed. Nellie Bowen had died peacefully in her sleep in the kitchen in Trout Lane, the day before the demolition bulldozers were due.

For Vera, the following couple of weeks passed in a haze of anxiety. After surviving the stroke with relatively little impairment, Eddy had several unexpected set-backs. The doctors' opinions became more guarded, and Vera's world dwindled to Eddy's room in the hospital; day after day, as he drifted in and out of consciousness, she willed him to fight, to hold on. After their years of estrangement, the determination that Eddy should live — and recover — had suddenly become the focal point of Vera's life. There was no question of her leaving to attend Nellie's funeral; distraught, not giving a thought to the glitzy social whirl that she had previously lived for, she dashed frantically between the apartment and the hospital. It was Ted, staying away from college to be with his mother, who kept in close touch with Megan and Owen.

When Eddy seemed, finally, to be improving steadily, Vera came back from the hospital at midday. The worry and the lack of sleep had taken a toll; she felt worn out. Putting on an old housecoat, she emerged from her bedroom and went into the study where she bumped into Ted.

'Look, Mom, they're pleased with him,' he said. 'I met one of the doctors in the corridor this morning. Now you've got to try to relax and take it easier.' He jiggled the change in his pockets and bent down from his huge height to give his mother a peck on the cheek.

'He *is* better. Thank God for that.' Vera sat down with a bump. She had no make-up on and her hair was ruffled out of its usual perfect shape. Deprived of powder and pencils, she had deep lines and creases round her eyes.

Ted, who had rarely seen his mother other than formally got up, thought she looked rather good. He sat on the arm of her chair, slinging his very long legs about, nervy, blinking. 'And you're not to make yourself sick with worry — Dad said that — or there'll be two of you up in that room.'

Never still for an instant, Ted began playing with a cigarette lighter.

'Do stop fidgeting, Ted,' his mother said sharply. 'You'll never do anything on the stage until you learn to keep still. I'd like to speak to Megan. I haven't properly, not with all this going on. Your father was asking about her.' She glanced at her watch. 'Two o'clock, seven their time. She should be home from her office by now. Why don't you try her, Ted? If you get that German housekeeper woman, Bertha, say we'll ring later.'

Ted loped over to the desk and seconds after, he was saying, 'Meg? Ted here. Yes, yes, I've just been there. Dad's really stabilized now after the blips and Mom wants to have a word with you.'

The stroke had been waiting to happen, Vera told Megan. She was sure Owen would agree. He'd had excellent, prompt care; it could have been a blessing in disguise. The fact that Eddy was taken ill only minutes after speaking to Megan, and learning of Nellie's death, was purely coincidental. 'And I've given up the business — completely. I've told Carl that he can do what he likes with it. Eddy's health and well-being are my one concern now.' Then, 'I've been so terribly distressed, I haven't been able to concentrate properly. Now tell me, Megan, everything — about Nellie . . .'

Vera learnt that Megan and the children had gone to Trout Lane late on that last Monday afternoon. After a lot of looking, Megan had found a small, well-run home — in the suburbs, no more than an hour's drive from the house — and made all the arrangements to move Nellie there on the Tuesday. She was taking the day off from work — which was going well, by the way, they were desperately busy — to settle Nan in herself. She had been dreading it, of course. It seemed pointless and cruel; but the row of small Victorian cottages was coming down and they had no choice. The problem was that Nan simply refused to believe it. She was staying in Trout Lane and that was all there was to it. Nothing Megan or Owen said appeared to get the reality of the situation through to her; whenever they tried to talk some sense into her, she covered her ears and 'Tra, la, la'd'. 'There's none so deaf etc., as Owen says frequently.'

As they had decided in the car, Harriet and Daisy kept Nellie occupied with tea and television while Megan crept upstairs and packed the few belongings she would need immediately. The important thing was to get Nan moved into the nursing-home, tomorrow, with as little fuss as possible. They left her, her usual cheery self, settled with a cup of tea in the fug of the kitchen, resolutely ignoring Megan's bright, 'See you in the morning, Nan.'

When old Mrs Brown from across the way looked in, as she did most days, Nellie hadn't stirred from her chair. The tea was still beside her. She looked so contented that it took Mrs Brown a while to realize that she wasn't just asleep.

Sniffing hard now, Megan said, 'She turned her toes up, Nan did. It happens sometimes, Owen says. She knew exactly what was going on with the street, whatever she pretended. She did it her way, to the end. So we can't really be sad for her, can we?'

Chapter 25

Ted's phone call caught Megan moments after she arrived home, still feeling the strangeness of her new working life. After, relieved to hear of Eddy's progress, she went straight upstairs to see the children; to ask about Harriet's school work (she was invariably top of her class) and Daisy's social life. Gwen Thomas never ceased to marvel at how different her two granddaughters were. Harriet was academic and self-contained, as Owen had been. Daisy dreamed and muddled her way through her work; but among her many acquaintances, boys and girls, no birthday party was complete without the pretty Daisy Thomas. And to everyone's surprise, she had come to terms remarkably quickly with her mother's working schedule. She had simply turned her baby blue-eyed charm on the besotted Bertha — who was now her willing slave. Harriet's attitude to her mother's job was, 'Why ever not? You won't catch me hanging around a house, stuffing a mushroom, not likely.' Owen, and his father, suspected that she already had medical leanings.

Megan had started work at Margot Spelling Inc. exactly three days after Margot's frantic call. A speedy worker, still as ambitious as when she was a girl, once Margot had taken the plunge, she immediately took spectacular office premises in Mayfair. 'It's important to make the right impression from the start,' she told Megan, gritting her teeth and looking fierce. While Margot worked round the clock, dealing with clients and hiring the best talent she could get her hands on, it was Megan's quiet efficiency and organization that got the operation running smoothly. In the weeks since the agency had started up, Megan reckoned that she had been doing much the same as any competent home maker would, only on a far larger scale: managing people adroitly. And it gratified her to discover how good at it she was.

Thanks to Bertha's solid support, the long hours exhilarated rather than tired her. And her clandestine, effervescent affair with Alain had also given her a giddy confidence. Making time to be with Alain on his lightning visits to London was so easy that it almost made her laugh. When he phoned the office — that seductive voice, her pulses racing — she had only to mention to someone (to Margot, or Bertha or Owen) a meeting that was running late or a problem that had suddenly cropped up. It baffled Megan that she felt no shame, no sense of betrayal. When they were together, anxieties fell away — his, as well as hers. It was as though their gaiety and their intense physical pleasure in each other were quite separate from their other lives; and in a way Megan couldn't explain, even to herself, it complemented them. Whenever she had seen Alain, however briefly, she felt as though she had drunk exactly the right amount of champagne.

Leaving Harriet deep in an essay and Daisy half asleep, she ran down to the kitchen. The children seemed to have accepted Nan's death quite naturally. 'I expect she was tired being so old, poor Nan,' Daisy said; Harriet wanted to know if the television had been on all night. Megan, while wholeheartedly grateful that she had been saved from taking her forcibly into the nursing-home, nevertheless felt the downward drag of sadness. For as long as she could remember, Nan had been the rock in her life — always there, always the same. And now, Megan thought, giving a tight little smile, now I have only my mother.

Bertha had taken on running the house, as well as looking after Daisy. When Megan came home, tired out, flopping down to chat to Harriet, delicious smells wafted from the kitchen. She was taking one of Bertha's mystery dishes out of the oven, when Owen walked in. He swung his briefcase on to the sofa and gave her a hug. The weather had turned sharply colder and there was colour in his cheeks.

After passing on the good news about Eddy, 'You're looking very chipper,' Megan said. 'What's up?'

'Two things. I finished the paper, in the library this afternoon. I cleared a few hours that I needed. And that was that. I have to go through it one more time, and then it will be typed.' He looked cheerful, relieved – and slightly smug.

'That's marvellous. Well done. What's the other thing?' Megan asked, guarded.

'It's Iris.' He sounded very crisp, very positive. 'I've fired her. She's clearing her desk at this moment. I'm paying her out her notice – and she's to go. Immediately. I've got a temp starting in the morning.'

'But Owen . . .' Megan was staggered. 'Why on earth . . .?'

'Her efficiency was a legend. But she was putting off the patients and getting people's backs up.' He picked up the evening paper. 'Finally, I didn't like the fact that when you wanted to speak to me, you couldn't get through. The Berlin wall, you said.'

So she had been right in thinking that he had been upset out of all proportion when she told him that. But all the same, it didn't quite make sense. For the last three years Iris had been such a paragon, perfectly organized, never putting a foot wrong. Even Megan, who instinctively disliked her, had a grudging respect for the way she juggled the strands of Owen's career. Something niggled unpleasantly . . . Surely her dismissal must be for more than the odd disgruntled patient or the crass way she invariably behaved to her? Owen hadn't complained before about the way she handled patients – or anything else, for that matter.

'But what will she do? Will she go back to South Africa?'

He turned on her, tetchily. 'I don't give a damn what she does. She can go to hell for all I care. Look, Meg, she's out of my life – for good. I'd rather we didn't go on talking about her. All right?'

Megan said, into the long silence that followed while she laid the table, 'Would you get me a drink? Sherry, I think. And perhaps you ought to see how Harriet is getting on with her essay. Incidentally, Vera said that she's given up that terrible Carl and the business. She's going to devote herself completely to getting Eddy better.'

They had decided to leave Bertha's rich apple strudel for tomorrow, and Megan was making the coffee, when Owen said suddenly, 'Meg, come with me to San Francisco, please. It's so important – and it would mean a lot to me to have you there. Particularly after Nellie, a week's change would do you good. I know the committee would be delighted if I brought my wife.'

This was the first Megan had heard of it. Their relationship had settled into a rut of cool, polite familiarity. Guiltily aware of her own relief, Megan thought, I can't remember when we last made love.

'It's a nice thought, Owen. But I'd be hopeless at giving you any help. I thought Iris . . . I mean, you'll need assistance, won't you? Someone to keep track of things, help with the slides.'

He slammed both hands, palms down, on the table. 'I am asking you to come as my wife. Simple. So will you – please?'

Measuring coffee and pouring boiling water, Megan prevaricated. This was the worst possible time for her to be away from the office. They were all working at full stretch, totally dependent on the bank manager's goodwill until the first fees came in. It was still touch and go and a lot of bravado; and she knew how much Margot depended on her being around. There was another reason, too. Alain was coming to London for a series of meetings around that date. He hadn't been absolutely sure of the timing. She was seeing him next week, she hoped; she would ask him then. And there, in her own kitchen, desire rose right through her; with Alain, she had discovered a world of the senses, beyond constraint, which she had barely glimpsed before.

'It really depends on the office,' she said, handing Owen a coffee, wide-eyed as Daisy at her wickedest. 'Can I think it over and talk to Margot? You won't need to know for sure for a couple of weeks, will you?'

'No – we can fix it up at the last minute, if need be. But do try, Meg. And we could come back via New York and drop in on Eddy and your mother.'

'Perhaps,' Megan murmured, stirring her coffee. 'Let's see how it works out.'

*

But it was ten days before Alain managed to get to London again. Something extraordinary had come up, he had told Megan, ringing her office from France. He simply couldn't get away. No, he couldn't tell her why, not like this; it was too important to him. She would understand when she knew it all. He sounded buoyant and elated. And Zillah was a little happier, he said; she was looking less drawn and talking about painting again.

So it was nearly the end of November before they met. Owen was still pressing hard for her to come to San Francisco and Megan was still dithering. She had mentioned it to Margot, who said, 'If you feel you must, Meg' — looking doubtful — and, for her, uncertain. 'I don't want to hold you back, and I can understand that it's a great honour for Owen, and that you'll be able to see your mother and Eddy in New York. All the same . . .'

Privately, for Megan, a lot depended on Alain and his whereabouts. She was thinking this as she drove from the office through the wild and windy dusk of the wintry afternoon towards his flat. 'It's been one of those days, Bertha,' she had told her earlier. 'But we've been paid by our largest account and we're all going to huddle in a plotting session at the wine bar round the corner. I shouldn't be too late. If you could hold the fort until Mr Thomas gets back and tell him . . .' True and not true; Megan didn't give a damn. The fees were beginning to come through, to her and Margot's huge relief, but she had left the office soon after four — and there was no 'session' planned.

It was raining hard, the windscreen wipers tracing arcs, last leaves spiralling down, lights quivering along the wet streets. Parking right outside the yellow door, Megan jammed in the key and fled through the hall, grabbing the banisters, up and up, heart thumping, breathless.

He was waiting for her in the doorway — darkly attractive and smiling.

'Darling one . . .' Her hand grasped his shoulder, the door closed, mouth on mouth. Megan's eyes were still closed when he pulled gently away from her. 'Come . . .' He took her hand and drew her into the room, helping her off with her streaming raincoat. 'I must tell you, now, that we haven't much time. I've only been in London for a few hours, for one meeting. I'm flying to Paris tonight. I must. I'll explain why later. And before I go, I have so much I want to say to you.'

There was an intensity about Alain that Megan had not seen before; everything about him emanated some inner, suppressed excitement. Megan felt herself faltering. Day after day, she had been longing for this moment.

She said, dismayed, 'But when, Alain? When are you going?'

Opening the wine, his back turned to her, 'My plane leaves at seven.'

'But Alain ... and I've hardly seen you ...' She could barely contain the panic that was bubbling up inside her. She was literally aching for his touch; over that, she had no pride.

He turned to her, holding out a glass, all charm: asking about the children, the office ...

'And it suits you, this working life,' he said, contemplating her appreciatively. 'You're looking lovely, my green-eyed one, and so chic all of a sudden. The flowery little-girl frocks and skirts have disappeared. Now, it's the *tailleur*.'

'I have to dress the part,' Megan told him demurely. 'And it's much easier with a pay cheque of my own.'

He laughed. 'But of course. And British men don't pay so much attention to these things. I'm thinking of Ceci and her wonderful pearls worn with those dreadful denim skirts.'

He settled himself beside her, his arm along the top of the sofa caressing her neck. He bent towards her, lightly brushing her lips.

'Now, you must listen, carefully.'

'What is it, Alain?'

This profound change which Megan sensed in him did not concern Zillah, as she had feared; it was to do with his father. He said gravely, 'I can't be positive, but I believe I now know what happened to him in that terrible bleak winter, when I first came to England, and eventually to Cloverley.'

The knowledge had come about because a young farmhand, friendly with the couple who tended the Gessons' vineyard, had come to see him one day – cap in hand, nervous. 'He stammered something about wanting to speak to me privately; and so, of course, I took him out on the terrace and brought out some good cognac. He seemed a decent fellow. After several slugs, he loosened up. And this is what he told me . . .'

Alain took Megan's glass and manoevred her round until they were lying in each other's arms along the length of the sofa. With her head beneath his chin, Megan could not see his face; but she could feel his warmth and his heartbeat against hers.

'He had a tale to tell, this young man, which he thought would be of interest to me. He had known for some time that one of the reasons we settled in these parts was because of my missing father. It's common knowledge, as I intended. But he had thought nothing in particular about it until, a month or so before this, his sick and elderly uncle had begun mumbling about a mysterious body that he had found, during the war, on the hillside overlooking their fields – the body of a man in his early forties, dark-haired, carrying no identity papers – not far from the Spanish border. He's not certain – he's dying of cancer, poor chap, and his mind is confused – but he believes that this was the winter of 1942. The man had been shot in the back; he must have died instantly. Fearful of the German patrols that roamed the countryside, feeling that such naked death was indecent, the uncle and his cousins waited until it was dark, then buried him in a hastily dug grave at the foot of the hill. The following day, they erected a rough headstone. It is there still. The young man took Zillah and me the next day. I am as sure as I will ever be – now – that I am living close to my father's last resting place.'

'How, Alain?' Megan whispered. 'How can you be so sure?'

'I have worked it all out. That's what I've been doing, walking the hills, looking up old timetables, drawing diagrams. It's all theory, but I believe it to be the truth. I think that my father somehow got aboard the train that was taking me from Perpignan to the Spanish border – that he dropped off once he was assured that I was across and safe – and began to make his way through the back country roads to Perpignan. I believe he was sighted by a German patrol and shot on the spot – where the farm hands found him. My mother must have been waiting for him in the cellar of the doctor's house. Undoubtedly, she was taken from there, alone, by the Germans – and sent to Auschwitz. Almost certainly not knowing that her husband was dead.'

'It's a tragic story.'

'Yes.'

'Yet you have survived, Alain.' Megan twisted her head and looked up at him. 'Something positive, at least, came out of all the horror. If what you believe is true, he died knowing that you were safe, that you had some chance in life. And that must have been what he hoped for above all else.'

They lay there together – peaceful, not talking much – until Alain said quietly that it was time for him to leave for the airport.

'I'll drive you,' Megan said. 'It's still quite early. And my car's outside.'

'You're sure?'

'Sure.'

On the way, he told her why he was flying to Paris.

'I'm meeting Zillah there,' he said. 'She and the nurse are going up by train. Tomorrow, we have an appointment with the psychiatrist who is looking after her.'

'But I thought she was improving?' Megan shot him an anxious look. 'You said she was happier.'

'Perhaps. Anyhow, she has come to a decision. And as long as the psychiatrist agrees . . .'

'Agrees to what?'

'That she throws away all the pills, stops the medication. It makes her better – quiet, calm, undemonstrative. There are no highs and lows. But the essential spark that is Zillah is missing also. She knows – and she won't permit that. So it's to be the old Zillah again, painting away, brilliantly alive, but unstable. Manic depressive, in a word.'

After a long time Megan said, 'That will be very hard on you, Alain. She only believes in you, no one else. You know that. You will have to watch her every moment.'

Alain was staring out of the window at the wild, dark night. 'I know,' he said at last. 'But it is the commitment I have made – for life.'

When they got to the airport, she stopped the car. He made no move to get out — and neither did she. Eventually, very slowly, he took out his diary, the way he always did, tentatively planning another meeting before the last had ended, making it easier on themselves. Their eyes met. As one, they moved and clung together. Neither could talk; they were both crying. In the only clumsy movement Megan had ever seen him make, he stumbled out of the car and slammed the door and she watched him walking into the departures hall, not once looking round, until he disappeared from sight.

Chapter 26

At the last minute, with only days left, Megan had more or less decided to go to San Francisco. Owen wanted her to, rightly; and she did, she thought wearily, have some conscience after all. Besides, she and Margot, the only two in the office who understood the financial structure of Margot Spelling Inc., were beginning to breathe more easily. Several of their new presentations had been accepted; and Margot had enticed a brilliant creative director from another agency, who would be starting soon. This coup had given the whole staff a boost. Surely Margot, who was clutchy and emotionally dependent on her in a way Megan couldn't fathom, wouldn't mind her being away for a few days now.

And it would probably, as Owen said, do her good. She still felt empty after Nan and the sad clearing-up in Trout Lane. Alain's continued absence had left her aching and flat. He had telephoned her office from Perpignan. For once, he sounded low; he was missing her — Megan knew — quite as much as she was him. Despite their stilted words, she felt very close to him. Since their long talk, she had thought endlessly about his father's story, and how he had pieced it together. The psychiatrist had concurred with Zillah's wishes, he told her. She was slowly being weaned off the medication. It was a difficult time and there were temperamental problems already. (He did not go into what these might be — and Megan didn't ask.) He was doing the best he could over his television work from France. He saw no way he could leave for the present.

Megan had a word with Bertha the next day.

'You go off with the mister,' Bertha advised. 'It's better that way. Your girls and I will manage beautifully. You'll see.'

'Thanks, Bertha. You know I couldn't do any of this without you. I'll speak to Mr Thomas tonight when he gets back from his meeting. I can't dilly-dally any longer. I'll have to tell them at the office and get a ticket and begin packing.'

When Bertha had gone off next door, Megan went upstairs to see Daisy. Harriet was spending the night with a friend, working on a school project. Megan found that Daisy had abandoned her homework, as usual, and was watching a daily soap opera — lying on the floor, rapt. Seeing no chance of getting her back to her reading, Megan sat and watched with her. They were both absorbed in the banal goings on when the front door bell rang. Daisy didn't even bother to take her thumb out of her mouth, but Megan, saying crossly, 'Now who on earth can that be?' got to her feet and went downstairs.

She switched on the outside light before opening the door. And when she did, there was a woman standing in the full white glare. Her mind was so taken up with matters which immediately concerned her — and she was tired — that for a second or two, Megan didn't recognize her. It was Iris.

After her stunned recognition, Megan said, 'Iris?' — almost a question, just to be absolutely sure. She could hardly have found anyone she had expected less on her doorstep. And when the woman said nothing — only stared — Megan found herself saying, 'Won't you come in?'

She led her through the hall into the sitting-room. Bertha had already drawn the curtains and put on the lights. It was a room that looked charming at any hour, in any light. After the dark November night outside, it glowed with warmth and colour.

'Do sit down, Iris,' Megan said pleasantly. 'Did you want to speak to Mr Thomas?'

Iris, her hands deep in her pockets, hugging her coat to her, stopped looking round as she had been doing from the moment she stepped into the house. She looked as Megan remembered her: late thirties, at least; mousy hair, white skin, brownish eyes.

Not fat, not thin; of average height; dressed in unflattering beige. Utterly unremarkable.

'No,' Iris said blankly. 'I know he's at that meeting — don't I? I want to speak to you.'

'I see . . .' Megan had already begun to get faint intimations that something was unpleasantly wrong. It had not occurred to her to ask Iris to take her coat off, or if she would like a drink or a coffee — something she would normally have done without thinking. 'What was it you wanted to speak to me about, Iris?'

'He sacked me. You know that. No reason — just wanted me out of there.' The flat, nasal accent had an impudent air.

Megan, sitting very straight on the edge of a chair, said coldly, 'Whatever goes on in the consulting rooms is my husband's business. If you've got any grievance, Iris, I suggest you take it up with him directly.'

Iris's face broke into a smile that had no mirth. 'He won't play. That's why I've come to you. Here. I think you might.'

'*Play*, Iris?' Megan was beginning to feel hot and uncomfortable. She didn't know when Owen was getting back from his meeting, but she hoped it would be soon. She wasn't enjoying this interview — and she had every intention of putting an end to it as soon as possible.

'That's right. That's just what I mean. You know how I came to work for him in the first place, don't you?'

'I don't — really, Iris,' Megan smiled briefly. 'Frankly, it's not of the slightest interest to me. You are no longer employed by my husband — and if you don't come to the point quickly as to why you are here at all, then I'm afraid I must ask you to leave.'

'Hoity-toity . . .' Iris leant back in her chair. Megan was fuming now. She had never liked her; she was nothing to do with either her or Owen now. How dare the creature force her way into their home like this . . .

'Right then. Here's the point. I came to him through my sister, Diane.'

All the heat left Megan's body; she could feel the chill creeping up from her toes, to her knees.

'She's an old friend of Owen Thomas's, Diane is. She used to be a dancer but she never quite made it, one way and the other. Ask him to tell you about her some time.' She was enjoying the growing horror which Megan could not hide.

'Get out of here,' Megan hissed through clenched teeth. 'Get out of here, I say.'

'Well — you would, wouldn't you?' Iris glanced at her contemptuously. 'I mean a lady like you, all got up, looked after, everything easy. "Is Mr Thomas likely to be late again tonight, Iris?"' mimicking Megan devastatingly. She sat bolt upright. 'You bet he's going to be late, Mrs Thomas, you bet. And why? I'll tell you why ... Because he's screwing his receptionist — me — on the floor of his precious consulting room, the way he likes it — fast and furious and bang and out through the door.'

Megan stood. Breathing heavily, she said icily, 'I do not believe one word of this filth. Now get out of here this instant or I'll call the police. Do you hear me?'

Iris laughed — genuinely. 'Come off it, Mrs Thomas. A fat lot the police care — about me being here or what your hubby gets up to behind closed doors. But I've enjoyed telling you this, wiping the smile off your pretty, ladylike face. I have — really.' She leant towards Megan. 'And you know it's the truth — I *know* you know. He did Diane wrong years ago. All right, she went to the bad, she got hooked on the wrong things. But he didn't have to drop her like a piece of dirt the moment he decided he'd had enough. And he didn't have to do the same to me. But he did.'

Megan had crossed the room and picked up the phone. She could hear the theme tune from another soap that Daisy must be into now floating down the stairs. It crossed her mind: thank God Harriet's not here, lurking about, listening.

'Look, that will do you no good at all. Do you really want the coppers here — with the kiddies upstairs? So you can put it down.' Iris folded her arms as Megan, to her fury, did just that.

'What do you want of us?' she asked roughly.

'Money,' Iris said calmly. 'I don't think Mr Thomas's colleagues would take kindly to being shown one or two of the photographs I have in my possession — do you? Not now, not when his career is going the way it is. Ever so bad it would look. I know all the medical bigwigs. And they wouldn't like it, they wouldn't like it at all. Now would they, Mrs Thomas?'

'Blackmail . . .'

'OK.' Iris shrugged. 'It's a word like any other. But you got the point. Diane's in trouble again. Can't seem to get off the drugs. I'm not asking for the moon — just something to tide us over, get me back to South Africa, set us up a bit. She's never had much luck, Diane hasn't. I'm thinking of more than the few quid he gave me when his conscience decided he didn't want me around, bugging it, any longer. He's used us — Diane and me — plenty. So I think that's reasonable enough. And if you and I play ball, there'll be no trouble with the pix, if you get my meaning.'

She got up, taking her time, still looking round inquisitively.

'Nice place you've got here . . .'

Megan stalked to the door ahead of her, flinging it open, her face averted.

'I don't know how he married a nice girl like you, dear. It's tarts he likes. Works off all that tension that goes with the job. No involvement, no talking. I can't say I blame him. He works damned hard. And it's a scary line of business he's in. But you didn't know, did you? The wives often don't, they say. Funny that . . .'

When Megan had stopped being sick in the downstairs cloakroom, she washed her face and combed her hair and went back upstairs to Daisy.

'Bedtime, Daisy,' she said, snapping off the television in the playroom. 'Do your teeth — and be quick about it.'

'You do look awful,' Daisy said with distaste as Megan tucked her up. 'All white and funny. Ugh . . .'

Still feeling queasy, her legs decidedly weak, Megan remembered to give Harriet a ring at her friend's house before she went down to the kitchen. Owen came home quite soon after; she could hear him whistling loudly as he let himself in. The conference in California only lasted three days, but he had set up a lot of other engagements and he was clearing everything so that he could have two full weeks in the States. Megan knew how much he was looking forward to it.

'Meg? Hello there . . .' He came clattering down to the kitchen. He looked happy and cheerful and eager. And Megan always liked him best in a plain blue shirt. 'Something smells good. Bertha been trying her hand again?'

This was the moment when Megan had intended to tell him that she would, after all, go with him; that they would have to organize her ticket in the morning. His arm around her shoulder, she turned to him. He saw her face — and stepped back.

'I've just had a visitation — from Iris,' she said unsteadily. 'And I think we must sit down at once and talk about it.'

They sat for two hours, perhaps three. It was a ghastly episode for both of them. Long stretches passed without either of them saying anything. Owen denied nothing. He sat with his head in his hands, saying dully — over and over again — 'It had nothing to do with my feelings for you, Meg, absolutely nothing.'

Later, Megan said, 'She said you like tarts. Is that true?'

He sighed like a tired old man. 'It helped a bit when I was young. You know I had a problem coming to terms with — well, a lot of human situations that a doctor has to face.'

'Yes, I know that.'

'I had a sort of breakdown. I suppose I should have told you — but it always seemed rather shameful to me.' Every syllable was agony for him; he was twisting his hands together. 'I was involved with — Diane — at the time. I suppose that didn't help. My parents certainly thought not. I recovered, but I couldn't quite — extricate myself from her.'

'From Diane?'

He nodded.

Megan shut her eyes. A confused picture came to her from years ago: the sluttish girl in the crowded coffee bar; his abject confession before they were married; Gill's offhand remarks . . .

'And after I realized I'd fallen in love with you, that was it, Meg, I swear.' He looked at her directly for the first time since she had dropped the bombshell into the domestic warmth of the kitchen. 'Until she wrote — Diane did — from Johannesburg.' He dropped his head again. 'Her sister was in London, desperate for a job, she said. She had excellent references in the medical field. A good worker, they all said that when I took them up, and extremely efficient. It was just what I was looking for. And that was the time Mrs Butter was getting worse and worse.'

'When did you start sleeping with her?'

'I can't remember. Soon, I suppose. It didn't happen very often. Christ, how I hated myself — after,' he said bitterly.

'I think you should give her some money,' Megan said stonily — surprising herself. 'Enough to get her back to South Africa, keep her going for a bit. She said she won't use the blackmail photographs then. And I believe her.'

They quickly gave up any attempt to eat Bertha's herby stew and settled for coffee and a biscuit. After Owen had stared at the kitchen table, saying nothing, for a long time, he got up abruptly, left the room and came back carrying his briefcase. Opening it, he pulled something out and flung it on the table. Megan gasped. She had seen it so many times in the past weeks — maroon-coloured, slim and expensive; against the tablecloth at San Lorenzo, in the lamplight beside a bed. It was Alain's personal diary.

'I took your car one day last week — mine was low on petrol,' Owen said quietly. 'It slipped out from under the front seat. I've been debating what to do with it, turning it over and over in my mind. I had decided to do nothing. I don't want any explanations. I care too much, far too much, for that — it would only make things worse. But I want to know one thing . . .' He was watching her intensely, all his being given up to that moment. 'Do you love him, Meg?'

Neither slept much. The strange and stilted language that had suddenly come between them, frightening and unrecognizable, dried up altogether. They got through what was left of the evening in silence. Curled to one side of the familiar bed, Megan was chilled to the bone, almost shivering. It was some time in the greyish half light of early morning — when she could tell from his breathing that Owen had dropped off — that an idea came to her. Grasping at it, astonished that she hadn't thought of it before, she immediately fell into a deep, late sleep.

By the time she woke, in a lather of panicky anxiety, Owen had already left. There was a brief note on her dressing table.

'I can never apologize enough for what you had to go through last night. The very thought of it sickens me. Please believe that I have always loved you – and I always will. Owen.'

Megan thought, stricken: and what of Alain and his diary?

When Bertha had taken Daisy off to school, she spoke to Margot. '... a splitting headache, I hope I'm not coming down with a flu ...' And to Margot's dubious questioning, 'No, I'm not going to the States after all. I'll ring in later ...'

She gave a crestfallen Bertha the day off and spent the morning wandering round the house, doing nothing, quickly losing the thread whenever she made the effort to think coherently. Around midday, concentrating hard, she made herself a cup of coffee and with shaking fingers, dialled her mother's number in New York.

'This is the Mortimer residence ...'

She was put through to the bedroom, where Vera was sitting propped up against daintily ruffled pillows with her breakfast tray in front of her.

'Heavens, Megan, this is a nice surprise, so early, and I must tell you ..' She was positively burbling. 'Now that we've got Eddy home, the physiotherapist is working miracles. He's going for walks, a little longer every day. We had a quiet dinner out last night. And at last, he's agreed to be fitted with a hearing aid. He's right back to the old Eddy – the relief of it ...' There was a silence at the other end of the line. 'Megan? Are you there? Is something wrong?'

Out of a burst of sobbing came, 'I'm in such a mess ... *we're* in such a mess ... I don't know what I'm going to do ...'

Vera immediately cleared her mind of Eddy – something she hadn't done for weeks. She then quickly ascertained that none of them was ill or had had an accident, and that Megan was phoning from the house.

'Answer me this, Megan,' she rapped out, all attention. 'Are you properly dressed?'

Taken completely by surprise, Megan stopped weeping and said, 'No,' quite distinctly.

'In that case,' her mother went on crisply. 'I suggest you do just that. Pull yourself together, fix your face and go straight into the office. Moping about like that won't do anyone any good, whatever the problems are.'

'But...'

'Are you coming over here with Owen next week?'

The gulp sounded like a vehement negative.

'I see. In that case...' Vera was thinking rapidly. Eddy's therapy... Ted was due down from Yale for a few days... For the first time in her life, it was apparent that her daughter needed her – badly. In a split second, she made the decision that she had spent half a lifetime avoiding.

'Listen Megan,' she said. 'As soon as I've sorted a few things out at this end, I'm going to make a very, very quick trip to London.'

Part 5

The Daughter

Chapter 27

Three days later, Owen left for San Francisco. At full stretch, keeping even longer hours than usual so that he caught up with as much of his work as possible, he returned to the hospital each night after supper. This was a relief to them both. The evening before he went, he met Megan as she came up the stairs on her way to put Daisy to bed. He had an armful of shirts which he was about to dump into a suitcase.

'Meg,' he said quietly, forcing her to meet his eyes briefly. 'There's something I want to say to you.' Harriet and Daisy were trading childish insults from the top of the house to the bottom. 'In here.' Stiff with resentment, wrung with unhappiness, she followed him into their bedroom. He banged the door shut with his elbow and stood facing her.

'What?'

'It's agony for me to leave you like this, Meg, with so much unresolved between us.' His eyes, beneath the tousled hair, bored into her. And when she didn't reply, 'I did what you said you wanted me to. I gave her a certain sum of money – Iris. She says that's the end of it.' His voice rasped with self-disgust. 'I suppose one can assume that it is. And she also said, about you, "I didn't expect to like her, but I did".'

Megan looked straight at him then. His expression was as vulnerable as a wounded animal's.

'I see.' She nodded.

'I can't say more than I have, Meg – that I'm so desperately sorry, and that you mean everything to me, everything.'

He had played his part, done what *he* could to repair the

damage. And yet she could not answer the simple question he had asked her in the kitchen – Alain's diary lying like a sword between them – late on that ghastly night. *She could not.* Through all this turmoil, their lives turned upside down, the sheer joy that Alain had brought her hovered like a blessing. Even the thought of the diary, stuffed in the back of a little-used drawer in the kitchen – and Owen's pain – didn't change that. Without a word, she rushed out of the room, clattering down the stairs, calling to Harriet.

Going over the latest bank statement at the office with Megan, early the next week, Margot thought: There's something going on with the Thomases, I swear it. It was nothing Megan had said, or even hinted. But Margot's sharp eyes had noticed Megan's secretive phone calls, taken hunched over her desk. On certain days, she looked radiantly beautiful; on others, like today, she was wan and worried. She couldn't make up her mind about going to San Francisco where Owen was to be one of the stars of the conference. Of course she was pleased that she hadn't had to do without her, but she wasn't sure it was right ... And now that mother of hers, who Megan had never had much time for – over the top, Margot had thought, meeting her at her wedding, bumping into that ridiculous hat – had descended on London.

When Megan had finished with the facts and figures, Margot put her mind to what they were doing and said, 'What you mean is, we're still afloat, and the shore line that bit nearer. Is that it?'

Megan, who was gathering up the files and papers, didn't quite meet Margot's frank, humorous look. 'You could say so.'

Around lunchtime, seeing Megan flash past in the corridor, Margot sang out, 'Hey – have you heard the good news?'

Megan stopped and stuck her head round the door. She could see that Margot was bubbling over with excitement.

'What's that?'

'The Bollier people accepted our presentation first go. So we'll all be drinking pale blue fizzy bottled water round here now.'

'That's great, Margot,' Megan said, perking up. 'Can we have a chat about it later? I've got to dash now. My mother's only here for a day or two.'

When Megan arrived at the hotel which the Mortimers called home whenever they were in London, her mother was waiting for her at the door of the suite. Almost running from the lift, Megan did something she had never done before: she flung herself at her.

'I'm so glad you're here,' she gulped, as Vera, slightly unnerved, removed Megan's arms from around her neck.

'So I can see, dear,' she murmured.

'Well,' Vera said, once the exquisite cold lunch had been served and they were left on their own, 'I haven't got a lot of time, so we'd better get down to business. I can recognize the sound of trouble in a marriage when I hear it.'

Megan quailed.

'Owen's in San Francisco receiving tributes from his colleagues and you're in London.' Vera picked up a slice of lemon, pricked it with her fork and squeezed hard. 'You phone me up at some unearthly hour in the morning, crying across the Atlantic, telling me that you're both in a terrible mess.' She eyed Megan sternly over her glasses. Her hair was unrelieved grey now and she was plainly dressed in a simple navy suit that Megan remembered from years ago. 'Don't you think you had better tell me what it's all about?'

When Megan, pushing the food about on her plate, had stammered out the trauma which began when Iris arrived on her doorstep, Vera said thoughtfully, 'The trouble was, you were so young, and so absurdly innocent, when you married him. You saw Owen as a knight in shining armour, swooping down to rescue you, your life smugly mapped out for ever and ever — not as a flesh-and-blood man with his own strengths and weaknesses. I was worried then that you would be hurt.' Megan, her face drawn and colourless, watched her mother across the beautifully appointed table. She waited while Vera finished off the salmon and picked up her napkin. 'I feel sorry for Owen,' she said.

'For Owen? And what about me?' Megan blazed.

'I can quite understand that you had a nasty shock – very nasty. We all have our failings, and we all let people down from time to time, even people we care about.'

She sounded regretful. Coming from Vera, this was an admission – of sorts. For years she had gallivanted around with Carl, regarding Eddy as a tiresome burden, to be looked after by strangers – housekeepers or nurses or secretaries – who were paid for that purpose. Rarely by his wife.

'I realize that.' Megan looked down; the room, scented by fresh lilies, felt stuffy and cloying.

'And Owen obviously has had a weakness. He's a devoted husband to you and a good father to the children. But he's attracted to – well – casual sex. A lot of men, perhaps most men, are. There was that girl he was involved with years ago for quite some time, you said. I smelled a rat there all right. I wondered how that would resolve itself.'

'I can tell you,' Megan shot back spiritedly. 'The girl was Diane, Iris's sister. That was how Iris got the job.'

'Quite. So Owen behaved foolishly, not for the first time; absurdly so for a man of his intelligence and in his position. As if that meant anything – he's human, after all. And you learnt about it in a very sordid way – that creature coming to your house, wanting money. I'm shocked about that. Personally, I would be very surprised if Owen hadn't learnt his lesson – and about time, too. He must be appalled at the way you were dragged into it.'

'He is.'

'All the same, I still feel sorry for him.'

'Why?'

'He's a brilliant man who is helping humanity. They're performing miracles in heart surgery these days, miracles.'

This touched a raw nerve in Megan.

'Do you think I don't know that?' she said passionately. She put her elbows on the table and leant forward. 'Almost all of Owen goes into his work, his patients. I understand, I suppose, but it's not easy to live with. Sometimes it's – it's – impossible.

He's moody, shut up inside himself . . . even I can't reach him. In Wales, it's better: he gets back to his real self there. And I knew things weren't going right between us. I knew it, long before this Iris business. And I did try. There's a cottage near the Thomases, one Owen has always loved. It came on the market this summer and I thought, perhaps, we could buy it, have somewhere of our own where we could get away, be alone together. We need this above everything. But Owen wouldn't hear of it. I think what I mean is . . .' Even to herself Megan sounded desperate. 'We can put the Iris situation behind us. I know that. But we don't seem to have the same priorities, Owen and I. I don't know how much longer I can go on always taking second place to my husband's work, when *I* need his love and attention, too.'

The relief of getting it into words, of saying things that she hadn't even known she felt — above all else, saying them to her mother — was overpowering.

After a moment or two, Vera got up and rang the bell. 'You've hardly touched your lunch, Megan,' she observed coolly. 'And I thought the salmon was excellent.'

When the dishes and the trolley had been ceremoniously dealt with, and coffee brought, Vera said, 'I remember, Megan, you said *we're* in such a mess — that you didn't know what *you* were going to do.'

'Yes . . .'

'And I fancy this isn't solely because of the horrid business with the Iris woman?'

Megan said nothing — and Vera sighed.

'I thought not,' she said, giving Megan, whose eyes seemed to be fixed on the spoon she was stirring her coffee with, a shrewd look. 'It wouldn't have anything to do with that attractive neighbour of yours, would it?'

Megan at last looked up. Her outburst, and just the mention of Alain, had brought life and colour to her face. 'Alain? I adore him,' she said quietly.

For the first time, Vera showed genuine dismay. 'Does Owen know?'

'Yes,' Megan said candidly. 'Yes — I think he does . . .'

'I could do with some air,' Vera said, pushing back her chair, looking distracted. 'All that time sitting about on planes ... I wanted to get Eddy and Ted a cashmere sweater each, at that good shop – Fisher's, isn't it? – off Bond Street. You don't have to be back at work yet, do you?'

Megan shook her head. 'Margot knows you're not here for long. So I'll come with you.'

They walked silently along the crowded pavements in the crisp, wintry gloom. The spirit of Alain Gesson, and Megan's feelings for him, drifted between them. Always decisive, Vera chose the sweaters quickly, and within minutes, they were standing outside the shop again.

That was when Vera said abruptly, 'I want you to come back to the hotel with me, Megan. Your work can wait for a while, surely. I'm leaving tomorrow – I don't like being away from Eddy any longer. I want to talk to you, now, to tell you certain facts. I believe I would have anyhow, now, but I think it might give you a – a perspective on what is happening between you and Owen, on your own life.'

Megan – literally – shrank; she could feel her shoulders curving inwards. She knew exactly what her mother was, at last, going to tell her; the emotional gaps between them, yawning through the years, were closing fast. She clutched her mother's arm.

All her instincts were to resist – and at all costs.

'I can't – I don't want to – the office – Margot – please – I must go . . .'

'I told you, Megan, years ago' – there were people, strangers, all round them; a woman, laden with packages, barged into Megan's side. Her mother's voice seemed to be coming from a long way away – 'that the right was mine, if I chose, when I chose.'

After a lifetime of hopeless wondering, an aching void somewhere in the centre of her being, the question she had despaired of knowing the answer to was going to be answered.

And now that it was upon her, Megan could not bear it. Her mother's distant past – her parentage – was the very last thing she wanted to know about. Ever.

In real distress, she said, 'Please, no, I don't want it ... It's better this way, for both of us ... you were right, after all ...'

But Vera's mind had been made up for some time. After talking to Megan today, she was more than ever convinced that the timing was right. And as an actress — which she supposed she was still — her timing had always been faultless. She hailed a taxi, even for that short distance, pushed Megan in, gave instructions to the driver. Megan, gripped with speechless panic, sat rigid on the slippery leather seat. Her ears were ringing and her heart seemed to be pushing right up her throat and there were funny black spots floating in front of her eyes. Tense, neither saying a word, they bumped and rattled through narrow side streets.

It seemed an age — paying the taxi, through the hall, up in the lift, the door closed on the rest of the world — before Vera finally said, 'You know very well what I want to tell you, Megan — while I can, while there's still time.'

Megan put her hands over her ears and cried out, anguished: 'Stop it ... stop it ... stop it ...'

Something, perhaps the sound of her own voice, steadied her. Vera put out both her hands — which she took. They stood together in the centre of the elegant sitting-room. It was very quiet; anonymous. The London traffic rumbled somewhere beyond the windows and the heavy curtains. It was only mid afternoon, but already the light was beginning to fade.

'I want to tell you, Megan, how I came to meet — and to fall in love with — your father.'

Every syllable dropped, precisely, into the electric air between them. As one person, they separated — Megan to curl up in a corner of the sofa, Vera sitting ramrod straight on a highbacked chair. Megan's eyes never once left her mother. And Vera saw that now Megan had lost her youthful curves, she resembled her father more than ever: those dense green-grey eyes; the slanting brows; the high cheekbones. In that still, silent room, it was as though her emotional life had come full circle.

'It was at a lunch party at the Savoy, in the spring of 1939.

We only met briefly, towards the end; although I'd noticed him, of course – it was impossible not to. He telephoned the next morning and invited me for supper.'

'Did it begin at once – the affair?'

'Oh, immediately. That night.' Vera's thoughts seemed to be wandering; she turned towards the darkening window.

'Go on.'

Never articulate, Vera spoke haltingly – and much of what she said was oddly disconnected. But the gist of the story was unmistakable: the passion, the tempestuousness, the awkwardness of their vastly different backgrounds. 'He was rich, very much part of the landed gentry. And I was an actress – got on – from the East End. It mattered then – you can't imagine how much. It was his mother who decided, before he did, that I really wouldn't do.' She touched, vaguely, on his strange political leanings ('I thought them quite mad at the time'); the beautiful country house, she couldn't remember the name – 'and he lived a lot of the time in London, in Chester Square'; the urgent sense everyone had in those days of living on borrowed time, the war overtaking their lives.

'And when you found out you were pregnant – with me . . .?' Megan whispered.

'It was all over by then, the affair, although I didn't know it,' Vera said with a sad little smile that went through Megan like a knife. 'He arranged the abortion before he left for France with his regiment. He even had his butler drive me there.'

'*What?*' In one bound, Megan had left the sofa and was kneeling by Vera, her hands on her knees.

'But I couldn't do it.' Vera looked down at Megan. 'I couldn't,' she repeated. 'I – just – left . . .'

'And what about – him?' Megan demanded. 'What did he do then?'

'Nothing. Not a word. I don't believe my letters ever reached him. But I don't believe it would have made any difference if they had.'

'But he let you down,' Megan burst out – violent, accusing. 'He behaved dreadfully.'

'Perhaps. I suppose you could say that. Although these things are never so simple.' Great waves of love and empathy — and admiration — were breaking over Megan. Everything in her life, her life itself, she owed to her mother. 'I had Nellie — and soon after you were born, I met Eddy. But leaving you, in Trout Lane ...' Her composure was going now and her voice was shaking. 'You must believe me when I say that that was the hardest thing I ever did in my life.'

Some time later — they were sitting in semi-darkness — Megan lifted her face from her mother's lap.

'Did you see him — after?' she asked gently.

'Once, near the end of the war. He came to my dressing-room. I was very successful then, you know.'

'I know you were. And did you tell him? About me?'

'Yes. Yes, I did. I was very bitter, of course. He was like a mad thing, pacing up and down. He wanted to help, he insisted. It was what he wanted more than anything else, he said. And I believed him.' She sat fractionally straighter. 'But I refused. I wouldn't tell him anything. You see, I knew he was married by then. I saw it in the paper, a few days after you were born.'

'Oh my God ...' Bleeding with her mother's hurt, Megan shut her eyes briefly. 'And was that the last time you saw him?'

Vera hesitated. She had intended keeping their last meetings, in New York, to herself. They concerned nobody else — and in ways she didn't fully understand, they had gone a long way to healing the past. But now, with Megan ...

'We met again in New York, not very long ago. Mutual friends ... a party ... We had lunch alone ...' She looked down at Megan's face in the dimness — white; eyes great grey pools. 'I told him a little about you, of course. There was a lot of — something — between us still. And he said ...' Although she couldn't see her face clearly, Megan knew that she was smiling. 'He said, "If I had to do it all over again, I would have done it very differently." And it's nice to dream, isn't it?'

Megan never knew how long they stayed like that, her cheek

resting on her mother's hand; but she was aware of a change in the traffic sounds — street lights shining; the frenetic crush of the rush hour beginning.

'There's one thing you haven't told me,' Megan said.

Gathering her thoughts, which had been miles and miles away, Vera asked, 'What's that?'

'His name.'

'Of course. I haven't mentioned that, have I?' She placed both her hands on Megan's head. There was a world of peace and understanding between them. And into it she dropped two words: 'Robert Brandon.'

When the world had stilled and the blackness that had come crashing down on her lifted a little, Megan found that she and her mother were both — inexplicably — sitting on a sofa; Vera had her arm around her and seemed to be rocking her. Megan had no recollection at all of where she was or what she was doing there. In her confusion, the only thing that puzzled her was, why are we sitting in the dark?

'It's the shock,' her mother was saying, somewhere near her head. Shock? What shock? And why was she sounding so concerned? 'You went all faint on me, but I got you up somehow. Now sit very still. If you feel it coming on again, push your head down between your knees . . .'

And that was when it all came flooding back: where she was — and the conversation that had led to this moment. From one second to the next, her mind focused. *Robert Brandon was her father.* Everything else in her consciousness — her home, her family, Alain — had been wiped clean, like a slate. Turning towards the shadowy form that was her mother, Megan cried — and her voice was as clear as a peal of bells —

'Robert Brandon . . . But I know him — I've met him. It was Ceci Brandon who took Alain in when he came from France as a child in the war. Zillah was painting the gardens at Cloverley — that's the name of the house — when she became ill last summer. I went down with Alain to fetch her. And that was when I met him . . .'

It was Vera who was speechless then.

'And I liked him. He told me that he had had heart trouble and I said he should see Owen. Ceci swore that she was going to make an appointment. And he said I reminded him of someone.'

In a quick movement, Megan stood, pulling at her mother's hand. It was like a puzzle; a vital link locked in, all the other pieces moving inexorably into place. With only the slightest effort of the imagination, she could see them together, her mother and Robert Brandon, as they must have been at the beginning of the war — ill-starred, romantic, and a couple: her parents. When he had seen her at Cloverley, he had sensed something.

Her voice full of laughter, dizzy with overwhelming joy and relief, Megan cried out, 'We can't go on sitting in the dark like this. Let's go home. The children will be back and Harriet is longing to see you. I've got a very special letter I want you to see, if I can find it . . .'

Hunting through her desk, Megan at last found what she had been looking for: Robert Brandon's letter from Cloverley. She rushed straight down to the kitchen where Vera and Harriet were huddled in a long, serious talk.

'What are you two up to?' Megan enquired. 'I've got something rather important that I want to show Vera, Harriet.' She looked a different woman from the one who had been dealing with the figures of Margot Spelling Inc. that morning — eager, vibrant, clear-eyed.

'Oh, leave us *alone*,' Harriet said crossly. 'You had Vera most of today and she's going back to New York tomorrow.'

'Later, Megan,' Vera said over Harriet's head, looking about for her glasses. 'Now wherever did I put them? I've got my diary here, Harriet. We're plotting a scheme for next summer.'

Watching the two of them, Megan thought, I never believed I'd see my mother as a middle-aged woman, enjoying being with her grandchild, but aching to get back to her home and her kind and gentle husband. She had completely given up smoking after Eddy's stroke; Megan hardly recognized her without a cigarette.

'Why don't you go up and see if Daisy has done her homework?' Harriet asked. 'We've nearly finished.' Harriet, who never showed much affection, except to Owen, leant closer to Vera.

'Here are your glasses. Stick them on, and we'll write the dates in a red pencil.'

Megan found Daisy reading in bed. To her surprise, every bit of homework had been done. After Megan had commented, pleased and surprised, Daisy said, yawning, 'Bertha gives me treats when I do it. But I do miss making up the excuses in class.'

When even Harriet had at last gone up to bed, Megan poured a glass of wine for her mother and herself. She had laid the table in the kitchen while Vera made a long phone call to New York from her bedroom.

'Harriet has a way of eavesdropping on the stairs,' she explained, shutting the door firmly after Vera had come back down to the sitting-room and sunk into a comfortable chair. 'And she always wants to monopolize you.'

'She's going to spend a month with us in Connecticut this summer. That's what all the whispering was about. I said I was sure you wouldn't mind. It will be good for Eddy, and I'll enjoy having her about, too. Everything's fine there, by the way, and they both send you their love. Ted is keeping Eddy company until I get back.' Vera took the glass of wine. 'Harriet's very adult for a girl of her age, isn't she?'

'Very.'

'And I can never help thinking — you'll agree with me now — how much she resembles Robert.'

Megan laughed.

'Our eyes, and Owen's hair, and a maddening amount of assurance.' The knowledge of her father was still so breathtakingly new to her; would she ever get used to the idea of it? 'I did find the letter — I knew I'd kept it. Here . . .'

As she was still wearing her glasses, Vera read it — and re-read it — and handed it back to Megan. 'He's a great charmer, even now. Didn't you think so?'

'I did. Everyone says that about him. And he's also considered cold and arrogant . . . ruthless. Politicians have to be, I suppose.'

'When I knew him — and I don't believe we change much — he was all of those things.'

'And handsome.'

'Oh, devastating,' she agreed. 'Utterly.'

Vera sat back in the chair. She hadn't realized how weary she was — the jet-lag, the searing emotion of the day . . . She watched Megan, who was standing in front of the fire, with pleasure.

'But he left you,' Megan said. 'And me. And in a particularly cold-blooded way. That was ruthless enough.'

'I've told you, Megan.' Vera sighed. She really was feeling very tired indeed. 'Human relationships are never simple. You know that — or you should do. And remember, we were living through an abnormal time. There must be no looking back, in bitterness, for either of us.'

Sampling one of Bertha's specials as they sat down for supper, Vera said, 'What a treasure that woman is. This is quite delicious.'

'Isn't it? It's her spicy goulash. I couldn't work without her,' Megan said. 'She looks after us all. Just as she used to look after Zillah.'

'And you'll keep on working, will you? I've noticed a distinct improvement in Daisy, by the way.'

Megan smiled ruefully. 'She's much less spoilt, despite all Bertha's attention. That's what Owen says. And I enjoy the work, so I will keep it up. I believe in Margot and the way she goes about things. I think we're a good pair — and with luck, the agency will go right to the top. It won't be Margot's fault if it doesn't.'

'Did I mention that when I spoke to Ted just now, he had heard from Owen?'

Megan tensed. 'No — no, you didn't. He phoned here just to say he had arrived in San Francisco. That was all.'

'The conference was very successful, apparently, but he's leaving as soon as he can. And he's spending a couple of nights with us in New York. He has other appointments the following week, I believe. Now listen, Megan,' Vera lowered her voice; she had been wanting to say this all evening. It seemed to her of crucial importance. 'I don't wish to interfere, but I know about your feelings towards Alain Gesson, and Owen's transgressions, and

I'm not unsympathetic. I can't tell you how to live your life, but . . .'

'No,' Megan agreed coolly, getting up from the table. 'No, you can't . . .'

Waiting for the taxi, to take her back to the hotel, Vera said slowly, 'I suppose you will go down to Cloverley, on the pretext of seeing the portrait, won't you?'

'Yes. I must. Just to be with him for a little while, knowing all I do now – and there may not be a lot of time.'

'I've been afraid of that, of course. Vera Hansard told me that he had a minor heart attack quite recently. That was when I first started to think seriously about telling you.'

'Did he? I wonder if Owen is looking after him? I do hope so. He never says, not unless I ask, and particularly if it's someone well known.'

'I hope so, too. But when all the other troubles came along, and I knew you were – you are – going through a difficult patch, I thought, I must; however hard, I really must be strong, and face it, with you.'

Megan put out her hand to her mother's. 'I'm glad,' she said simply, 'for both of us.'

'Let him wait,' Vera ordered, after Megan had answered the cabbie's ring. 'I can't leave without saying one more thing to you – and you may take it as you will.' She stood, tall and imposing, still a woman of striking appearance. 'I've chased a rainbow all my life – I expect you can see that now. Regretting, desiring, thinking of what might have been . . . For a very long time, I didn't see, or want to see, the goodness and the happiness that was right in front of me. And oh, Megan, it would be the death of me to watch you doing the same.'

When Vera had left, Megan sat down and wrote a note to Cecilia Brandon, at Cloverley, telling her that she expected to be in the area on Saturday afternoon and could she take up her husband's kind offer to show her a particular portrait? She hadn't heard from Alain recently, she said, but she believed that Zillah was improving, and happier.

When she had finished, she went straight to a drawer in the kitchen. Pulling out Alain's diary, hardly looking at it, she stuffed it into an envelope. From that first heart-stopping moment when Owen produced it, Megan had known that this was what she must do. Yet, she had procrastinated — day after day; postponing the painful letting-go. There was no need for a note or an explanation. Alain would understand — as she did now. He loved Zillah, she was certain of that, but he needed his occasional diversions. A dalliance with a pretty woman was meat and drink to a man of his temperament. For her — looking across the kitchen, eyes blurred with tears, unaware of the old familiar objects around her ... 'Memories,' she said aloud. 'Memories, and a rainbow to be chased ...'

Shutting her mind to everything else in her life, picking up both the envelopes, she let herself out into the dark, quiet night and ran up the road to the postbox.

Chapter 28

Always warm and spontaneous, Ceci Brandon telephoned the same evening she got Megan's letter.

'How good to hear from you – and do please drop in on Saturday. Any time in the afternoon. Robert hasn't been at all well, so we've been taking things quietly. Come whenever it suits you.'

It was a bitter, grey day, with an icy wind tearing through bare, blackened branches. But even in that harsh light, Cloverley's warm, pinkish stone and the eccentric charm of its turrets and odd windows still glowed. Driving slowly through the park, quivering with apprehension, Megan couldn't help wondering how her mother had come upon the house in the autumn of 1939. Had its beauty, and tranquillity, overawed her? Had she and Robert been happy that day? She had only been there once, she said; she couldn't even remember the name.

Driving from London, Megan had been on the point of turning back at least twice. She was playing with fire; she knew that. And was it wise? 'There may not be a lot of time,' she had said to her mother. She had known that she must do it quickly – or not at all. And a perfect opportunity had presented itself. Nobody seemed to be about in the bleak late afternoon; there were lights already on in the house. Taking a grip of her nerves, Megan flung a warm, cherry red cape round the shoulders of her grey suit and walked confidently across the crescent of the driveway.

Ceci Brandon must have heard the car because as Megan approached, the great door was flung open and she called out in her loud, pleasant voice, 'Megan, come in at once. It's freezing out there,' enveloping her in her messy, friendly, country-house aura. And with Ceci fussing about her being cold and the dogs yapping and snuffling and the ghostly ambiance of the ancient hall around her, Megan thawed. She was there as a guest, as a friend of the family. Nobody else in the world — except her mother, who was now back in New York — knew the poignant undercurrents that had forged this extraordinary meeting.

Removing the cape, smiling back at Ceci, she said boldly, 'My husband is away in the States and my children are doing things with their school. So I came to see an old schoolfriend who lives quite near and I thought I would take you at your word.'

They went straight into the library which was lit by a few blurry lamps and the blazing warmth from a huge log fire.

'Robert, Megan Thomas is here.' A tweedy figure, tall and a bit bent, rose from a great leather armchair. He was noticeably more fragile than when Megan had first seen him, in the spring.

'My dear, a pleasure . . .'

His hand, in Megan's, felt like porcelain.

'It's so kind of you,' Megan said, looking him full in the face. It was all there — the eyes, the thick hair springing back from the forehead. Megan had no feeling of shock; only recognition. Her loyalty given totally to her mother, she wanted to be armoured against his craggy good looks, his assurance. She was not. His fragility smote her.

'You remembered to write, about the picture; and as I was near by . . .' She faltered.

He was looking at her with an absorption quite as intense as hers. 'We're so glad you looked us up, particularly since the name "Thomas" has become a byword in this house. That's right, isn't it, Ceci?'

Ceci, who was carrying off Megan's cape, glanced carelessly back at them over her shoulder. 'You may not know, Megan, but we took your advice, and Alain's, and Robert consulted your husband at once. I really insisted. And he found him most impressive. He's now under his very superior care. He's his guru, you might say.'

'Really?' Megan's face lit up. 'I am *so* pleased,' she said fervently. 'He's the most wonderful doctor. All his patients adore him.'

'I can see why. He's really very attractive. I've always been mad about red hair.' Ceci came back in and sat on the shabby old leather fender. Her hands were stuck into an outsize woollen cardigan, which could well have been an old one of her husband's or her sons'. 'We've been up to Harley Street several times since the summer, haven't we, Robert? And we've got another appointment next month.'

Drinking tea, drenched in the fire's heat, they chatted about the Gessons and Zillah's precarious mental health.

'We hear she's painting again,' Robert said. 'Although her pictures are a bit modern for my taste.' Ceci winked at Megan as she refilled her cup. 'She's enchanting, of course, but a very unstable creature. It's hard on Alain.'

'Oh, he asked for it,' Ceci said, feeding crumbs of biscuit to the dogs. 'We all thought he was far too hasty in marrying her. Even Millie had her doubts, and she thinks there's no one on earth like Alain. Although they're a good pair – and they seem exceptionally happy together as long as Zillah isn't having one of her terrible down swings. Millie asked to be remembered to you, by the way, Megan.'

'Oh, do give her my love. I liked her so much.'

'I will. She's had both her hips done and she's hopping round like a two-year-old. She's in charge of the kitchen here, now, and we're having the first decent food we've had for years. It seems as though Alain's stuck in France indefinitely. He simply dare not leave. So Millie is going out to visit them. That should cheer him up. He sounded very gloomy on the phone the other evening. I don't think I've ever heard him so sad.' Ceci looked at Megan thoughtfully, weighing her up. 'My poor Alain . . .'

Even his name sent a tremor through Megan; perhaps it always would. 'It's a difficult situation. I know that,' she said, meeting Ceci's eyes.

'There's no shortage of funds,' Robert added impatiently, reaching forward to put his cup on the table. 'They live marvellously well in France, I'm told. It's a huge estate old Amos bought them.'

'He might have bought it, but Alain did all the restoration work,' Ceci snapped.

'All Werner money, my dear.'

'I happen to think that Alain has squandered his talent. He only gets those television shows because he looks so good and he still has that accent.'

While the Brandons squabbled amiably, Megan stared into the brilliant, leaping flames and wondered restlessly whether the diary had reached him yet. And what he would feel when it did.

Having exhausted the Gessons as a conversational topic, Ceci said to Megan, 'I'm so sorry Harry and the twins aren't down. I'd have liked you to meet them. There's much more life about the place when they're here. Our old Nanny, who brought them up, is still living with us — in her dotage.' Megan had noticed various silver-framed photographs of dark-haired young men, all the spitting image of their mother, dotted around tables in the room. Getting up to chuck another log on the fire, Ceci said, 'Harry is farming in Scotland and the twins say they want to be lawyers — that's the latest. They're terribly naughty, always wanting things.' She glanced defiantly at her husband. 'I adore them. Now do tell us about yours — two little girls, isn't it?'

Soon afterwards, Megan made a move to leave. She wanted to get some of the journey behind her before it was completely dark.

'But we've forgotten the portrait,' Robert cried. 'Good heavens, we can't miss that. It's what Megan came for.' He got up, laboriously, and walked ponderously out of the library while Ceci and Megan climbed the shallow steps to where the portrait hung. Robert watched from the hall below.

'He's not terribly good on stairs now,' Ceci murmured to Megan. 'In fact, we've really been very worried about him.'

'I know,' Megan replied quietly. 'He does look frail. I can see that.'

'And he still gets so worked up about things — it's terribly bad for him.'

When they reached the landing, Ceci shouted out, 'Here we

are, Robert, here's Cordelia Brandon,' her words reverberating around the huge, high space. They looked up at the picture, which Megan remembered vividly. The formal creamy satin dress, the pearls ... From this angle, the willowy height of the young woman, already accentuated, seemed almost a caricature. It was the dark hair, the eyes, and the unusually slanted brows which riveted Megan's attention. Some way down, Robert called out.

'Stand right underneath, Megan. Like that ... Out of the way, Ceci.' Irritably, he motioned her to one side with his hand. Taking up the portrait pose exactly, Megan raised her chin, half turned, and gazed across at the minstrels' gallery at the further end of the hall.

It was Ceci — looking around, beginning to be bored — who saw him: right hand across his left chest, bent over, stifling a moan. She and Megan flew back down the stairs, both reaching him at the same moment, physically preventing him from falling. Supporting him by his arms, they helped him back to the library and into his chair. He was terribly pale and his lips had a bluish tinge. Within seconds, Ceci was in full command, doling out pills, pouring water, reaching for the phone.

'I don't want to see that damned man, Ceci,' he spluttered, grimacing from the pills, his hands trembling, 'so put the bloody phone down. I don't mean your husband, Megan, it's the local quack she's after.'

Megan watched him anxiously. The only sounds were the licking flames and the wind keening outside. Exhausted by all the effort and the pain, he put his head back and closed his eyes. Muttering to herself, Ceci had abandoned the phone and seemed to have gone in search of some different tablets.

'So sorry, my dear,' he croaked to Megan. 'I do get these turns. I'll be all right in a short while.'

'It was me — and the portrait, wasn't it?'

She couldn't help herself. The words, after all, meant nothing in particular — except to her. And to him, perhaps? She thought they did; after seeing the way he reacted, she was almost sure. Although he made no sign, she knew he'd heard. Still with his eyes shut, he put out his hand to her. Megan's heart thudded over. She took his hand and held it and placed it flat against her cheek.

'Look after yourself,' she whispered, her voice catching helplessly. She stayed like that for several minutes, but he seemed to have drifted off to sleep, so she put his hand gently back at his side and tiptoed out of the room.

Driving back to London through the stormy darkness, Megan worried away about Robert; guilty feelings nagged her conscience. He'd had a nasty bout, seeing her standing directly below the portrait. And emotion often brought on these attacks. How much, if anything, did he know? Or suspect? The truth, she thought – but she would never be certain. Ceci seemed concerned and competent; but she knew from Alain that she lived her own life now and was often away from Cloverley for days at a time. She hated to think of him being on his own there, in the huge, draughty house, with the wind shrieking round it; no one to give him warmth and comfort – except dear Millie Frampton, perhaps.

Sharp images of the afternoon came back to her: the fire blazing orange in the great hearth; Ceci's welcoming warmth; the papery feel of Robert's hand when she put it to her face. Crawling through the suburban traffic, she thought, seeing my father today – knowing – was like being shown a baby for the first time. You wondered how you could ever have imagined that he – or she – would be anything other than themselves.

Once she was sure that Robert was stable – and he still refused point blank to call the doctor – Ceci shot off upstairs to change for a dinner-party. It was being given by a local farmer and his wife who lived some ten miles away. Her friend and lover, Bert Woods, would be there – they all hunted together – and it promised to be a jolly evening. It wasn't Robert's cup of tea, even if he were well; and Ceci had pooh-poohed the idea of inviting him. When she had put on a long black skirrt and the inevitable

'It's absurd to stay here, Ceci. I'm perfectly all right — just feeling a bit weak. They'll bring me something on a tray if I ring. And I'd like a good whisky.'

As soon as she had brought him his drink, he seemed anxious to be rid of her.

'Now go on,' he told her testily. 'Enjoy yourself. I may, or I may not, be up when you get back. And for God's sake stop treating me like some elderly ruin.'

Knocking back his drink, he waited until he heard her car zoom off before pulling the phone over to his chair. Then, using a magnifying glass as well as his normal reading glasses, he eventually found the number he was looking for. He dialled. By some miracle, he immediately reached Veronica Hansard in New York. Using all his old wiles, exerting every ounce of charm he still possessed, he asked a few precise questions concerning Vera Mortimer's past. Other people's secrets were Veronica Hansard's prey; she scented them out like a bloodhound. Nothing much escaped her — and let her make what she would of his curiosity. She didn't disappoint him. Well satisfied, he thanked her effusively and collapsed back into the comfort of the chair he had known all his life.

He couldn't be positive; but it all fitted. The timing of the second marriage; the child's age, although Veronica didn't know her name; brought up in London by some shadowy grandmother, she believed. Cockney most likely, somewhere in the East End; like Vera. He would never know anything of this, of course; all those years were lost to him. It was the portrait, finally. But it was more than that. Even last summer, that first casual meeting, brought about through the Gessons, and Zillah's collapse — and it was on these extraordinary coincidences that everyone's life turned, if you came to consider it — even then he had sensed some familiarity.

Steady, he told himself, his breathing laboured, steady . . .

He was as sure as he would ever be that Megan Thomas was his daughter. She knew it, too; he was certain. Vera, who never did anything without a reason, had told her. And a very charming and beautiful young woman she was, too, with a splendid husband, a distinguished physician – *his* doctor. A good chap; he'd got on with him very well indeed. He felt a spasm of genuine yearning – for the years that had gone by, for Vera, for so many things. But as his breathing became gradually more relaxed, still thinking of Megan, a feeling came upon him that he had rarely experienced in all his life: profound satisfaction.

Also in New York that evening, Vera watched her son-in-law prowl about her formal drawing-room, where everything, down to the last lamp and ashtray, had been brilliantly thought out by an army of interior decorators.

'Owen, dear, do take a drink and sit down somewhere – anywhere.' Vera clinked the vodka and ice in her glass. He had arrived that morning, fresh from what was clearly a triumph in the most rarefied medical circles; although watching him, no one would believe it. Since Vera had looked him in the eye and told him that she had just returned from a flying visit to Megan in London, he had behaved like a man going through some acute personal crisis. Even the studied, professional composure had cracked – and he hadn't shown a great deal of interest in Eddy's prognosis either, Vera thought, miffed.

'We've been looking forward to having you visit with us, Owen. And Ted will be down from New Haven tomorrow,' Vera said serenely. Privately, she had every intention of giving him a piece of her mind, sharply and concisely, when the right moment came.

'What about a vodka?' she asked. Anything to get him to behave normally for a bit. 'Or would you prefer wine?'

Owen stopped his pacing and poured himself a drink. Swivelling round, looking desperate, he blurted, 'She's not going to leave me, Vera? Is she?'

At that moment, Eddy shuffled into the room, moving carefully, using a stick. Tall and benign, and rosy-cheeked, perfectly dressed by the best outfitters in London, he was better looking than he had ever been as a young man, despite his physical disability.

'Leave – what's that, Owen?' Eddy's state-of-the-art hearing aid was switched on for once. 'Why, you've hardly got here, and we want to hear all about the conference, don't we, dear? We surely are very proud of you. That article in the *Times* now...'

Vera shushed him and kept her hand on his arm. 'Owen's not talking about leaving us, darling,' she said, raising her voice slightly. 'He's afraid that when he gets home, Megan will have decided *she's* leaving *him*. Owen, would you please get Eddy the weakest possible scotch and water?'

Looking bemused, Eddy sat in the chair next to Vera's. And Vera decided that the time for her plain talking had come.

'It's my fault, that's what you really think, isn't it?' Owen gave Eddy his watery drink and turned back to Vera. 'I'm a workaholic, too wrapped up in what I'm doing, Megan feels shut out, neglected. Is that it – really?' He sounded close to despair. 'Is that why she turned to – Gesson?'

Vera said cautiously, 'I think it's part of what has gone wrong between you.'

But he interrupted, flinging himself into one of her pretty bergère chairs. Vera thought, that hair will never lose its colour completely; but there's a lot of white mixed in now – it tones it down, improves his looks. Then she turned her attention to the torrent of words pouring out of him concerning the crisis in his relationship with Megan, and his desperate hopes for putting it right. When he had finished, and during the silence that followed, Vera decided, brilliant he may be, but as Nellie Bowen would have said, common sense is not so common. To Vera, it seemed a matter of accommodation on both their parts, his and Megan's. At the same time, what he had just told them showed imagination.

And the idea he had floated would appeal to Megan. Vera was definitely encouraged.

'What's that, Owen?' Eddy leant towards him, blinking. 'You're getting into real estate, did you say? Isn't that rather out of your field?'

Vera patted his arm.

'I think,' she said to Owen, rather as though she was talking to a not very bright child, 'I think it would be an extremely good idea if you and Megan...' She paused. Now there was a word –

Megan had used it — that perfectly expressed what she was trying to get across to Owen, who, for all his brains, seemed to be rather dim in certain matters. It came to her. *'Priorities,'* Vera crowed triumphantly. 'That's *exactly* what I mean. It's high time you got your priorities straight, both of you. And for God's sake tell her what you've done.'

Waking in a sweaty panic, his heart banging, Robert Brandon started up in the chair. He had had some fearful dream, as he often did after one of his attacks; it was still at the edge of his consciousness. It involved a car, a crash, some unspeakable disaster. He said aloud, 'Megan?' Somehow, she had figured in the nightmare. Was she all right? Had she got home safely? Fumbling for his glasses, sorting through a pile of letters with shaking hands, he found her note to Ceci. He grasped the phone.

'Hello, this is Harriet. Who's there? Who are you?' A child's voice, probably about twelve; surprisingly competent. His throat was tight and he was uncomfortably breathy. 'Here, you'd better take it, Mum. Whoever it is doesn't seem to want to talk.'

After a brief pause, Megan said politely, 'Hello? Can I help you?'

'I — I only — wanted . . .' But the agonizing pain was creeping up his arm, across his chest, snuffing out the air. Wincing, he fell back, dropping the receiver. After some seconds, hardly daring to breathe, he lost consciousness.

'It must have been a wrong number,' Megan said, frowning. Strange calls always disturbed her, although Owen had told her, crisply, that she shouldn't worry. 'Emergency calls almost always get through somehow,' he said.

'If it's important, they'll ring back, won't they?' Harriet asked reasonably. 'Why don't we get Daisy and have a game of Scrabble?'

'All right.'

And when Harriet had summoned Daisy with an ear-splitting whistle, 'When is Dad coming back?'

'I don't know for sure, Harriet. The week after next, I think.'

Robert was peacefully asleep in the chair when Ceci came in and found him just before midnight. The phone was still dangling where it had fallen. She had tried to reach him several times, each time getting the engaged signal. She had left the party, which she wasn't enjoying, soon after dinner.

Hearing the door, and her footsteps, he opened his eyes.

'*Robert* – you gave me the most terrible fright. What happened? I haven't been able to get through to the house. And the office didn't answer at this hour.' She looked shocked. 'I thought – I don't know what I thought . . .' Even her usual high colour was blanched.

'I expect you thought I was dead,' Robert said equably, wide awake by then. 'And a very reasonable assumption, too.' He pushed at the receiver and immediately remembered Megan's voice. And the child's. 'I must have knocked this damned thing off. But I assure you I am not – dead, that is. I had a very good rest and I'm feeling rather well. I'm already looking forward to whatever it is Millie proposes to give us for lunch tomorrow. Pheasant, I think she said . . .'

Chapter 29

Owen arrived at Somerset Terrace shortly after eight o'clock on Monday morning. It was blowing a gale, raining hard and still almost pitch dark. He had cancelled the second half of his American tour, left the Mortimers after only one day, and travelled overnight from New York, taking the first flight he could get on. He was hollow-eyed and unshaven; he looked as though he hadn't slept for a week. His damp raincoat seemed to hang off him and he was carrying a case in either hand. Opening the door on him — and she hadn't the least idea he was planning to come home so soon — Megan stepped back in astonishment. They glared at each other, while the gusty rain came slanting in. Upstairs, Daisy was complaining loudly and tearfully; and Harriet, usually so controlled, was having one of her rare but violent tantrums, which seemed to concern schoolwork that had gone missing. There was a strong acrid smell of burnt toast.

Megan and Owen stood there for at least a minute, the wind licking round their legs, before they both spoke at once, very fast.

Megan said, 'I've sent the diary back. It's over.'

Owen said, 'Priorities. That was my fault. And I've bought Pear Cottage.'

They were so intent on spitting out what they had to say — to get it over with — that each scarcely heard the other. So they then said, again simultaneously, 'What?'

At that moment, all the lights in the house flickered and went out.

Owen came in, banged the door shut, dropped his luggage

and made straight for the cupboard where a torch was kept for such emergencies. Whatever had passed between them on the doorstep — searing as forked summer lightning — would have to wait.

'You'd better go and have a look at Daisy,' Megan said coldly. 'She's got a temperature and I've been up with her most of the night.'

She felt her way along the wall and started up the stairs.

'Where's Bertha, for God's sake?' Owen called out from below.

Crashing and cursing, he stumbled out with the torch which he shone on Megan, who was near the top of the stairs. She had never looked so plain; her hair hung lankly and her face was pale and puffy.

'She was called to Germany last night. Her sister has shingles.' She looked as though she was about to burst into tears. 'I've rung up an agency to try to get someone to stay with Daisy.'

Harriet was now screaming hysterically. 'I can't see, I can't see. And I worked all the weekend on it. It's a French essay, the longest I've ever done. I can't find it. If it's anything to do with Daisy, if she's done anything to it ... And what's happened to the lights?'

Megan edged gingerly into her room. 'Calm down, Harriet,' she said sharply. 'There's obviously been an electricity cut. And Dad's back. He's going in to see Daisy. Where did you have it last, the essay? Owen, Harriet must be able to see.' She went back out to the landing, snatched the torch from him and gave it to Harriet. Close to demented by now, Harriet totally ignored her father. Megan said with a composure she was far from feeling, 'Look right through all the papers, carefully, Harriet, one more time.'

Daisy was sobbing pathetically, 'It's all dark, and I'm hot, and I feel sick.'

Owen went in and closed the door. At once, Harriet found her essay — exactly where she had put it the night before, as far as Megan could tell. She then helped her find her boots and raincoat and an umbrella and saw her off to school. Harriet remembered Owen's reappearance as she was leaping down the front steps.

'Tell Dad I'll see him tonight,' she called back, running down to the gushing street.

Megan slammed the door shut, and was heaving a sigh of relief — at least Harriet was dealt with — when the phone rang. It was Margot calling her back. She had spoken to her earlier about the domestic crisis caused by Bertha's sudden absence and Daisy's bad night.

'Listen, Meg, don't even think of getting someone to stay with Daisy. You must be worn out. It's a lousy morning, the traffic will be hell — stay at home and have a day off. Have several if you want to. I still feel guilty that you didn't go to the States with Owen.'

Megan said faintly, 'Thanks Margot. I'll see how it goes. Stay in touch' — and rang off.

Did Owen say he had bought Pear Cottage — or had she imagined it?

They met on the landing where an eerie grey light was beginning to filter in through the windows.

'Daisy's got chicken-pox,' Owen said flatly. 'Textbook case. She's rather proud of herself.'

'Oh, the poor love . . .'

'Daisy can wait.' He caught her arm as she pushed past him and they ended up sitting on the top stair, not touching. Reassured by Owen's attention, Daisy had gone quiet.

'I put in a ridiculously low offer,' he said stiffly. 'For Pear Cottage. I'd forgotten all about it, my mind was so full of everything else. Gwen nursed it through. I was going to tell you that night.' He wrenched his head round to her. 'The night I came home and you told me that Iris had been here.'

Megan remembered that he had been whistling as he came in, unusually for him. 'I told you, I sent the diary back,' Megan said dully. Her eyes were fixed on the wall opposite. 'I'm sorry . . . sorry, sorry, sorry . . .'

'I wasn't guiltless over that,' Owen said steadily. 'I knew I was overextended professionally, that things were going cold between us. What happened with both of us — or so I pray — were the symptoms, not the causes. Vera told me you said "priorities" —

and it's true. It's not going to be easy, but I'm going to cut down whatever I can, resign unnecessary committees, limit the research and travelling, concentrate on my patients. I think, after all, that's what I'm best at. And I've had my hour in the sun.'

'But I'm terribly proud of your work, Owen — of all you're achieving. I always have been,' she said — quickly, wretchedly.

He longed to reach out and touch her. The cat, in obvious distress, stalked around them. 'I know that, Meg,' he said humbly. 'But in the process, I've taken everything at home — you particularly — very much for granted.'

'And Pear Cottage?'

'You were right in thinking it could play a part in balancing our lives. Particularly with your own work now. And the children. I've been going over the possibilities in my mind — endlessly. We can make a go of it, still, sort out what's important in our lives, despite all the pressures. If we care about each other, enough, to want to. That's the point, really, isn't it, Meg? As for the cottage, it's yours anyhow — whatever happens.'

And still she wouldn't look at him. Hugging her knees, she said, 'How ill is Robert Brandon?'

'Brandon?' He looked at her as though he hadn't heard her correctly — or as if she had suddenly gone mad. '*Robert* Brandon?'

'How ill?' she insisted.

He was baffled, staring at her oddly. Nothing in his mind was making sense any more.

'I — we — well, no one can be sure, of course, but if he does what he's told, he should have several more good years. But why, Meg?'

She turned to him then. She said, with enormous pride, 'Because he is my father.'

They were still sitting there, not saying anything, when Daisy started coughing hard. Getting to his feet Owen muttered distractedly, 'I'll dose her up with aspirin. She needs to sleep. And we ought to let the school know. I suppose Harry will get it next — or has she had it?'

By the time Megan had settled Daisy with a hot drink and made them coffee and carried it upstairs to their room, Owen had showered and shaved and was padding about in jeans and a sweater. He looked younger and healthier, and there was a buoyant air about him. The desperate expression he had arrived with had gone.

'Is that what Vera came to London to tell you, Meg? About Robert Brandon — your father — at last?'

Megan nodded.

'I'm not thinking straight — my brain hasn't caught up yet — but it fits, doesn't it, in every way?'

'Oh yes — yes, it does.' She sensed that he hadn't quite taken it in, the enormity of what she had just told him. He was still acting like a sleepwalker.

He said slowly, 'And all the time I was imagining that you'd sent for Vera to say — to say — that you were leaving me — for Alain Gesson ...' Megan hardened herself against the pang which she expected — but didn't happen.

'I told you, it's finished.'

'I've been to hell and back, Meg.'

'I know ...'

Megan raised her head. Great weights were dropping from her shoulders. She had learnt so much, so quickly; and all of it from her mother. About chasing rainbows, for instance; about guts; about her background and her beginnings, the daughter that she was, which made her uniquely her. That would remain a secret; she and her mother both agreed. It was something to ponder endlessly, with Owen, perhaps over long, quiet weekends in Wales — away from work and away from the children, in the peace of Pear Cottage.

But before she could say any of this, as she suddenly, desperately wanted to, Owen had got on his knees and was rootling round in his open suitcase in the leaden gloom.

'Your mother asked me to give you something.' He sounded frantic. Discombobulated with the time change, the Robert Brandon thunderbolt, and a chronic lack of sleep, he was flinging things out all over the room. Megan knelt close beside him.

'What, Owen?'

'This. Here it is.' He held up a small, worn leather box. 'She said it was given to her during the war, in the winter of 1939. She said she wanted you to have it – that you'd understand.'

Megan took the box and opened it. The delicate, diamond star brooch sparkled against the black satin lining. Very gently, his strong, competent hand perfectly steady, Owen took it out and pinned it to Megan's sweater.

'My father must have given it to her,' Megan whispered. 'When she was in that play . . . about the time that . . . Don't you think?' Their faces were only inches apart. They were both on the verge of laughter and tears.

And that was when the lights came on.